VILLAGE OF THE
GHOST BEARS

VILLAGE OF THE GHOST BEARS

a novel

Stan Jones

Published by
Soho Press, Inc.
853 Broadway
New York, NY 10003

Library of Congress Cataloging-in-Publication Data

Jones, Stan, 1947-
Village of the ghost bears / Stan Jones.
p. cm.
ISBN 978-1-56947-606-2 (hardcover)
1. Police—Alaska—Fiction. 2. Arson investigation—
Fiction. 3. Alaska—Fiction. I. Title.

PS3560.O539V56 2009
813'.54—dc22
2009014736

10 9 8 7 6 5 4 3 2 1

To the people of Northwest Alaska

ACKNOWLEDGMENTS

THE AUTHOR WISHES TO thank Deputy Fire Marshal Donald C. Cuthbert of the Alaska Department of Public Safety for generously sharing his off-duty time to explain the ins and outs of arson investigation in rural Alaska.

The author also extends his deepest gratitude to Kent Sturgis, who gave the book a professional edit.

"Earth and the Great Weather," the song in Chapter Twelve, was recorded by the Danish explorer Knud Rasmussen during his Fifth Thule Expedition early in the last century and attributed to an Eskimo woman named Uvavnuk. It is sometimes known as the "Song of Uvavnuk."

"The ghosts of dead bears have, it is said, their own village far off on the ice of the ocean."

—Nuligak, in *I, Nuligak*

A NOTE ON LANGUAGE

"ESKIMO" IS THE BEST-KNOWN term for the Native Americans described in this book, but it is not their term. They call themselves "Inupiat," meaning "the people." "Eskimo," a term brought into Alaska by white men, is what certain Indian tribes in eastern Canada called their neighbors to the north. It probably meant "eaters of raw flesh."

Nonetheless, "Eskimo" and "Inupiat" are used more or less interchangeably in northwest Alaska today, at least when English is spoken, and that is the usage followed in this book.

The Inupiat call their language Inupiaq. A few words in it—those commonly mixed with English in northwest Alaska—appear in the book, along with some local colloquialisms in English. They are listed below, along with pronunciations and meanings. As the spellings vary among Inupiaq–English dictionaries, I have used the most phonetic of the spellings for the benefit of non-Inupiaq readers.

A Northwest Alaska Glossary

aaka (AH-kuh): mother

aana (AH-nuh): grandmother; old lady

aaqqaa! (ah-KAH): it stinks!

alappaa! (AH-la-PAH): it's cold!

arigaa! (AH-de-gah): good!

arii! (ah-DEE): Ouch! I hurt!

ataata (ah-TAH-tah): grandfather

atchak (AH-chuk): aunt

atikluk (ah-TEEK-look): A light summer woman's parka, usually in a flowered pattern. It has no opening in front, but is pulled on and off over the head.

can't-grow: a small dog

Inupiaq (IN-you-pack): the Eskimo language of northern Alaska; an individual Eskimo of northern Alaska

Inupiat (IN-you-pat): more than one Inupiaq; the Eskimo people of northern Alaska

iq'mik (ICK-mick): a form of chewing tobacco made by combining leaf tobacco with the ashes of burnt tree fungus, usually birch

katak (CUT-uck): fall

kinnaq (KIN-ock): crazy; a crazy person

kunnichuk (KUH-knee-chuck): storm shed

malik (MULL-ick): accompany or follow

miluk (MILL-uck): breast

muktuk (MUCK-tuck): whale skin with a thin layer of fat adhering; a great delicacy in Inupiat country

naluaqmiiyaaq (nuh-LOCK-me-ock): almost white; an Inupiaq who tries to act white

naluaqmiu (nuh-LOCK-me): a white person

naluaqmiut (nuh-LOCK-me): more than one white person; white people

nanuq (NA-NOOK): polar bear

polynya: a lead in the sea ice kept open all winter by winds and currents

qavvik (KAH-vik): wolverine

quiyuk (KWEE-yuck): sex

taaqsipak (TOX-ee-puck): the color black; an African-American

ulu (OOH-loo): traditional Inupiat woman's knife, shaped like a slice of pie with the cutting edge at the rim and a handle of horn, ivory or bone at the point

umiaq (OOM-ee-ak): whaling boat, made of a wooden frame and covered with the thick, tough hides of walrus or bearded seal

Village English: a stripped-down form of English used by older people and residents of small villages in northwest Alaska

VILLAGE OF THE GHOST BEARS

CHAPTER ONE

"SEE WHY THEY CALL it One-Way Lake?"

Cowboy Decker rolled the Super Cub into a slow arc as Alaska State Trooper Nathan Active peered over Grace Palmer's shoulder. One-Way Lake was a blue teardrop cupped in the foothills of the Brooks Range, with caribou trails lacing the ridges on either side. The outlet, One-Way Creek, lined with stunted black spruce and a few cottonwoods gone gold, threaded south across the rusting fall tundra toward the Isignaq River. At the lake's head, wavelets licked a fan-shaped talus under a steep slope of gray-brown shale. More caribou trails cut across its face.

Grace was wearing the intercom headset, so Active was obliged to shout at the back of the pilot's head. "Looks pretty tight," he said.

"Yep," Cowboy shouted back. "One way in, one way out. You land toward the cliff and take off going away."

Active lifted one of the headset cups away from Grace's ear. "What do you think?"

She shifted on his lap in the cramped back seat of the Super Cub and turned her head toward him. "I'm game. Anything to get out of this damn airplane."

"Let's do it," Active shouted.

Cowboy leveled the wings and flew a half-mile down

One-Way Creek in the slanting fall sunlight, then swung back for the approach to the lake. He came in low, floats barely clearing the treetops along the creek, chopped the power, and dropped the Super Cub onto the water, throwing up spray that painted a brief rainbow in the air.

Cowboy slowed to taxiing speed and pointed the nose at a spot on the bank that boasted a tiny gravel beach and a stand of spruce on high, dry ground suitable for camping. The floats crunched into the shallows and Cowboy shut off the engine, ushering in a sudden and deafening silence broken only by the slap of their own wake reaching the shore.

Cowboy popped open the Super Cub's clamshell doors, letting in the smell of the Arctic—the wet, fertile rot of tundra vegetation, a hint of resin from the spruce, and something else—something sharp and cool that Active associated with autumn in the mountains near sunset. Winter, perhaps, hovering just over the ridges to the north. It was already a couple of weeks late and couldn't be far off.

Cowboy, wearing jeans and the usual bomber jacket and baseball cap, pulled up his hip waders and jumped into the shallows. He grabbed the nose of a float, tied on a yellow polypropylene line, and dragged the plane forward a few yards, then walked into the trees and snubbed the Super Cub to a spruce. He returned to the beach and surveyed the lake with an air of great satisfaction. "You get into One-Way this time of year, you got caribou walking by; you got grayling in the creek, maybe some Arctic char, maybe some pike in the lake; and you got the best blueberries in the Arctic." He raised his eyebrows and grinned. "And you got total privacy. There's only a couple guys can get in here, and you're looking at half of 'em."

Not for the first time, Active marveled at the pilot's intuition, and at his utter lack of discretion in dealing with the insights it brought him. Cowboy might sense that fishing, berry picking, and caribou hunting were the least of their reasons for coming here, but it was none of his business. "We probably oughta get unloaded," Active said.

He helped Grace climb onto a float, then extricated himself from the torture chamber that is the rear seat of a Super Cub and clambered ashore, stamping and stretching to unkink his muscles.

Cowboy walked onto the float and began emptying the cargo pod under the Super Cub's belly and the space behind the back seat: food in cardboard boxes, two cased rifles, two fishing rigs, a bright orange Arctic Oven tent, a Woods Yukon single-double sleeping bag, camp stove and fuel, cooking gear, and all the other impedimenta required to support human life in the Arctic.

Active and Grace ferried gear ashore until finally the plane was empty. Cowboy untied the Super Cub, waded into the shallows, walked the plane back until it floated free, then swung the nose around to point across the lake. "Okay, you two, I'll see you in a week. Enjoy yourselves, huh?" His eyes twinkled behind his steel-frame glasses, and the grin reappeared.

It was not reciprocated.

Cowboy shrugged. "If you run into any trouble, just set off your EPIRB, and somebody'll be along to check on you." They nodded, and he climbed into the plane.

He cranked up and taxied to the foot of the cliff, then turned and put on full power, filling the bowl with the roar of his engine as he accelerated down the lake. They watched as the pilot got onto step, lifted one float clear of the water, then the other, and cleared the trees at the outlet.

As the red-and-white plane shrank to a dot in the sky, Active put his arm around Grace's shoulders, breathing in the scent of lavender. "What do you think?"

She shrugged stiffly. "I don't know yet."

He gave her a squeeze. "Don't sweat it. Good fishin', good huntin', good berry-pickin', good weather, good company—who needs the other?"

She looked at him with a quicksilver flash from the corner of her eye. "Every couple does. Otherwise they're just. . . ."

"Roommates?"

"Don't say that. I hate that word."

"It's all right if we're roommates for a while," he said. "It'll happen when it happens."

"Feel free to shop elsewhere."

"Thanks, but no thanks."

She turned into his arms and pulled him down for a kiss. "Thank you," she said after a long time.

When they separated, he cleared his throat. "I guess we should do something about getting a camp together."

She nodded. "I'll organize some dinner if you want to set up the tent."

She busied herself putting up a Visqueen awning for the camp kitchen while he stamped about the mossy floor of the spruce grove, looking for the flattest spot big enough for the Arctic Oven. He found one a few yards off, requiring only that he dig out a few rocks and pitch them aside. Then he tugged the tent out of its pouch and spread it on the moss as the sun drifted below the ridge and the basin sank into blue shadow.

Later, in the tent, came the conundrum of the Woods single-double. Each half could be zipped into a bag for one person, or the two halves could be zipped together for a couple.

"One bag or two, madam?" he asked without much optimism.

He studied her face in the buttery light of the propane lantern as she turned it over in her mind. The hunger for normalcy showing as always in her eyes, the desire to please him, and the dread that, if she let him take her, he would be transformed somewhere deep in her wounded psyche into her father, who had been the first man to do so.

"One, I think, kind sir, but no guarantees." Like him, she was playing it light, keeping the escape route open.

"None needed."

He unrolled the bag and zipped it together, stripped down to his shorts and T-shirt, and crawled in. Then he watched her next internal debate: undress with the light on, or off? Put on the long johns, or go for broke in panties and one of his T-shirts?

She looked at him, stuck out her tongue like a twelve-year-old, and closed the valve on the lantern. He listened in a kind of fever-dream as clothes whispered off in the darkness and something was pulled on. Long johns, or a T-shirt?

She slid into the bag, and he felt a smooth, hot thigh against his own. She turned toward him for a kiss. Her lips soft and wet, a flicker of her tongue. But when he slid his hand under her T-shirt, she stiffened, quivering. As usual.

He eased his hand off her breast, stroked her hair, and felt her relax. He kissed her cheek and tasted salt.

"Sorry, baby," she said.

"All in good time."

"You know I've started seeing Nelda Qivits again."

"Okay."

She put her hand on his chest, scratched him lightly, sighed, and let the hand trail southward. "Liar."

"Eh?"

"I see things are not altogether all right down there."

"What are you—"

"I think I could—"

"Mmmm, oh, God. . . ."

"You should register those hands with the FBI," he said a few minutes later. "They're lethal weapons."

"That would explain why I won the shoot-out," she replied with a giggle.

He laughed out loud, pleased that her joke was dirtier and more original than his own. But how to get into the real issue? "Am I imagining things, or did we just have a breakthrough?"

"Progress, at least." She shifted to put her head on his chest.

He was silent for a time. "What do you think accounts for it?"

"It's just different out here. I don't know."

"Maybe it's being out of that house."

She stiffened again. "Don't overanalyze it. Leave it be."

"I withdraw the remark, your honor."

"Noted." A long moment passed. Then she relaxed again and rolled toward him a bit. The tent was filled with the smells of lavender, sex, and his own sweat, now cooling.

"It was nice, but it does seem a bit one-sided," he ventured at length. "Anything I can do to reciprocate?"

She shrugged. "Someday, maybe. For now, your pleasure is my pleasure."

He flipped back the sleeping bag to cool off and—now

that his eyes had adjusted—to admire the curve of her calf thrown across his thigh in the dim light seeping in from the evening sky.

"You know something?" She was serious, suddenly.

"Mmmm?" He was drowsy and hoped this wouldn't get too deep.

"You're so polite."

"Mmmm." He tried to stay drowsy, thinking they could work this out tomorrow, whatever it was. But "so polite"?

He opened his eyes, resigned to it. "Meaning?"

"I mean, you keep trying, but not too hard. Sometimes I'm not sure how much you want me. With my past, I could understand. . . ."

"Well—I mean, my God, look at you. You're the most beautiful . . . what man wouldn't. . . ."

She was silent, slightly tense against his side and chest.

"I—are you saying you want to be taken?"

"I don't know. Maybe it's what I need. Some women do."

"By force?"

"Sometimes. If it's someone they trust. They want to be wanted that much."

"Are you one of those women?"

"I don't know. I want to be normal, is all. I just don't know what that is." Her hand drifted south again. "But I see the idea interests you at least a little?"

"Of course." He moved the hand back to his chest. "But I'm not the caveman type. For us, what we have is normal, for now."

"Well, then, have some more of it, on me." She rolled over and kissed him, hard, her hand moving south again. This time, he let it roam.

ACTIVE AWOKE when the sun got high enough to heat the tent and spent a few minutes studying her face, the foxlike set of her eyes, her hair lying against the honey-dark skin of her neck in the orange half-light. Finally he eased outside, clothes in hand so as not to wake her by moving around in the tent. Everything looked blue until his eyes adjusted to normal light, and he did a hop-dance on the cold, damp moss as he dressed. At least there was no frost yet. Maybe Indian summer would last out their week at One-Way Lake.

He was scrambling eggs and frying bacon on the camp stove when she came out, yawning and pulling on a jacket against the last of the night chill. "That smells good." She sniffed hungrily. "What time is it?"

He shrugged. "I wouldn't know. My watch is in my pack, and that's right where it'll stay till Cowboy picks us up."

"You put away your watch? I'm amazed."

"I'm smitten," he said. "And I cook." He waved a spatula at the eggs and bacon.

"Where you been all my life?" She squatted, stole a rasher out of the pan, and ambled to the shore. She stood looking out over the water, chewing as breakfast popped and sizzled in the skillets. "Nathan, do you think bliss is achievable as a permanent condition? Or do we just have to content ourselves with a random series of singularities and contingencies?"

"Say again, please? In English?"

"I feel helplessly happy. Think it'll last?"

"I wouldn't know," he said.

"Even if it doesn't, I can't complain. I slept like a zombie."

"Me too. I felt oddly drained."

She giggled.

He dumped the eggs onto their plates, tossed two slices of bread into the skillet, and was turning down the gas when she called out.

"Hey, look at that!" She was pointing across the lake.

He turned and swept his eyes over the water, seeing nothing out of the ordinary. "What—"

"Up on the ridge."

He scanned the crest and saw them, a string of caribou filing south toward the Isignaq, headed for Jade Portage and the wintering grounds across the river. From this distance, they looked like bugs crawling along the edge of the sky. He was reminded of a phrase he had once heard an old Inupiat hunter use for caribou: earth-lice.

There was indeed some resemblance, Active saw now. Plus, as the old man had pointed out, the Inupiat of long ago had eaten their own body lice as well as earth-lice. Now that everyone was civilized and bathed regularly, the old man had reflected somewhat gloomily, body lice were no longer on the menu, but at least the earth-lice were still plentiful, and as tasty as ever.

Active went back to the tent and fetched his binoculars for a closer look. The males were in full fall regalia, with towering antlers and thick coats of gray-black fur except for the white capes shining practically incandescent in the morning sun. The females ran more to brown and gray, with spindly, twig-like antlers.

"How about some caribou for breakfast?" Grace asked. There was fire in her eyes of a kind he had not seen before. Her Inupiat half coming out, surely.

"You bet," he said, hurrying to the tent to uncase the guns. "We'll have to cross the creek and come up farther along the ridge to get ahead of them."

They loaded quickly, slung the rifles over their backs, and sprinted along the lakeshore to the outlet, then worked down One-Way Creek until they found a spot shallow enough to ford.

He was halfway to the opposite bank, eyes on the ridge, measuring their pace against that of the caribou, figuring the odds of getting up the slope in time, something about the creek trying to get his attention, when she called out behind him.

"Nathan, look!"

He turned. She was pointing at a dark object a few yards downstream. He had caught it from the corner his eye before, but in his hurry had passed it off as rocks or a log. Now he saw what she had seen—a pack frame strapped to a figure lying face-down in the stream.

They splashed through the creek, their Sorels taking on water, and rolled the corpse over. The head flopped forward with the current, as if the neck were without bones, and they both recoiled.

"Oh, God," she said. "Where's his face? And look at his hands. The flesh is just . . . gone. What would do that?"

"I don't know," he said. "I've never seen anything like—wait, didn't Cowboy say something about pike in the lake back there?"

She nodded, and Active moved closer to the head of the corpse, now lying on its side in the shallow water. "Pike supposedly eat everything. Even their own young."

Grace looked nervously at the water rippling over her Sorels, then at Active, and edged toward the bank. "Are they in here now?"

"I don't think this happened to him here," Active said, feeling himself shift back into work mode. "He must have been in the lake for a while. That's when the pike would have gotten at him. Then he drifted into the outlet and got stuck here in these shallows." He studied what was left of the man's face. Nothing but grinning bones with a few shreds of flesh attached, but he still had his ears and most of his straight black hair, probably because the hood of his anorak had protected them from the pike. "Anything about him seem familiar?"

Grace stepped a little closer and studied everything but the missing face. "Not really. But he's obviously from around here."

Active nodded. The anorak had a duct-tape patch below one shoulder, and the man wore a faded Nike sweatshirt underneath, plus insulated Carhartt jeans and Sorels like their own. "Not a stitch of Eddie Bauer or Patagonia on him. But nobody's been reported missing."

"Maybe he's not overdue yet. I wonder how long he's been here."

Active shook his head. "Not long, probably. He's dressed for cool weather."

"But how did he die?"

As one, they turned to stare out over One-Way Lake toward the cliff looming at its upper end.

"Beats me." Active scanned the lakeshore for any sign of a camp or boat, then shook his head. "Well, I'll go through his pockets and pack and see who he was. Let's get him over to the bank." At Grace's look of reluctance, he added, "You can take the feet."

Ten minutes later, Active shook his head in mystification and began stuffing the hunter's belongings back into his pack.

"No I.D., huh?" Grace said.

"Nothing. No wallet, no name on his clothes or tent or sleeping bag, nothing. Weird, huh?"

"Not that weird. A lot of guys from the villages don't carry I.D. when they're out in the country. Just one more thing to lose."

"Good point," he said. "What do you make of this?"

He pulled the soggy remains of a box of two-seventy ammunition out of the pack and held it up for inspection.

"I guess he was hunting," she said. "Why else would he be up here?"

"Exactly. Caribou, probably, or maybe sheep. So where's his rifle?"

They looked across the lake again, then at each other. "All right, you take the right bank, I'll take the left, and we'll meet at the upper end," he said. "Give a shout if you find his gun, or anything else man-made, or anything that looks like a recent campsite."

Forty-five minutes later, they were standing together on the rubble at the foot of the cliff, as puzzled as ever. Active looked down the lake toward the outlet, then at the mountain behind them, and swore softly to himself as he pulled the binoculars hanging around his neck from the folds of his coat and raised them to his eyes.

"You think?" Grace said.

He nodded, sweeping the mountainside with the glasses. There was a relatively gentle slope at the top, where caribou trails cut through the tundra carpet, then bare gray and brown rock, steepening to a near-vertical cliff that ended at the talus fan. "There we go," he said finally, pointing at a spot uphill and to their right, a few yards above the talus.

He handed her the glasses and she scanned the slope. "I don't—oh, yeah, I see it. What—"

"Water bottle, maybe."

"Umm-hmm." She handed the glasses back to him.

"You wait here," he said. "I'll go up and have a look."

"Careful. You don't want to end up like him."

He grunted, handed her his rifle, and started up the slope. The going was rough enough on the talus fan, and it became impossible when he reached the cliff itself. He glassed the object again, now much closer, determined that it really was a water bottle—actually, a plastic Coke bottle—and started back down.

He was halfway to the lake when he spotted the two-seventy Winchester, wedged muzzle-down in a crevice between two rocks. He pulled it out and studied it. The scope was gone, the barrel was bent slightly, and deep gouges scarred the weathered wooden stock. The sling, if the rifle had ever had one, was also gone.

He picked his way back to where Grace was waiting and showed her the gun. "He must have been crossing the slope on those caribou trails and lost his footing," Active said. "Looks like he bounced all the way into the water. That would explain the broken neck."

Grace gazed at the slope, then down the lake to where the brush concealed the hunter's body. "Poor guy. Can you trace the gun and figure out who he is?"

"Not likely. There's a million of these Winchesters around, and most of them were bought before there was any kind of gun registration. We'll put the word out to the villages and wait for somebody to realize they haven't heard from this guy in a while."

"What now?" she asked as they started back to camp.

He sighed. "We set off the EPIRB and wait for somebody to show up to see what the problem is."

She shivered. "We have to stay on this lake with him?"

"'Fraid so," he said.

A DEAD man for a neighbor, they discovered, didn't affect their appetites. So, after Active found the EPIRB in one of their bags and set it off, they reheated breakfast and began wolfing it down on the lakeshore.

"How long does that thing take to work?" Grace waved at the bright yellow EPIRB hanging from a spruce tree. It looked like a walkie-talkie.

"I'm not sure," he said. "Never had to set one off before. A satellite picks up the signal, then it tells the Rescue Coordination Center, then they have to decide if the signal is for real and where you are . . . several hours, probably. A day, maybe."

"I thought it could tell the satellite exactly where you are."

"Some do," he said. "The newer ones."

"But they cost more."

He nodded.

"So you kept that one. And here we sit."

"Ah-hah."

"So cheap." She shook her head and took a swallow of coffee.

"We probably should wrap him up," Active said.

"*You* should," Grace said. "While I clean up here. And we should stop calling him 'him.' He needs a name."

"A name?"

"It's disrespectful if he doesn't have one. Also, it might jinx him in the afterlife."

"I didn't know we Inupiat believed in the afterlife."

"When it suits us."

"All right," he said. "A name. How about Henry?"

She grimaced and stirred her coffee with a spruce twig. "How about One-Way? In honor of the place of his demise."

"No-Way."

"Why not? What's wrong with One-Way?"

"No, I mean how about 'No-Way' for the name?"

"No-Way? Wha—oh, I see. Once he got into One-Way Lake, there was no way out."

"Uh-huh." He nodded.

"Excellent. No-Way it is, then. You go bundle old No-Way up for transport, and I'll take care of the breakfast dishes."

She stacked the plates, coffeepot, and skillet, and started for the lakeshore. He didn't move.

"What?" she said.

"It strikes me that the division of labor here is very much along traditional gender lines all of a sudden. Maybe I should do the dishes while you—"

"No way," she said with a huge grin.

"Precisely," he said with an equally huge grin.

He dug through the duffel bags again, came up with the roll of Visqueen and a hank of nylon camp cord, and set off along the shore toward No-Way's resting place.

He was knotting the last loop of cord around the Visqueen-wrapped remains when he realized the buzz poking at his subconscious wasn't a late-season mosquito, but an airplane—a Super Cub, from the sound of it.

He stood, made a visor of his hand, and peered southward, toward the sun. A Super Cub swam out of the glare and into focus. A red-and-white Super Cub on floats, in fact, unmistakably the Lienhofer Aviation Super Cub flown by Cowboy Decker. Active checked his watch, realized he wasn't wearing it, and started for camp.

Cowboy came straight in over the trees at the outlet and splashed down, then taxied toward their camp, cut the engine, and grounded the plane in the gravel shallows. He was climbing out as Active hurried up.

"That was fast," Active said. "It can't be more than an hour and a half since I set off the EPIRB. How'd you get here so soon?"

"EPIRB?" the pilot said as he waded ashore. "I don't know anything about an EPIRB. You got a problem up here?" He scanned them up and down. "You both look all right."

"We're fine," Active said. "But we found a dead hunter in the creek." He pointed at the cliff. "Looks like he fell up there and broke his neck, then drifted down the lake and got caught in the shallows at the outlet."

"No shit. Who is it?"

Active explained about No-Way's missing I.D. and face.

Cowboy grunted. "Pike'll do that, all right. Look, Carnaby

sent me to get you. The Rec Center burned down last night and, ah, well, ah—"

"And what?" Active said, noticing now that the pilot was red-eyed and grimy and smelled of smoke.

"We've got seven or eight people dead and two in the hospital and one that's not expected to live being medevacked to the burn unit in Anchorage."

"Jesus!" Active said. "Anybody I—Who's dead?"

Grace didn't speak, but she pressed a hand over her mouth.

"They haven't identified 'em all yet or even counted 'em for sure," Cowboy said. "But one of 'em was Jim Silver."

"Jim?"

Cowboy nodded.

Active was silent for a long time, gazing sightlessly at the hillside across the lake. "And was it arson?"

"They don't know yet," Cowboy said. "Call came in around ten-thirty last night. I rolled out with the Volunteer Fire Department, but by the time we got there it was already too hot to go in. All we could do was try to keep it from setting off the Center's stove-oil tanks or spreading to the other buildings around there—what we call a surround-and-drown. The city cops are on it, and the Troopers, and one of your arson guys is coming out from Fairbanks. And Carnaby wants you back to work on it."

"Of course, yeah."

"Come on, I'll help you pack up," Cowboy said. He walked over and began breaking down their camp kitchen.

Active and Grace went into the tent together and began cramming clothes and books back into nylon stuff bags.

"Jim Silver," Grace said.

"Yeah."

"I'm so sorry."

"Yeah."

"Is that it? 'Yeah'?"

Active shrugged. "He, he. . . ."

"Go on."

"He made sense."

"What?"

"I don't know that he was the best cop I ever met, but he was the one that made the most sense. Of Chukchi, you know. When he explained Chukchi to me, I would think I got it. It was like life was a story for him, and Chukchi was the most fascinating chapter he ever ran across, and being police chief was the best way to appreciate it. You know what he said to me once?"

"Mmm."

"It was when we were out on the ice after old Victor Solomon was harpooned at his sheefish camp and I was whining about the cold, and Jim says, 'If you weren't suffering, how would you know you were alive?' And then he laughed that big belly laugh of his and, you know, all of a sudden it made sense. The ice, the cold, the west wind, Chukchi—even the bad stuff. But this." He stopped and shook his head. "I need to get out of here. We need to."

Her face tightened in the familiar way, but she said nothing.

"Listen to me. I'm sorry."

"It's all right."

"Nah, I gotta act like a cop now," he said.

"Not with me, baby. You can act however you like."

He pinched the bridge of his nose. He wasn't crying, exactly, but the corners of his eyes were wet. Grace looked away while he wiped them. "Thanks," he said, and kissed her.

They crawled out of the tent, hauled out their gear, and collapsed the Arctic Oven as Cowboy ferried loads to the plane. Finally, everything was aboard and Cowboy told them to climb in.

"What about our friend?" Active pointed toward the outlet.

"Sorry," Cowboy said. "No can do."

"What if something gets to him? A bear or foxes or something?"

"Ordinarily, I'd tie him on a float and we'd be fine," Cowboy said. "But not on One-Way Lake, not with you two and your gear in the plane. We'd never make it over the trees."

"I wrapped him up pretty good," Active said. "I guess he'll keep."

"Yeah, with the weather this cool," Cowboy said. "I'll get back in here as soon as I can."

As they took off over the trees, Active peered down at the shiny bundle of Visqueen on the creek bank and wondered again who No-Way had been.

CHAPTER TWO

COWBOY FLEW SOUTH ALONG One-Way Creek, the overloaded Super Cub laboring to gain altitude. When they could see over the ridge west of the lake, Active spotted a small band of caribou grazing on a sunny hillside, apparently in no hurry to get to the Isignaq River and cross to the wintering grounds on the south side. He touched Grace's shoulder and pointed, and she shifted on his lap to watch the little herd until it passed out of sight behind them. It looked like the same band they had seen on the ridge before they found No-Way.

When they reached the Isignaq, Cowboy swung west, following the big brown river as it meandered toward the coast. The tundra crawled past, the wind-ruffled lakes glinting gunmetal blue under the autumn sky. At the upwind end of each lake, a crescent of calm water, like a shard of mirror, nestled in the lee of the tundra bank. At the opposite end, the wind piled up a moustache of white foam along the shore.

A family of swans—two adults and a cygnet—patrolled one of the lakes. They were ice-white in the cold, hard light. There was something anxious in the scene, as if the parents, feeling the earth tilt away from the sun, could not impress upon their child strongly enough the urgency of starting south ahead of winter.

As the Super Cub neared the sea, the sky gathered itself into an overcast, the lakes dulled to feathered slate, and rain streaked the windshield. Cowboy dropped down to an altitude of a few hundred feet and worked his way through the scud until they reached the shore of Isignaq Inlet. Over a couple of miles of gray chop, they could just see the Burton Peninsula, a long fat finger of rolling tundra with the village of Chukchi at its tip.

Cowboy crossed the water to the peninsula and swung northwest toward the village. Active spotted the smoldering Rec Center soon after they passed over Nimiuk Creek, which trickled into the inlet a few miles southeast of town. A tendril of white smoke spiraled up, then vanished on the west wind.

Active heard Grace speaking to Cowboy but couldn't make out what she was saying. Then she removed the intercom headset and passed it to Active. He slipped the big foam cups over his ears and heard the rasp of the pilot's voice finishing a question: ". . . a look?"

"Say again?" Active said, using the phrase Cowboy used when he couldn't make out something coming over the radio.

"I said, you want to make a pass over the Rec Center and take a look?"

"Good idea," Active said. Then he thought of another bit of pilot-ese he'd heard when Cowboy talked to the FAA, and added, "That's affirmative."

They crossed the lagoon to the spit on which Chukchi lay and sailed above the village's meandering streets and wooden houses, gleaming wetly in the gray light. Soon the ruins themselves passed under the wing. Cowboy rolled the plane into a tight circle, and Active studied what was left of the Rec Center.

Two scorched walls still stood at the northwest corner of the debris field, swaying in the wind as a city fire crew with a yellow truck hosed down the remaining hot spots. The roof and the other walls had fallen in, leaving a rectangle of smoldering black debris where once had stood a gymnasium that doubled as a bingo parlor to help pay the bills, a couple of exercise rooms where Active had worked out three nights a week, a racquetball court, showers, lockers, saunas, and two small offices.

Cowboy eased out of the turn, swung into the traffic pattern for the airport, and put the little floatplane down on the lagoon, just south of the big asphalt east–west runway that marked the southern limit of the village.

After a brief discussion, it was decided that Cowboy would drop Active off at the scene, then take Grace to the home of Martha Active Johnson, Active's birth mother, to check on her and her family, as well as on Grace's adopted daughter Nita, who had been farmed out to Martha while Active and Grace went camping at One-Way Lake. There was always the infinitesimal possibility that one of them might, for some reason, have been at the Rec Center the previous night.

A few minutes later, Active stepped out of Cowboy's van and leaned back in to kiss Grace, whose hand had tightened into a clawlike clamp around his as they approached the site of the fire. Now her face was masklike, nearly frozen. "You all right?" he asked.

"I will be," she said. "Let's just go, Cowboy." The pilot shot a mystified glance at Active and slipped the van into gear. Active watched as they pulled out of sight in the drizzle that was slanting out of the silt-colored sky. He filed

Grace's reaction away at the top of his get-to-as-soon-as-possible list.

Then he turned and surveyed the wreckage of the Chukchi Community Recreation Center. It had been a wooden structure with aluminum siding, and scraps of the stuff still clung to the two standing walls, flapping and rattling in the wind. The interior was a rubble of burnt, fallen timbers and exercise machines covered with a black paste of congealed ashes. Even with the wind hurrying the smoke away, the air smelled of wet ash and something like a barbecue. Active tried not to think about it.

An ambulance manned by two paramedics was parked nearby, as was the blue, black, and white Trooper Suburban. A dozen or so people watched from the edge of the street, some of them crying and clinging to each other. Between the civilians and the ruins, yellow crime-scene tape surrounded a cluster of four-wheelers. Near the four-wheeler corral he saw his boss, Captain Patrick Carnaby, talking to two other men and studying the ruins.

Active recognized one of the men as Alan Long, an officer with the Chukchi Police Department. The other, a stranger in a Trooper uniform, was leaning on a shovel.

Carnaby turned, spotted Active, and waved him over. "Nathan, this is Fire Marshal Ronald Barnes from Fairbanks."

The name, Active did recognize. Barnes was famed as the best arson investigator the Troopers had, a man who lived fire, loved fire, ate, slept, and breathed fire, understood fire like Heisenberg understood uncertainty.

Barnes undraped himself from the shovel, stuck out his hand, and said, in a Western drawl, "Pleasure, Nathan. Call me Ronnie."

That drawl. Montana? Was that where Barnes was from? Active shook the hand and nodded. Barnes certainly didn't look like a legendary arson investigator. Active had imagined someone resembling Carnaby, chief of the Chukchi detachment. Carnaby was tall, broad-shouldered, and gray at the temples, and he wore a bristling salt-and-pepper moustache—the walking embodiment of duly constituted state authority. A Cop with a capital C.

But Ronnie Barnes was wiry and sandy-haired, five-eight or five-nine, with pale blue eyes, a drooping handlebar moustache, and shoulders that seemed to droop a little too. He didn't look like the embodiment of anything, unless it was white trash.

That was it. Ronnie Barnes looked like somebody who'd be swearing at the camera on *Cops* as he was hauled out of a trailer park in the Montana pines, clad only in jeans, tattoos, and handcuffs while a pregnant girlfriend watched from the stoop and pressed a bloody Kleenex to her nose.

Active and Alan Long, the city cop, exchanged nods. Long, an Inupiaq like Active, was round-faced and buck-toothed, a former Army MP. Normally, he was annoyingly enthusiastic, but not today. Today he was grimy and red-eyed, like Cowboy Decker, and smelled of smoke.

"Sorry to hear about Jim," Active said. "He was, he was. . . ."

"Yeah," Long said. "I know."

Nobody said anything for a while. Barnes jabbed the dirt with his shovel a couple of times. Carnaby turned away and cleared his throat. After a decent interval, Barnes said, "I was just telling Alan, we need to get the names of the people standing around here."

Long scanned the gaggle of spectators. "I know them

all," he said. "I'll make a list." He pulled out a notebook and began writing.

Barnes nodded. "Your true pyromaniac has a sexual disorder. He'll come watch the fire to get his rocks off. You see somebody in the crowd with his hands in his pockets, masturbating, that's him."

Active, recognizing this as something he'd learned in a course on fire investigation at the Trooper Academy, ran his eyes quickly over the crowd. Most had their hands in their pockets, all right, men and women alike. But in the pockets of their coats, not their pants. And a few were bobbing up and down, but that was just what you did if you stood in the west wind in Chukchi for very long.

Barnes followed Active's gaze and shrugged. "I know, I don't think he's here either. But if it was arson, he was probably here last night, when it was really rolling." He looked at Long. "Was anybody taking names then, Alan?"

Long's chipmunk cheeks sagged.

Barnes patted him on the shoulder. "Don't worry about it. Was there a cat?"

"A cat?" Long said.

"Or maybe a dog?"

"A cat," Active said. "But how did you know?"

Barnes shrugged. "Just a hunch. Most big public facilities have one or the other. Did it get out?"

Long shook his head. "Who cares? We've got more important things—"

"If it did, whoever took care of it probably set your fire," Barnes explained in a patient tone. "Usually, the arsonist will make sure his pets get out."

"I didn't see any cat come out," Long said.

"I'll look for it when I go through the building," said Barnes.

Active thought about the Rec Center cat. A light yellow calico. Who had he heard calling the cat? Who had he seen opening a can of tuna and setting it on the office floor?

"Well, we ought to get to work," Carnaby said.

"Damn right," Long said. "Jim Silver was the best boss I ever had. As chief, I can tell you that everything the city has is at your disposal."

"Chief?" Active asked, eyebrows raised in surprise.

"Acting chief," Carnaby said. "Alan talked the mayor into appointing him this morning when we got the news about Jim. But it's only until the new borough assumes public-safety powers and hires a real chief. Right, Alan?"

Long gave a stiff little nod.

"And the mayor asked us Troopers to take the lead in this investigation. Right, Alan?"

Long looked even more crestfallen. "Absolutely, Captain."

"Okay," Active said. Then he looked from Barnes to Carnaby. "So we think it was arson?"

Barnes scraped at the gravel with his shovel. "Doesn't do to start with a big load of preconceptions, but most structure fires are."

Active had heard this in his fire-investigation course too. "How long till you can get in?"

Barnes shrugged and studied the ruins. "Couple hours, maybe. They're going to keep the hoses on it a while, then I guess the state's sending over a dozer from airport maintenance to take down these last two walls?" He looked at Carnaby.

Carnaby nodded. "It's on the way."

Active looked at Barnes. "What do we do till then?"

Barnes looked at the gawkers again. "Not we. It's you guys, mostly."

"But you're the expert, right?" Long asked.

"Arson investigation is twenty-five percent physical evidence and seventy-five percent interviews," Barnes said. "And in a village . . . trust me, it's better if you guys handle the interviews and I handle the shovel." He jabbed it into the dirt for emphasis. "People don't want to talk to a stranger at a time like this."

"You're it?" Active asked. "I thought you guys traveled in teams."

"Hah," Barnes said. "Do the words 'Republican governor plus Republican legislature' mean anything to you? You're lucky there was enough travel budget to send *me*."

"What about the Feds? With this many fatalities, doesn't the Bureau of Alcohol, Tobacco, and Firearms usually come in?"

"Hah," Barnes said again. "Maybe if we told 'em al Qaeda did it. These days, it's no terrorism, no Feds, except for maybe a little consult over the phone if I need it. Basically, I'm it."

"Cowboy said we've got two survivors here and one at the burn unit in Anchorage?"

Carnaby cleared his throat. "Two here and none in Anchorage, as of about forty-five minutes ago."

Active shook his head. "Can the two here—who are they, anyway?"

Carnaby looked at his notebook. "Jack Stocker and Enos Rexford. Couple of teenagers." Active recognized the surnames as belonging to Chukchi families, but he didn't know either boy.

"Can they talk?"

"They can and did," Carnaby said. "Alan interviewed them this morning."

"And?"

"They weren't much help," Long said. "They were playing one-on-one in the gym when smoke started pouring in and they heard Cammie Frankson screaming for help."

Cammie Frankson was a senior at Chukchi High who worked nights at the Rec Center. Active remembered a plump face, bright eyes, optimism, and a red MP3 player dangling between her breasts like her heart had popped out. "So Cammie's not one of the survivors?"

Long shook his head. "They took her to Anchorage, but. . . ."

"I think she wanted to be a nurse," Active said. "She was going to the university next year." The memory came to him now, and he grimaced. "And she took care of the cat. Its name was Pingilak. It means 'ghost' in Inupiaq."

"Uh-huh," Barnes said in a tone that indicated he was being patient about the detour, but hoped it would end now.

"The last Jack and Enos saw, she was running toward the locker rooms," Long said. "They tried to go after her, but the fire was too much for them. They got out through the rear door of the gym. They're not burned much, but they breathed in a lot of smoke."

"And Cammie?"

Carnaby spoke. "The fire department found her on the front steps there"—he pointed at what was left of the wooden stairs—"about halfway out the door. Unconscious and pretty much burned all over. Hair gone, most of her clothes."

Barnes spoke up. "Anybody else come into the hospital with a burn last night?"

The other three looked at him, then Long pointed at the ruins. "They're all still in there, as far as we know."

Barnes gazed again at the little crowd of onlookers. "Starting a big fire is tricky if you don't know what you're doing. A lot of times, the arsonist will get burned himself if he uses gasoline or some other accelerant. So we always check the emergency rooms the morning after."

"Would you take care of that, Alan?" Carnaby asked.

Long nodded, called Dispatch on the Bluetooth cell-phone headset he'd taken to wearing lately, and gave the instructions. He signed off and said, "Someone's on the way."

"Any chance you've had a string of arsons or unexplained fires recently?" Barnes asked.

The three cops thought for a moment, then shook their heads in unison.

Barnes grimaced slightly and looked at Long. "Any of your firefighters get here before anybody else was on scene, maybe forgot his turnouts?"

"Eh?" Long asked.

"Firefighters love fire," Barnes said. "Sometimes one of them will get to loving it a little too much and start one when things are slow."

Long reflected for a moment, then shook his head. "When I got here, there were four guys on it. All in turnouts. But I'll ask the fire chief if he noticed anything."

Barnes nodded. "Probably nothing there. But you gotta touch the bases."

The west wind subsided for a moment, and the smell of barbecue and wet ash got stronger. Active turned away from the ruins. "Cowboy said we have eight dead here, not counting Cammie. If they're all still in there, how do we know?"

Carnaby pointed at the ATVs in their circle of yellow tape. "It's an estimate. We initially had five four-wheelers, meaning at least five people right there, plus Chief Silver is six, plus Cammie is seven at least. But some of the four-wheelers might have had two people on them. And there could have been some walk-ins."

"We may never know for sure," Barnes said. "Sometimes in a fire this hot they're so burned up or melted together, you can't get an exact body count."

"Wait a minute," Active said. "Jim Silver never drove a four-wheeler. How do we know he was inside?"

"His city Bronco was parked out front, but we moved it already," Long said. "We checked with his wife, and. . . ." He shook his head.

"How's Jenny taking it?"

"I heard she's going up to Cape Goodwin." Long shrugged. "Her mother and sister live up there, one of her and Chief Silver's daughters too. I think their son is coming up from Anchorage."

Active waved at the four-wheelers. "Maybe a couple of these belong to Jack and Enos."

Carnaby shook his head. "Nope, they were on Jack's Honda, and they drove it to the emergency room. That's how we got the alarm. The ER called 9–1–1."

"How about Cammie? Did one of these belong to her?"

"No telling till we talk to her family," Carnaby said.

Active studied the ATVs. "So how do we find out who owns these? They don't have plates."

The captain grimaced. "Nobody registers an ATV

around here. We'll just have to wait for people, family members, to realize somebody never got home last night and come check. We put out the word on Kay-Chuck."

Active glanced at the ATVs in the circle. "There's only three machines now. The other two have already been claimed?"

Long nodded, flipped open his notebook and showed Active a page with six names on it. Cammie Frankson, Jim Silver, and the two survivors in the hospital were at the top. Below them were Augie Sundown and Rachel Akootchuk, who, Long reported, had been identified when their four-wheelers were claimed.

"Augie Sundown?" Active said. "Ouch."

Long nodded again. "That family."

"First Edgar and now Augie," Active murmured.

Augie Sundown was—had been, Active corrected himself—the hottest thing ever to come out of high-school basketball in bush Alaska, where the game was a religion, played under street lights or moonlight or the northern lights on iron-hard frozen snow with gloves for protection when it couldn't be played inside.

Augie, known as "Mr. Outside" for his ability to score from beyond the three-point line, had played four incendiary seasons for the Chukchi Malamutes, then gone off to the University of Alaska Fairbanks to play for the Nanooks. There he was a starting point guard by the end of his first season, despite the fact that he stood just under five feet, eight inches. He had come home for the summer to teach at a basketball camp sponsored by the city and apparently had ended up at the Rec Center at exactly the wrong moment.

"Edgar?" Barnes said. "Who's Edgar?"

"Augie's father," Active said.

Edgar Sundown had vanished with his brother-in-law Cecil Harris during a seal hunt on the spring sea ice the previous year. The official search had gone on for thirteen days, nonstop, before the Troopers called it off, though volunteers had continued to patrol the ice in skiffs and bush planes till the last floe had melted and the Chukchi Sea rolled unencumbered from Point Hope in the north to the Bering Strait in the south.

"Wow," Barnes said after hearing the story from Long and Active. "Living in Fairbanks, I sure as hell knew who Augie Sundown was, but I never heard about his father and the uncle. You never found anything?"

"Not a trace." Active said. "They had two snow machines with dogsleds, a kayak—but we never so much as picked up a jerry jug off the beach."

"Two older guys, out in the country all their lives, the right gear—everybody kept thinking they could handle anything; they must be camped on the ice somewhere out there, waiting for the weather to lift or somebody to come by, but. . . ." Long fell silent and shook his head.

"Anyway, this was right before Augie graduated," Active said.

"With honors," Long added.

"It's like he had Role Model coded into his DNA," Active said.

"First kid from Chukchi ever to get a full-ride sports scholarship anywhere," Long said. "And then Edgar disappears."

"Everybody wondered if Augie would crash," Active said. "Just hang around town, shoot hoops in the city league—"

"Get drunk," Long interjected.

"He didn't, obviously," Barnes said.

"Not Augie," Long said.

"He's gonna leave a hell of a hole in the Nanooks lineup." Barnes didn't seem to notice the outraged stares produced by this remark as he took Long's notebook with the list of victims.

"You guys know anybody who's mad at any of these people? You got a police chief here, some other teenagers besides Augie, sounds like. How about it, Alan, anybody ever threaten your boss? Either of these girls have a bad breakup with a mean boyfriend lately?" He looked at the three officers.

Carnaby sighed. "Yeah, I guess we've got some interviewing to do."

"How about we all meet again around five, see where we are?" Barnes suggested. "Your office, Captain?"

Carnaby nodded. "We Troopers can take the interviews with Augie Sundown's family and Rachel Akootchuk's. Alan, do you need to stay here with the ATVs, or can you work some of this?"

"The paramedics can watch the four-wheelers." Long gestured at the ambulance. "They'll radio in the names as people come by and claim them."

"Okay, then how about you check around Public Safety, see if anybody was madder than usual at Jim? Talk to the other cops, the dispatchers, jailers, that kind of thing."

"Sure," Long said. "And I'll work back through the files and see if anybody he put away got back on the street recently."

"Good idea," Carnaby said, not sounding very optimistic.

"It's a moon shot, but you never know." Long trotted off to the ambulance and huddled with the paramedics.

"I think I'll get something to eat," Barnes said. "Anybody

around here serve steak and eggs?" Carnaby directed him to the Korean hamburger joint near the state court building, and Barnes set off on foot.

Active turned to Carnaby. "He seems pretty calm about it all."

"Barnes? Guys like him are like that."

"Like what? Cold-blooded, you mean? Abnormally detached?"

Carnaby shook his head. "It's not that simple. It's just—well, I never met an investigator worth a shit who was motivated by anything other than ego."

"Ego?"

"Ego. Not pity for the victims, not revenge, not a passion for justice. Intellectual vanity, pure and simple."

Active swiveled to watch Barnes's departing back. "It doesn't seem natural, though."

"You're like that yourself, you know."

"Me?"

"Let me ask you this: when a case isn't going right, do you get madder at the bad guy for what he did, or at yourself for not being able to figure it out?"

Active thought for a moment, then shrugged in acknowledgment.

"So," Carnaby said. "You want to talk to Augie's family, or Rachel's?"

"Augie's, I guess," Active said.

Carnaby nodded. "I heard he was staying with his grandmother. Green house up on Second Avenue, kind of behind the tank farm. Dead Cat in the yard."

Active gave Carnaby a blank look.

"As in D-8," Carnaby said. "You know, yellow, treads, a blade?"

"Ah, right, the dead Caterpillar," Active said. "I do know the place."

"I'll send Dickie Nelson to talk to Rachel's family, then. Why don't you take the Suburban and drop me at headquarters? You can swing by Grace's place to get out of your camp clothes and clean up before you get started, if you want."

"Yeah, I guess a shower wouldn't hurt," Active said. "It's starting to look like a long day."

"Lots of 'em, probably," Carnaby said.

"Oh, hell." Active frowned in irritation. "We forgot about No-Way."

"What?" Carnaby said. "Who?"

"No-Way," Active said, and told Carnaby about the dead hunter at One-Way Lake.

"Who was he?" Carnaby asked.

Active shrugged. "There wasn't any I.D. on him, no initials on his clothes or gear."

"Inupiaq or white?" Carnaby asked.

"Inupiaq," Active said. "From one of the villages up the Isignaq, I'd guess."

"Well, the lack of I.D.'s not that surprising, then," Carnaby said. "Your average village guy tends to figure the Fish and Game Troopers are out to bust an Eskimo the minute they get an excuse, so he doesn't carry any. That way, it's more hassle for the Fish and Game cops, more forms to fill out. Maybe they'll let him off with a warning."

"Not worth the paperwork?"

Carnaby nodded.

"Yeah, but hunting without a license?" Active asked, annoyed as usual by how people not from Chukchi always seemed to know more than he did about how things worked on his alleged home turf. "That's a fairly serious bust."

"Oh, most of 'em get their licenses," Carnaby said. "They just don't carry them. Makes it even more annoying for Fish and Game."

"So how do we figure out who this guy was?"

Carnaby brushed his moustache with his fingers and thought it over. "Sorta like with the four-wheelers over there, maybe? Put a message on Kay-Chuck that someone was found dead on One-Way Lake and if anybody doesn't come back from hunting, people should report it to their Village Public Safety Officer or the Troopers. Then maybe they can identify him by his stuff."

"If we can get him out of there," Active said.

"Yeah, okay," Carnaby said. "After you drop me off, run by Lienhofer's and see when Cowboy can go back up there and bring him in. Then you can get cleaned up and go see Augie's grandmother. By the time you're done, the paramedics should have some more names for us."

Active nodded, and they climbed into the Suburban and rumbled down Third Avenue toward the Chukchi Public Safety Building.

A few minutes later, Active pulled up at the Lienhofer offices and hangar on the north side of the airport. He went inside and tensed up when he saw that the only occupant was Delilah Lienhofer, who owned fifty percent of the business and one hundred percent of the worst disposition that Active had ever encountered in a member of the human species, or any other.

Her husband, Sam, owned the other half of the business; but Sam, according to Cowboy, had become a full-time drunk as the Chukchi winters rolled by and nowadays did far less than half the work of keeping Lienhofer's going, though he spent far more than half the money. Sam's high overhead was due to the fact that Chukchi had voted itself dry a couple of years earlier. Now drinking meant doing business with bootleggers, which meant prices four or five times what they had been when Chukchi was wet.

Delilah, once as much of a drinker as her husband, had dried out about the time Chukchi did, though no one knew if that was because of the new law or because she figured out the business was in a nosedive and needed at least one sober principal if it was to stay aloft. Now she was that most toxic of personalities: the drunk who had reformed without the benefit of AA or any other program and lived with a mate who hadn't.

All of which, Active agreed in theory, provided ample justification for her evil temper. But this insight was no comfort if you were the person facing it.

Which he assuredly was at this particular moment. "Can you tell me where Cowboy is?" he asked.

"The fuck you want him for now?" Delilah said from her desk behind the counter. She was a squarish, strong-looking woman with collar-length gray-brown hair. Her only concession to vanity was a carefully maintained set of long red fingernails. Now she was leaning forward in her chair, hands gripping the armrests, as if preparing to leap over the counter and use them to rip out Active's jugular. "He wakes up, he's gotta go up to the Gray Wolf mine and pick up a load of GeoNord executives from Anchorage."

"He's asleep?"

"Back there in the hangar," she said. "But don't bother him. Like I said—"

"It's just a quick run up to—"

"No, I said! No more nickel-and-dime Super Cub shit for the Troopers today. This trip to the Gray Wolf is in the twin, and that airplane not only costs a lot more than a Super Cub, but GeoNord pays its bills with a lot less paperwork and no damn whining about the state budget."

Cowboy poked his head in from the hangar. "Hey, Nathan," he said.

"Get back in there and shave and brush your teeth and wash that soot off your face," Delilah said. "You're not going anywhere but the Gray Wolf today. And find one of our jackets with the epaulets."

"We've got to get that guy out of One-Way Lake," Active told the pilot. "If you could just. . . ."

"Sorry, man, it'll have to wait till tomorrow," Cowboy said. "He's not going anywhere, right?"

Active frowned. "I still don't like leaving him up there. This time of year, everything's on the move and hungry. Bears, wolves, foxes, ravens. Wolverines too."

Cowboy gave him a what-can-I-do? shrug. "One more day won't hurt."

"I don't know," Active said. "What about somebody else? Didn't you say there were a couple guys that can get in there?"

"Usually there is, but right now there's only me."

"Why's that?"

"You know Dood McAllister?"

The name sounded familiar. He must have heard it around town—maybe on the Mukluk Messenger service on KCHK. Sooner or later, everybody's name appeared in one of Kay-Chuck's Mukluk messages, anything from a birthday wish, to an arrival or departure time for a snowmachine trip between villages, to a request to pick up or send something at the airport, to a funeral or birth announcement. But Active couldn't recall ever having met the man. He shook his head.

"He flies for us sometimes when he's between clients in his guiding operation. Unfortunately, right now his Super Cub's parked out on the Katonak Flats with busted floats. His engine quit on him a couple days ago, and he couldn't make it to anything wet, so he had to put her down on the tundra."

"He wasn't hurt?" Active didn't remember anything about a crash. Usually the Troopers were notified.

Cowboy shook his head. "Dood's rolled up a plane or two, like anybody, but, well, like they say, you don't fly a Super Cub: you wear it. He kept her right side up, but he did tear up one of his floats. Apparently he found the only pile of rocks in the Flats."

Cowboy chewed his lip for a moment, then rambled on, almost to himself. "He's got a Cessna 185 on wheels, and I guess maybe you could set down on that ridge above the lake, but then you'd have to horse the body all the way up there—nah, I think we're out of luck till tomorrow."

"Couldn't he take your Super Cub?"

Cowboy's face took on a pained and incredulous expression. Active raised his hands in supplication. Apparently he had proposed an unimaginable breach of the bush-pilot code. The Arctic had a way of making simple things complex, and this was another example. "Okay," he said. "Tomorrow it is."

"You coming?" Cowboy asked. "Kind of a job, dragging a corpse up the creek and then wrestling it onto a float by yourself." He paused. "Creepy, too."

"I doubt I can make it," Active said. "We're all on the Rec Center fire."

"How's that going? Your expert from Fairbanks come up with anything yet?"

Active shook his head. "He's just getting started. The site is still pretty hot."

"Sure." Cowboy rubbed his chin absently. "How big is the guy at One-Way, anyhow?"

"Average size Inupiaq," Active said. "About five-eight, five-nine. One-fifty, one-sixty, maybe."

Cowboy grunted. "I guess I can handle him by myself. But you owe me. This is when bush piloting gets to be un-fun."

"Nothing around here's going to be fun for a while, Cowboy."

The pilot looked at his toes for a few seconds. "How's Grace? She seemed a little—"

"Yeah, freaked out."

Cowboy nodded. "In the van, yeah."

"I don't know what that's about. It's new to me."

Cowboy nodded again, and Active sighed, then forced his mind back to business. They agreed that Active would arrange to have No-Way flown to Anchorage on Alaska Airlines' evening jet the next day. That would give Cowboy time for the round trip to One-Way Lake, even if the Arctic threw him a curve or two before the trip was done, as was highly likely.

Active signed the paperwork for the charter, then set off for the house Grace Palmer had inherited from her murdered father. It was a relief to be able to forget about No-Way for a while. If the Anchorage crime lab was as backed up as usual, it would be at least a couple of weeks before they heard anything. And by then, someone from one of the villages up the Isignaq River might have reported a friend or relative missing. With a little luck, Active would be able to scratch the dead hunter off the Trooper to-do list with almost no work.

CHAPTER THREE

WHEN HE LET HIMSELF in, Nita was watching the Animal Channel, the big blue backpack she had taken to Martha's on the floor at her feet. "Hi, Uncle Nathan," she said when she spotted him.

"Hi, sweetie." He bent and gave her a peck on top of the head. "Where's your mom?"

"Upstairs," she said, just as he'd feared.

He looked around for the remote to mute the TV. It was nowhere in sight, so he spoke over a story about the mystery of where ravens go at night. "I'll go up and talk to her."

Nita twisted to look up at him. "I think she's sad again. Is it because of me?"

"Of course not, sweetheart," he said. "You know how much she loves you."

"Mm-mmm," she said, sounding like an *aana* for a moment. "But why does she get so sad?"

Active thought about this for a long time before answering. "I don't know. It's just how she is sometimes."

Nita was silent, watching the show about the ravens, but not watching.

"Could you put your backpack away?" he asked finally, to get them focused on something mundane and manageable.

"Can I wait till there's a commercial?"

"Sure, that's fine."

Why does she get so sad? Telling Nita he didn't know was only partly a lie, he decided as he made his way up the stairs. He did know the name of Grace Palmer's demon, it was true. But the feel of it, what it was like to carry it around inside, always—of that he knew nothing, could know nothing.

He stopped at the door of the room he knew she'd be in—not the bedroom she used now, but her childhood bedroom, with the sports gear still piled in corners, the purple wallpaper, the posters of long-faded rock stars, the memories of the nighttime visits from her father.

He stepped insided. The blinds were drawn, and she lay on the bed in the dusk, still in her camp clothes, an arm thrown over her eyes. Her old Discman lay beside her, and she had earphones on. The case of an Enya CD was open on the nightstand, which was a good sign. Enya, bland as she might be, was at least optimistic, at times even uplifting.

Grace raised her arm, made eye contact, and pulled off the headphones. "Hi, Nathan," she said. "Shouldn't you be at work?"

"I have a few minutes." He smiled, bent, kissed her forehead, and put his hand on her arm. "You take something?"

"Some Tylenol PM," she said. "It'll kick in soon, and when I wake up . . . well, maybe it'll be gone. Fingers crossed."

He made Xs of the first and second fingers on each hand and held them up. "You want to talk about it at all?"

"He had my sister cremated, you know. Seeing the Rec

Center like that, it kind of . . . and his birthday's in two weeks. That always. . . ." She put her arm over her eyes again, and her shoulders shook.

He slid down beside her and worked his arm under her neck. She pushed the Discman aside, half-turned toward him, and put her head on his chest, eyes wet. "Your body is always so warm," she said, her voice low and drowsy, and snuffly with tears. "Your thermostat must be set different. Do they know who started it?"

It took him a moment to shift gears. "We're not even sure yet it was arson. Our fire expert from Fairbanks will go in as soon as it cools off enough. We're supposed to meet him at five for the report."

"Can you stay till then?"

"Ah, I have to go interview some of the families—" He stopped at the look on her face. "But I can lie here till you fall asleep."

"Sorry for all the drama. You should find someone normal."

"No, thanks," he said.

"Thanks." She slid a hand under his shirt and laid it on his chest. Her breathing slowed, and he was about to ease off the bed when she spoke again. "He must have had a boat."

"Who did?"

"Or a four-wheeler. How else would he . . . ?" She gave a deep, slow sigh and fell silent.

It was a minute before he realized she had meant No-Way, and another minute before he realized she was right. As he eased her hand out of his shirt and worked his arm from under her neck, he felt a little stupid for not thinking of it himself. The nearest of the upper Isignaq villages, Walker, was at least twenty-five miles from One-Way Lake. Nobody hiked that far to hunt caribou.

Active decided his money was on a boat *and* a four-wheeler. Load the ATV into the boat, take the boat to the right spot on the Isignaq, drive the ATV into the hills, and start shooting caribou. Then you've got a way to get the caribou to the boat without spending a week packing out meat. He made a mental note to catch Cowboy and tell him to scan the riverbank above and below the mouth of One-Way Creek for a boat and to search the area around the lake for a four-wheeler, or four-wheeler trails, or signs of a camp. Maybe there would be something to identify No-Way, or at least indicate which village he was from.

He would have thanked Grace and told her all this, but she had begun a series of tiny, delicate, endearing snores. He kissed her forehead, savored her lavender scent for a moment, and tiptoed out.

Active had no problem finding the green house on Second Avenue. The dead Cat in the yard was a dead giveaway. The problem was finding a place to park. A pickup and two four-wheeler ATVs filled the driveway, and three more ATVs lined the street out front. Active stopped the Trooper Suburban behind the ATVs on the street and walked up to the house.

The *kunnichuk* door was open, and the inner door swung open at his knock, disclosing a roomful of Inupiat women, most of grandmother age. "*Arii*, that Augie," one of them was saying as Active took off his hat and waited to be noticed. "You remember when Barrow got that big tall *naluaqmiu* on their team and he try to stop Augie that time and when Augie go around him, that guy's shorts are falling down on his ankles?"

This produced a shower of giggles from the *aanas,* another of whom picked up the story. "That *naluaqmiu* boy try say Augie pull his shorts down, but them referees never see nothing, so they couldn't even call him foul. *Arii,* that Augie!"

There was more of the silvery laughter, fading as the women sensed his presence.

"I'm looking for Lena Sundown?"

The woman who had told the first part of the story pointed through a doorway into the kitchen. "Lena," she shouted, "that Trooper is here."

A red-eyed woman came to the door, smiled in a small way, and motioned him through. "You could sit down," she said.

He took a chair at the table and watched as Lena Sundown worked at the stove, dropping batter into a pot. She had dark gray hair but was rather smooth-skinned and not fat. He doubted she could be much past fifty, which seemed a little young for the grandmother of a college kid. But, then, girls in Chukchi tended to become mothers at an early age. Suppose Lena gave birth to Augie's father, the late Edgar, at seventeen, and Augie was born when Edgar was likewise seventeen. Augie had probably been about nineteen when he died, which would make Lena only about fifty-three.

Fifty-three and bereft of both a son and a grandson— and possibly widowed too: he didn't recall hearing of Lena having a husband.

How to get into it? The Inupiat, particularly older Inupiat, were comfortable with long silences, but they gave him the fidgets, Anchorage-reared as he was. Suddenly he recognized the smell filling the room. And an opening.

"You making seal oil doughnuts?"

"Ah-ha," she said. "Couple minutes they'll be ready. You like 'em? Lotta people don't, especially if they're *naluaqmiiyaaq*."

Was she grinning a little? At a time like this? It was possible. He had never met an *aana* yet who could resist the temptation to rib him about his Anchorage upbringing. "Sure I like 'em. Everybody likes seal oil, right?"

Her face turned sad again. "Augie always like 'em, all right, ever since he's little. You want some coffee?"

He nodded, and she brought him a cup, black, which was how he liked it.

"Could I talk to you about your grandson?"

"*Arii*, I come back here to get away from those ladies because I don't want to talk about it no more." She turned back to the stove and dabbed at her eyes with the corner of a dish towel. "First my son Edgar, now it's Augie."

He drank some of the coffee before responding. She hadn't quite refused to talk. "Did you hear we think somebody might have started the Rec Center fire on purpose?" he asked finally.

"Who was it? You catch 'em yet?" She stayed busy at the stove, keeping her back to him, deciding whether to open up.

"Not yet. That's why we need to talk to people. To figure out who it was."

She slid the doughnut pot off the burner, turned to face him, and sighed. "*Arii*, that Rachel." She came to the table and sat across from him, her hands around her own coffee mug.

It took him a moment to make the connection. "Rachel Akootchuk?"

Lena lifted her eyebrows in the Eskimo yes. "Those *miluks*. I try tell Augie she's trouble, but he won't listen."

It took him another moment to sift through his tiny vocabulary of Inupiaq for the meaning of *miluks*. Breasts. "She was Augie's girlfriend? And she had—"

Lena lifted her eyebrows again and cupped her hands in front of her chest. Quite some distance in front. "They're like magnets for you guys, ah?"

"Well, some guys—"

Lena snorted.

"All right, most of us, but. . . . Wait a minute, are you saying Rachel started the fire at the Rec Center? But she was killed, too."

"Not her. That Buck Eastlake. You know him?"

Active struggled to place the name. "He was, wasn't he on the Malamutes before—"

Lena raised her eyebrows. "He's on the team, too, all right, pretty good player, but not like Augie. Try for team captain, but Augie get it."

"And Rachel—"

"That Rachel, she's with Buck till Augie gets team captain, then Augie get her too. Girls with big *miluks*, they sure like basketball players, ah?" She gave a little chuckle of what sounded like reluctant pride, then frowned again. "I tell 'im she's trouble, but he don't listen."

"Guys that age usually don't."

"Guys any age if a girl got big *miluks*, is what I see from my life."

Active couldn't think of a response, so he just raised his eyebrows.

"Ah-hah," Lena said with a nod. "That Buck, he's real mad about it, especially when Augie get that scholarship to go to Fairbanks and Buck don't get nothing. He blame Augie for everything, say he better look out. Buck try fight him couple times, but Augie don't want to and he's so fast Buck can't hit him, so there's no fight, what Augie told me.

"Anyway, Buck, he didn't get no scholarships, so he have to stay around town, get that cargo job at the airport."

"Ah," Active said. "That's where I've seen him." A face suddenly clicked into focus. A tall kid, especially for an Inupiaq, much taller than Augie's five-eight, yet it was Augie who'd gotten the limelight and the scholarship. And Rachel Akootchuk of the magnificent *miluks*.

Active pulled out his notebook and wrote down the name.

"Then Augie leaves for Fairbanks, and Rachel's still here," Lena continued. "She's mad because Augie never take her with him, so she goes back with Buck and I think if she doesn't turn up pregnant from Augie in couple months, everything will be good."

"And she didn't?"

Her face took on an expression of remembered relief. "Nope, no babies. She's here; Buck's here; Augie's in Fairbanks, so seem like it's all right. But then he come home this summer and, next thing I know, he's right back with that Rachel. And now he's talk about she might come back to Fairbanks with him!"

She gazed at him with a look of outrage and expectation.

"Imagine that." He gave his head a shake with a frown he hoped would convey an acceptable degree of disap-proval. "And Buck started threatening Augie again?"

"No, this time he never say nothing. He just have a look whenever I see him around town. Augie laugh when I try warn him, but I tell him, that Buck is a man that don't care no more."

Active stifled a sigh. "Where does Buck live?"

Lena put a finger to her chin, lost in thought. "Seem like him and Rachel have that little red cabin up by the radio towers. You know that place have all them old doghouses, that *naluaqmiu* musher used to live up there?"

Active thought he could picture a red cabin at the north end of town, surrounded by the oil drums cut in half that provided all the shelter a husky needed, even in an Arctic winter. He started to make a note of the information.

"And then she kick him out when Augie come home, and he's . . . where he's living?"

Active put down his pen and waited her out.

"His uncle's place, I think."

"Ah," Active said. "Uncle . . . ?"

"Sayers." She nodded in satisfaction.

He picked up his pen and wrote this in his notebook. Sayers didn't sound like a Chukchi surname. The uncle must have been an outsider who'd married an Eastlake female. "And his first name?"

"Ah-hah."

He looked at her, then at his notebook. "Mr. Sayers. Do you know his first name?"

She stared at him with a puzzled look. "S-A-Y-E-R-S, I guess."

"No, I mean—" Then he got it. "Sayers Eastlake is the uncle's name?"

Lena looked even more puzzled. "Didn't I say that already?"

"You did, but I—"

"But you're *naluaqmiiyaaq*. Everybody know that."

He gave his head a little shake to clear it and asked if she knew where Sayers Eastlake lived.

She put her finger to her chin again. "I think he live somewhere up there, too, but I don't know where. You could just go up there, ask around, ah? It's E-A-S-T-L-A-K-E."

"Thanks," he said.

As he made his way toward the door, the women in the living room were watching a video of a basketball game. He recognized Augie Sundown and the other Malamutes, but not the opposing team. The boys on it were all white and tall. Definitely not the Barrow team that had had only the one tall *naluaqmiu*. Probably from a Christian school in Anchorage or Fairbanks. Chukchi played in the small-schools class at state tournaments, and the Christian schools in Anchorage and Fairbanks were the only small schools in Alaska with white student bodies.

He watched for a few moments as Augie ran the team and the game, showing off the uncanny dribbling skills and the quick jump shot that seemed to come out of nowhere and had earned him the nickname Mr. Outside. Except he wasn't really showing off. He looked like a creature at home in its environment, doing what came naturally without much conscious thought. Like a seal in an open lead or a polar bear loping across an ice pan.

Active felt a touch on his arm and turned to see Lena behind him. She motioned for him to follow and led him down a short hall and into a bedroom.

At least, it had once been a bedroom.

"I call it the Augie Sundown museum," Lena said with

a sad little chuckle. "He always tease me about it, but I think he like it."

Active gazed around the little room. Trophies, medals, plaques, and photographs filled a floor-to-ceiling bookshelf. A scrapbook stuffed with newspaper clippings lay open on a table near the door.

"He always like basketball, even when he's little," Lena said. "We used to watch that NBA together on Saturdays. And he make me put up a toy basket out there in the living room when he's maybe seven years old. Every time he practice his jump shot, this old house shake and it turn on the furnace." She chuckled again, not quite as sadly. "Sure used to get hot whenever he play."

"I'm sorry for your trouble," he said.

"Me and Augie, we take care of each other. After my son Edgar split up with Augie's mom, Augie stay here because Edgar don't have no woman around and Augie's mom, she go to Nome."

"That was where she was from?"

"No, they got bars in Nome. That's why she go. She's still down there, what I hear, but Augie never see her in a long time." She paused. "I don't know if she even heard about our Rec Center fire yet."

"I'll have the Troopers in Nome contact her," Active said.

"I hope you catch that Buck Eastlake," Lena said. "Augie, he was a real good boy. He make some of these other boys around here think an Eskimo can do something, all right. Everybody like him, everybody but that Buck."

Active went out through the living room, where the *aanas* were still watching Augie on Lena Sundown's TV, and to the Suburban. He drove north up Third Street in a fall rain, cold and steady and wind-driven, the kind of rain that seemed like it would go on until it turned to snow and winter set in.

For lack of a better idea, he started at Rachel Akootchuk's red cabin, which was as vacant as the oil drums in the yard, then drove around the neighborhood looking for someone to ask where Buck Eastlake's uncle might live. But that turned out to be unnecessary, as the second house he passed bore a sign with "Sayers Eastlake" cut into the wood with a router.

A teenage girl answered his knock, a cordless phone pressed to her chest. When she saw his uniform, she put the phone to her mouth. "I'll call you back. There's a State Trooper here. What? I don't know what he wants. *Arii*, I said I'll call you back!"

She clicked the phone off, and he introduced himself. She said "Hi," but didn't offer her own name, so he plunged ahead. "I'm looking for Buck Eastlake, or Sayers?"

"They both went caribou hunting," she said. "At my dad's camp up by Katonak village."

"When did they leave?"

"Dad left three days ago, maybe. Buck, he only left last night. He had to work yesterday, so he couldn't go before."

"Buck left last night? What time?"

She chewed on the stubby antenna of the cordless. "Maybe about seven or eight?"

"By boat?"

She lifted her eyebrows, yes, then frowned in uncertainty. "How else would he go up there? Why you asking about my cousin?"

"He took a boat up there at night?" The Katonak River drained hundreds of thousands of square miles of prime caribou country in the Brooks Range north and east of Chukchi. Katonak village lay about fifty miles upstream from the river's mouth on Chukchi Bay. "That's a long trip in the dark."

The girl lifted her eyebrows again. "That Buck is always on the river if he's not working or playing basketball. He could do it at night, especially if the weather's good and there's a moon."

Active tried to remember. The weather had been clear in Chukchi the previous afternoon when he and Grace had crammed themselves into Cowboy's Super Cub for the trip to One-Way Lake. But had there been a moon last night? He tried to visualize the scene at One-Way Lake as evening came on. Yes, he was sure of it, a full moon gliding up from the southeast as the sun dropped behind the ridge and draped their camp in shadow.

So Buck Eastlake could have left Chukchi and navigated up the river by moonlight. He could have been fifteen or twenty miles away when the Rec Center went up in flames a little after ten. Or he could have parked the boat somewhere past the last houses at the north end of Chukchi spit and hiked back to the Rec Center to get even with Augie Sundown and Rachel Akootchuk before setting off for caribou country.

"Where's your father's camp? Upstream or downstream from Katonak village? And which side of the river?"

The girl shrank a little at this barrage of questions. "Why you want my cousin?"

"We have to tell him Rachel Akootchuk was killed in the fire last night." It wasn't a complete lie, Active told himself. Just a half-truth.

The girl put her hand over her mouth. "Rachel's dead?"

He lifted his eyebrows.

"That's sad, even if she was a tramp with that chest of hers. I always told my cousin she's no good and he should just let that Augie Sundown have her. But it's still sad she burned up."

Active felt an extra pang of sympathy for Rachel Akootchuk. Not only was she dead, but it appeared that, when she was alive, her *miluks* had earned her the undying enmity of every female she ever met.

"Very sad," he said in his gentlest voice. "Now can you tell me how to get to your father's camp?"

The girl closed her eyes for a moment, and he wondered if she was about to realize her cousin was a suspect and shut down on him. But, no, she opened her eyes and explained that her father's camp was on the north bank of the river, second or third bend above Katonak village. It was easy to spot, she said, because the cabin was up on a bluff and painted yellow, like their house, and there was a dead snowmachine in the yard. And there should be two boats pulled up to the riverbank.

Active thanked her, returned to the Suburban, and radioed Dispatch for the name and address of his next interview.

HE GOT to the five o'clock meeting a little early so he could report on the plan to retrieve No-Way the following morning. He dropped into an orange plastic chair in front of the boss's desk.

"It'll have to do, I guess," Carnaby said distractedly after Active had outlined the arrangements. "I just hope Cowboy gets to the guy before something else does. A family will never quite get to closure on a deal like this unless the remains are recovered and they can give him a proper burial."

"Anybody upriver been reported late from a hunting trip yet?"

Carnaby shook his head. "Not a peep. Kinda odd, huh?"

Active shrugged. "It's the Arctic. Everything takes two weeks longer."

"Tell me about it," Carnaby said. "What's he look like, anyway?"

Active was momentarily speechless. "Like I said, the pike—"

Carnaby waved him off. "I mean otherwise."

Active recited the same statistics he'd given Cowboy Decker, then filled in details about No-Way's clothing and rifle. "He seemed kind of light-skinned for a full-blooded Inupiaq," Active added as an afterthought. "Lighter than me, certainly. Maybe a half-breed or a quarter white?" As he spoke, he heard people in the outer office and Dickie Nelson asking Evelyn O'Brien, the Trooper secretary, for Carnaby.

Carnaby grunted. "Hard to guess, if he was in the water with the pike for a while. Anybody'd look like a ghost, probably." He rose to wave Nelson and Alan Long into the office.

Long took the other plastic chair near Carnaby's desk, turned it around, and sat with his arms draped over the backrest. Dickie Nelson was left with the choice of standing or taking the ancient green leather couch. He opted for standing—or leaning, actually—against a four-drawer file cabinet. They all knew the perils of the green couch: it tended to swallow its occupants, effectively excluding them from any conversation.

"How about we get going here?" Carnaby said. "Where's Ronnie, anyway?"

"Still finishing up at the Rec Center," Nelson said. "He said he'll see you by six at the latest."

"All right, so what have you three got?"

"As I think everybody knows," Long said, "all of the four-wheelers have been claimed except one."

"What do you make of that?" Carnaby asked.

"I don't know," Long said. "Maybe—"

Carnaby waved a big hand and said, "Never mind, let's go over the interviews first."

"Well, as I said, four of the five ATVs have been claimed," Long said. "And I think all the families have been interviewed." He looked at Active and Nelson for confirmation. Both nodded.

"Anything?" Carnaby asked.

"A possible," Active said as the other two shook their heads.

"All right," Carnaby said. "One at a time, then."

Each of the three reported on the interviews he had conducted over the course of the day, as more and more of the ATVs had been claimed and the paramedics had radioed the names of the claimants to Dispatch at the Chukchi Public Safety Building.

In addition to Lena Sundown and the girl cousin of Buck Eastlake, Active had also talked to a superintendent for the construction company rehabilitating Chukchi's decrepit elementary school. Two of the men on the job—a carpenter named Charles Hodge and an electrician named Roy Marks—had borrowed a company four-wheeler to go to the Rec Center for a sauna. Both had been in Chukchi less than a week, and the superintendent was pretty sure they hadn't had enough contact with the locals to get anybody mad enough to want to kill them.

Dickie Nelson had talked to the family of Rachel Akootchuk, who said she had gone to the Rec Center with Augie Sundown to watch him shoot hoops. Nobody at her house could imagine anyone wanting her dead. The name Buck Eastlake hadn't come up.

The owner of another of the four-wheelers found in front of the Rec Center had been identified as Lula Benson, who managed the bingo operation there. Her husband, a sixty-ish Inupiaq named Benjamin Benson, couldn't think why anyone would want to kill her, either.

Alan Long reported on his day's work, including the fact that one of the four-wheelers had indeed belonged to Cammie Frankson.

"So," Carnaby said when the round-robin was over, "we've got seven fatalities so far, counting Cammie and Chief Silver."

"Plus whoever was on the unidentified four-wheeler," Nelson said.

"In all probability," Carnaby agreed. "Plus maybe a walk-in or two. How does that square with what the paramedics took out of there?"

"They didn't yet," Long said. "Barnes hasn't released the bodies."

Carnaby frowned for a moment and finger-brushed his

moustache. "What do we do about that last four-wheeler?"

"I finished early," Active said, "so I went by the Rec Center and checked it out. Like Alan said, there was no I.D. on it, but it is a fairly new Honda, so I towed it over to the dealer's. They're going to see what they can figure out. Check serial numbers and so on against whatever they've got in their records."

"Cop time or village time?" Carnaby asked, not sounding very hopeful.

"They promised to have it done tomorrow," Active said.

"What else?" Carnaby said, looked around the three of them. "Dickie, what's left on your list?"

"Nothing, far as I know," Nelson said. "I'm ready for the next phase, whatever it is."

"Go ahead and knock on doors around the Rec Center, then," Carnaby said. "Maybe one of the neighbors saw something."

Nelson nodded and left.

Active pulled at his lower lip. "Did Jim go to the Rec Center much? I don't remember him ever mentioning it." He visualized the Chief's paunch-bellied middle-aged figure. "Or looking like it."

"Excellent point," Carnaby said. "I don't think he did hit the gym very often. What about it, Alan? You know if he ever went?"

Long wrinkled his nose and squinted: an Inupiat no.

"Maybe you should ask around the city force," Active said. "See if anybody knows why he was over there last night."

"You bet." Long scraped his chair back and stood up.

"And weren't you going to check on whether anybody who Jim had put away hit the streets recently?" Carnaby asked.

"I didn't get—" Alan Long shut up at Carnaby's look, then rushed to fill the resulting vacuum. "I'm on it, Captain. Cop time." He pulled on his coat and scooted out the door.

"He's on it," Active said.

"Silver used to call Alan his alpha pup," Carnaby said. Then he ruminated in silence and Active wondered if he was being dismissed too. Finally the captain shook his head. "He asked me to recommend him for Jim's job."

Active grinned. "Alpha pup, huh? You gonna do it?"

Carnaby frowned. "He might grow into it. People do that, you know."

"Or not."

"Or not," Carnaby agreed, with a burdened look. He was silent again. Finally he said, "Christ, I hope Barnes comes up with something."

Active raised his eyebrows in agreement. "Like maybe a short in the wiring at the Rec Center?"

"Something like that. Accidental origin would be nice," Carnaby said. "You think?"

"I don't think anything yet, but my gut says not."

"Mine, too," Carnaby said. "Dammit. Seven, eight people, whatever we end up with. How much do you like this Buck Eastlake? Worth flying up there to talk to him?"

"Probably, unless something better comes along," Active said. "It is kind of shaky, though. Couple kids bump chests over a girl with big *miluks* for what, two, two and a half years, then all of a sudden it turns into mass murder by arson?"

"Stranger things have happened," Carnaby said. "What else we got? I mean, who the hell would do such a thing? Whatever it was about, it can't possibly make any sense."

Active shrugged. "Most arsons are never solved. Remember the *Investor*?"

Carnaby winced at the name, as did most Troopers who had been in uniform at the time. Active had been only a kid then, but had heard plenty about the *Investor* fire when he hit the Trooper Academy several years later.

The fishing vessel had been set ablaze near the hamlet of Craig in Southeast Alaska. Eight people had died, including a family of four. No one had ever been convicted of the crime.

"God, I hope this doesn't turn out to be a rerun of that one," Carnaby said. "I didn't work the *Investor*, but . . . the guys that did, they still obsess about it. It's the kind of thing that stays with you your whole career. And after. All right, you get hold of Cowboy and see about getting up the river to Eastlake's camp after he gets your guy out of One-Way Lake tomorrow."

Active nodded.

Carnaby cleared his throat and looked at something scrawled on his desk blotter. "Listen, I had a call a couple hours ago from Harry Winthrop down in Anchorage. He was checking references."

Active's eyes widened, but he held his tongue.

Carnaby made him wait a good thirty seconds, then grinned. "I told him you weren't a total screwup."

Somewhat to his own surprise, Active found himself whooshing out a breath. "I finally have a shot at getting out of here?"

"More than, looks like," Carnaby said. "I got the impression it's just a matter of working the paper at this point. I imagine you'll be in Anchorage by Christmas."

"Thanks, boss," Active said.

Carnaby waved it away. "Ah, I'd never stand in your way. Just wish I could buy a ticket out myself."

Carnaby, as they both knew, was likely to finish his career running the Chukchi Trooper post. A few years earlier, he had been unlucky enough to bust a prominent state senator from Anchorage on cocaine charges and had barely escaped with his job when the jury let the senator off. It was unspoken but understood from the top of the Troopers to the bottom that the politicians would allow Carnaby to stay on long enough to get his pension if he did it quietly and at the maximum possible distance from Anchorage. Carnaby's family—a wife and a nearly grown son and daughter—still lived there, and Carnaby commuted home a couple of weekends a month.

"I don't know about this outfit sometimes," Active said.

"Yeah, but what human organization isn't at least twenty percent screwed up?" Carnaby said.

Active shrugged and changed the subject. "You want me to hang around till Barnes shows?"

They heard steps in the hall, and Carnaby sniffed. "I think I smell him now."

CHAPTER FOUR

RONNIE BARNES PUSHED INTO Carnaby's office without knocking, sagged into a chair, and took a long pull from a bottle of Diet Pepsi. Red-rimmed eyes peered from his soot-covered face like wolves in a cave.

He set his drink on the floor, pulled a tube of Rolaids from a coat pocket, broke it in half, and chewed about four of the tablets. "One in the women's sauna," he said. "Looks like the fire came up so fast, she couldn't even get out of the sauna. Just curled up in a corner like a kitten."

"That must be Rachel Akootchuk," Active said.

Carnaby nodded.

"Couple in the hallway outside the locker rooms too, stretched out like they were crawling for the exit when it got them," Barnes continued. "But the men's locker room. The guys in there were all stacked up at the doorway. Maybe the crime lab will be able to figure out how many, but I sure as hell can't. Three, four, maybe." He rubbed the grime on his face and drained the bottle of soda. "All burned and melted together like they were fighting each other to get out but the door wouldn't open. Now, why would that be, do you suppose?"

Carnaby opened his window, then his door, letting a little breeze circulate through the office. The smell of smoke thinned out somewhat.

"It was locked?" Carnaby said.

Barnes shook his head. "Not when I got there. The mechanism still worked fine." He reached into his coat again and came out with a plastic bag, sealed with evidence tape and tagged. "I think maybe this is why."

Carnaby took the bag and examined the contents: a twisted loop of blackened wire. "This? How?" He passed it to Active.

Barnes sighed. "Either one of you guys go there to work out?"

"I do," Active said. "Or did." It was hard to think of the Rec Center in the past tense. "Three or four times a week. Especially when the weather was bad and I couldn't run." He paused and counted back. "I was there three nights ago, I think."

"Lucky it wasn't last night," Barnes said.

Active cleared his throat and said nothing.

"See anybody weird hanging around, like they were casing the place?"

Active reflected, then shook his head.

"How about this wire here? Ever see anything like that around the door to the men's locker room?"

Active studied the contents of the plastic bag, trying to visualize the locker room entrance. It was down a hall, near the back of the building, opening to the right. "Don't think so," he said.

"Well, when I found those guys piled up there, I shoveled through the debris around the doorway and found that wrapped around what I think was the inside doorknob. The door was some kind of heavy-duty wood, so it was eventually consumed, just the doorknobs left and the lock and the hinges. And that." He pointed at the plastic bag with the wire in it.

"On the inside doorknob," Carnaby said.

Barnes nodded. "Which way'd that door open?"

Active closed his eyes for moment and remembered turning into the locker room. Pull the door toward him, or push on it? "It opened in," he said. "Hinged on the left as you entered."

"Thought so, but it's hard to be sure of anything in there now," Barnes said. He paused. "You'll see what I mean in the pictures." Then he shook his head as if to clear it. "Suppose you wrapped a loop of wire around the inside doorknob, then shut the door on the wire so it came out on the other side, right by the outside doorknob?"

Active and Carnaby nodded. "And then?" Active asked.

"Exactly," Barnes said. "And then what? Was there some kind of hook or something outside the door he could have anchored the wire to so nobody inside could get the door open and, after everything burned up, all we'd have is this little piece of wire?"

Active thought for a moment and shook his head. "I don't remember anything like that. But I might not have noticed." He shrugged. "You know how it is. You don't see things after four or five times. You didn't find anything like a hook in the debris?"

Barnes shook his head. "Nope. Just the wire."

"Didn't that place used to be the Air Guard Armory before they built the new one?" Carnaby asked.

"I think I did hear that," Active said.

Carnaby looked at Barnes. "The wire might not mean anything, Ronnie. It could have been lying around ever since the Guard was in there. Maybe the door jammed by itself. From the heat. Or maybe those guys panicked and jammed it trying to get out."

Barnes gave his head a slow wag, reflecting. "Anything's possible. But I don't think so."

"Is there any other sign of arson?" Active asked. "Other than the wire?"

"I can't say it's unambiguous," Barnes said. "The fire appears to have started in the southeast corner of the building. That's where the furnace and the water heater were, right?"

Active nodded. "I think so. I know there was some kind of utility room at the back of the building, right behind the men's locker room. You could hear equipment running in there a lot of the time. Especially when all the showers were on and using hot water."

"And that was a forced-air heating system?"

Active nodded again.

"Mm-hmm," Barnes said. "That explains why the fire seems to have broken out in several other places in the building as well. As the fire built up in that utility room, the ductwork would have carried superheated air all over the building until the fan overheated and quit. That old wood was probably bone-dry, and that was that."

"But you think the utility room was the original source?" Carnaby asked.

Barnes rubbed his face again, moving some grime from his moustache to his cheekbones. "There was a big heat trail in there. It ran—"

"A heat trail," Carnaby echoed. "You mean—"

"The floor was saturated with an accelerant," Barnes said. "Something set it off and the scorch mark still shows on what's left of the floor. It probably only took two or three minutes before the situation was out of control." He made an erupting gesture with his fingers. "Whoosh!"

Carnaby was taking notes now.

"Anyway," Barnes continued, "this heat trail ran from under a fuel pipe on an exterior wall, across the floor, and to the base of the wall between the furnace room and the men's locker room. Seems like the floor kind of sagged there along that wall?"

"A lot of the old buildings around here are like that," Carnaby said. "They heat up the permafrost, it melts, and they start to settle. The middle's the warmest, so it settles fastest."

"Mm-hmm, we get that in Fairbanks too," Barnes said. "So if you pour something on the floor at an outside wall, it's naturally gonna run to the middle. My guess would be, the base of that common wall was pretty well saturated with stove oil. That locker room probably became an inferno almost instantly."

"So they all headed for the door," Active said.

"Only to find it wired shut," Barnes said.

"Maybe," Carnaby said. "Let's hear about the fuel pipe."

"There's your ambiguity," Barnes said. "That pipe brought in stove oil from those tanks back of the building. Just inside the wall was a 'T' fitting, with one pipe going to the furnace and another one to the water heater."

The other two men nodded.

"Well, one of the couplings in that fitting was loose, and there was still oil dripping out of it when I got there."

"Shit," Carnaby said. "You stop it?"

"Uh-huh. I closed the valve outside at the tank."

Carnaby was silent for a time, then shook his head. "I'll say it's ambiguous."

"Yup," Barnes said. "Guy uses an accelerant that's

available at the scene, it's a bitch to prove anything. I pulled up some of the floorboards to test, but I'm figuring it's about a hundred to one I'll find stove oil."

"The way maintenance is around here, that fitting could have been like that for months," Carnaby said.

"Uh-huh," Barnes said. "Until finally conditions reached the point where the furnace or the water heater set it off, and here we are."

"But you don't think so," Active prodded.

"Nope. I don't like the wire." Barnes frowned. "I think our guy comes in the back door to the furnace room, opens that fitting till it's gushing, makes himself a trail over to the locker room wall, and then tightens the fitting back down till it's just dripping a little, like when I found it. And then—Nathan, was there a door to the furnace room at the end of that hall?"

Active visualized the layout again. He imagined himself moving down the hall, stopping at the locker room door, turning in. But if he kept going, would he hit a wall, or a door?

"Yes," he said finally, with a nod. "There was a door at the end of the hall. I never tried it, but I think it would have had to go into the furnace room."

"Right," Barnes said. "So our guy sets up the furnace room, then comes into the hall through that door, and there's the door to the men's locker room just a few feet away. He opens it a little bit, wraps his wire around the inside knob, and—" Barnes shook his head and looked out of his cave again. "—and somehow wires the damned thing shut."

Suddenly Active snapped his fingers. "Hang on," he said, and left Carnaby's office. He walked to the supply cabinets behind Evelyn O'Brien's desk and rummaged for a moment, then returned, hands behind him to conceal what he had found in the cabinet. "Turn your backs," he told the two men in the office.

As the secretary got up to watch, they obediently turned away and Active brought a roll of package twine out from behind him. He looped a piece around the inside knob of Carnaby's door, pulled the twine past the edge of the door and closed it. Then he took the eighteen-inch ruler he'd found in the cabinet and lashed it in position so that one end was braced against the door frame, and the other against the middle of Carnaby's door.

"All right," he yelled through the door. "See if you can get out without breaking anything."

The two men in the office pressed against the window in the upper half of the door, craning their necks in a futile effort to see what Active had done. They gave up and Barnes reached for the doorknob. He pulled, producing only a slight bend in the ruler. He pulled harder, then jerked, and the ruler snapped. The two halves fell to the floor.

"Well, I'll be damned," he said as he opened the door.

"Thanks," Evelyn O'Brien said, as she picked up the broken ruler.

Barnes pulled the twine off the doorknob and dangled it in front of him. "So he uses a piece of wood—maybe a chunk of two-by-four—as a brace on the outside of the door like Nathan did with the ruler. It burns up in the fire, and there's nothing left but this." He picked up the wire in its baggie and held it beside the string. "Shit, it could be."

"Or not." Carnaby shook his head. "Those guys in that room were bush Alaskans. At least half of them had to have a Leatherman on their belt, and the rest had knives. No way they couldn't have gotten through that wire."

"You ever been in a burning building, Captain?" Barnes asked. Carnaby shook his head. "I thought not. Well, in a fire like this one, you got about ninety seconds from the moment you smell smoke before the room is so hot you can't breathe and so full of smoke you can't see. All you can think about is smashing your way out."

Barnes fell silent. "More likely arson than not," he said eventually. "That's my opinion, and that's what my report'll say."

"Let me see that." Active took the bag containing the wire from Barnes. "Look how tight it's twisted together to close the loop."

"So he used pliers from the furnace room," Barnes said.

"No, it's too neat. Like a machine did it. And wouldn't you expect more damage from the heat? It looks almost untouched except for the soot on it."

Barnes shrugged. "I'll send it to the crime lab, see what they come up with. You guys have any luck today?"

"Eh," Active said with a shrug of his own.

"Maybe," Carnaby said. "Nathan here might have turned up a jealous ex-boyfriend."

Barnes's eyes widened in inquiry, and Active recounted the saga of Buck Eastlake, Augie Sundown, Rachel Akootchuk, and the *miluks*.

"Wouldn't be the first time a guy went nuts over a pretty face," Barnes said. Then he grinned. "Or a nice set of *miluks*. Never heard 'em called that before. It's a good name."

He looked at Active, serious again. "You get a moment, let me know what you make of this Eastlake guy after you go up there. Maybe I can help you get a fix on him. Especially if he shows any sign of a burn injury."

"Sure," Active said, mildly annoyed that Barnes would tell him for the second time to be on the lookout for scorched suspects.

"You're done here?" Carnaby asked.

Barnes nodded. "I think so. I'm on the noon plane tomorrow. I'll spend a couple more hours over there in the morning, but unless I turn up something new, probable arson is what you're going to get. I'll e-mail you my report from Fairbanks. The crime lab will send their report to both of us."

He shook their hands. "It's up to you guys now," he said. "If it's not your Buck Eastlake, find out who our arsonist was after, and you'll find out who he is."

After Barnes left, they needed to talk about something else to ease themselves out of that locker room with the burnt bodies piled up at the door. So they chatted about Active's shot at the job in Anchorage. Carnaby spoke highly of the salmon fishing on the Kenai River to the south of Anchorage and the moose hunting in the Talkeetna Mountains to the north, neither of which interested Active very much. Carnaby also mentioned that he thought somebody at the Anchorage post was organizing a Trooper hockey team for the Anchorage City League, which interested Active a great deal.

Finally, they locked the office and headed for the stairs, but before they got there Alan Long emerged from the well and waved a manila envelope.

"I knew there was something," he shouted. "The chief must have been psychic. Couldn't be more than a couple weeks ago he asked me to check if this guy was out."

Active and Carnaby looked at each other. They exchanged eye rolls, and Carnaby unlocked his office again. Once they were seated around the captain's desk, Long dumped out the contents of the envelope.

The two Troopers flipped quickly through the pile: paperwork from a federal Fish and Wildlife case and mug shots of an Asian named Jae Hyo Lee. The perp looked vaguely familiar, Active thought, but, then, all Koreans still looked pretty much alike to him. After he'd known more of them for a while, he supposed, their features would come to seem as individual as those of whites or the Inupiat. But, for now, Lee just looked . . . Korean.

"You didn't check then?" Carnaby asked.

Long's face fell. "Well, I got busy, and the chief didn't necessarily say it was a priority. Plus—well, anyway, I found it on his desk. Maybe he decided to do it himself."

Carnaby waved a weary hand. "Why did he want to check on this—" He studied the name, shook his head, and continued. "—on this Mr. Lee?"

"That's my point," Long said. "It's what I was coming to tell you. Jae Hyo Lee went to prison for trafficking in bear gallbladders, and he blamed me and Jim. Jim figured there might be trouble when he got out."

Carnaby was rubbing his chin. "Do I remember this case?"

"I think it was right around the time you got assigned here," Long said. "And before you came, Nathan."

"Must be," Active said. "It's all new to me."

"Wait a minute, I think I remember it," Carnaby said. "The Feds didn't say anything till they made the case and arrested the guy. Then I got a courtesy call from an agent in Anchorage."

"Sounds right," Long said. "You know how the Feds are."

Carnaby nodded. "So the guy is out now?"

Long bobbed his head vigorously. "Yep, he was released from the federal prison in Sheridan, Oregon, about three weeks ago and hasn't been heard from since."

"You checked?" Carnaby asked.

Another nod. "I called the prison and caught his case officer on her way out the door. She said Lee was due to check in with his parole officer in Anchorage two weeks ago, so I called the guy at home, and he hasn't heard a peep from Mr. Lee yet."

"Maybe he slipped back into Korea," Carnaby said. "I would, if Alaska didn't work out for me."

"I don't think so." Long shifted in his chair and began straightening the papers from the Jae Hyo Lee file.

"Why not?" Active asked.

"This is not going to put the chief in too good of a light," Long said.

Carnaby sighed and pinched the bridge of his nose. "All right, Alan. Back up, start over, and tell it all, in chronological order. The bear gallbladders, Jae Hyo Lee, why he'd blame you and Jim, and how any of it puts the chief in a bad light."

Long chewed his lip for a moment. "Also, it's kind of a Cape Goodwin deal."

"Oh, no," Active said.

"Oh, God," Carnaby said. "Cape Goodwin. What's the saying? Famous for twins and schizophrenia—"

"And polar bears," Active finished. The village of Cape Goodwin, poor, tiny, and afflicted with a terminal case of beach erosion, lay sixty miles up the coast from Chukchi, just north of the landmark for which it was named. In a few years, the village was to be moved inland because of its disappearing beach, if the money could be found. If not, Cape Goodwin would presumably disappear also.

"Oh, it's not so bad," Long said. "I got an uncle up there, an aunt, some cousins. I go whaling with them sometimes. They're pretty normal."

"Sorry, Alan," Carnaby said. "I was just repeating what I'd heard."

"I know a lot of people say it," Long said.

"But polar bears—wasn't there a deal up there a few years go?" Carnaby asked. "I remember there was a big writeup about it in the *Anchorage Daily News*. Some guy's walking down the street with his pregnant wife, and a polar bear jumps them, right there in the middle of the village?"

Long raised his eyebrows. "That was Ossie Barton. I knew him for a couple years when his parents sent him down here for high school. He was a good guy."

The story was a new one to Active. "So, what happened? He shoot the bear?"

Long shook his head. "He didn't have his rifle along, so he tells his wife to run and he pulls out a pocket knife and takes on the bear with that. She gets to a house, screaming for help, and the guy inside grabs his rifle and comes out and shoots the bear, but it's already too late for Ossie. At least he got the bear, though. He worked it over good enough with his knife that it had nearly bled to death by the time they shot it."

"Christ," Active said.

"Uh-huh," Long said. "So they do a necropsy, and the polar bear is real skinny and there's almost nothing in his stomach. It was like he couldn't hunt like a regular polar bear, so he started coming into the village, taking garbage and dogs and what-not like they do, and then he made the mistake of taking on Ossie."

They were all silent for a moment. "At least there's Ossie Junior," Long said. "She's a legend up there because of what her father did to make sure she'd be born. Little *Nanuq*, they call her."

"Her? Ossie Junior is a she?" Active asked.

"People are pretty traditional in Cape Goodwin," Long said, raising his eyebrows. "They still think that when somebody dies, the soul will come back in the next baby that's born, so they give it the dead person's name. That's why you'll hear the old *aanas* up there call some kid 'my little husband' or 'my little mother.' They think the person has come back."

Carnaby pinched the bridge of his nose again. "How'd we get on this?"

"You're the one that asked," Active said.

Carnaby shook his head, then bicycled his hands at Long in a move-it-along motion. "And this relates to Jae Hyo Lee how?"

"All right, all right," Long said. "I'm getting to it. Jae came up here eight or ten years ago to work for Kyung Kim." He paused and looked at Carnaby and Active questioningly.

The two men nodded. Kyung Kim owned the Arctic Dragon restaurant and every other restaurant in Chukchi, as far as Active knew, plus the town's only janitorial service. Active thought he'd also heard Kim owned the Arctic Arms eightplex, one of the few apartment buildings not run by the Chukchi Region Housing Authority. Kim was probably the biggest private businessman in town.

Most of his employees were allegedly relatives, though not necessarily present in the United States legally. Not long after Active's arrival in Chukchi, immigration agents had swooped down on the Dragon and carried off most of Kim's kitchen help.

"Jae is another one of Kyung's cousins or nephews or something," Long continued. "Most of them stay a couple years, then move on. Too cold for them, I guess."

He grinned at Carnaby and Active. Neither grinned back. Carnaby rolled his eyes and made the move-it-along motion again.

"Okay, okay," Long said. "Jae didn't leave. He got into the life. Hunting, fishing, trapping. A lot of your Koreans are totally psycho about fishing, but they don't hunt much and I never heard of one running a trapline before. But Jae did it all. And those Koreans, you know how they don't mix much, with us or with the whites, how they keep to themselves? Jae wasn't like that either. Next thing you know, he's taken up with a local girl and moved out of those trailers that Kyung puts his help in, and they've got their own place on the beach down south of the airport, living in somebody's fish camp. A little cabin there, a couple of wall tents, not bad if you like that life. But that's where the problem started."

There was a loud squeak as Carnaby shifted in his seat. Active scraped his own chair back and stood up to give his sitting muscles some relief.

"What problem?" Carnaby asked.

"With Chief Silver," Long said. "Jae's girlfriend was the chief's oldest daughter. Ruthie."

"Ah," Carnaby said.

Long raised his eyebrows and went on. "The chief was

kind of prejudiced against Koreans, because of how they keep to themselves, you know? If there's any kind of crime involving a Korean, you can never get any of them to say anything, and the chief hated that. Plus, he just didn't want Ruthie living the village life. His idea was, she'd go to college and end up in Anchorage being a lawyer or something or maybe come back here and work for Chukchi Region or the Gray Wolf mine. But some girls, you know, the first thing they'll do is the last thing their father wants?"

"Tell me about it," Carnaby said, with feeling.

"Uh-huh," Long said. "Well, there Ruthie was. Living in a fish camp and the chief going crazy thinking he'll have a half-Korean grandkid before he knows it. So he goes down there and gets into it with Jae and ends up flat on his back in the snow, because Jae is tough and he has a hell of a temper too. So then the chief starts leaning on Jae for any little thing he can find—speeding tickets on his snow-machine, littering, uncontained trash, I don't know what all. Made his life miserable, anyway. So you can probably guess what happened?"

"Jae and Ruthie didn't split up, I'm thinking," Carnaby said.

"Not a chance," Long said. "Ruthie's mom being from Cape Goodwin—"

"Look out," Carnaby said.

Long lifted his eyebrows again. "Exactly. Jae and Ruthie took off up there, and they moved in with Ruthie's grandmother for a while, till they found some kind of place of their own."

"They ever marry?" Carnaby asked.

Long squinted no and shook his head.

"I'll bet the chief loved that," Active said. He had a vague recollection of hearing about a daughter in Cape Goodwin, but these details were new to him. Silver had never mentioned any of it. Too painful, maybe. Every family had its secrets.

"He was pissed," Long said. "But what could he do? The women in his family got together and outsmarted him, and he knew it."

"I imagine they thought he'd come around eventually," Carnaby said.

"Well, he never did," Long said.

"Tough one," Carnaby said. "All right, let's see. Jae's in Cape Goodwin, so are a lot of polar bears, and he's Korean."

"Exactly," Long said. "It takes money to live, even in Cape Goodwin, and Jae didn't have much. What he did have was an uncle down here in Chukchi—Kyung Kim—who everybody suspected was dealing in gallbladders."

The other two men both said a silent prayer of thanks that the polar bear gallbladder trade was a matter for the U.S. Fish and Wildlife Service, not the Alaska State Troopers. Bear gallbladders supposedly sold for upwards of three thousand dollars in Korea, where they were turned into stomach medicine. Alaska was assumed to be supplying much of the market, but poaching and trafficking cases were notoriously hard to make.

"So pretty soon Jae is buying gallbladders from the guys up in Cape Goodwin, who are always killing nuisance bears around the village anyway, so why not turn a little cash at the same time? Sweet setup all the way around, other than being illegal."

Active and Carnaby nodded.

"Except things kind of got out of hand," Long said. "You know that big lead off the Cape that the currents keep open pretty much all winter?"

"The Cape Goodwin polynya," Carnaby said.

Active had been to a whaling camp on the Cape Goodwin lead during the Victor Solomon case. But he hadn't known it stayed open all winter, qualifying as a polynya.

"Of course, having that much open water in the middle of all that ice is a magnet for anything that swims or flies— seal, beluga, ducks, polar bears—so pretty soon the guys from the village are out there at the lead, killing polar bears for their bladders and selling them to Jae. Word filters out, and eventually the Feds get interested."

"So, how'd they get him?" Active asked.

"That's where I came in." Long sounded proud. "I was just out of the MPs then, and I was talking to various law-enforcement agencies about jobs when U.S. Fish and Wildlife asked me about a one-shot undercover deal for them. It turned out to be the Cape Goodwin case. I told them sure, as long as I didn't have to bust any of the local guys. The Feds got hold of some gallbladders, and I sold them to Jae."

"It was that easy? He didn't recognize you?"

"Nah, we're different ages, so we never hung out. I didn't even know about his deal with Ruthie Silver till after the case broke, and the chief finally told me about it when he heard I had been undercover. Anyway, us Eskimos probably all look alike to Koreans, huh?" Long chuckled.

Nobody else did, and he continued. "Yeah, it was pretty easy. The Feds flew me and a snowmachine up to Nuliakuk one night in January when it was colder than hell and I rode down the beach to Cape Goodwin. I poured some Wild Turkey on my shirt, took a couple of swallows, and found Jae's house and told him I had two gallbladders for sale. He didn't want anything to do with me because he didn't know me, but I acted belligerent—like a village drunk will. Finally Jae told me he'd give me three hundred bucks apiece for the bladders if I'd go away. I made one more sale a month later, and he said he'd feed me to the polar bears if I came back again. I was wired, of course. The U.S. Attorney in Anchorage got an indictment and arrested Jae a couple months after the second buy. I was already on the force here by that time. It took forever to get him to trial—he had a hell of a lawyer, which we never found out how he was paid—but Jae was finally convicted and sent off to the federal prison in Oregon."

Carnaby frowned. "The Feds can do that? Sounds like entrapment."

Long chewed his lip for a moment, lost in thought. "Let's see, how did they get around that? If they can show a predisposition to do it, it's not entrapment. So the Feds forced some of the Cape Goodwin guys to testify that Jae bought bladders from them too, and that seemed to cover it. I remember Jae lost an appeal on that point."

Carnaby raised his eyebrows and grunted. "But they couldn't bring down Kyung and the rest of the pipeline to Korea?"

Long squinted in negation. "That's right. Jae never cracked. He took it all himself."

"I can understand why Jae would want to nail you," Active said. "But why would he be after Jim? Was he involved in it somehow?"

Long shook his head. "The chief didn't know about it till it went down. The Feds didn't tell the city cops any more than they told you Troopers. But Jae was convinced Jim had set him up because of, you know, the thing with Ruthie. And pretty soon the word's trickling down from Cape Goodwin that Jae is going to get even with Jim and me. And now he's had a couple years to sit in his cell in Oregon and stew about it. My guess is, the Rec Center is his payback." Long was silent for a moment. "Maybe it's my fault. If I'd have checked like Jim said—"

"Don't go down that road, Alan," Carnaby said. "What's done is done."

Long cleared his throat.

"If it wasn't through Jim, how did the Feds get onto the Cape Goodwin deal?" Active asked.

"They never told me who tipped them off," Long said. "They operate on a need-to-know basis."

"How about the bladders you sold to Jae? Where'd the Feds get them?"

Long shook his head and shrugged.

"Well, they have their ways," Carnaby said. "But I guess Jae has to be somewhere near the top of our list for the Rec Center fire right now. You talk to Uncle Kyung?"

"I called him after I talked to the prison people," Long said. "I got basically nothing. Kyung was pretty much in 'Jae who?' mode. You know how those Koreans are."

"You check with our Village Public Safety Officer up in Cape Goodwin?" Active asked.

"He's moose-hunting up the Goodwin River," Long said. "But I got hold of his wife at home. She hasn't heard of Jae being in the village. And I would have heard if any of our city officers had seen him down here."

"You've been busy, Alan," Carnaby said in a tone of somewhat grudging admiration. "Very thorough."

Long beamed and said thanks.

"But how could Jae get into town without somebody spotting him?" Active asked. "He'd have to come through the airport, right?"

Long shrugged. "Probably. Or he could have come along the coast from Nome or Barrow in a boat, maybe."

Carnaby looked at Long with a skeptical frown. "He's that good in the country?"

Long lifted his eyebrows. "From what I hear, yeah."

Active considered the possibilities and gave up. It didn't make a lot of sense, but when had revenge and logic ever paddled the same kayak?

"So the chief's daughter is still up there?" Carnaby asked.

Long lifted his eyebrows.

Carnaby looked at Active. "Unless somebody's got a better idea, I guess you better head up there tomorrow and have a talk with Ruthie, Nathan." Then he looked at Long. "Sound right to you, Alan?"

Long looked a little disappointed. "Jae is kind of my deal, so I'd like to go, but—"

"But you helped put him away, so Ruthie's not likely to talk to you."

"Yeah," Long said.

"All right, then, we're—"

"What about Buck Eastlake?" Active asked.

Carnaby drummed his fingers on the desk blotter for a moment. "He'll have to wait, I guess. Jae Hyo Lee seems to make more sense."

The other two nodded.

"What else?" Carnaby asked. "Alan, did your guys check the ER like Ronnie Barnes said? In case somebody came in with a burn last night or this morning?"

Long stood and gathered up the Jae Hyo Lee file. "I'm on it, Captain," he said and headed for the door.

"Hang on a minute," Carnaby said.

Long paused in the doorway and turned back.

"Close the door."

Long closed it.

"Let's go back to something that came up just now." Carnaby rubbed his chin and looked at Long. "Jae Hyo Lee said he was going to get you too?"

Long swallowed. "Well, yeah, but—"

"We obviously can't assume it was just talk," Carnaby said. "I mean, look at what happened to. . . ."

Long nodded, his face losing some of its eagerness. "Chief Silver."

"Uh-huh. You still living with your mom?"

Long nodded again. "But he wouldn't—"

"If he'd do the Rec Center fire, he would," Active said.

"You guys back to twenty-four-hour patrols now?" Carnaby asked.

"Uh-huh," Long said. "Chief Silver got a grant from somewhere. Homeland Security, I think."

"Yeah, well, wherever," Carnaby said. "Have your guys patrol your mom's house a couple times an hour, eh?"

"I guess I better," Long said.

CHAPTER FIVE

THE PALMER HOUSE ON Beach Street was silent when Active let himself in for the second time that day. No TV, no radio, no kitchen sounds. It was a little after seven. He tried to remember if this was one of Nita's basketball nights and finally decided it was.

He tiptoed up the stairs. The door was open to Grace's childhood bedroom, and it was empty now. Active relaxed a little. She must be doing better, he thought.

Then he saw light under the door of her parents' old bedroom and heard muffled TV sounds coming from inside. He relaxed some more. She was herself, or as close as she got, when she slept in her father's bed. She had taken to sleeping there after his murder, seeming to regard the bed as conquered territory.

He knocked and poked his head in.

She was watching a home-remodeling show on cable, the volume lowered to near-inaudibility. He couldn't remember the name of the show, but it involved people redoing rooms in each others' houses with camera crews recording it all. And it was, as far as he could determine, irresistible to any female who tuned in to it. His mother was also addicted.

"Hi," he said as she muted the TV. "How you feeling?"

"Better," she said. "Did you find out who he was?"

He sat on the bed. She was rubbing on lip balm.

"The arsonist? No, and we're still not sure it was arson in the first place."

She shook her head with a sympathetic smile. "Bad day, huh?"

Active let out a long breath and rubbed his eyes, noticing now how tired he was. "Alan Long thinks maybe it was a Korean if it was arson. You ever know a guy named Jae Hyo Lee?"

She thought for a moment, then replied, "Don't think so. They tend to keep to themselves, you know."

"So I hear."

"Why does Alan think he did it?"

Active laid out what they had learned that day, and waited for her take on it.

"Wouldn't somebody have seen him around if he was back in town?" she asked.

"You'd think, and we'll probably do some more checking. But I don't know. Maybe he was just here long enough to set the fire. Alan Long's hot on him, and I guess I'm starting to come around myself. Oh, and by the way—"

"This is all secret Trooper stuff, and we never had this conversation, ah?" She was smiling.

He smiled back and lifted his eyebrows in affirmation.

"So Carnaby wants you to go up to Cape Goodwin tomorrow?"

"Uh-huh. Know anybody up there?"

"Not really. Everybody says people from Cape Goodwin are a little different."

"I've heard that too," he said. He was silent, thinking of how to break the news about Anchorage.

"How about No-Way?" she said before he could speak. "Did you find out who he was?"

"Well, no. Cowboy's not going up to get him till tomorrow, then we have to send him to the crime lab in Anchorage. It'll be a few days before we know anything."

"Anybody reported missing from the villages upriver?"

"Nope."

"Mmm-mm."

He shifted his position to look at her more directly, studying her quicksilver eyes for a moment. "Carnaby talked to me about something else just now too."

She looked up at him, her face tightening. "You got the transfer."

"Apparently."

"When?"

"By Christmas, probably."

Her gaze shifted to the remodeling show, still muted. "I don't know how I'd do in Anchorage. Too many memories."

"How are you doing here?"

She didn't answer, but her face got a little tighter.

"You need to get out of this house. This room."

"I know. But not yet. Don't crowd me."

"I don't mean to."

"I don't know what you see in me."

He was silent for a long time, trying to explain it to himself so he could explain it to her. Finally, he said, "I'm not so lonely now."

"Oh, baby, neither am I. Come here." She opened her arms, and he leaned in for a hug that became a kiss, then a hug again. She un-muted the remodeling show. "Let's finish this, then I'll go down and make us something to eat. How does that sound?"

"It sounds fine." He shifted around to face the TV, counting the remodeling show a small price to pay for her company.

THE NEXT morning, Active was not surprised to learn that getting to Cape Goodwin to see Ruthie Silver would not be easy. Chukchi had two small airlines that ran commuter flights to the outlying villages. Neither, he discovered, could get into Cape Goodwin just then. The ticket agent at one said that half the Cape Goodwin runway had been eaten away by a fall storm two weeks earlier, and what was left of it was too short and rough for a standard nose-gear airplane. Until the runway was fixed, you needed an old-fashioned taildragger, a Super Cub or maybe a Cessna 185, to get into Cape Goodwin. Unless you wanted to take a floatplane and land in the lagoon behind the village. "Cowboy Decker goes up there in the Lienhofer Super Cub," the agent concluded.

Active sighed and hung up, resigning himself to another run-in with Delilah. Maybe her disposition would be better today.

It wasn't.

"First you want Cowboy to go up to One-Way Lake and fly out a dead man," she said from behind the

Lienhofer counter, "and now you want him to go up to Cape Goodwin instead? The fuck for? Somebody dead up there too?"

Active shook his head. "There's been a change of plans. It's Trooper business. That's all I can tell you."

"Doesn't matter anyway. Cowboy already left for One-Way."

"Already?" Active looked at his watch. "It's not even nine o'clock yet."

Delilah shrugged. "I guess he's not running on village time today. Anyway, he probably won't be back till around noon, or a little after."

"That long, just to One-Way Lake and back?"

"Don't forget, he's got to tie a dead man on a float. And didn't you ask him to look for a boat or something?"

"Oh, yeah." Active drummed his fingers on the counter until Delilah shot him one of her glances. Something was tugging at his memory. "So, is there any other way to get up to Cape Goodwin?"

The phone rang, and she booked a charter to Ebrulik before answering him. "There is no other way to get to Cape Goodwin that I know of," she said after she hung up. "And I am kind of busy right now?"

"Wait a minute," Active said. "What about Doug McAllister? Didn't Cowboy say he's got a Cessna 185?"

Delilah shrugged. "It's Dood, not Doug, and yes, he has a 185. But I don't think he wants any charters today. He gassed up at our pumps a few minutes ago and said he was gonna be hauling supplies out to his hunting camp on the Upper Katonak. See?"

She pointed at a line of planes tied down between the Lienhofer hangar and the runway.

Active saw a squat, potbellied man loading boxes from a pickup into the back of a shiny blue-and-white taildragger with a cargo pod under the belly. It was noticeably larger than a Super Cub.

"Maybe he could drop me on the way," Active said.

"I doubt it," Delilah said.

"Well, if I can talk him into it, will you send Cowboy to pick me up when he gets back from One-Way?"

Delilah glared at him for a moment, then walked to the flight board on the wall at the end of the counter and made a note with a black marker. "I see you leave with McAllister, I'll book it," she said. "Will that be all, officer?"

The phone rang again, and he turned to leave, but stopped when she said, "Hold on, he's right here." She waved the phone at him. "It's for you, and don't tie up my line, all right?"

"You want to look for a stolen boat as you head up the coast?" said the voice of Alan Long.

"What boat?"

"Somebody stole a boat off the beach two nights ago."

"The same night as the Rec Center fire?"

"Yep."

"And it just got reported now?"

"No, it was reported yesterday, but everybody was too busy to pay attention. The report just hit my desk this morning, and I'm thinking maybe Jae took it to make his getaway."

"But if Jae came in by boat, why would he need to steal one to get out?"

Long was silent for a moment. "Good point."

Active sighed. "All right, what's it look like? I'll keep an eye out."

"Blue wooden dory, eighteen-footer, white Johnson outboard on the back. Owner's a guy named Roland Miller. Went out yesterday to load up for a caribou hunt, and it was gone."

Active left the office still writing the description in his notebook and headed for the blue-and-white Cessna. McAllister turned to watch as he walked up. "Help you?" the guide said.

Active introduced himself. "I need to get up to Cape Goodwin. Delilah says you're heading up to your camp, and I thought you might be able to drop me off."

Up close, McAllister didn't seem so much short and potbellied as tough and compact. He smelled tough too, like gas, sweat, wood smoke, and something else—animal blood, maybe? Camouflage anorak, rust-colored Carhartt jeans, hip waders folded down to the knee, the hilt of a hunting knife sticking out of a sheath on his belt. Dark, fleshy, leathery face, maybe a quarter Inupiaq, maybe half, careful eyes in what looked like a permanent squint, no sunglasses.

"Sorry. I've about got a load here, all right." McAllister gestured at the groceries in the pickup and the plane.

"Relax. I'm not doing any Fish and Game enforcement today."

McAllister shrugged. "I'm not doing any violations today. Or any other day."

Besides groceries, the pickup held four jerry jugs of gas, Active saw, and what looked to be a case of wine labeled "Solare." Active had never heard of Solare, but he guessed it was expensive. It was well known that sportsmen willing to pay fifteen or twenty thousand dollars for the Arctic Quadruple—moose, caribou, grizzly, and Dall sheep—liked their comforts, even in the wilderness. For the most part, Chukchi law enforcement looked the other way and let the local guides fly in their clients' liquor unmolested, as long as none of it hit the black market in Chukchi or the surrounding villages.

McAllister finished loading the groceries and heaved two of the jerry jugs into the back of the plane.

Active leaned on a fender of the pickup and dangled a hand over the Solare. "And the city cops are in charge of enforcing the liquor ban. But this probably isn't wine anyway, right? Probably just an old case you're using to haul groceries, right?"

McAllister muttered something Active didn't catch, lifted the case out of the pickup, and held it against his chest. He looked at Active with a little smile. "This case?" he said, and then he dropped it.

Active jumped sideways to save his feet. There was a crash of breaking glass, then a clear, red liquid began trickling out. The tang of wine reached Active's nose.

"Whoops," McAllister said, still wearing the little smile.

"That was no accident."

"That uniform doesn't mean you can fuck with people, *naluaqmiiyaaq*."

"I could bust you for the wine."

McAllister shook his head with a disgusted look. "I didn't know it was wine. The client said it was camera gear."

"I could bust your client. How would that be for—"

"Client's not here yet. And he won't be if I tell him there's a Trooper hanging around with a hard-on."

Active rubbed his forehead. "All right, I was out of line. Sorry."

McAllister hefted the last two jerry jugs into the plane. "Somebody dead up there?"

Active shook his head. "Nobody dead, but that's all I can tell you. It's Trooper business."

McAllister muttered under his breath again, then looked at Active, head tilted. "Wait a minute. From what I hear on Kay-Chuck, all you Troopers must be working on that Rec Center fire. Somebody up there set it?"

"I told you, it's Trooper business."

"All right, I'll take you if that's what it's about. And if you'll stay out of my face."

Active was tempted to ask why McAllister wasn't worried about overloading the plane any more, but decided he needed the ride more than the information. "No problem."

"Is anybody going to be shooting at us when we land?"

Active stared at McAllister, who appeared to be serious about the question. "What for?"

"They don't like strangers in Cape Goodwin. I've had my tires cut when I left my plane on the runway overnight, and I wasn't bringing in a Trooper to arrest anybody. They see your uniform, they might shoot, all right."

"Don't worry about it," Active said.

"In Cape Goodwin, you gotta worry about everything," McAllister said. "I land; you jump out; I take off. That's that."

"I'm not going to arrest anybody," Active said. "I just need to talk to them. And they don't know I'm coming."

"Okay," McAllister said. "But I'm not shutting my engine down. And how you getting out of there? I'm sure not coming back for you."

"Cowboy Decker will pick me up in his Super Cub this afternoon."

"Well, you better be out at the lagoon waiting for him. If he has to go into the village looking for you, he's liable to have holes in his floats when he comes back."

Active watched as the guide shoveled the remains of

the Solare back into the bed of the pickup. Then they climbed in and buckled their seat belts. The Cessna 185 was luxurious compared to Cowboy's Super Cub. Its skin was metal, not fabric, and it seated four, not two, with room at the back for the groceries and extra gas McAllister had loaded in.

McAllister handed Active a headset, and he listened as the guide talked to the FAA station across the field. Then they took off into the west wind beneath an unfriendly gray sky that seemed to promise more rain or perhaps snow. Maybe the weird, warm fall was finally breaking.

McAllister climbed out over Chukchi Bay, then swung right until the nose pointed due north, across the Sulana Hills toward the Katonak Flats. Cape Goodwin was to the northwest, directly up the coast from the far shore of Chukchi Bay. Active studied the shoreline curving into blue-gray haze off their left wing. No sign of coastal fog, so why was the pilot heading north instead of taking the direct route to Cape Goodwin?

He was about to ask when McAllister came on the intercom in a spray of static. "I gotta go by the Flats and check on my Super Cub."

"I heard you went down," Active said.

"Mm-mmm."

"What happened?"

From the corner of his eye, Active saw the pilot shrug. "Engine quit. Happens sometimes."

Active turned to study McAllister. Most bush pilots never passed up the chance to tell a flying yarn, but maybe McAllister was different. Active thought about the case of Solare the guide had wasted and decided he was definitely different.

Soon they were circling McAllister's Super Cub, which

was blue and white like his Cessna. The little plane was stranded in a patch of brush, one float showing a long gash down the side. The struts between that float and the fuselage had crumpled too, leaving the plane tilted about thirty degrees, the left wingtip nearly touching the tundra. Over the intercom, Active heard the pilot muttering to himself again.

"What's that? I didn't hear you."

McAllister looked at him, as if in surprise, before speaking. "Doesn't look like anybody's been fucking with it. You gotta watch 'em."

The plane was at least a quarter mile from the nearest water, a long and relatively straight stretch of one of the sloughs that meandered through the pothole lakes on the Katonak Flats.

"How will you get it out?" Active asked. "Helicopter?"

McAllister snorted over the intercom. "Right, me and my million dollars. Nah, I'll wait till freezeup and take it out on skis."

Active studied the terrain around the Super Cub. It was rough and covered with brush, fall-dappled in red and gold. "You really think the Flats will get enough snow to smooth all that out?"

McAllister said, "I'll cut enough of a trail through the brush that I can winch it out to the slough, then take off from there. All I need is a few days of hard freeze, and it looks like we're about to get it."

McAllister rolled out of his circle and pointed the nose west, straight at a low range of coastal hills, the slopes splashed with autumn reds and yellows, the ridgetops mostly barren gray rock dusted with snow.

"Too bad about Jim Silver, ah?" McAllister said over the

intercom. "He was a pretty good guy, all right. For a *naluaqmiu*, anyway."

"You know him at all?"

"Couple times he busted people that were robbing from my planes when they were parked on the ice in front of town there." McAllister grunted. "The other cops we used to have wouldn't bother with that kind of stuff, but he got me back a rifle and a couple of those Woods sleeping bags them kids took. I took him up on the Isignaq, got him a spring bear after that. He was pretty skookum out in the country, all right."

"You didn't charge him for the hunt?"

McAllister grunted again.

Active took that for a no, and decided after a moment that it probably hadn't been unethical for Silver to take the free trip. Not that it mattered now.

"It's tough he had to die like that," McAllister said. "Him and those other people. You got any ideas yet who did it?"

"It's Trooper business."

McAllister grunted again. "You I.D. them all yet?"

Active studied the guide and thought it over. On the one hand, it was Trooper business. On the other hand, some of the victims' names had already been aired on Kay-Chuck, and the village gossip circuit would swiftly broadcast the rest. McAllister undoubtedly knew just about everyone in the village. Not only that, but also their family histories, who they were sleeping or feuding or drinking or hunting with. Everything.

Active reeled off the list of the victims who had been identified so far. "Know why anybody would want to burn any of them up?"

McAllister frowned and thought it over. Finally, he shook his head. "Unless somebody was after Chief Silver maybe?"

Active thought some more and decided McAllister was likely to know as much about Silver and his family as Alan Long did. "You know a guy named Jae Hyo Lee?"

McAllister grunted. "That Korean that took up with Silver's daughter. Didn't he blame Chief Silver for that gallbladder deal in Cape Goodwin?"

"Uh-huh. You know if he's back in the country?"

"I thought he was still in prison."

"He's out," Active said. "As of about three weeks ago."

"You think he came back and started the Rec Center fire?"

Active said nothing. McAllister turned to stare at him, then directed his gaze back to the horizon.

A few minutes later, they crested the coastal range and saw a belt of stratus along the shore and, beyond that, the ocean, a limitless expanse of white-streaked steel. At its far edge, the lemon glare known as iceblink signaled pack ice over the horizon, gliding down from the north with the approach of winter.

The coast here consisted of a chain of long, low barrier islands separated from the mainland by shallow, brackish lagoons. The village of Cape Goodwin lay on one such island, a few miles north of the protruding headland for which it was named. Under the stratus, a quartering surf curled into pearly breakers before splashing onto the gravel beach.

"There it is," McAllister said. "It's famous for—"

"Yeah, yeah, I know," Active said. "Twins, polar bears, and schizophrenia."

Active studied the village as they crossed Goodwin Lagoon. A line of wooden houses straggled along the shore, dominated at one end by a cluster of fuel-storage tanks and at the other by the school, which, as in most villages, towered above everything else. The runway started just beyond the fuel tanks, and the village cemetery lay between it and the lagoon.

McAllister crossed the beach a quarter-mile from the village and rolled right to line up with the runway.

"Wait a minute," Active said suddenly. "Let's take a look at that boat."

McAllister dropped a wing and rolled into a circle around the blue dory with the white outboard beached a few hundred yards down the shore from the village. "Hey," the pilot said, "that's Roland Miller's boat. What's he doing up here?" He glanced at Active. "Looks like it's swamping."

McAllister was right. The surf was coming over the transom, and the dory was half-full of water and sand. "Wonder why he left it there," the guide said. "Normally they pull into the lagoon and land on the back side of the island."

Active looked up the beach toward the village. A dozen or so boats were beached or riding at anchor in the sheltered waters of the lagoon. A man was loading supplies into one from a small trailer attached to a four-wheeler, and another boat was making its way across the lagoon toward the mouth of the Goodwin River. A few yards in from the lagoon, the frames of several of the whale boats known as *umiaqs* rested upside-down on driftwood platforms.

Active refocused on the blue dory. "Let's make a couple more circles. Maybe it capsized and washed ashore."

"I don't think so," McAllister said. "See those?"

He pointed. A faint string of tracks dimpled the silken sand near the water before fading out in the loose gravel higher up the beach. "Probably just quit on him," McAllister said.

"Yeah, probably," Active said.

McAllister shot him a glance. "The Troopers interested in abandoned boats these days?"

"Only if somebody gets hurt."

McAllister glanced at him again, then shrugged and pointed the Cessna at the runway once more. Like every bush pilot Active had ever ridden with, McAllister made a low pass to check the airstrip before landing.

"Shit," he muttered over the intercom.

"What?" Active said.

McAllister pointed down. "Look at that. This is bad."

Active stared out at what was left of the Cape Goodwin airport. The system of lagoons and barrier islands was great country for nomadic hunters who subsisted on seals, whales, and seabirds, but it was implacably hostile to any effort to raise a permanent settlement. Unlike the somewhat sheltered recess of Chukchi Bay, the coast here was defenseless against the late summer storms that boiled up from the Bering Sea to the southwest. The one that had hit the village a few weeks earlier had chewed a huge chunk out of the island at the north end of the runway. The surviving section of the strip was appallingly short and appeared to be covered with some kind of steel matting that undulated with the natural contours of the beach and hung, twisted, over the gap left by the storm. Getting down would be like landing on an aircraft carrier, but without the tailhook.

"We don't have to do this," Active said as the Cessna

shot past the end of the strip and McAllister rolled into a turn over the lagoon.

"Shit," the pilot said. "I don't have time to take you back to Chukchi. And I ain't taking you to camp."

"What about landing on the beach? I can walk in."

"Too soft," McAllister said. "We'd nose over. That's why they have the matting. Brace yourself."

McAllister made a circle and came up the beach again, low and slow. He chopped the engine over the fuel tanks, banged the plane onto the runway, and rode it like a bronco as it bucked over the heaves in the steel matting. Active found himself jamming his feet against the floorboards in an unconscious effort to help with the brakes as the Cessna rolled and pitched toward the newly carved dropoff into the Chukchi Sea. Active had his seat belt off and his mind on swimming when McAllister finally got them stopped a few yards from the water.

Both were silent for a time.

"Shit," McAllister said finally. He revved the engine and pivoted the plane on its left main gear to point back up the runway.

"Can you get off again?"

McAllister chewed his lip, peered through the windshield at the strip, said something under his breath, then spoke up: "Without your weight, yeah. I think."

He taxied slowly past the cemetery, marked by a man-high arch formed of two bowhead jawbones, to the start of the runway. "Here ya go," he said, not killing the engine. "Have a nice visit."

Active grabbed his pack, popped the door open, and was about to step into the propwash when he realized he didn't know which of the rundown houses in the little village was occupied by Ruthie or by her grandmother. Or, for that matter, by Jim Silver's widow, Jenny, who supposedly had flown home to Cape Goodwin the morning after the Rec Center fire.

He closed the door again. "Know where I can find Ruthie Silver?"

McAllister studied him a moment. "Why d'you want her?"

"Troo—"

"Yeah, yeah, I know, Trooper business," McAllister said. "I think she stays with her grandmother down by the school." He pointed along the gravel street that rambled through the center of the village, generally paralleling the beach. "That way."

CHAPTER SIX

McALLISTER'S ENGINE ROARED, AND the plane quivered in place as the pilot held it with the brakes and let the RPMs build. Then he let go, and Active watched the plane bounce down the matting and stagger into the air just before the dropoff into the sea.

Feeling suddenly grateful that Cowboy Decker would be picking him up in a floatplane from the lagoon, Active turned and started down the street, the knee-length breakup boots that were part of his uniform from spring to freezeup sinking into the beach gravel.

From ground level, Cape Goodwin looked deserted. No four-wheelers moving, nobody walking. Just the wind off the ocean, a fine rain stinging his face, and a skein of seagulls riding the updrafts along the tideline. No sign of polar bears, but then, none was to be expected until the sea ice closed in for the winter and brought the animals ashore.

Well, the kids would already be in class; most of the men were probably upriver hunting, like the Village Public Safety Officer; and it was early enough in the day that everyone else, operating on village time, was probably still in bed.

He made his way to the school and saw several houses that could be Ruthie's grandmother's place, but none that seemed likelier than another. From the corner of his eye, he sensed a flicker of motion at a window as he passed a cabin that looked to have been built of driftwood logs. He turned to catch a glimpse of a heavy-jawed oval face, but it vanished before he could raise a hand to wave or turn toward the door to knock.

He was about to go into the school and ask for directions when he heard the stutter of a four-wheeler near the shore of the lagoon. He watched as the driver rode it up the slope to the street and parked beside a house. The man pocketed the key and started back the way he had come, avoiding eye contact all the while.

He could hardly have missed an Alaska State Trooper in uniform on the village's only street. "Excuse me," Active shouted.

The man accelerated his pace toward the lagoon, Active now recognizing him from his clothing as the man who had been loading his boat as they circled to land. Active trotted down the slope to where the man was untying the boat, another of the homemade plywood dories favored in the coastal villages. This one wasn't painted, just covered with a clear varnish that glistened in the rain.

"Excuse me," he said again. "I'm Trooper Nathan Active."

The man cut him a sideways glance and tossed the rope into the boat without a word.

"Can you tell me where Ruthie Silver lives?"

The man was short and mahogany-faced with close-cropped white hair and dark glasses. He wore a raincoat, hip waders, and a baseball cap with "Native Pride" stitched on the crown. He gripped the prow of the boat and heaved, grunting loudly. It didn't budge. Evidently the tide, such as it was at this latitude, had ebbed since he had beached the boat.

Active seized a gunwale and heaved too. The dory scraped backward and then was afloat. Active grabbed the prow to keep it from drifting away. The man climbed in.

"Ruthie Silver?" Active asked again, without much hope.

"Got a whalebone in front, all right," the man said, pointing toward the school.

Active thought he remembered a bowhead vertebra beside the door of one of the houses near the school.

"Thanks," Active said. He decided to press his luck. "There's a blue dory swamped on the beach down there." He pointed south. "You know whose it is?"

The man was at the back of the boat now, squeezing a rubber bulb in the fuel line to prime the engine. "Not me," he said and yanked the starter cord. The outboard sputtered to life, and he backed the dory away from the beach, then threw the engine into forward and started across the lagoon to the mainland.

Active trudged through the gravel to the cluster of houses near the school and found the one with a whale vertebra out front. It looked like a huge, three-bladed outboard propeller carved from porous, cream-colored pumice.

He stepped through the *kunnichuk* to the inner door, knocked, waited, and knocked again, trying to imagine living on village time. Up till two or three in the morning, sleeping till noon. There were days when it sounded pretty nice. In the Arctic, it was dark all winter and light all summer. The diurnal cycle was pretty much an abstraction, another *naluaqmiut* invention of marginal utility.

Finally the door opened to reveal a gray-haired Inupiat

woman wearing a tired, kindly face and the lightweight, flower-patterned, all-purpose parka known as an *atikluk*. She took in his uniform in silence.

A tiny white dog burst yapping into the room from somewhere in the back of the house and headed for Active's ankles. The woman bent and scooped him up. "You, Jackie, you shut up now!" She cradled the animal to her chest until he calmed down. At last, he was only a silent bundle of white fur with two glaring, black BB eyes.

"*Arii*, this little can't-grow," the woman said. "He think he's great big husky, all right."

"I'm Trooper Nathan Active," he said. "I'm looking for Ruthie Silver."

"I'm Blanche Ahvakana," she said. "That Ruthie, she's still asleep I think. You don't need to bother her. She's too sad, all right."

"It's about her father."

Her eyes narrowed as she studied his. "You find out who burn him up yet?"

"Maybe Ruthie could help us."

The woman considered this for a moment, then lifted her eyebrows. "I'll get her. You could come in."

Active shut the door behind him as the woman shuffled through a doorway to the rear of the house. He was in a combination kitchen, living room, and dining room: gouged wooden dining table with mismatched chairs; an oil stove for heat and cooking; a sofa and easy chair, both old and brown; a big gray plastic trash can in a corner that probably held drinking water; clothes drying on a wooden rack behind the stove; a pair of jeans and a sewing kit on the table; a radio on a counter tuned to Kay-Chuck; a wall covered with family snapshots and a tapestry of the Last Supper.

The four quarters of a dressed-out caribou hung from eyebolts screwed into the ceiling joists. They were dripping blood onto a green tarp, but not much. The animal must have been cooled out before it was brought in for Blanche Ahvakana to cut up. A second caribou was in the process of dissection on another tarp on the floor. It had been gutted and the legs severed at the knees, but the skin was still on, except for a flap peeled back from the right foreleg. An *ulu*, the traditional pie-slice-shaped Inupiat woman's knife, lay in the chest cavity.

He took a seat on the sofa. The door from the rear of the house opened and Active rose as Blanche Ahvakana led a sleepy-eyed young woman into the room. "This Ruthie," she said. The older woman went to the stove and moved a teakettle onto a burner.

Ruthie Silver looked to be about twenty-five. Short black hair, freckles on her nose and cheekbones, a chin like her father's, a squarish, pleasant face that looked as if it might have been merry before life got so complicated. She wore black sweatpants and the heavy-ribbed white top from a set of thermal underwear. Her pajamas, Active surmised.

"I'm Trooper Nathan Active," he said.

"I know," Ruthie said. "My *aana* told me. Did you find out who, who. . . ." Her grandmother passed her a handkerchief, and she wiped her eyes, then her nose.

Active shook his head. "Not yet."

She dropped into the armchair, and he settled onto the sofa again.

"That's why I'm here," he said. "We thought you might be able to help us."

"My dad and me, we were so mad at each other. We, we—"

"Too much alike," Blanche growled from the stove. "Stubborn."

"We didn't get to say good-bye," Ruthie said. Then, after a long pause: "You worked with him, ah?"

Active nodded. "He was a good man and a good policeman."

"He ever talk about me?"

"Sure," Active said. "He talked about how much he loved you and missed you, and he said he hoped that one day you two would get over your fight and be . . . like you were before."

"Dad said that?" Ruthie sounded disbelieving, but not suspicious. More like a dream was coming true.

"Lots of times," Active lied again, with not a murmur of protest from his conscience. In reality, Silver had never mentioned this daughter who had run off with an unsuitable suitor, but why not give her the comfort she needed? Besides making her feel better, it might increase the chances that she'd talk. "He said maybe he was too hard on Jae; maybe he could help Jae get on his feet after he was released."

"Really?" Ruthie sobbed and snuffled and used the handkerchief. "I sure miss him."

Active thought of asking which one, but decided against it. He cleared his throat and dived in. "We were wondering if your dad worked out at the Rec Center a lot."

Ruthie thought it over, then squinted a no. "Not when I'm living there. I don't think he ever went."

"Do you have any idea why he would have gone the night it burned?"

She squinted again. "I hadn't talked to him since last week."

"How about Jae? Have you heard from him since he got out of prison? Is he back in Cape Goodwin yet?"

Ruthie's face froze for a moment, then collapsed into tears again.

"She never hear nothing," Blanche said, handing each of them a cup of tea. She knelt by the caribou on the floor and resumed separating the hide from the flesh with the *ulu*.

"He called me a few days before he was getting out," Ruthie said from behind the handkerchief. "He said he'd be here in a couple weeks, but he never did come, and he hasn't called, and now I don't know what happened to him. That's why I called Dad last week, to see if he would check on Jae, but he just hung up on me. Can you find Jae?"

Active considered. She was almost certainly too distraught to lie. Still, it wouldn't hurt to push a little. "We heard Jae thought your father was the one who reported him and got him arrested?"

Ruthie lifted her eyebrows. "He's almost as bad as Dad when he gets an idea in his head. I tried to tell him Dad didn't do it, but at first he wouldn't listen. Then, couple months ago when he called from prison, he said it's all right, now he knows who turned him in, and it wasn't Dad."

"He changed his mind?"

Ruthie raised her eyebrows again.

"Did he say why? Or who it was?"

"No, he just say he found out the truth, and he's sorry he thought it was Dad."

Active was silent for a long moment. How much pain could he inflict? "Did you believe him?"

"Of course. Why wouldn't I?"

"Before he changed his mind, was he angry enough to want to hurt your father?"

Ruthie's face froze again as she realized what this visit was about. She set her teacup on the floor with a loud rattle and some spillage. "You think Jae started that terrible fire?"

"We have to check all the possibilities."

"No, he. . . ." Active watched as Ruthie searched for solid ground and couldn't find a spot to put her foot. "But he said. . . ." She looked at her grandmother. "*Aana?*"

Blanche put down her *ulu* and looked at her granddaughter as if they were now separated by a huge polynya. "He's one of them Koreans," she said finally. "You know how they are. If he was going to do this thing, he wouldn't want you to know."

"Don't tell Mom it was Jae," Ruthie said. Then she buried her face in the handkerchief again.

Blanche came over and put an arm around Ruthie's shoulders. "She'll have to know sometime." Then she turned to Active. "My daughter Jenny, that's Ruthie's mom, come up here yesterday. She's at church right now."

Active set his teacup on the floor and stood. "There's one more thing. Somebody stole a boat from Roland Miller and drove it up here two nights ago, when we had the fire in Chukchi. It's swamped on the beach down that way." He pointed south. "Have you heard who brought it up?"

Blanche wrinkled her nose no. "We never hear nothing about that," she said.

Was it possible that somebody could bring a boat to a hamlet like Cape Goodwin and not be noticed? People were nosy and gossipy everywhere, but nowhere more so than in the tiny Inupiat villages of the northwest coast.

The boat thief would have arrived at night, admittedly, and the boat had been beached out of sight and sound of the houses. Perhaps he could have walked into the village without being noticed, but then what?

"Any strangers show up in the village yesterday?"

Blanche squinted no again.

Active thought it over and suddenly felt stupid. The thief had to be somebody *from* Cape Goodwin. He'd simply landed, walked home, and gone to bed. This was starting to sound like a drunk story. Maybe the theft was more like an involuntary loan. The guy would probably sober up, dig the boat out of the sand, take it back to Chukchi, and have a good laugh about it with Roland Miller.

He looked at the two women, both watching him, waiting for him to go. "Anybody come home from Chukchi yesterday, maybe they've been drinking a little?"

Another pair of squints.

He left his card, asked them to get in touch if they heard from Jae, and took his leave.

Outside Blanche Ahvakana's house, he put his baseball cap back on and pulled up the hood of his anorak against the rain and wind, both of which seemed to have picked up while he was inside.

"Nathan? You're up here? Did they find out about, about . . . ?"

He turned and found himself facing Jenny Silver, who looked like an older and more Inupiat version of her daughter.

"Jenny, I'm so sorry about Jim. I—"

She moved toward him a little and, without thinking, he opened his arms. She stepped into them, and they huddled for a moment against the weather, like mother and son or sister and brother. "*Arii*, how am I going to live without him? We're married twenty-eight years next month. He was taking me to Hawaii."

"Is there anything I can do?" he murmured after a few seconds.

"You could catch whoever did it."

"We're trying." He patted her back and relaxed his embrace.

She took the hint and stepped back, though she retained a grip on his elbow, as if unwilling to be without human contact for the moment. She peered into his eyes with a directness uncommon for any Inupiaq, particularly a woman. "You find out anything yet?"

He shrugged helplessly and squinted a no. "We're just getting started, but. . . ." He paused, momentarily frozen by the desperation in her eyes. "But we're wondering if Jae Hyo Lee could have done it. We understand he blamed Jim for—"

"Not any more. He tell Ruthie he found out it was somebody else."

"But he might lie if he was planning to do this."

Jenny Silver became still, then lurched back as if he had shoved her. He put out a hand and caught her shoulder. "You think he would—you never tell this to Ruthie, did you?"

"I'm sorry. I—"

"I have to go in there." She pulled her shoulder free and turned toward the house.

"Jenny, wait, I—there's one more thing."

She faced him again. "Ah-hah?"

"Did Jim go to the Rec Center a lot?"

"He never go. Only that one night."

"Did he say why?"

She squinted. "Just that he have to talk to somebody up there."

"He didn't say who? Or why?"

Another squint. "He'll never say much about anything he's working on, until it's finished."

She turned and hurried through the door of her mother's house.

Active started past the school toward the water, turning his face a little to the side to keep the weather from blowing into his hood.

At the beach, he swung left and headed for the blue dory, just visible through the mist, perhaps three hundred yards away. He descended the gravel slope to the packed sand near the water, where the walking was better, and trudged along, seagulls over the tide line shrieking at the intrusion, little breakers washing onto the beach with a sound like a long sigh of exhaustion.

Thanks to the ebbing of the tide, the dory was now just above the water line, the waves no longer coming over the transom. First he studied the tracks leading from the dory to the upper beach. Rain and wind had done their work, leaving only faint depressions in the sand that offered no clue as to what kind of footgear had made them.

Then he turned to the dory itself. An empty green jerry jug floated on the water that had washed into the boat earlier, as did a red-and-white Monarch vodka bottle, which he pocketed, and a red steel gas tank, still connected to the Johnson outboard by a black rubber hose with a squeeze-bulb primer in the middle. "R. Miller—Chukchi" was hand-lettered in black paint on the tank and on the jerry jug. A spare propeller lay mostly buried in the sand flushed in by the surf. A red plastic toolbox was buried up to its lid, also labeled "R. Miller." He dug it out and, inside, found two screwdrivers, four small wrenches, vise grips, and a pair of spark plugs.

The upper half of a gallon plastic jug, the mouth still capped, was tied to a gunwale. It was the Chukchi version of a bailer, used to clear the boat of water that came in via rain, spray, or the odd wave while under way. He used it to attack the sand in the bottom of the boat but quickly discovered the plastic was too soft. He dropped the bailer and combed through the sand with his fingers, but came up with nothing else.

He stepped out of the dory and looked up the beach toward the village. It would be a couple of hours till Cowboy showed up, maybe more. What to do? Every village had at least one small store. He'd find it, buy something to eat, maybe a sudoku book too, and figure out a place to wait.

He remembered from his telephone conversations with the Village Public Safety Officer that the man worked out of the same building that housed the health clinic and the city clerk's office. He could hole up there. Wherever he was in Cape Goodwin, he'd certainly hear when Cowboy Decker buzzed the village in his Super Cub.

CHAPTER SEVEN

"THINK THEY WERE TELLING the truth?" Carnaby asked. They were gathered in the Trooper captain's office for what threatened to become a standing afternoon meeting on the lack of progress on the Rec Center fire.

Active nodded. "Struck me that way. I don't think they've seen or heard from Jae since he called Ruthie before he got out."

"And he told Ruthie he'd changed his mind about Jim Silver turning him in? What do you make of that?"

Long broke in. "Like the grandmother said, of course he's going to tell them that if he's planning this thing. Otherwise they're gonna know he did it."

"And Jim didn't tell Jenny anything except he was going to the Rec Center to see somebody?" Carnaby asked. "Nothing about Jae Hyo Lee?"

Active shook his head.

Carnaby swiveled his chair to gaze out a window. Across the lagoon and the rolling folds of tundra, a wet, gray night was gathering in the east. "So where the hell is Jae Hyo Lee?" He swiveled back and looked at Alan Long. "Alan? You're the only one here who's ever met him."

Long shrugged. "Like I said, he's really good out in the

country. He could be anywhere by now if he has a boat and travels at night."

"That reminds me." Active looked at Long. "I found your stolen dory. It's swamped a few hundred yards down the beach from Cape Goodwin."

"No joke? The village, or the Cape itself?"

"The village. Looks like the guy parked it there and hiked into town. I couldn't find out who he was, but I found this sloshing around inside it." He pulled the vodka bottle from his anorak and held it up.

Long looked disgusted. "You know, it's hard enough getting a boat up that coast and around the Cape even if you're sober and it's daylight. And some drunk does it by night. I'll let Roland know he'll have to go up there and get it."

"All right," Carnaby said. "What else we got?" He studied a sheaf of notes on his blotter. "Let's see, Dickie Nelson knocked on doors around the Rec Center. None of the neighbors saw anything till they heard the sirens and looked out their windows."

The other two nodded.

"And how was your day, Alan?"

"Not a lot better," Long said. "I confirmed that none of our officers have heard anything about Jae being in town, and I checked with the ER at the hospital. No burn cases the night or morning of the fire. But we think we've got an I.D. on the owner of the last four-wheeler. The Honda dealer says he sold it to a guy named—" Long paused and flipped through a notebook. "—Tom Gage?"

Carnaby and Active looked at each other and shook their heads.

Long studied the notebook. "I didn't know him either,

but the name sounds kinda familiar. The dealer says Gage teaches aviation technology at the Tech Center. Or did teach it. White guy."

"Any family?" Carnaby asked.

Long grimaced. "I went to his house back on the lagoon. Nobody home, small place, all right, looks like maybe he's the only one that lives there. The Honda guy thinks he remembers Gage was in the middle of getting divorced when he bought the four-wheeler about a year ago, and the ex-wife-to-be had already gone back Outside."

"Any sign of a girlfriend?" Active asked.

"I don't know," Long said. "Place didn't look very feminine from what I could see through the window. No vehicles around except for a pickup on jacks with the rear wheels off and the brakes pulled apart."

"Should we let the ex-wife know?" Active asked. "The Tech Center would probably have her on file as the next of kin."

Carnaby thought for a moment. "Let it ride for now. Put a message on Kay-Chuck for Gage to contact us. If we don't hear from him in a day or two, then we can let his family know he probably died in the fire."

"All right," Long said, writing in his notebook.

"Where do we go from here?" Carnaby asked.

Active chewed his lip for a moment. "If Jae did start this fire, seems like he would have to have been planning it for a while. Maybe he talked to somebody about it. He was shooting off his mouth before he went away, right, Alan?"

Long raised his eyebrows yes.

"So, we should talk to the prison in Oregon," Active said. "Find out about his mail and visitors and phone calls, huh? See if the prison will interview his cellmate for us? You ask the prison about that, Alan?"

Long looked chagrined. "I've been busy. I was in a hurry."

Carnaby sighed. "Take care of it, will you, Nathan?"

Active looked at his watch. It was almost five-thirty and in Oregon it was an hour later. "Sure, first thing tomorrow."

"What else we got on our list?"

Active spoke. "Jae blamed Chief Silver for getting him busted, but Jim told Alan he didn't do it. And Jae ended up telling his girlfriend the same thing. What if he was leveling with Ruthie? What if the chief wasn't the target at all?"

Carnaby frowned skeptically. "And Jim just had the bad luck to be in the Rec Center the night Jae made his move on the real snitch?"

"Everybody there had the same bad luck, except the snitch," Active said.

"Good point," Carnaby said. "All right, Alan, you get on that. See if the Feds will tell us who their source was when they busted Jae."

Long pulled himself up and looked a little more official. "Absolutely, Captain. First thing tomorrow."

After taking his leave, Active drove the Suburban to his birth mother's house.

When he was born, Martha Active had been only fifteen, interested mainly in partying and sleeping around. So she had turned him over to two of her teachers at Chukchi High. Officially, his adoption by Ed and Carmen Wilhite had been *naluaqmiut*-style, complete with lawyers, court proceedings, and documents on long paper. In practice, it had operated more like a village adoption, even after the Wilhites moved to Anchorage. They let him keep his mother's last name, and he saw her from time to time when she came to the city. She sent him Christmas and birthday presents, and Carmen made him send her thank-you notes.

In time, Martha had tired of strange beds and stranger men. She had gotten her GED, then a job as a teacher's aide at Chukchi High. The Wilhites had taken him to Chukchi for a visit about then, but for the entire visit he had refused to speak to the woman who had sent him away.

Martha had finally married, about the time he was old enough for Little League. The groom was one Leroy Johnson, an electronics technician at the nearby Air Force radar site that had peered across the Chukchi Sea for Russian bombers and missiles until the Cold War ended. Two years after the wedding, the Wilhites had reported to a sullen Nathan that he had a half-brother in Chukchi, but he hadn't set foot in the village again until the Troopers, with the ancient and faceless perversity of bureaucracies everywhere, posted him to Chukchi for his first assignment.

And now Martha and Leroy were solidly ensconced in Chukchi's version of married, middle-class comfort. He delivered stove oil for the local Chevron dealer and hunted and fished more than a lot of Inupiat, while she headed the teacher-aide program at Chukchi High. They lived in a modern house on a quiet back street. Leroy bought each of them a new snowmachine every year, plus a new Ford Ranger every other year, and maintained a shifting population of boats and four-wheelers.

Active parked the Suburban in front of the house, went

past a pair of four-wheelers into the *kunnichuk*, knocked on the inner door, and braced himself for the discussion that lay ahead.

Martha, he knew, held the view that only one final detail needed nailing down to make her life perfect: persuading her older son to give up his ambition of a transfer to Anchorage and settle down in Chukchi with a suitable wife, one who was smart, educated, and not too much of a village girl, but nonetheless willing to make a home, a life, and a family right here on the shores of the Chukchi Sea.

And now—the inner door swung open to reveal Sonny Johnson, gym bag in hand and dressed for the rain that seemed to be increasing as the wind diminished. He slipped off the earphones of an iPod and said, "Yo, Nathan! Whaddup?"

Sonny, like every teenage male Active had encountered in the past few years, was into hip-hop music. "Not much, man, whaddup with you?" Active responded.

Active could tell from his half-brother's look that it hadn't come out quite right, and he vowed never to try to talk like a teenager again. Better to slide into the irrelevance of adulthood in dignified silence.

Sonny, however, was an exceptionally polite teenager and ignored Active's gaffe after that one brief flash of scorn. "Not much, dog, not much. I'm on my way to the gym. City League basketball starts tonight."

Then the boy's face clouded and he forgot his hip-hop for a moment. "That's terrible about Augie and everybody at the Rec Center, ah? You guys find out who did it?"

Active shook his head. "We're not completely sure anybody did it. The fire may have been accidental."

"I hope so," Sonny said. "Augie was our coach in basketball camp this summer. He was sure good at it. I'd hate to think anybody around here would do something like that."

"Me too," Active said. "I've got to talk to Martha, then maybe I'll come up and watch the game. Who you playing?"

"Nuliakuk," Sonny answered with a feral expression.

"You'll crush 'em," Active said.

"Word to that," Sonny said with a grin. "They're just a bunch of village boys."

As the teenager slipped around him and left the *kunnichuk*, Active pondered the phrase: *Word to that.* It signified emphatic agreement, clearly, but how could a simple, everyday noun like "word" have taken on such a load of meaning? Active shook his head and pushed open the inner door to the house.

"Hi, Sweetie!" Martha said, hurrying to him for a hug. "Good to see you!"

As usual after not seeing her for a few days, he was struck by her youthfulness. She was in her mid-forties, but she carried it well. No middle-age fat, black hair still glossy except for the first hint of gull-wings at the temples, smooth-faced except for the laugh lines around her mouth and sparkling black eyes.

"Hello, *aaka*, it's good to see you."

She frowned. "Isn't it terrible about the Rec Center? You figure out who did it?"

He gave her the same non-answer he had given Sonny, then changed the subject. "What's that I smell?"

She led him into the kitchen and lifted the lid from a pot on the stove. "Moose stew. Didn't I tell you Leroy got one?"

Active tried to remember. "Probably."

"Oh, it was lotta trouble. It ran into a lake after he shot it. He and Sonny had a terrible time getting it out. Leroy will tell you all about it when he gets back from caribou hunting."

"I can't wait."

Martha shook her head. "Same old smart-mouth, ah?" She filled two bowls from the stewpot and set them on the table, along with a box of the CD-size saltines known as pilot bread. "How you going to be a real Eskimo if you don't hunt?"

Active realized the moment had come, but he didn't quite have the nerve to seize it. Instead, he filled his mouth with stew and pilot bread, eyes on the bowl.

Martha, of course, spotted the stall instantly. "What? You can't look at me?"

He chewed slowly, stretching it out.

"Whatever you don't want to tell your mother, that's what she needs to hear."

He met her eyes, finally. "I got my transfer. I'll be moving to Anchorage around Christmas, probably."

Martha's spoon halted halfway to her mouth and hovered there. "No," she said.

"What?"

"No. You can't go."

Active had never seen her look so upset. "But I. . . ." He filled his mouth with stew to gain time. What to do next?

She put down her spoon and stared at a spot in a far corner of the room. "But what about Gracie and Nita and . . . and everything?"

"And everything," Active understood, meant "and what about me?"

"I don't know yet about Grace and Nita. Grace is a little scared about it, but I need to get her out of here."

"Maybe if you just got her out of that house."

"Maybe. But I don't want to stay in Chukchi all my life. Look at it."

She was silent, eyes liquid and dark. "It's not so bad if you're used to it," she said eventually. "I thought you were getting to like it."

He shrugged. "A little bit, maybe. Sometimes. But I have to make my way in the Troopers."

"You want to get away from me, ah?"

"Of course not. I'll come back for—"

"Because I gave you away, ah?"

"*Aaka*, please. Don't say that again. You know I—"

"Well, it seemed like the right thing at the time. I couldn't take care of any baby. I was too young and *kinnaq*, like any girl that's fifteen."

"I know, *Aaka*, and—"

"And weren't Ed and Carmen good to you?"

"Of course they were." This was like a catechism now, a ritual exchange they had to reprise every few months. His role was to give the right answers and hold his resentment in check, so he no longer added "but not like real parents" to the obligatory praise of the Wilhites' child-rearing abilities.

"Well, then, why?"

"*Aaka*, Anchorage is my home. It's where I grew up." He braced himself, belatedly realizing how Martha was likely to take this.

She blinked rapidly for a few seconds, then took a spoonful of the moose stew. "You can't go away again," she said. "It's bad when I let them take you when you're baby, it's bad when you come visit me when you're little boy, and . . . no, you can't go again."

"You can come down and visit us."

"No."

"I'll come up and visit you, then."

"You can't go."

They both fell silent. Martha dabbed at her eyes with a napkin. After a time, she blew her nose into the napkin and tucked it into the pocket of her jeans.

"Gracie doesn't have any women still alive in her family, ah?"

"Not that I know of." Where was this going?

"Maybe when you guys have baby, she'll need me to come down, help her out, ah?"

"Let's not get ahead of ourselves," he said, trying not to think of how many bridges he and Grace would have to cross to reach that point. Then he saw the effect of his words on his mother. "But, when the time comes, I'm sure Grace would like that."

She ate silently for a few moments. "You tell your *ataata* yet?"

Active shook his head. "Not yet. I will. He talking to you these days?"

She squinted the Inupiat no and said nothing.

Exactly why Jacob Active didn't speak to his daughter wasn't clear to anyone, except perhaps Jacob, who never explained anything. According to Martha, the silence had started after the stroke that had deprived him of most of his English but left his Inupiaq intact. But the root cause, she believed, was the fact that Leroy Johnson was white. Jacob Active's contempt for *naluaqmiuts* like Leroy was unshakable. Martha thought the stroke had also deprived Jacob of what little ability to mask his feelings he had ever possessed.

"*Arii*," Martha said. "My father doesn't talk to me, and now my son is leaving."

"I said we'll visit back and forth."

Martha's expression brightened, but not by much. Active decided to change the subject, and perhaps get a little work done as well. "What are people saying about the fire?"

She brightened a little more. Seeking her advice usually had that effect.

"They're real mad to think someone around here would do that."

"Like I said, we're still not sure how it started."

"They think, if Jim Silver was alive, he would figure it out. But they aren't so sure about that Alan Long. So I tell them, my son Nathan will catch 'im."

"Who do they think it was?"

"Nobody knows. We never had anything like this in Chukchi before."

CHAPTER EIGHT

ACTIVE WAS AT HIS desk at eight the next morning, on the phone to the Federal Correctional Institute in Sheridan, Oregon. After navigating a tortuous voice mail system and undergoing several interrogations as to who he was and what he wanted, finally he was connected to a businesslike female voice that identified itself as belonging to Correctional Treatment Specialist Lana Bickford.

"Jae Hyo Lee? Yes, I was his case manager," she said. "We let him out a few weeks ago. Didn't you guys call about him a couple days ago?"

"Right, that would have been Officer Alan Long. He's also working this case."

"And what is it you guys want with Mr. Lee? Let's see, I think his file is still on my desk here somewhere." There was a thunk as she laid the phone down, then a rustle of papers.

"Here we go," she said at length. "I have my notes now. He's an arson suspect, Officer Long said?"

"A person of interest," Active said. "For now, we just want to question him."

"Well, all right. Lessee—uh-huh, he's the one was in for poaching bear gallbladders. We don't get many of those. Although they're usually Koreans when we do. Anyway, what can I tell you about him?"

Active sketched out what they needed to know—anything available about Jae Hyo Lee's visitors, mail, and phone calls.

Bickford blew out a long breath. "Some of this I can help with, some of it I can't be much use to you. Letters, we read anything coming in or going out, but we don't keep any record unless we find something fishy, and there's nothing like that in Mr. Lee's file."

Active, scribbling notes on a legal pad, nodded, then remembered he was on the phone. "Uh-huh."

"Phone logs . . . ah, here we are. Looks like he called a Ruth Marie Silver about every two weeks the whole time he was here. And he called a Kyung Kim a couple of times."

"Uh-huh. That's his girlfriend and his uncle. Can you give me the dates?"

Active copied as Bickford read off the last few. Lee's last two calls had been to Ruthie Silver and to his uncle, a few days before he got out of prison. Arranging his homecoming, no doubt.

"Any visitors?"

There was a long pause, with the sound of paper crackling in the background.

"Oh, yeah, here we go. Looks like he only had one visitor the whole time he was here."

"Close-knit family, eh?"

"I don't think it was a family member. A fellow from up your way looks like, Chukchi, right? He was logged in as, geez, this handwriting. Some of our correctional officers—a Thomas Gaines?"

"Thomas Gaines? I never heard of any—" Active stopped in mid-sentence. "The handwriting is bad?"

"Like a doctor's."

He could hardly bring himself to ask. "Any chance that's Gage instead of Gaines? Thomas Gage?"

"There I go again," she said. "I had a hard time reading it when the other guy called last week."

"Officer Long? I thought he only called day before yesterday."

"No, somebody else called before that. Now, what—uh-huh, here it is. Your police chief up there, a Jim Silber?"

"Silver? You told Jim Silver that Tom Gage visited Jae Hyo Lee?"

"I DIDN'T want to know this," Carnaby said after Active broke the news a few minutes later.

"Me either," Active said.

Carnaby ticked points off on his fingers.

"So Tom Gage goes to see Jae Hyo Lee in prison—when?"

"About two and a half months ago."

"Then three weeks ago, Jae gets out of prison."

Active nodded.

"And last week Jim Silver finds out about Gage's visit?"

Active nodded again. "I guess he was checking on Jae like his daughter asked."

"And three days ago the Rec Center burns down and Silver and Gage both die?"

"Thus killing the only visitor Jae had, the entire time he was in Sheridan," Active said. "And the cop who called to check up on him."

Just then the phone rang. Carnaby picked up and listened for a few seconds. "Yes, Senator. I know. We all feel the same way. But these things take. . . . Well, thank you, but we have all the resources we need for now." Carnaby paused, listening, and rolled his eyes at Active. "Yes, I'll certainly keep you posted."

Carnaby hung up. "Our own Senator Darryl Beaver, wanting to know how we're doing with the investigation. And letting me know in the kindest possible way that it'll be very difficult for him to defend the line item for the Chukchi detachment if this thing is still hanging fire when the legislature convenes in Juneau."

"Hanging *fire*? He said that?"

Carnaby grimaced. "Uh-huh. Oh, and the mayor also called this morning, by the way, and he says there's a celebration-of-life memorial service thing tonight at the high school. And Roger Kennelly from Kay-Chuck called for an update. And Lena Sundown, and—" The captain stopped and shook his head. "Jesus. Jae Hyo Lee and Tom Gage. What the hell is this about?"

"Maybe Gage and Lee were in it together, and Gage isn't really dead: he just left his four-wheeler in front of the Rec Center to throw us off."

"But why? Was he in the gallbladder thing with Jae? And if he's not dead and he did help Jae set the fire, where is he?" Carnaby thought for a moment, then answered his own question. "With Jae, obviously, in this infamous boat he's running around in. And now what? They're sailing off somewhere to start a new life together? Shit."

"Yeah," Active said. "So maybe instead—"

"Maybe he was working with Jae, all right," Carnaby said with a look of inspiration. "But he really did get trapped and die in his own fire. Didn't Ronnie Barnes say that happens sometimes?"

"Yeah," Active said, "but why would he park his four-wheeler out front? Wouldn't he come up on foot, sneak into the furnace room from the back, and do the whole thing with the 'T' fitting and the wire on the door?"

Carnaby shook his head. "None of it makes a damned bit of sense."

"Wait a minute," Active said. "What if Tom Gage was the Feds' source in the gallbladder bust? And then Jae finds out about it and burns down the Rec Center to get even."

Carnaby was silent, turning this over in his mind. "Yeah, it holds together a little better than anything else we've come up with. He did tell Ruthie he found out it wasn't Jim who turned him in, right?"

Active nodded.

"But it still doesn't explain Gage's trip down to the prison to see Jae. Or why an aviation instructor would be involved with a Korean gallbladder smuggler."

Active sighed. "Nah, it doesn't."

Carnaby picked up the phone. "Let me get Alan in here. He's supposed to be talking to the Feds today to see if they'll tell us their source in the gallbladder thing."

A few minutes later, Long was seated beside Active at Carnaby's desk, asking them what was up.

"Tom Gage visited Jae in Sheridan?" he said after hearing what they had learned. "Jesus."

Carnaby outlined their theory that Gage had been the

federal source in the gallbladder case, then looked hopefully at Long.

"It's a little complicated," Long said. "They won't tell me outright who the source was, but they did agree to look at our list of fatalities and I.D. him if he's on it. Plus they'll call in the FBI to help catch Jae if it looks like he killed their source. So I faxed them our list."

Carnaby and Active exchanged uneasy glances. The FBI commanded vast resources and was good at many things, but working rural Alaska was not one of them, according to Trooper lore. Carnaby looked at Long again. "And? Was it Gage?"

"They haven't called back yet."

"Let's give 'em a try," Carnaby said, pushing the phone across the desk to Long.

Long pulled a notebook from his pocket, found the number, and dialed. "Alan Long for Tony Ehrlich," he said after a moment. "Yes, I'll hold."

The moment dragged on. Long put his hand over the phone's mouthpiece. "Tony was my handler in the gallbladder case."

Active shifted in his chair and doodled on the legal pad.

"Yeah, Tony," Long said finally. "You get my fax? Uh-huh, and. . . ."

Fifteen seconds passed in silence.

"You sure?" Long asked. "None of them? How about Tom Gage specifically? It turns out he visited Jae Hyo Lee in Sheridan a couple months ago."

More silence.

"Really? Well, thanks." Long hung up and looked at them, shaking his head. "They never heard of Tom Gage till they got our list."

They looked at each other gloomily. "I'm out of ideas," Carnaby said at length.

The other two raised their eyebrows in agreement.

"Tom Gage is about all we've got," Carnaby finally said. "Full-court press here. Alan, you get over to the DA's office and tell Charlie Hughes we need a search warrant for Gage's place, and—"

"Why?" Long interrupted. "If he's dead, why don't we just break the lock and go in?"

"He's not dead till the coroner says so," Carnaby said with a glare. "And who knows how long that'll take? Besides which, what if he does turn up alive? Then whatever we find in there becomes useless to us because we didn't have a warrant. Nope, Gage had recent contact with our suspect, and that makes him a suspect or at least a material witness, so a search warrant it is. Dead or alive. Okay, Alan?"

Subdued, Long nodded.

"Nathan, you talk to the Tech Center. See what they know about Gage's background. But most important, find out how to get hold of his ex-wife."

ACTIVE LOPED down the stairs of the Public Safety Building and climbed into the Trooper Suburban. He was headed up Third Street, toward the Tech Center at the north end of town, when he remembered he had a lunch date with Grace. With a sigh, he swung into the parking lot of the Bible Missionary Church, looped around a pair of four-wheelers, pulled back onto Third Street, and headed south toward GeoNord's Chukchi headquarters.

Grace had started as an administrative assistant in the human resources department of the company that ran the Gray Wolf mine, mainly as something to do while she decided how long to stay in Chukchi after the deaths of her parents. But with her intellect and organizing abilities, she was soon functioning as office manager. And then the head of the department—a white man from Anchorage—had begun spending more time at the Chukchi dump shooting ravens and foxes than at his desk solving GeoNord's personnel problems. Concluding he had endured more seven-month Arctic winters than he could handle, the company had sent him back to Anchorage, and Grace Palmer had become the new director of human resources.

The GeoNord elevator was out of service, as usual, so Active clumped up the two flights of stairs to her office, which, like Grace, smelled delicately of lavender. She was in the middle of a phone call but waved him in past the receptionist. "Hold on just a second," she said into the phone and put her hand over the mouthpiece. "Got the mine on the line. Is it lunchtime already?"

"Not quite. But I have to go up to the Tech Center and I don't know if I'll have time after."

She raised her eyebrows, told the mine she'd call back later, and stood up, stretching and twisting her neck.

"Long morning?"

She raised her eyebrows again: yes. "And you? Any progress on the fire?"

He shrugged. "You know. You put one foot in front of the other and hope you eventually get somewhere."

He helped her into her coat, and they made their way downstairs. "Mind if we hit the Pizza Palace?" he said once they were in the Suburban.

She rolled her eyes. "Again? Do you ever not work?"

"We have to eat somewhere," he said. The Pizza Palace was one of Kyung Kim's properties, and it was common knowledge that one of his cooks was selling liquor on the side. The knowledge just wasn't common enough for the Troopers or the city cops to make an arrest yet. "You never know when somebody—"

"We both know he's not going to sell any liquor out the back door with a Trooper in the dining room."

"Exactly. So if somebody comes in, spots my uniform, and takes off without ordering anything, what's that tell you?"

She sighed. "Have it your way, Dudley Do-Right. Would this mean we'll be parking a discreet distance from the premises, yet again?"

"If they see this Suburban at the Pizza Palace, they won't come in, will they?"

"One can only hope." She grinned and punched his shoulder.

He parked in a slot at the state court building, which sat diagonally across the intersection of Caribou and Second from the restaurant.

Grace gestured at the big building perched on stilts to keep it from melting its way down into the permafrost. "This is why, isn't it?" she said. "You Troopers just can't stand the thought of somebody bootlegging in plain sight of the courthouse."

"Should I be able to stand it?"

She hooked an elbow through his, and they angled across the intersection and pushed through the *kunnichuk* and into the dining room of the Pizza Palace. They found a booth and examined Kyung Kim's schizophrenic menu. The left-hand page was burgers and pizza, in keeping with the name of the place. The right-hand page offered a long list of Chinese dishes that were, as Active knew from experience, remarkably good.

They agreed on the snow pea shrimp, and he went to the counter to order, peering at the back of the cook working over the griddle. Was it Tae Ahn, the bootlegging suspect, or not?

An Inupiat girl whom Active knew only as Googie came to the counter to take his order. "Is that Tae back there?" he asked.

"Tae's off today," Googie said. "You want something?"

"We'll split an order of snow pea shrimp," Active said. "When Tae comes in, tell him that Trooper Active said 'hello,' ah?"

"*Ee,*" the girl said, raising her eyebrows without a hint of expression. Active wondered if she was in cahoots with Ahn or maybe a customer. Or maybe just oblivious. Active filled two cups with coffee, put four packets of creamer in his shirt pocket, and returned to the booth.

"Not if you're going to be you," Grace said as he slid onto the bench across from her. A smile played at the corners of her lips.

He tried unsuccessfully to remember what they had been talking about before he went to order. "Not if I'm going to be me what?"

The smile took over her lips completely and the fox-eyes sparkled in their quicksilver way. "That makes absolutely no sense, you know."

"But something tells me you understood it perfectly."

She raised her eyebrows, still smiling. "You shouldn't be able to stand the thought of Tae Anh selling liquor in sight of the courthouse. Not if you're going to be you."

"Ah."

"Which I hope you are."

"Are what?"

"Going to be you."

"Totally," he said. "I promise to be me twenty-four/seven." They dumped the creamer into their coffees. "Look, I need to talk to my *Ataata* Jacob about, um. . . ."

Her smile vanished. "About going to Anchorage?"

He raised his eyebrows.

"And you need a translator."

He raised his eyebrows again.

She was silent for a moment. "Can you find someone else?"

"He likes you."

"How about Lucy? She's good at it."

Active flinched inwardly. Lucy Brophy, nee Lucy Generous, was his ex-girlfriend. Her journey toward that status had begun the moment he had seen the mural-sized photograph of Grace Palmer in her Miss North World days on the wall at Chukchi High. The problem was, it had taken both of them some time to grasp the enormity of his obsession with Grace Palmer, though Lucy had figured it out first. The breakup had been slow and agonizing, though it hadn't ended as badly as it might have, all things considered. They were still . . . not friends, exactly. Amicable ex-lovers described it best, he supposed. Lucy was now married to Dan Brophy, a fourth-grade teacher at Chukchi's elementary school and—

"Isn't she due soon?" Grace asked.

Active had greeted Lucy at the dispatch station in the Public Safety Building just that morning. He tried to visualize how big her stomach was. "Couple months, I think."

"You haven't answered my question. Still too touchy there?"

This was the way with women. No woman would ever ask a question about a man's old girlfriend that was merely about what it appeared to be about. He thought it over and decided to be honest, which he tried to make a firm policy with Grace.

"When I see Lucy looking so happy. . . ."

She waited a decent interval. "Yes?"

He studied his coffee, thinking, then decided to start over. "When I see that sunny normalcy of hers, I do sometimes think of the life I'll never live with her. It's like—"

"Would you rather be living it?"

He looked up in shock at the suggestion, then realized that was exactly how his rambling must have sounded to Grace. "You kidding? No, no way. This thing that we have—" He stopped, searching for the words.

"Yes?"

"I think it's like your sexual orientation. Or being right-handed or your eye color, you know?"

She frowned. "Not exactly."

"I mean, there's no choice about it. Once I saw that picture of you at the high school and your father asked me to find you, that was it. That other life—"

"With Lucy?"

"Uh-huh. That other life, it's off to the side of all this"—
he gestured around the Pizza Palace, but knew that she knew
he meant to take in the entirety of things—"to the side of
this life I have now. It's like an abandoned river channel in
the tundra. It's over there and its day is past, and you're here,
and this is now.

"Besides," he continued, after some thought, "there was
an imbalance in the relationship. She was more into me
than I was her. I was afraid I was just using her for sex."

"Nathan, don't ever get arrested. You wouldn't last ten
seconds under interrogation."

An image of Lucy naked and astride him—her favorite
position—suddenly came into his mind, and he found
himself at once embarrassed and aroused. "Well, yeah. But
I, I mean, ah, we, ah, she—"

Grace patted his wrist. "It's all right, Nathan. I have it
on good authority she enjoyed it as much as you did.
Probably more. Normal girls do."

"You talked to her? Women talk about that stuff?"

Her fox-eyed smile was back. "Women talk about
everything. Constantly."

"Jesus. That's terrifying."

She lifted her eyebrows, then fell silent, swirling a
spoon in her coffee. "Sunny normalcy, huh? Is that what
you need? Because I doubt I'm capable of it. I think you
know that."

"What I need is you. Period."

She was silent again.

"How'd I do?" he asked finally.

"Not so bad, Trooper."

Something in the street caught her eye, and she
frowned. "Is that Alan Long in Jim Silver's Bronco?"

Active glanced out and nodded, trying to place the girl in the passenger seat next to Long. "I didn't tell you? The mayor made Alan acting chief."

"No."

"Indeed."

"And is that Queenie Buckland with him?"

"So it is," Active said. "I couldn't recall at first. Isn't she supposed to be Calvin Maiyumerak's girlfriend?"

"She was the last I heard. But Calvin's only got that old Yamaha four-wheeler."

"Ah. You're thinking she. . . ."

Grace's face lit up in a huge grin. "Yep, I think she's upgraded. All the way up to a Bronco, complete with a cop who has a Bluetooth headset and wears a great big gun on his belt."

Active shuddered. "Don't remind me."

"Some girls," Grace said.

Googie deposited two bowls of white rice on their table. Active dribbled some soy sauce on his. "About my grandfather. I don't want to crowd you. I can probably get one of the *aanas* at the Senior Center to translate."

She shook her head. "No, I'll do it. Call me when you're done at the Tech Center. I'll take my four-wheeler and meet you at the Senior Center."

"Thanks," he said.

She nodded silently. They unwrapped their chopsticks and put away a few bites of rice. She paused and looked into the bowl. "The Anchorage thing has to be faced."

"It does," he said as Googie brought the shrimp. "Is it too much?"

"I don't know yet."

THE ARCTIC Technical Center lay on Beach Street at the north end of town, just past the high school. It was a rambling complex of two-story wheat and slate-blue cubes on stilts. There, residents of Chukchi and surrounding villages learned how to tune up cars, set up computer networks, rebuild snowmachines, and fix or fly airplanes.

Active steered the Trooper Suburban into a visitor slot near the main entrance, between two four-wheelers.

Inside, a receptionist directed him to the office of a Gilbert Cividanes, head of the aviation program. Cividanes was in his mid-forties, Active guessed, balding, running to fat, but well-dressed and well-groomed for Chukchi, almost professional-looking in a blue sport shirt open at the neck and jeans pressed to a crease. How had a Hispanic yuppie ended up in Eskimo country? The only other Hispanic Active knew of in Chukchi was Hector Martinez, the Honda dealer, but he was no yuppie. Martinez wore cowboy boots and a Stetson, except in the dead of winter, and ate *muktuk* the year round.

"You're sure it was Tom?" Cividanes asked after Active had identified himself and explained his mission. "I heard they hadn't identified all the bodies from the fire yet."

"Not a hundred percent sure," Active said. "But what are the odds? His four-wheeler was out front, and he hasn't shown up for work, right?"

Cividanes sighed. "I suppose. We better start looking for a new aviation mechanics instructor, I guess."

Active raised his eyebrows in the white expression of surprise and disapproval.

"I didn't mean to seem callous," Cividanes said in an apologetic tone. "It's just that I didn't know him very well. None of us did."

"How long did he work here?"

Cividanes furrowed his brow and glanced at some papers on his desk. "Seems like . . . yeah, he started a couple of years ago. His marriage broke up about a year later and I don't think he was handling it very well."

"No?"

"I suspected he was drinking pretty hard. You know, Monday-morning flu every few weeks, looked haggard most of the time. Bags under his eyes, kind of pasty-faced. Always smelled like gasoline and wood smoke or something. Of course, he liked to get out into the country, too—had his own plane, boat, snowmachine, so maybe. . . ."

"So maybe he just didn't have time for details? Or sleep?"

Cividanes shrugged.

"He have any kids you know of?"

Cividanes scratched his temple and nodded. "Seems like the beneficiaries on his life insurance were kids."

"It wouldn't be the ex, I gather."

"No, I shouldn't think," Cividanes said. "You want me to look it up?"

"It's not important," Active said. "I'll talk to the wife. You've got the contact information I called about?" He pulled out his notebook, but Cividanes waved him off and handed him a sheet of paper.

"I printed it out for you."

"Thanks." Active rose and shook Cividanes's hand, then walked out studying the paper. The ex-wife's name was Donna and she lived in Vancouver, Washington. There were phone numbers for home and work.

ACTIVE PULLED the Suburban into the parking lot of the Chukchi Senior Center. Like nearly every other building in town, it boasted T1–11 plywood siding and a shingle roof. A gaggle of four-wheelers was parked in front, along with a pickup and a green van with a dire case of body rot.

The center was a wheel with three spokes and no rim. Each spoke was a wing where the residents had their bedrooms. The cafeteria, TV room, and administrative offices filled the hub.

Grace met him at the door, and they found Jacob Active in his wheelchair in the TV room, watching, or appearing to watch, *Animal Planet*. With most of his English lost to the stroke, perhaps he could only watch shows where the words didn't matter.

Jacob Active had creased brown skin stretched tight over his cheekbones and a shock of white hair that stood straight out from his head like dandelion fuzz. He wore a hearing aid in his left ear. The lobe was missing, taken by frostbite on the trail long ago. The right side of his face still drooped a little from the stroke, though not as much as when Active had first come to Chukchi.

Active knelt beside the wheelchair and spoke into the hearing aid. "Hello, *Ataata*."

The old man turned, blank-faced for a moment, then smiled, mostly on the left. His mouth had the caved-in look that meant he had forgotten to put in his dentures.

Grace spoke to him in Inupiaq. Active could follow it enough to understand that she was telling him his grandson had come to talk to him. Jacob said, "*Arigaa*," and lifted his spiky white eyebrows.

Active took the handles of the wheelchair, and they rolled to the cafeteria. He went to fetch tea while Jacob and Grace chatted with a pair of aides taking a break at the next table.

"He already heard you're leaving," Grace said as Active set three mugs of tea on the table. "He thought you wouldn't say goodbye."

"Tell him I'll come back to visit all the time."

Grace delivered the message, and Jacob responded in his reedy old-man's voice, then chuckled.

Grace smiled. "He says maybe you'll bring him some new teeth from Anchorage. The ones they gave him here don't fit."

Active grinned back and raised his eyebrows.

Jacob spoke again, and Grace translated. "He says, when are you leaving?"

"Tell him around Christmas, maybe right after."

Grace stared at him a moment, then turned back to the old man and spoke a few syllables.

Jacob responded with another question. Active caught enough to understand that his grandfather was asking if Grace would move to Anchorage also.

Grace's back stiffened as she answered Jacob in a low voice, too low for Active to make out.

Jacob looked at Active, back at Grace, then reached out and touched her hair. The old man spoke again.

"What did he say?"

Grace squinted a no and shook her head.

"Come on. What kind of translator are you?"

A little sigh escaped her. "He said he'd make me go if it was him."

"Tell him at his age he should have learned that no man can make a woman do anything, unless she wants him to."

She translated, and the mood lightened a little. They chatted for a few minutes, then Jacob abruptly closed his eyes and fell silent in the middle of a long, meandering story about seal hunting with his father in the old days, when snowmachines hadn't come along and everybody still used dog teams.

Active looked at Grace in alarm. "You think he's all right?"

The old man emitted a thunderous snore.

"*Arii*, that Jacob," said one of the aides at the next table. Her name tag identified her as Della. "He always do that when it's nap time." She stood, pushing back her chair. "Here, let me take him to his room."

Active and Grace watched her wheel him away, then walked through the Senior Center doors into the fog sweeping across Chukchi on the west wind. His cheeks felt wet, but he couldn't tell if it was rain or just the fog condensing on everything it touched.

Grace pulled up the hood of her anorak. "See you after work, huh?"

He nodded and bent for a kiss, then watched as she yanked the starter cord on her Honda, swung into the seat, and headed for GeoNord.

"*Arii*, you gonna make her sad too?"

Active started, recognizing the voice. He turned to see the familiar stooped figure of Pauline Generous, grandmother of Lucy.

"It's good to see you again," he parried.

"Ah-hah. I came to play snerts with them old ladies."

Active sensed a potential distraction and was preparing to ask her to explain the rules of snerts, which was the favorite card game of elderly Inupiat females in Chukchi and the villages in its orbit but appeared to be played nowhere else. Pauline, however, was not to be diverted.

"You gonna make her sad too, like with Lucy?"

"I thought Lucy was happy, with the baby coming and all."

Pauline glared at him through the huge, thick glasses that gave her eyes an unnerving size and intensity. "Pretty happy. She love that Dan Brophy, all right. But no girl ever really get over the first man she love. I think she miss that other life she never gonna have with you now."

Active, as usual, was a little spooked by Pauline. She had put it almost exactly the same way he had.

"Well, I'm with Grace."

Pauline looked at the four-wheeler disappearing down Fourth Street into the mist. "She's pretty, ah?" She turned back to him.

He raised his eyebrows, unable to think of words to describe the being that was Grace Palmer.

"You think she kill her father?"

"I don't believe so. I hope not."

"Sound like he had it coming, all right."

"People say that."

"Hmmph. You still talk like a *naluaqmiiyaaq*. You'll fit right in at Anchorage."

"Well, I—"

"She'll *malik* you to Anchorage?"

"Yes, I hope she comes with me."

Pauline was silent, studying him with her eyes narrowed. "What if she don't? You gonna leave her here by herself?"

"I don't know."

THE WORK number in Vancouver rang three times, then a female voice said "Harney Elementary."

Active identified himself and asked for Donna Gage.

"Hold on," the voice said. "I think it's her prep time."

The phone clicked onto a feed of elevator music, then the voice came back. "Yes, I can put you through to her classroom now."

Active remembered that Tom Gage's ex-wife probably hadn't heard about the fire yet and was trying to figure how to get into it when a new and younger female voice broke into the elevator music.

"Donna Gage," it said around what sounded like a mouthful of food being chewed.

Active identified himself and said he was calling from Chukchi.

Donna Gage swallowed audibly. "Yes?"

"I'm afraid I have some bad news about your ex-husband, Mrs. Gage."

"Good," she said. "The worse the better. He finally crashed his plane and killed himself, I hope?"

"No, actually—"

"Broke through the ice on his snowmachine, then?"

"No, we don't have any ice yet. It's still—"

"Open water? He flipped his boat and drowned?"

"Mrs. Gage, somebody burned down our Rec Center three nights ago. It looks like eight people were killed. We think Tom was one of them."

"You mean you can't tell if he's dead or alive? That's Tom, all right." She laughed unpleasantly. "He never could commit."

"Ms. Gage—"

"I'm sorry, ah, Trooper Active, was it? You probably don't want to hear all of this. Or need to. As you may have guessed, our marriage didn't end well."

"So I understand. His boss here said he was drinking pretty hard."

"He was?"

"According to Gilbert Cividanes."

"Really?"

"That surprises you?"

"Well, I don't think it was because of me. He was happy as a clam when I told him I was clearing out. Maybe after I left, he realized . . . nah, the prick was glad to be rid of me." She was silent for a few seconds, then spoke more softly. "I lost him to the Arctic, you know. He took to it like a duck to water, out in that damn plane hunting and fishing all the time, like he had come home to a place he'd never seen. He had this student from Cape Goodwin who invited him up there for whaling and . . . after that, the girls and I hardly ever saw him. He wanted to live like an Eskimo, think like an Eskimo, hunt like an Eskimo. If they had DNA transplants, he would have had himself turned into an Eskimo."

Active felt a slight chill between his shoulder blades. "Did you say Cape Goodwin?" All the roads in this case seemed to lead there, but they never quite intersected.

"Mm-hmm. He eventually fell in love with a girl from up there but, really, it was the country that seduced him. When he looked at me, it was like he'd run into an old flame but couldn't quite remember her name. Or what he ever saw in her. So I took my daughters and left." She paused. "Shit, I'm going to have to tell them."

Active cleared his throat. "Your husband had a girlfriend in Cape Goodwin?"

"Some little slut he met in whaling camp, I think."

"Do you remember her name?"

"By that point, I was trying to ignore as many details as I could. I didn't need them."

"Anything? A first name?"

"Let me think." She was silent again. Then, "Buddy . . . Booger . . . Buster . . . Buzzy . . . Beanie, I don't know. One of those cute little village nicknames."

"You don't know her last name?"

Another silence. "Apparently not. I must have heard it, but . . . well, she was killed in a plane crash just after I moved out. I never did like to think about her, and after that I didn't have to. Although I do admit drinking a toast to the fates that arrange such things when I heard about it."

"Tom crashed his plane and killed his girlfriend?"

"Actually, I don't think I ever heard who was flying, just that it was way up on the North Slope somewhere. Don't I wish it was him, though? Wouldn't it be sweet if he crashed and killed her?"

Now Active was silent, impressed anew by the damage one human being could do to another without really intending much harm. "Did he ever know a Jae Hyo Lee?"

"Jay who?"

"Jae Hyo Lee. A Korean who lived in Cape Goodwin." Active described Lee's arrest for gallbladder trafficking and Tom Gage's visit to the prison in Oregon.

"Did you say Sheridan?"

"Right. Sheridan, Oregon."

"So that's what that was about."

"What was?"

"Tom came down early this summer to visit the girls," she said. "He borrowed my car one day, wouldn't say where he was going, but a few weeks later I started getting these notices about an unpaid parking ticket in Sheridan."

"Did Tom ever buy or sell polar bear gallbladders that you knew of?"

"Why would he tell me if he did? Isn't that illegal?"

"So you have no idea why he'd visit Jae Hyo Lee in prison?"

"Absolutely none. I never had much of an idea why Tom did anything, once we hit Chukchi. Any more questions, Trooper Active?"

"Been up here lately?"

She laughed without mirth. "Haven't been, won't be, no way, never. Why on earth would I—oh, you think I set your fire to kill my ex? Seriously?"

"Stranger things have happened."

"If only. But when you find whoever did, thank 'em for me, will you?" She was silent for a moment. "I'm sorry I said that, Trooper Active. Maybe if it was only Tom. But seven others? I was mad about the divorce, all right, but not that mad. I can't imagine that much rage."

They hung up, and Active studied the five words at the bottom of his notes from the mystifying conversation: Buddy-Booger-Buster-Buzzy-Beanie.

CHAPTER NINE

As Active walked across the reception area to Carnaby's office, he saw that Alan Long was already there, a legal document laid before him.

"Our search warrant?" Active asked as he took a chair beside Long.

"Got it," Long said. "Shall we?"

"Hold on a minute," Carnaby said. "Let's hear what Nathan found out first."

Active frowned. "Very little, I'm afraid. Gage's boss at the Tech Center said he took the divorce hard, seemed to be drinking. Ex-wife says good riddance, may he burn in hell, and would we please thank whoever did it when we catch him. She confirms he went to Sheridan this summer, has no idea why he'd visit Jae Hyo Lee or if he was trafficking in gallbladders."

The other two looked downcast, which was becoming the default expression at any meeting about this case.

"There was one thing, though," Active said. "Tom Gage used to go up to Cape Goodwin a lot. Even had a girlfriend up there, according to the ex."

The other two perked up. "Now, that's interesting," Carnaby said. "Let's find her and—"

Active held up a hand. "She was killed in a plane crash

around the time Gage's wife moved out, which would make it at least a year ago. Long before any of this got started."

"Plane crash?" Carnaby said. "You guys remember a crash up around Cape Goodwin a year ago?"

Long shook his head.

"No," Active said. "It was somewhere on the North Slope."

"Ah," Carnaby said. "That would explain it. If there was an investigation, it would have been the North Slope Borough cops. Gage was the pilot?"

"Don't know," Active said. "The wife couldn't remember hearing who was flying. I got the impression she's trying to put Chukchi and everything about it out of her mind as fast as she can."

"Yeah, this isn't really your average white woman's country," Carnaby said.

"What was the girlfriend's name?" Long asked. "Maybe I knew her."

"The ex pretty much drew a blank on that too," Active said. "Couldn't remember the last name, if she ever heard it, and wasn't sure about the first name. Or nickname, actually. Buddy, Booger, Buster, Buzzy, Beanie, something like that."

Long got a faraway look for a moment, then shook his head. "Rings a bell, somehow, but I can't quite pull it up. Want me to check around?"

"Leave it," Carnaby said. "We're not quite to the point where a victim's long-dead girlfriend is our best lead. Too bad about her, though. If she was still around, maybe she could tell us what the hell this is about."

He looked at the other two, as if hoping one of them

would do so in the dead girlfriend's absence. Finally he shrugged. "All right, I guess we can head over to Gage's house. The place locked, Alan?"

"Yep," Long said. "Padlock on the door. I got bolt-cutters from the city shop already."

Carnaby raised his eyebrows.

"And I got another lock to close it back up."

Carnaby nodded his approval, and they left the Public Safety Building and piled into the Trooper Suburban.

The sky had cleared and the wind had swung around to the north, driving the temperature below freezing. The streets glittered under a pellicle of ice, and the lagoon was edged in crystal as they followed Long's directions to Tom Gage's place, a rust-colored cottage with T1–11 siding and a tarpaper roof, no shingles.

As Long had said, a pickup was on blocks in the driveway, rear wheels off and the brake drums missing. A padlocked shipping van stood beside the north wall of the house. A canvas-covered snowmachine squatted next to the van, secured to it by a heavy chain and padlock through the undercarriage. Behind the house, a big dory with an outboard was pulled up on the shore of the lagoon.

Nearby were several other driveways leading to gravel pads, but none had houses on them yet. Gage's place was pretty much isolated. Active tried to remember if he had heard anything about the little subdivision on the lagoon. Hector Martinez owned it, he thought. But was it a new venture with as yet few takers, or an old one that had fizzled out with Tom Gage the only buyer?

Probably the latter, Active decided. The ground here was pure tundra, a mosquito swamp in summer. Anyone local would know the gravel roads and driveways and house pads, together with anything on them, would sink into the muck at a fairly rapid pace. Gage obviously hadn't put much money into the place. Perhaps its chief appeal for him was its location on the lagoon. He could pull his boat up to the back door in summer and park his Super Cub on skis there in winter.

Long applied his bolt-cutters to the padlock on the front door, and they went in through the *kunnichuk*. Carnaby flipped on the lights, and they peered around the little dwelling. One big room in front served as a combined kitchen and living area, with an oil heater at the back near a second exit sealed shut with yellow spray-on insulating foam. The furniture consisted of a dining table with three chairs, a sofa with a sleeping bag and pillow on it, and a desk littered with mail and other papers. Four dirty plates and a miniature Stonehenge of empty Budweiser cans littered the dining table. Three more Budweiser empties stood on the floor beside the sofa, as did a bottle of vodka, a quarter full.

Two doorways led to other rooms. Both were open, one showing a bed with another sleeping bag on it, the other a tiny bathroom with a toilet and shower but no sink. "I guess he brushed his teeth in the kitchen," Carnaby said, pointing.

"Doesn't look like he even lived here," Long said. "More like he dropped in once in a while when he needed a room for the night."

"The ex-wife said he was out in the country or up at Cape Goodwin most of the time," Active said.

"What are we looking for, anyway?" Long asked.

Carnaby took off his hat and swept his eyes over the

place. "Anything that would connect Tom Gage and Jae Hyo Lee, or Tom Gage and bear gallbladders, or Tom Gage and anybody who might want to kill him—or who he might want to kill." He looked at Long, who lifted his eyebrows. "Or anything else interesting."

"I'll take the bedroom," Long said.

Active took the desk, while Carnaby roamed the rest of the main room. The clutter on the desk was unremarkable. Bills from Visa, Chukchi Electric, Chevron; a birthday card from Gage's daughters; a letter from the state about twelve hundred dollars in overdue child support.

A couple of dozen snapshots were tacked to the wall over the desk. One was of a white man with two little girls; they had to be Gage and his daughters. Another showed him dropping a packload of caribou meat and antlers beside a Super Cub on a gravel bar, with a river, tundra, and mountains in the background, all splashed in fall colors. Still others showed Gage in whaling camp helping to cut up a bowhead and then push the huge mandible into the sea in the ancient Inupiat ritual of respect for the spirit of the animal. The final shot in what appeared to be a series showed Gage posing with a group of Inupiat beside a stack of *muktuk* slabs. Probably whalers, Active surmised, except some of the Inupiat in the picture were women. He had the impression women were taboo on whaling crews.

Another photo showed Gage on a polar bear kill far out on the sea ice, grinning at the camera and holding up the long snakelike neck and head so the bear looked at the camera too. The same Super Cub, this time on skis, was visible in the background. Active called Carnaby over and showed him the shot.

"Illegal as hell," the captain said.

"Uh-huh," Active said. "He's lucky the Feds didn't bust him along with Jae." Federal law barred anyone but the Inupiat from hunting polar bears.

Carnaby grunted his assent. "Think we should believe the Feds when they say he's not the one turned Jae in?"

"Beats me. You know anything about this Tony Ehrlich, the Fed Alan was dealing with?"

"Never met him."

"I guess we have to trust him," Active said.

"Provisionally," Carnaby said.

"I trust him," said Long, who had wandered up while they were looking at the photographs.

Active pointed at the pictures from the whaling camp. "Think Gage was in the boat when they got that one?"

Carnaby shrugged. "Who knows? Another violation if he was."

Long leaned in for a closer look at the group shot of the whalers. "Gage is the white guy?"

"Presumably," Active said.

"Budzie!" Long said suddenly. "Budzie Kivalina."

The other two looked at him.

"Budzie Kivalina. That's her right next to Gage. She must have been the girlfriend the ex-wife was trying to remember. Now that I think of it, seems like I did hear she was killed in a plane crash up on the Slope a while back."

Long tapped one of the women in the snapshot. Carnaby and Active bent closer to see what Budzie Kivalina had looked like. But the print was small; it was a group shot, not particularly well focused; and the whalers had been backlit by the sky, so it was hard to tell much about her. Active had a vague impression of an animated and slightly simian face, nothing more.

"You think she was on the crew?" Active asked.

"On it?" Long said. "She was the captain. About the only woman I ever heard of that had her own crew. That's probably how a *naluaqmiu* like Tom Gage got on it, if they were sweethearts."

"Probably," Carnaby said, turning away from the photographs. "But that's neither here nor there. Either of you guys find anything to explain why anybody would want to kill Gage bad enough to take out all those other people in the process?"

"I'm not done in the bedroom," Long said, and wandered off again.

Active shook his head. He pointed at the sofa with its sleeping bag and trio of empty Budweisers. "Looks like Gage had company, though."

"Yeah," Carnaby said. "New girlfriend, maybe?"

"A girlfriend who sleeps on the couch? What would be the point?"

Carnaby pondered for a moment. "Maybe they had a fight."

"And she decided to kill him and a half-dozen other people? Doesn't sound like a girl crime to me."

"Nah, you're right. A woman gets that mad, she's more likely to hurt herself than the guy." The captain swung his eyes around the room again. "Anyway, there sure hasn't been any woman living here. Or even visiting more than a couple hours. Look at this place."

"So it was a guy?"

"Had to be."

"We have to talk to him, obviously."

"Yeah, but who is he?" Carnaby said. "If he wanted to talk to us, he would have come in as soon as we put Gage's name out on Kay-Chuck, right?"

"Which makes him all the more interesting, eh?"

Carnaby peered out one of the front windows. "We could canvass the neighbors, if Gage had any. Or we—"

"Jesus, look at this!" Long shouted from the bedroom.

Active and Carnaby crowded through the door. Long stood at a chest-type deep-freeze along the wall opposite the bed. The lid was open, and several folds of frost-covered black plastic were flopped over the rim.

"I found something wrapped in trash bags in here, so I unwrapped it," Long said as Active and Carnaby reached the freezer.

"Is that a wolf?" Carnaby said.

"What the hell happened to it?" Active grabbed the trash bags and lifted the head out, then motioned to Long to close the lid.

He set it on top of the deep-freeze, pulled the plastic away, and stepped back. They all stared in silence. The neck had been severed just above the shoulders. The left eye was missing, just a bloody socket. There was a hole, also bloody, in the fur a couple of inches behind and below the eye. The jaws were closed, an inch or so of frozen tongue protruding out one side.

"I think it was a husky," Long said.

Active decided he was right. Under the blood and frost, the fur appeared to be a mix of gray, black, and brown, and the remaining eye looked to have been blue.

"Somebody shot out its eye," Long said in a tone of wonder. He touched the hole behind and below the empty socket. "This must be the exit wound."

"And then they cut off its head," Carnaby said.

"And brought it home and put it in the freezer," Active added.

They looked at each other, then at the thing on the freezer.

"This Tom Gage, whoever he was, was one strange guy," Carnaby said.

"Yeah, but he was a hell of a shot," Long said.

Carnaby and Active stared at him.

"Well, you gotta give him that."

Neither man responded.

Long turned back to the dog's head. "So what do we do with it? Is it evidence?"

"Of what?" Carnaby said. "It's not illegal to shoot your dog or keep the head in the freezer if you want, just weird and mean. Put it back in there and leave it. We'll let whoever has to clean the place up worry about it. Maybe the ex-Mrs. Gage?"

He looked at Active, who shook his head. "No way she's coming back up here."

"What if somebody breaks in?" Long asked.

"Don't worry about it," Carnaby said. "We'll put that lock you bought on the door, and we'll nail up a sign telling people to keep out." He looked at the dog's head again. "And if they do break in and open the freezer, this'll probably scare 'em right back out again."

After determining that the house held nothing else of interest, they went through Gage's pickup, without useful result, then cut the lock off Gage's shipping van and went through it as well. It was crammed full of tools, winter clothes, camping gear, a stack of two-by-fours, five sheets of T1–11, airplane parts, car parts, a half-dozen caribou hides, one yellow-white polar bear hide, several cans of aviation gas, and a snowmachine that appeared to be in the middle of an engine overhaul. None of it shed any light on the cause of Tom Gage's demise or on his role, if any, in the Rec Center fire.

"Sheesh," Carnaby said as they stood on the gravel pad in front of Gage's house, taking a last look around, their backs to the wind boring in from the north. "What a waste of a perfectly good afternoon. You got a crime with this few clues, you do start to wonder if it wasn't an accident after all. You know?"

Active nodded. "Except for the Jae Hyo Lee thing. Where the hell is he?"

Carnaby grimaced. "Maybe in Vegas getting the taste of prison out of his mouth while we chase our tails up here. Asians like blackjack and blow jobs as much as anybody, right?" He looked at Active and Long. "Maybe it's time to think about that run up to see Buck Eastlake at caribou camp?"

"What if we call Ronnie Barnes first, go over it with him one more time?" Active suggested. "See if there's something we should be doing that we're not."

"Can't hurt," Carnaby said. He looked at his watch. "Ah, it's too late now. We gotta get over to that thing at the school. Let's keep our eyes open, see if we can pick up anything, then get a good night's sleep and hit it again tomorrow, eh?"

They climbed into the Suburban. Active steered it out of Gage's nearly abandoned subdivision, then along Church Street to Second Avenue and up Second to Chukchi High on its forest of pilings at the north end of the spit. The school's gymnasium had been deemed the only place in town large enough for the crowd likely to be drawn to the memorial service for the Rec Center fire victims. When the three of them walked in, the gym was already packed and as steamy as a sauna from body heat.

They stood at the back and peered over heads and shoulders as best they could. There had to be six or seven hundred people in the bleachers and on the gym floor. Long gave a little cough of disgust and nudged Active. "Fat chance of spotting anything in this mob, huh?"

Active and Carnaby grunted in assent. It was impossible to see anything except the people onstage.

Carnaby sighed. "Alan, let's you and me circulate through the crowd. Nathan, how about you hang around here, see who comes and goes?"

Active lifted his eyebrows and watched as the other two disappeared into the crowd. Then he studied the group on the stage at the end of the gym. He spotted Chukchi's mayor and a middle-aged Inupiat he recognized as Hubert Skin, pastor of the Friends Church, the biggest denomination in town. Behind them stood a choir of women in blue robes, hymnals in hand. One of them was Lena Sundown.

The proceedings began with a prayer from the Reverend Skin, who expressed confidence that God would speedily receive into heaven the souls of the victims of the fire, regardless of past sinfulness or church membership, as the suddenness with which death had overtaken them had deprived them of any chance to repent or accept the Lord as their savior.

Then Skin led the choir in "I'll Fly Away" and "Amazing Grace." After that, he got to the real point of the event—inviting anyone so inclined to come up and offer a testimonial on behalf of a loved one who had died in the fire.

He lowered the microphone to the floor in front of the stage, and people began lining up. Lena Sundown left the

choir and came down in her robe to speak first. She told
the story about Augie shooting hoops in her living room
and triggering the furnace, drawing a scattering of chuckles
and "amens" from the crowd. A man in Carhartts and
Sorels stepped up next. "I'm Benjamin Benson," he said.
"Lula Benson was my wife thirty-nine years before this fire.
We had good times, and we had bad times, but she loved
me, and I loved her. Now I know she's with the Lord, but
I miss her anyway and I hope she's hearing me tonight.
That's all I have to say. Thank you very much."

And so it went for an hour, then two. Active hovered
near the entrance as instructed, scanning the late
arrivals, observing absolutely nothing out of the ordinary,
and wishing he was home with Grace and Nita, anywhere
but here.

Finally, the last person in line, an *aana* in a calico *atikluk*,
took the microphone and spoke in Inupiaq for a long time,
her old, whispery voice barely audible over the bustle of the
crowd and an occasional wail from a baby nestled in the
back of its mother's parka. Active caught the word "Rachel"
and concluded that the *aana* was part of the Akootchuk
family. The crowd grew quieter as she went on. Men cleared
their throats, and women pulled out tissues and dabbed at
their eyes and blew their noses.

The *aana* stopped and shuffled away from the microphone,
and the crowd fell silent for a few moments. Then,
somewhere on the floor, a woman began to sob.

Skin looked around the room and, when no one else
moved toward the microphone, pulled it back onstage. He
glanced at the mayor, who nodded and came forward.

The mayor of Chukchi was a forty-something Inupiaq
named Everett Williams. He had dark skin and curly

hair and was said to be descended from an African-American crewman on a long-ago whaling ship. He was so popular that he was mayor not only of the city of Chukchi, but of the new regional government known as the Aurora Borough as well.

Williams was also, as he reminded the crowd, the uncle of Cammie Frankson, the Rec Center clerk who had died in the fire, apparently after trying to save the men trapped in the locker room. "A lot of our family's hopes died with Cammie that night," Williams said. Then he spoke for a few seconds in Inupiaq. Active caught enough to know that he was repeating his remarks in the only language many of the elders in the room could understand.

"Cammie was a good girl. She didn't drink or run around, she helped her mom with the other kids at home, she had her job at the Rec Center, and she was going to college," Williams continued, translating into Inupiaq as he went.

"We're all shocked by what happened because we never had something like this in Chukchi before. But we who are left behind here, we have to go on and make the best of life that we can, because we never know when our day will come, like Cammie didn't know—" Williams coughed, pulled out a handkerchief, wiped his eyes, and went on. "—didn't know when she went to work the other day that she wouldn't be going home again. We are all facing in that direction, and that same day is ahead of every one of us."

The big room was silent again. Williams stepped away from the microphone and Skin came up to it, presumably to end the service with a prayer.

But a man's voice called out from the steaming anonymity of the gym floor: "I see the cops are in here tonight, sneaking around among us. How about they get up there and tell us why they haven't caught anybody yet?"

A wordless rumble of assent rose from the crowd like river ice going out.

"Well, that's not the purpose of this gathering," Skin said. "We're here—"

"Yeah, get 'em up here!" a different male voice called out. The rumble grew louder.

"They should talk to us!" a woman yelled.

Skin looked uncertainly at Williams, who returned to the microphone, looking as uneasy as Skin while the calls from the floor continued to build.

"Well, maybe Captain Carnaby of the Alaska State Troopers could come up here and say a few words," Williams said. "I see him right over there." He pointed to where, even from the back, Active could see Carnaby towering over the crowd.

Carnaby made his way to the stage and came to the microphone, looking off-balance and unprepared. He recapped what little had already been made public about the fire and extended his condolences to the families of the victims. "We have the Trooper arson specialist from Fairbanks working on it, and we're following up all the leads that come in, and if it turns out this was arson, you can be sure we'll find and arrest the person responsible."

"You're getting nowhere," a man shouted from the floor.

"You should bring in the FBI," a woman joined in. "If it was a bunch of white people at Anchorage that burned up, the FBI would be taking the case, all right."

The mayor raised his hands, and the rumble subsided slightly. Williams leaned toward the microphone. "The

Troopers and our city police are doing all they can," he said. "We all know that. I see Alan Long out in the crowd from our city force, and there in the back is Trooper Nathan Active. They're Inupiat, like most of us. And many of the victims in the Rec Center fire were white. We all know that. So instead of dividing ourselves up tonight, let's try and come together until Chukchi is through this and life can start to get back to normal again. Captain Carnaby, did you have anything more to say?"

The rumble grew again, with individual voices rising above the din now and again to complain about the lack of progress on the case and the stupidity and indolence of the investigators. Carnaby stood silently at parade rest, shoulders squared, hands locked behind him, a neutral expression on his face, eyes on the crowd, waiting. After a minute, perhaps realizing he looked too military for the situation, he took off his hat, shifted his weight to one hip, tilted his head to the side, and softened his expression. Finally the crowd quieted again.

"Let me just repeat that we do have some good, solid leads," Carnaby said. "Of course I can't go into detail about them, but I'm confident we'll get to the bottom of this soon, especially if you can help us. If you have information that might help, please let us know about it. Anything at all, like if you saw someone hanging around the Rec Center about the time of the fire, or if someone said something funny, or if someone is acting funny since the fire."

The crowd rumbled again, but the tone was different, more thoughtful now.

"You can call our anonymous tip line if you don't want your name known," Carnaby went on.

Williams stepped up to the microphone. "And I'm sure most of you have heard the Lions Club and the Fire Department have a five-thousand-dollar reward for information leading to the arrest of the person responsible for the fire," he said.

Now the rumble was just a murmur as heads nodded in the crowd.

Carnaby gave the tip line number twice, then moved back from the microphone with a look of relief.

Active feared the mayor would call him up next, or perhaps Alan Long as acting police chief. But Williams evidently figured enough had been said, because he asked Skin to give a closing prayer.

Active wanted to slip away while everyone's heads were bowed, but decided he should stay on post as people left the gym. Who could say when the thought of five thousand dollars for a boat or snowmachine might undermine family or romantic loyalties long enough for someone to whisper in the ear of law enforcement?

CHAPTER TEN

EARLY THE NEXT MORNING, Active braked to a halt at the little cabin on Second Street where Nelda Qivits lived and checked his coat to be sure the foil packet was still there.

Satisfied, he climbed out of the Suburban and walked to the door. Like the rest of the place, the door might once have been brown, but was now pretty well paint-free. But a lot of old buildings in Chukchi were paint-free, and it didn't seem to hurt them much. Being deep-frozen eight or nine months a year probably offered as much protection from the west wind and driving snow as anything the petrochemical industry could come up with.

He let himself into Nelda's *kunnichuk* and knocked on the door to the cabin proper.

"Who's that?" Nelda croaked from inside.

Active heard a TV in the background. Nelda was probably in her easy chair, as usual. He nudged the inner door open. "It's me, Nathan."

"*Naluaqmiiyaaq!* Good to see you!" She fumbled in the folds of her dress, came up with a remote, and clicked off an ancient *Dukes of Hazzard* rerun on the state's bush television channel.

"Good to see you too, *atchak*. Look what I brought you."

Her eyes lit up at the sight of the packet. "You found *iq'mik* again? Where you get it this time?"

"One of our Troopers went to Bethel a few days ago. I asked him to look in the store there."

"*Arigaa!* Long time since I had *iq'mik*, all right." She struggled up from the chair, Active checking the impulse to extend an arm. He knew from long experience that she would reject, with profanity, any such foolhardy offer.

"I'll make us some sourdock tea," she said, hobbling toward the kitchen. "And I gotta get some water for my *iq'mik*."

Iq'mik was a noxious chew made by mixing cigarette tobacco with the ashes of burnt tree fungus. It was acutely unhealthful and apparently about as addictive as heroin. Though nearly unheard-of around Chukchi, it was wildly popular in the Bethel area, where, Active knew, a much younger Nelda Qivits had spent several years as a cook in a government hospital. He felt only mildly guilty for feeding her habit. For one thing, he could only get it a couple of times a year. How much of an addiction could that cause? For another, Nelda was well past eighty, as best he could determine. If *iq'mik* hadn't done her in yet, what were the chances it would carry her off to the Inupiat hereafter before some more natural process did so?

In any event, she was a doctor of sorts—a tribal doctor, actually—and she deserved to be paid. Sometimes he left money, which she seemed to resent. When he happened to come into possession of fish or game, he'd leave some of that, which she liked a great deal. But nothing made her happier than an ounce or two of *iq'mik*. Who was he to deny an old lady her pleasures?

He followed her into the kitchen, where she was dipping

a spoon into a bowl of water and dribbling a few drops at a time into the *iq'mik*. She stirred the stuff around in the foil, rolled a pinch between thumb and forefinger in appraisal for a few seconds, then tucked it into her cheek with an expression of anticipatory bliss. "*Arigaa,*" she said again. "You want some?"

"No, thanks," he said. "I, ah—"

"You think you'll puke it up like before, ah?" She chuckled and dropped some sourdock root into a teakettle, lowered it into the sink, and turned on the faucet.

"I wouldn't want to mess up your couch again, no. I should probably stick to the sourdock." He nodded toward the kettle.

"*Naluaqmiiyaaq.*" She turned off the faucet and set the kettle on a burner.

They made small talk for a few minutes, primarily about the delayed onset of winter and the likelihood that it was caused by, in Nelda's phrasing, "that global warning, what them *naluaqmiuts* call it."

Finally the sourdock tea was ready. Nelda poured out two cups, and Active took a swallow from his. It was vile and bitter, though nothing compared to *iq'mik*. Nelda claimed sourdock could cure nearly anything. Active didn't know if it could or not. It was true that he never seemed to get sick now that he drank it regularly.

Nelda, meanwhile, was gulping hers with gusto as she made her way back to the easy chair. He wondered how she was getting the sourdock past the *iq'mik* in her cheek. Chewers like Nelda must have solved the problem long ago, he concluded.

He perched on the couch, near the stain from his experiment with *iq'mik*, and sipped a little more sourdock as Nelda's eyes played over him. He had learned there was no use saying anything before Nelda finished her intake exam. It seemed to be her equivalent of a *naluaqmiu* doctor checking your temperature and blood pressure, even if you came in for a sprained ankle.

Finally her eyes settled on his. "Grace tell me you want to take her and Nita to Anchorage."

He lifted his eyebrows. "The Troopers want to send me there."

"What I heard, you're the one want it."

He lifted his eyebrows again, trying to decide if he'd been caught in a lie. "I'd be getting a promotion in the Troopers."

"You're still too much *naluaqmiiyaaq* for Chukchi, ah?" She sighed and smiled in a familiar way. He had come to recognize this smile as indicating that Nelda Qivits, with the perspective of eighty-something years of life, was resigning herself to the fact that human nature was not to be changed, only abided.

"How do you think they'll do down there?" he asked. Grace and Nita both visited Nelda for the Inupiat version of counseling, and she possessed insights into their souls that astonished him. Better yet, unlike a white counselor, she would discuss these insights with him.

"That little Nita, she'll probably be okay anywhere if Grace is around, and you."

He lifted his eyebrows again. "And Grace?"

Nelda thought it over for a while. Then she said, "No *quiyuk* yet?"

He shook his head. "Not exactly."

Nelda's wise old eyes burned into him. "Ah?"

His face turned hot, and he was sure he was blushing. "She, ah, she used her hands on me at One-Way Lake."

"First time?"

He raised his eyebrows yes. "I think it was because she wasn't in her father's house."

"She let you do anything for her?"

He squinted no. "She still freezes up when I touch her . . . her, anywhere below the neck."

"*Arii*, that Gracie." There was another long silence. Nelda looked into her sourdock, took a swallow, then did something with her mouth that puzzled Active until he realized she was shifting the *iq'mik* from one cheek to the other. "You know why she still want to live in that house, after what happen?"

He wrinkled his nose in negation and dismay. It was a painful subject. "I've never understood it. And she's never explained it to me."

"That's because she never understand it herself."

He waited out another long silence, knowing they were inevitable in any conversation with an elderly Inupiaq. At last he could stand it no longer. "And you do?"

She lifted her eyebrows yes. "That house, it's kind of like her daddy to her. Long as she's there, it's like he's still around."

"But why would she want that, after what he—after she. . . ."

"Ah-hah," Nelda said. "After he do what he do to her when she's little girl, then she go on Four Street in Anchorage all that time what they call her Amazing Grace, then she come back and try kill him, but her mother do it first?"

Nelda phrased it as a question, though she knew Grace Palmer's history as well as he did. As usual, the old lady didn't flinch from looking at things straight on. The question she was really asking was, "This is what you can't bring yourself to say?"

He nodded, feeling numb.

"Ah-hah," Nelda said again. "A girl need her daddy. Down deep inside, she know he should take care of her. That's his job, and that's what she need, no matter what. If he don't, she'll think it's something wrong with her; maybe she'll never get over it. Boyfriend rape her, uncle rape her, probably she'll be okay someday maybe. But if it's her father, maybe not."

She peered intently at him with a questioning look: did he understand?

"But I don't—"

She held up a finger to stop him.

"If she's got his house, if she's safe and warm, maybe if you're there too, then in her mind it's kinda like she can make her daddy do right after all this time. She's making him take care of her like he should, even if he never do that when she's little girl."

She sipped the sourdock, gazing at him over the rim of the cup.

He gazed back in his usual amazement at the things she came up with. What Nelda said sounded right. He seemed to remember reading somewhere that the human psyche could rebuild itself after most forms of emotional trauma. But father–daughter incest was the hardest. "I have to get her out of there."

Nelda shrugged. "If she get ready to leave on her own, that'll be good. It'll mean she got better from what her father did."

"And if she's not ready?"

"If you make her leave, maybe it's good for her, she'll get over him faster. But maybe not too. She might leave Anchorage, come back up here to that house. Or maybe she'll go back on Four Street again. It's full of girls like her, what I hear."

He took a swallow of sourdock, wishing real life were more like police work. In police work, you investigated a case and closed it. Or, if you couldn't close it, it cooled off and you forgot about it eventually. But in life, no issue could ever be completely closed, or completely forgotten. One way or another, it would come up again and again.

"You go to that meeting at the school last night?" Nelda asked.

"Mm-mm. It was really crowded in the gym."

"Ah-hah. I listen on Kay-Chuck, all right. So sad about all them people burn up, ah?"

He lifted his eyebrows.

Nelda was silent for a long time, sipping sourdock and staring into the blank face of the television. "You never catch 'im, things will be bad around Chukchi for long time. Maybe never get better again."

It was said in a way that didn't require a response. He sighed, set his cup on the floor, and stood up.

"Who you fellas think it was?"

"You know I can't talk about that. It's Trooper business."

"Ah-hah. But you'll catch 'im soon, whoever start that fire?"

"We're doing everything we can," he said, embarrassed by the fatuity of the officialese. He took his leave from the old lady. As he closed the outer door of the *kunnichuk*, he heard the television click back on, this time to what sounded like an iPod commercial. What could Nelda Qivits possibly imagine an iPod to be?

It was almost nine by the time he got to work, shucked his coat, checked his e-mail and voice mail, and—Diet

Pepsi in hand—joined Carnaby and Long in the captain's office.

"That deal at the high school was brutal," a red-eyed and slightly groggy-looking Carnaby was saying as Active slid into a chair. "I felt like a deer in the headlights."

"No joke," Long put in. "I'm just glad the mayor didn't call me up there. As it was, I couldn't get to sleep until three or four."

"I guess people need to vent," Active said. "Did you notice anything from the stage?"

"Nothing but grief," Carnaby said. "More grief than I, I. . . ." Carnaby shook his head and gulped his coffee until the cup was half-empty. "Times like this, I remember why I got into the business, and I wish I hadn't."

Long just lifted his eyebrows.

Active nodded as if he felt the same way. He didn't, not yet, but the Rec Center fire was a start.

"How about you guys?" Carnaby asked. "Spot anything from the floor, Alan? Or by the door, Nathan?"

Neither of them spoke.

"Nothing?" Carnaby said. "All right, then, who's gonna do this?"

It took a moment for Active to remember their reason for gathering was to call Ronnie Barnes and go over the evidence from the fire scene again.

"I brought Barnes's card." Active patted his shirt pocket. "I guess I could."

"Feels kind of pathetic," Long said. "Like we're panhandling for a break in the case."

Carnaby frowned. "Alan, the first thing that pops into your head shouldn't necessarily be the first thing that pops out of your mouth."

"Sorry, Captain." Long hid his face by taking a slow pull at his coffee cup.

"Especially when everybody else is thinking the same thing," Active said.

Carnaby's frown deepened, and he glared at each of them in turn. "I don't know which one of you two is worse." He sighed. "Both, I guess."

He looked at Active again. "All right, Nathan. You call him. Alan and I will just listen unless we think of something to say." He turned his glare on Long. "Something helpful and intelligent, right, Alan?"

Long lifted his eyebrows.

Active pulled out Barnes's card and had laid it on the desk when Evelyn O'Brien rapped on the captain's door and stuck her head in. The three of them relaxed slightly at the reprieve.

"Call for Nathan."

"Take a number," Carnaby said. "He can call them back."

"It's the crime lab in Anchorage," O'Brien said. "They've got an I.D. on the body we sent down there."

The three men looked at each other. "What body?" Carnaby said.

Several seconds of silence passed before it dawned on Active. "Maybe it's No-Way. I completely forgot about him."

"No-Way?" Carnaby asked. "Oh, the guy from One-Way Lake. Really?"

Active counted backward in his head. "But we only sent him down there, what, two days ago? The crime lab couldn't have worked him already, could they? "

"Nah," Carnaby said. "It normally takes them at least a

week to get around to one of our bodies. Look, you better go straighten them out. They must have switched the toe tags or something."

Active trudged across the reception area to his own office, picked up the phone, and punched the line that was blinking. "Active here," he said.

"John Park," said a faintly Asian voice. "From the state crime lab?"

"Right," Active said. "Our secretary said you had an I.D. for us, but we're thinking there must be a mixup. We did send a body down, but it was only a couple days ago."

"Yeah," Park said. "The guy from the lake, right?"

"You worked him already?"

"Sure. We had an opening, so I slipped him in. Happens sometimes."

"And?"

"The I.D. is a little complicated, so I'll do the cause of death first. That part was easy."

"Okay."

"Broken neck, to put it in plain English. Kind of a rotational thing, like his head was twisted. Did he take a fall or something?"

"That's how it looked," Active said. "His rifle and some other stuff were scattered down the face of a cliff, like he lost his footing higher up the slope and basically cartwheeled down into the water. Whatever he hit or got caught on that made him lose the rifle, it ripped the sling out of the stock."

"Sounds right," Park said. "That could have done it."

"So he didn't drown in the lake?"

"Nope, no water in his lungs. Which is why he floated around in the lake for the fish to eat his face. Pike, I'm guessing?"

"That's what we think," Active said. "They're thick in those lakes along the Isignaq. But who was he?"

"That's the hard part," Park said. "The fish ate most of the flesh off his hands along with his face, and there was some decomposition as well, but we did get a reasonably good impression off his right thumb."

"And?"

"I ran it through the system, and it came back with five possible names. I can give 'em all to you if you want, but only one of them is even from Alaska, much less your area up there, so I figure he's gotta be your guy."

"Gotta be," Active agreed. "Go ahead."

"He's a long-lost cousin of mine," Park said.

"Eh?"

"I mean, he's Korean too."

Ah, Active was thinking, that would explain the slight accent. His brain skidded to a halt as Park said the name, then began to list the other four possibilities.

ACTIVE WAS still more or less deaf and blind as he walked back to Carnaby's office a few minutes later. He banged a knee on a corner of Evelyn O'Brien's desk and failed to respond in kind when she snarled at him as he rubbed the spot before limping on.

"What?" Carnaby said after a look at Active's face.

"Well, we found Jae Hyo Lee."

"What?" Long said. "They picked him up? Where? Did he confess?"

"Oh, shit." Carnaby met Active's eyes, then looked away in pain. "No!"

Active nodded.

"What?" Long said.

Carnaby cleared his throat. "Alan, I think Nathan is trying to tell us that the guy in One-Way Lake was Jae Hyo Lee." He looked at Active, eyebrows raised in the white expression of inquiry.

Active nodded again, Long's mouth shut with an audible pop, and a depressed silence settled over the room.

"Let's hear it," Carnaby said finally.

Active sketched Park's findings on the cause of death and explained that a thumbprint had identified No-Way from One-Way Lake as Jae Hyo Lee from Cape Goodwin, thereby depriving them of their only suspect in the Rec Center fire.

"Only the one thumbprint? Any room for doubt there?" Carnaby asked, not sounding very hopeful. "What about the other possibles?"

Active shook his head. "One of them is in custody in Reno, one's a female bank embezzler on parole in Chicago, one's a sixty-year-old Russian pimp from Brooklyn—admittedly between jail stretches at the moment—and the other's a black kid from Omaha."

They pondered the implications.

"But if Jae. . . ." Long said at one point, but was unable to proceed farther.

"And then who. . . ." Carnaby mumbled a little later, then sank back into the silence.

Finally Carnaby sighed. "So, when did he die?"

"According to Park, he was in the water a couple weeks, plus or minus a couple days," Active said.

Carnaby looked at the calendar on his desk blotter, and, with a pencil, tapped his way backward through it. "In other words, he was in that lake within a week of getting out of Sheridan."

Active nodded. "Plus or minus."

"And he died of a broken neck? Not drowning?"

Active nodded again.

Carnaby toyed with the pencil a moment, then began ticking the sequence off on his fingers. "Let's see. He gets a visit in prison from Tom Gage, he gets out of the system a couple months later, then turns up in One-Way Lake with a broken neck a few days after that. And by the time you stumble across him up there, Nathan, Tom Gage is dead too, as is Jim Silver. Anybody want to bet Jae Hyo Lee dived off that cliff by accident?"

"He didn't necessarily break his neck coming down the cliff," Active said.

"No?"

Active shook his head. "I asked Park if he was sure Jae broke his neck in the fall. He said, 'All I know for sure is, he wasn't breathing when he hit the water.'"

"You think he was dead before he fell, then?"

"You think we can rule anything out in this case?"

Carnaby grimaced. "You're right. But there's a hell of a cliff there, right? If he was already dead, how would anybody get him up that slope from the lake?"

Active thought it over. "I don't think anybody could. But they might have brought him in along the face of the slope somehow and let him go. Maybe they came through the mountains by four-wheeler?"

"Could be," Long said. "Those guys up there all use 'em to hunt."

"Cowboy spot anything like that when he went back in to get the body?" Carnaby asked.

Active shook his head. "He said it was hard to read. Four-wheeler trails all over, like Alan says, but nothing special around the lake. No camp or anything."

"What about somebody flying him in? Any way to land a plane up in those hills above the lake, maybe haul him down to the edge of the cliff and let him go?"

Active visualized the country around One-Way Lake and tried to imagine setting a plane down among the crags above it. "I don't think so," he said. "I don't think even Cowboy could get in up there."

Something was nagging at him, though. He was trying to tease it out of his memory when Carnaby sighed again.

"Look," the captain said. "Could a guy want to go hunting that bad? So bad, it's the first thing he does out of prison? Is it possible Jae just wanted to get away for a while, spend some time alone out in the country? He's rusty and maybe out of shape from prison, and the terrain gets ahead of him? Could it be that simple?"

The other two shrugged.

"Whatever," Long said. "But if Jae didn't start the Rec Center fire, we don't have anybody but Buck Eastlake."

"Yeah," Carnaby said. "But let's not let go of Jae quite yet. First let's have another talk with Uncle Kyung."

"Sounds right," Active said.

"I could," Long said. "He wasn't much help the first time around, but—"

"I'll go," Active said. He tried to think of something more to say, but decided there was no way to soften it: he didn't want Alan Long questioning Kyung Kim or conducting any other important interview in the case.

"What!" Long had stood to pull on his coat. Now he dropped back into his chair and laid his hands on Carnaby's desk, palms up. "Captain, I already talked to him. I know how to read him and—"

"You can go," Carnaby said. "But let Nathan do the talking. You keep quiet and observe the subject's demeanor, then report your findings to Nathan afterward."

Long clearly wasn't happy, but all he said was "Yes, sir." Carnaby's shower of officialese had probably been too much for him. He rose again and left the office.

Active stood and pulled on his own coat, looking at Carnaby. "Observe the subject's demeanor?"

Carnaby shrugged, appearing rather pleased with himself. "Worked, didn't it?"

ACTIVE PULLED up in front of the Arctic Dragon and shut off the Suburban. He looked over at Long, who held up a hand.

"Don't say it. You ask the questions. I listen."

Active nodded. "And Uncle Kyung answers, hopefully."

"Hopefully." Long swung open his door and climbed down from the SUV.

Kyung Kim was at the counter, a dozen or so receipts spread out before him, when they stepped into the restaurant. Kim was Korean, and so were the cook at work in the kitchen and the waitress watching CNN on a wall-mounted TV from a table near the counter. But the wall décor at the Arctic Dragon ran to medieval tapestries replete with knights, maidens, and unicorns. And the menu had become more American and less Chinese even in the relatively short time Active had been in Chukchi. Today, at any rate, the place smelled of frying fat, like any other diner in America. The Arctic Dragon, it appeared, was assimilating.

Kim spotted them, nodded brusquely, and said something in Korean to the waitress. She hurried over and pointed to a booth by a window looking out on Beach Street. "Table for two?"

"That's okay," Active said and slid around her to the counter.

Kim didn't look much like an uncle. He was too young, Active thought, then decided he probably didn't know enough Koreans to judge the man's age. Kim was short and slight, but, even so, his head looked too small for his body. And the back of his skull was flat, as if he'd slept on a board all his life.

"Can I help you?" he said, snapping a rubber band around the receipts. "I already talked to this officer on the phone." He cut his eyes over Active's shoulder, toward Long.

"Maybe we could go in your office." Active jerked his head toward a tiny cubicle near the counter. It contained a desk with a calculator and computer on it and one chair that he could see.

"My office is very small," Kim said. "Maybe better over there." He pointed at the same booth the waitress had indicated.

"Your office will be fine." Active put out his arm as though pointing. In reality, it was to leave Kim nowhere else to go.

Kim gave a small shrug of resignation and walked into the cubicle. He took the chair and watched them squeeze in and close the door. His face was a mask now. It reminded Active of the look an Inupiaq got when crowded by any-one official, especially a *naluaqmiut* official. The Eskimo mask, Active called it.

Long and Active loomed over Kim in his chair. With the three of them inside, the little office began to heat up.

"We found your nephew," Active said after a lengthy silence.

Kim's mask remained impassive.

"That was him we pulled out of One-Way Lake a few days ago. You heard about it on Kay-Chuck?"

"The radio said he was Eskimo."

"We thought he was, because the fish ate his face." Still no flicker of expression from Kim. "But we got a fingerprint off his thumb, and we made a match in our computer. It's Jae Hyo Lee."

"And you are sure?"

Active nodded. He thought a small sigh escaped Kim.

"How did he die?"

"What was he doing up at that lake? Why didn't he come here when he got out of prison? Or go up to Cape Goodwin to see his girlfriend?"

"I wouldn't know about that. Can you tell me how he died?"

"His neck was broken."

"Ah, yes, I think the radio said he fell from a cliff."

"When was the last time you heard from him?"

Kim paused. Active sensed he was calculating whether the two officers were likely to know about the call from Jae Hyo Lee shortly before his release from prison.

"He called from Oregon to tell me he was getting out," he said finally. "He said he might see me here, or he might go on to Cape Goodwin if the plane schedule was right."

"And did he see you here?"

"No. I didn't hear from him."

"Nothing at all? Weren't you worried?"

"I thought he went to Cape Goodwin and he must have better things to do than call his uncle after being in prison so long." Kim gave a small, experimental smile, then resumed the mask when neither Long nor Active returned it.

"Did you know Tom Gage?"

"Not much. I heard his name on the radio after the fire, though."

"Uh-huh. Did you know he visited your nephew in prison a few months ago?"

Active thought he sensed Kim calculating again, but the expression, if it could be called that, flickered off his face before Active could be sure.

"No, I don't think Jae told me that."

"So you wouldn't know what they talked about?"

"Of course not."

"Did you know Jim Silver?"

"The police chief? Of course. He didn't like Koreans much."

Long stirred behind Active, but held his tongue.

Kim gave a slight, quick nod. "I should not have said that. I'm sure he was a very good police chief."

"Well, Jim Silver called the prison about your nephew

a couple of weeks ago, and now they're both dead," Active said.

Kim nodded again.

"And Tom Gage went to see your nephew, and he's dead too."

Another nod.

"And you talked to your nephew a little before Jim Silver did, but you're still alive."

Kim didn't nod this time.

"And I'm guessing you want to stay alive. Is that it?"

No answer, but perhaps that flicker of calculation again.

"Mr. Kim, is there any way we can help you with that? Staying alive, I mean?"

"Leave me alone to run our family's businesses. We have many properties in your city, and your fire department is somewhat inefficient."

This produced a sharp intake of breath from Long, but he didn't speak. The office was beginning to smell, but Active couldn't tell if it was Kim sweating or Long.

"You think your properties might catch fire if you help us?" Active asked.

Kim's face was a mask again.

"Mr. Kim?"

The face didn't flicker. Active fished out a business card and dropped it on the desk. "You can call me if you think of anything."

No response. Active pushed the office door open, admitting a wash of relatively fresh air. "You knew that was your nephew in One-Way Lake before we came in, didn't you?"

Kim remained silent.

They walked to the door of the restaurant and Active took a look back. Kim was at the counter again, still watching from behind his mask.

"He knew," Long said as they climbed into the Suburban.

"Yep."

"And he's scared shitless."

"Yep."

"But who of?"

"Exactly."

"So you didn't get much more out of Kim in person than Alan did on the phone." Carnaby said this with a slight twinkle in his eye after hearing their report. "And did you observe anything significant in the subject's demeanor, Alan?"

Long suppressed a chuckle and Active tried to think of a comeback. Failing, he just said, "Maybe we should call Ronnie Barnes now."

Long stared at him.

"What?" Carnaby said.

"We were about to get on the phone to Barnes when the guy from the crime lab called. Go over the case with him, pick his brain a little?"

"Oh, yeah," Carnaby growled. "Right. Go ahead, Nathan. Smile and dial."

While the phone was ringing, Active switched it to speaker mode. In a few moments, they heard the familiar drawl. "Ronnie Barnes."

Active identified himself and informed Barnes of the presence of Carnaby and Long. "We were just wondering if you came up with anything else on our fire," Active said.

"Not much," Barnes said. "Just one little thing I was going to e-mail you with later today."

"Uh-huh?"

"Turns out you were right about that wire, Nathan. There was something funny about it."

Active remembered the wire loop that had possibly secured the locker room door in place and doomed the men inside. He even remembered noticing something odd about it, but not exactly what. "Go ahead," he said, covering. He could catch up as Barnes went on.

"You were thinking the way it was twisted looked like a machine did it?"

Now it came back to Active. "Right, it looked too neat for a guy to do with pliers."

"Uh-huh," Barnes said. "You know what a safety-wire twister is?"

Active looked around the desk. Carnaby and Long shook their heads. "No idea," Active said.

"Me too," Barnes said. "Until I showed the wire around the office and one of the guys here's a pilot. He recognized it. It's aviation safety wire. Airplane mechanics use it to tie down the heads of bolts so they won't vibrate off in the air, everything from Super Cubs to 747s, which would explain why it wasn't affected by the fire; it's made to withstand high temperatures. Now, I guess you could put it on with regular pliers, but airplane mechanics use something called a safety-wire twister. It's kind of like a vise grip where you lock the jaws onto the wire and then it has this shaft that you pull to make it spin and twist the—Ah, hell, I'll e-mail you a picture of one, all right?"

They all grunted their assent, impatient for Barnes to finish.

"The point is, it's a really fast way to wire something down tight, and you get the kind of neat and tidy twist that that wire from the Rec Center had on it. I got some safety wire and a twister from the guy here and tried it myself, and it came out exactly like what I pulled from the ashes out there."

Nobody said anything for so long that it was Barnes who broke the silence.

"You guys still there? Hello?"

"Yeah, we're here," Carnaby said. "So an aviation mechanic started our fire?"

"Or somebody who stole his wire twister," Barnes said. "Unless that piece of safety wire was still lying around from when that building used to be, what was it, your Air Guard Armory?"

"Uh-huh," Carnaby said. "You got anything else for us?"

"Nope, that's it," Barnes said. "Look for an e-mail, all right? And I'll send the wire down to the lab in Anchorage, see if they can find any tool marks. You guys find a wire twister, maybe they'll match. Anything else I can do for you?"

Carnaby cleared his throat and looked at Active. "You remember Buck Eastlake, the—"

"Right, the jealous boyfriend," Barnes said. "You guys talk to him yet?"

"Not yet, but he's starting to look pretty good. Turns out he's a cargo handler for Alaska Airlines."

"So he might have had access to a wire twister," Barnes said. "But—"

"Yeah," Carnaby sighed. "If you were plotting a major arson, where would it enter your head to steal a wire twister from your employer for the project?"

"Exactly," Barnes said. "I'd say he's not a real hot prospect, but if you got nothing else, you might as well go on up to that camp so you can check him off your list."

Active was about to push the Release button on the speaker phone when Barnes spoke again. "Just going down my own list here. You guys checked for burn cases the night of the fire, right?"

"I did," Long said. "No burn cases of any kind that night or the next morning, aside from the two survivors."

"Okay," Barnes said. "I guess that's one I can cross off."

CHAPTER ELEVEN

ACTIVE STOOD. "I SUPPOSE I ought to get hold of Cowboy about a ride up the Katonak."

"An aviation mechanic," Carnaby said.

Active sighed and sat down again. "All right. An aviation mechanic."

"Tom Gage," Long said.

Carnaby's eyes lit up, and his brows rose. "He could have flown his Super Cub up to One-Way Lake and dropped Jae off that cliff, all right."

"Not if he was on floats," Active said. "Nobody could haul a hundred-and-sixty-pound corpse up that cliff, trust me."

"What if he was on wheels? You sure there's no place to land up there?" Carnaby asked.

Active tried to picture the terrain again, started to shake his head, then remembered what had been nagging at him before. "Wait a minute. There's a ridge alongside the lake where you might be able to get in on wheels. And from that ridge, yeah, you could pack a body along the caribou trail to the top of the cliff and drop it into the lake. If you were reasonably determined and reasonably strong."

"So it is doable." Carnaby brightened slightly as he said this, then sobered again as the next thought came to him.

"But why would he haul a body all the way out there to get rid of it? There's gotta be a hundred easier ways."

Active pulled at his chin. "They had to be up there to start with," he said at length. "Maybe Gage never planned to kill him, but something went wrong, and he did, and throwing Jae in the lake was the best thing he could think of."

"Maybe," Carnaby said.

"It makes a certain amount of sense. Hardly anybody goes up there, so the chance of someone finding the body any time soon was pretty low. It was pure luck that Grace and I stumbled across it. And with the broken neck, it did look exactly like an accident."

"Which maybe it was." Carnaby looked gloomier than ever. "Maybe Gage and Jae were just pals, it's as simple as that. They plan a hunting trip to celebrate Jae's release, Jae puts his foot down wrong on the caribou trail, and there you are, right down the cliff. It happens."

"And then Tom flies back to town and never tells anybody his hunting partner died?" Long said.

"And then a couple weeks later he starts the Rec Center fire to kill himself out of grief and remorse?" Active said.

"All right, all right," Carnaby said. "I admit it doesn't totally add up, but it ties together more of our loose ends than any other theory I've heard." He looked from Active to Long and back. "Am I right?"

The other two raised their eyebrows in acknowledgement.

"So," Carnaby continued. "Jae dies in the mountains, and a couple weeks later Tom Gage dies in the Rec Center fire. But what if Tom didn't start it after all? What if he didn't get caught in his own arson?"

"Eh?" Long said.

"Maybe it was revenge. Maybe Tom really did kill Jae, and somebody figured it out and killed Tom to even the score."

Active had to admit it made as much sense as anything else in the case. "And took out all those other people—"

"To leave us exactly where we are right now," Carnaby said. "Absolutely nowhere."

"It has to be Kyung Kim," Long said.

The other two stared blankly for a second.

"He had to be Jae's partner in the gallbladder business," Carnaby said thoughtfully.

"And he wouldn't talk to us either time," Long said.

"It could add up," Carnaby said. "Nathan?"

"And where would Uncle Kyung get an aviation safety-wire twister to seal up the locker room at the Rec Center? Raise your hand if you think he even knows what a wire twister is."

"Argh," Carnaby said. "You're right. We're looking for an aviation mechanic."

"Maybe Kyung hired one," Long said.

Carnaby massaged the bridge of his nose. "Alan, if you're looking to hire an arsonist, why on earth would you want him to be an aviation mechanic too?"

Long looked somewhat chastened but stubborn. "I'm just saying, is all."

Carnaby's face softened slightly. "Either way, all that matters is, we're looking for an aviation mechanic. Soon as we check out Buck Eastlake, we're twenty-four/seven on the aviation mechanic angle. Hit Lienhofer, the other charter services, Alaska Airlines, the Tech Center. Ask if anybody's missing a wire twister, see if the FAA has a list of everybody in town who is or ever was an airplane mechanic, canvass the outfits that sell these things to see if they have customers in Chukchi—the whole sushi roll, right?"

"An aviation mechanic or somebody who hung out with one!" Active said, almost shouting. "Damn it, the roommate! Jesus, hand me that phone book, will you?"

Carnaby swiveled around and pulled the flimsy Chukchi Region directory from the shelf behind his desk. "The roommate? Do we know who it is? Who are we calling?" he asked as he swung back and pushed the directory across the desk.

"The village clinic in Cape Goodwin. Remember the damned boat? Shit!" Active flipped the book open, found the Cape Goodwin listings, and ran a forefinger down to the line for the clinic. He dialed, praying the village phones would be up, the power wouldn't be down, and the health aide wouldn't be out moose-hunting or playing bingo. He switched the phone to speaker, breathed a line of thanks when he heard the first ring, and mouthed a fervent, if silent, "Amen" when a woman's voice said, "Health clinic."

Active introduced himself, and she told him her name was Molly Booth. He gave her the date of the Rec Center fire, then asked if she could check her records to see if anyone had showed up with a burn the next morning.

"I don't need any records," she said. "That was Pingo Kivalina. His left arm was kinda burned, all right, but not too bad. I put some medicine on it and give him some pills for the pain and tell him to go home and stay out of trouble."

"Pingo Kivalina?"

"Ah-hah. His real name is Frederick, but they always call him Pingo for some kinda reason."

"Did he say how he got the burn?"

"He tell me he fall on the fire while he's moose-hunting, but I dunno. He's pretty hung over, all right. I think maybe he fall asleep with a cigarette and catch himself on fire or something."

"Has he been back in?"

The health aide was silent a moment. "No, I never see him since then. Seem like I hear he took off with Icy Cape that same day, maybe—or, no, next day I think."

Icy Cape Aviation in Barrow served the entire North Slope, from the Canadian border on the east to the North Slope Borough's southwest tip at Cape Goodwin. Or at least it had, until the storm that damaged the Cape Goodwin airport.

"Icy Cape is still getting in there, with your runway all torn up?"

"Mmm," Booth said. "They got a Cessna 206 on floats up at Point Hope, all right. They come down here with that, land on our lagoon, at least till it freeze up."

"Ah. And this Pingo went to Barrow?" Active asked.

"Must be," she said. "Don't know why he'd stay in Point Hope or any of them other villages up there."

Active ended the call and looked at the other two, a bell tinkling faintly in his head. He read aloud the name he had scrawled on the desk blotter. "Pingo Kivalina."

"I remember him," Long said in a tone of wonder. "That's Budzie Kivalina's twin brother."

Carnaby leaned his forehead on his palm and sighed heavily. "Where the hell does this end? We got Tom Gage visiting Jae Hyo Lee in prison, we got Gage killing Lee at One-Way Lake, and now we got Gage being burned alive by Pingo Kivalina, who just happens to possibly be Gage's roommate, not to mention the twin brother of his dead girlfriend. Am I leaving anything out?"

"Unless Pingo was really after Chief Silver all the while," Long said. "Or somebody else in the Rec Center."

"I don't want to think about it," Carnaby said. "I just know we gotta find Pingo Kivalina. Alan, go tell Evelyn to put out a BOLO for him in Barrow—get hold of North Slope Public Safety and the Trooper detachment up there."

Long nodded and headed for the secretary's desk as Active suppressed a chuckle at the ludicrous acronym that had replaced the old APB—All Points Bulletin—in copspeak. BOLO stood for "Be On the Lookout." The Troopers in Southeast Alaska even had a drug-sniffing dog by that name. Active had read or heard the term a hundred times at least, but it still sounded too comical for the gravity of its purpose—bringing in people suspected of robbery, mayhem, and murder. In this case, multiple murder by arson.

"And you, Nathan—log on to the system and see what you can find out about this guy."

Active paused for a moment, looking at the captain. "And you, boss?"

Carnaby extracted a section of the *Anchorage Daily News* from the clutter on his desk. It was open to a crossword puzzle, half-finished. He brandished it at Active. "I'm gonna take this down the hall and try to spend ten minutes thinking about something other than is this Pingo Kivalina real, is he still in Barrow, and, if he's not toes-up in a snowbank, does he have anything whatever to do with this goddamn case?"

ACTIVE AND Long returned to Carnaby's office within a minute of each other and with the same information. The crossword, Active saw, was finished.

"They've got him," Long said.

"Who does?" Carnaby said.

"North Slope Public Safety," Active said.

"He's in the Barrow jail," Long said. "They busted him yesterday for—"

"He was trying to sell three bottles of Monarch vodka to some teenagers up there," Active said. "He told the cops he needed the money to get to Anchorage."

"Wait a minute," Carnaby said. "Didn't you find a bottle in that boat at—"

"Right, at Cape Goodwin," Active said. "That was Monarch too. It's in a bag in my desk. You want to—"

"Yeah, we'll send it down to the crime lab for prints," Carnaby said.

Active slapped his forehead. "And wasn't that another Monarch bottle—"

"—at Gage's place," Carnaby finished. "I'll send Dickie Nelson over to get it and we'll send it down too. But first things first. How long is Pingo in for?"

"He's being arraigned later today," Long said. "He might bail out. Or sometimes they just let 'em out on their own recognizance in these minor bootlegging cases."

"No good, no good," Carnaby said. "Look, I'll talk to Charlie Hughes and see if we can get an arrest warrant for

Pingo on what we know so far. At least Charlie ought to be able to call his opposite number in the prosecutor's office up there and get them to stall things a few hours while we get this figured out."

He looked at Active and Long, drumming his fingers on the desk. "How are the connections to Barrow on Alaska Airlines these days?"

"They suck," Active said. "When I took that prisoner up there last spring—"

"Oh, yeah," Carnaby said. "You had to go through Anchorage, right?"

Active nodded. "Or Fairbanks, sometimes. And if you don't hit it right, you may have to overnight along the way. We should charter with Cowboy Decker. It's only about three hundred miles if you go straight over the mountains. Less than two hours in the Lienhofer twin. A little longer in the 185."

"Go ahead," Carnaby said. "By the time you get up there, maybe we'll have our arrest warrant. At least you ought to be able to interview the guy before he gets out."

"What about me?" Long asked.

"Yes?" Carnaby lifted his eyebrows in inquiry.

"I mean, I know Pingo a little from Cape Goodwin. Plus if we bring him back, it's a prisoner transport. Wouldn't hurt to have a second officer along."

"He's got a point," Active said.

"Sure, you go too, Alan." Carnaby waved his hand expansively. "What cop wouldn't want to be in on the bust in a case like this? But it's Nathan's interview."

"I'll get my stuff." Long bustled out, his chipmunk face split in a huge grin.

Carnaby leaned to one side and yelled past Active into

the reception area. "Evelyn, get on the horn to Lienhofer's and see if Cowboy can do a charter to Barrow today, ideally within the next hour. Two going, three returning."

"Prisoner transport?" the secretary asked.

"Yeah, but don't mention it unless they ask," Carnaby said. "Maybe they won't tack on the surcharge."

"Fat chance, if Delilah's on duty," O'Brien said as she picked up her phone.

Carnaby turned to Active. "Pack a toothbrush," he said. "Looks like you guys'll be there overnight, at least."

Active was silent, pulling at his lip.

"What?"

"Budzie Kivalina. Her name has come up again."

"Yeah, so? Look, the gene pool's only about an inch deep in Cape Goodwin. You get involved with one of 'em up there, you're involved with all of 'em." Carnaby paused. "You've heard the joke, right?"

"Do I want to?"

"About why you can't solve a rape case in Cape Goodwin?"

"Now I'm sure I don't want to."

"All the DNA's the same."

"Very funny."

"You're not smiling." Carnaby paused again. "All right, what are you thinking?"

"I don't know. It's just that she keeps coming up."

"I know what you mean, but—" Carnaby paused, thinking. "Okay, Pingo doesn't pan out, she's next on our to-do list, after Buck Eastlake. Okay?"

Active left the Public Safety Building, went by the Trooper bachelor cabin where he technically still lived to collect his things for the trip to Barrow, and realized that most of what he needed was still at Grace's house. He climbed back into the Suburban and headed for Beach Street.

It was not until he spotted Grace's four-wheeler in front of the house that he realized it was lunchtime and then some, and they were supposed to be having it together at home that day.

He found Grace at the kitchen table, holding a half-eaten tomato-and-cheese sandwich and frowning in concentration at her laptop. A Microsoft Word document was open on the screen. She closed it as he came in.

"That your journal?"

The journal had been Nelda's idea. Even with the old tribal doctor, Grace had trouble talking about Jason Palmer and the circumstances of his death. So, Nelda had said, "You could write it, ah?" Nowadays, that meant on a computer, not in a spiral notebook. Grace took the laptop to her sessions with Nelda, but never showed Active the entries.

She nodded. "I'm sorry. I—it's the Anchorage thing, you know."

"It's all right. I don't need to read it. You'll tell me what you want me to know."

"And that's really okay?"

He was seated beside her now, in front of the tuna sandwich and iced tea she'd set out for him. He nodded and leaned in for a kiss. "You talk to Nita? How's she doing with it?"

Before she could answer, the door of the *kunnichuk* slammed, then the inner door creaked open and banged shut.

"Uncle Nathan! Are we moving to Anchorage?"

Active turned and opened his arms. Nita raced down

the hallway, shrugged off her backpack, and dived into them, then took her usual seat on his left knee.

"Probably maybe," he said. "Whattaya think?"

"You and Mom will both be there, right?"

Active lifted his eyebrows yes.

"Of course," Grace said.

"*Arigaa*. But nobody else from Chukchi?"

"Sometimes Chukchi people might visit us when they come down," Grace said.

Nita wrinkled her nose in rejection and dismay, then looked at Grace. "I don't like them. Sometimes they always tease me a lot. They say mean things about you and my Aunt Ida, how she kill Uncle Jason."

Grace's face took on the stricken expression that appeared whenever this subject came up. "But you don't believe them, right? You remember what I told you about what really happened?"

Nita raised her eyebrows. "He was showing her how to clean the gun, and he dropped it, and it went off and shot him, right?"

Grace relaxed slightly and nodded. "Well, if you don't want to see any Chukchi people, we won't."

"Nobody will know us down there?"

"Nobody except Nathan's *naluaqmiut* mom and dad. You like them, ah?"

Nita beamed. "Remember when we went to Chuck E. Cheese? Can we go there again?"

"Every Saturday," Active said. "We'll all go together."

Grace rolled her eyes at this but smiled. "You hungry, sweetheart?"

Nita glanced at the third place set at the table, and her eyes lit up. "Macaroni and cheese!"

"Yes-a-roni," Grace said. Nita giggled as she shoved in the first bite.

Over Nita's head, Grace grimaced in mock embarrassment. The stuff was Nita's favorite dish, one she'd eat three times a day if Grace would allow it. In fact, it was Grace's favorite too, though she wouldn't have admitted it to most people. "Comfort food for the soul," she called it.

Active smiled and applied himself to the tuna sandwich. He still had a third of it left when Nita swallowed the final spoonful of her macaroni and cheese and downed the last of her apple juice.

She jumped out of her chair and raced for the stairs. "I'm going to play Nancy Drew till it's time to go back."

"Yeah, okay, fifteen minutes, then it's off the computer and out the door, young lady!" Grace yelled as the girl clumped up to her room.

"Full speed as usual," Active said.

"Absolutaroni."

He smiled.

Grace was silent for a moment. Then she said, "Nita's all right with the Anchorage thing, obviously. I guess I'm seriously outnumbered."

"Two to one, looks like." He paused, thinking about how to get into it.

She turned her amazing quicksilver eyes full on him. "What?"

"I talked to Nelda."

"About the Anchorage thing?"

He raised his eyebrows.

"And?"

"She seems to think that, at some level, this house represents your father to you," Active said. "When you're here, running this place, you feel like you're in control, you're getting love and comfort from him the way you never did when he was alive."

"We've talked about that," Grace said. "Makes sense at an intellectual level, I know, but I can't say that I actually feel it. It's just an idea to me."

"She said if I make you leave this house, it might be good for you. It might help you finally make that break with . . . with everything here."

"But it might not?"

"If it's too soon, you might leave me and come back to the house. Or even go back to Four Street."

Grace fidgeted, picking at the latch on the front of the laptop. "I think about that sometimes."

"Going back to Four Street?"

She nodded, more to herself than to him. "It's comfortable there, in a way. You don't have to try to do or be anything. Nobody expects anything. They don't judge you. They just want to drink with you."

She saw the look on his face and said hurriedly, "Not that I ever would, of course. With you and Nita in my life, I never would, not now."

She paused, lost in thought again, her fingers busy with the latch.

"I'll go if you make me," she said at length.

"But if I have to make you, will it really—how will you—"

"I think that would be the way to do it, is all." She was smiling, tears glistening at the corners of her quicksilver eyes.

When she spoke again, her tone was reflective, inward. "You know, I think I might be able to have sex in Anchorage.

Maybe Nelda's right. If I get out of here, maybe I'll have a shot at being normal."

"That's how I interpret that lovely experience at One-Way Lake."

She went on as if he hadn't spoken. "I think I could have done it that night I tried to seduce you in Dutch Harbor, but I was your murder suspect at the time, and you turned me down. Remember that?"

"Don't remind me."

"Maybe you'll get a second chance if I'm not in Chukchi."

"We could all use a second chance."

She raised her eyebrows in assent, then looked around the kitchen and down the hall. "Maybe I should burn it."

"Burn what?"

She shrugged.

"You mean this place? You want to burn your own house?"

"Sure. To complete my recovery."

"But . . . it's probably against the law."

"Why? I own it outright. There's no mortgage. I could cancel the insurance first. Maybe it's the only way I'll ever be free of it all. Burn it, like he did my sister."

"It might endanger the neighbors." He pointed out the kitchen window at the house next door. It was rented by a couple who taught at the elementary school. "Like the Olsons there."

She shrugged again. "Maybe I'll talk to the fire department. They could set it on fire and put it out for practice. This is a pretty big lot and they could do it in the winter, when everything's covered with snow. That should be safe for the neighbors, eh?"

He was still groping for a response when she spoke

again. "Speaking of fires, you guys getting anywhere on the
Rec Center case?"

"Oh, yeah," he said, almost shouting from relief at the
change of subject. "I'm going to Barrow. We actually have
a lead."

Her eyes widened in interest, and he sketched the latest
developments for her, the prospects seeming dimmer the
farther he went. A village drunk from Cape Goodwin in
the Barrow jail for bootlegging—that was their best lead,
with second place going to a caribou hunter in camp on
the Katonak River. "Pretty depressing, huh?" he said at
the end.

She pondered for a few moments, shrugged, and smiled
in sympathy. "Finish your lunch. You won't solve anything
on an empty stomach. I'm going to go up and kick Nita off
the computer and pack you a bag for Barrow."

She headed for the stairs, and he downed the rest of tuna
sandwich without tasting it. She had just proposed setting
her own house on fire. Was that her way of telling him that
she—no, of course not. She had been in the sleeping bag
with him at One-Way Lake when the Rec Center went up
in flames. She couldn't have been involved. Her father's
house was the only thing she wanted to burn down.

At first thought, it seemed bizarre and crazy, pure
pathology. But maybe the idea made sense. Maybe it would
be therapeutic. Grace's knack for getting straight to the
heart of a thing was a little spooky sometimes. Maybe he'd
see what Nelda thought when he got back.

Grace came downstairs with Nita, handed him a bag,
and kissed him good-bye. "Maybe I'll book us a house-
hunting trip to Anchorage for when you get back from
Barrow."

"I might be back tonight," he said when he found his voice. "Or tomorrow at the latest."

"Okay," she said. "I'm probably going to have to make a trip up to the Gray Wolf tomorrow. Can Nita stay with your mom?"

"I'm sure it'll be fine—just check with her."

Nita asked him for a ride, so they walked out to the Suburban together and she chattered about Chuck E. Cheese and the other delights of Anchorage as he drove her back to Chukchi Middle School and marveled at the speed with which Grace Palmer was capable of moving.

His amazement still hadn't fully subsided an hour and a half later when he climbed into Cowboy Decker's Cessna 185 with Alan Long and they lifted off into the clear, windy sky of an Arctic early afternoon. Cowboy pointed the plane northeast, toward the great stone spine of the Brooks Range. They climbed steadily as they passed the Sulana Hills across the bay from Chukchi and then the Katonak Flats. The departed storm had dusted the hilltops and upper ridges white, though the lower elevations still wore the dead, flat brown of late fall. The tundra ponds on the Flats were glazed over now, and pan ice was running in the Katonak River.

To their left, over the coastal hills marking the western edge of the Flats, Cape Goodwin was just visible as a row of tiny, fragile boxes on the rim of the Chukchi Sea. Farther out, a white line stretched along the horizon where the ice pack rode down from the north on the same wind that rocked the Cessna from time to time.

Cowboy leveled the plane and clicked on the intercom. "So, why are we going to Barrow?"

"Trooper business, Cowboy." Active glanced into the

rear seat to make sure Alan Long wouldn't tell the pilot more than he needed to know. Long was asleep, head resting against one of the Cessna's Plexiglas windows, mouth slightly open. It made his chipmunk face even more childlike.

"Who we bringing back?" Cowboy asked. "You have to tell me at least that much, right?"

Active thought it over and decided Cowboy had a point. "Pingo Kivalina. We hope."

"Kivalina, huh? From Cape Goodwin, right?"

"Uh-huh. You know the guy?"

Cowboy was silent, adjusting the controls. The Cessna's nose dropped slightly and the pilot nodded in satisfaction. "Don't think I know Pingo, but the Kivalinas that I do know . . . well, they're different. But so is everybody in Cape Goodwin. What did this one do?"

"Like I said, it's Trooper business."

"He your guy on the Rec Center fire?"

"What makes you think so?"

"Why else would the Troopers pay for a charter to Barrow? And what else are you guys working on these days?"

Active said nothing, and Cowboy didn't ask any more questions. He was silent until they crossed the crest of the Brooks Range and the North Slope unfolded before them. Here in the uplands, the country was already asleep for winter, the terrain a titanium white, the lakes frozen over. Most of the streams were iced in, too, except for the occasional waterfall or stretch of rapids.

"Hungry country," Active said.

Cowboy grunted through the intercom. "I'll say. Hardly any place to land up here till the ice on the lakes gets thick enough."

Active peered down at the terrain. Not trackless, exactly, with all the streams cutting through it, but it might as well have been. The peaks, ridges, and rivers formed an endlessly iterated pattern of arteries and capillaries, meaningless to his untrained eye. "So what would you do if this thing quit on us right now?"

Cowboy glanced at his instruments, then at the map on his knee. "Right now? We'd probably luck out. There's an old oil company strip called Driftwood about three or four miles behind us on the Utukok River. We might be able to glide that far. Otherwise, you got your choice: set her down on the tundra and nose over, or take your chances on a lake and cross your fingers about the ice."

"Yeah, but—"

"Let's talk about something else," Cowboy said. "That's the Utukok over there." He pointed under the left wing. "It runs north into the Arctic Ocean, and so do all the rivers west of it—the Kokolik, the Kukpowruk. But that one up ahead there, that's the Colville. It runs a couple hundred miles east before it turns north and goes down into the Beaufort Sea."

Cowboy dropped the right wing slightly and pointed at a brush-lined furrow threading a snowy valley below them.

Active grunted in acknowledgment but said nothing, letting Cowboy have his change of subject.

"You know about the redwoods, right?" Cowboy asked.

Now Active was slightly interested. "Redwoods?"

"Yup. There's a place on the Colville where redwoods are coming right out of the bank and falling into the river."

"Fossils, you mean."

"No, redwoods. As in wood. They been frozen all this time, and they never fossilized. Or rotted."

Active thought this over. It might be true. The Alaskan Arctic had had a much balmier climate in the dinosaur era. Redwoods could have grown here, and they could have been frozen when the climate changed.

On the other hand, Cowboy Decker's critical thinking skills weren't exactly robust. "Did you see this with your own eyes?"

"Absolutely," Cowboy said. "Few years ago, I was flying support for a bunch of paleontologists who were in there studying those redwoods. I brought back a chunk and made it into a lamp."

Active turned to stare at the pilot. "Did the paleontologists know this?"

Cowboy shrugged.

"Is that legal?"

Cowboy shrugged again.

Active shook his head and returned his attention to the corrugated landscape. Here the bare, jagged peaks were a savage reminder of the ancient forces that had thrust and tumbled and smashed this particular chunk of the earth's crust into the Brooks Range millions of years ago.

As they pushed on, the terrain calmed down and began to look like tundra was supposed to look—flat and lightly bearded with dwarf willow. The snow thinned out, and the land was brown again, except for the blind white eyes of the countless frozen ponds and lakes of the coastal plain.

By the time Cowboy made his call to the FAA for the landing at Barrow, sunset was blooming behind them. A few minutes later, the lights of the village twinkled in the cold night air as Cowboy swung the Cessna onto final approach and dropped it onto the runway.

"Five above, eighteen knots of wind," Cowboy said over

the intercom as he turned off the runway. "Welcome to beautiful downtown Barrow."

The pilot taxied to a set of gas pumps in front of a hangar with "Icy Cape Aviation" painted on the doors and shut off the engine. "They'll call you a cab." He pointed at the office beside the hangar as the propeller shuddered to a halt. "I'll gas up and tie down and hang around here a while. We going back tonight?"

"Probably not," Active said. "This may take some time. There's paperwork involved."

"Suit yourself," Cowboy said. "I'll just grab a cot in the hangar here. We let their guys sleep in our hangar if they get a charter to Chukchi."

Active thought for a moment, then looked at the salmon sky over the tundra to the southwest. "Should we go back tonight? Will this weather hold?"

Cowboy nodded. "Clear and cold through the night, according to the weather service. Some stuff moving in tomorrow afternoon, maybe, but we should be in Chukchi by then."

"All right, we'll plan on going back in the morning. It's already been a long day, and it's not over yet, so we may as well get some sleep before we start home."

CHAPTER TWELVE

TWENTY MINUTES LATER, A tiny van with an inadequate heater dropped them in the hard-frozen gravel parking lot in front of the Barrow jail, a new-looking two-story building with yellow-brown walls and a blue roof, all made of shiny metal.

"Look," Long said. "No stilts."

As in Chukchi, most buildings in Barrow perched on the shoulder-high pilings necessary to keep the permafrost from melting and swallowing anything that stood on it. The jail was one of the few structures they'd seen in Barrow that sat right on the ground.

"I guess they must have found a spot with no permafrost," Active said. This was rare in the Arctic, but not unheard-of.

"Either that or they don't care," Long said. "They got so much money up here, they can just build a new one if it sinks." The Prudhoe Bay oil fields lay within the taxing jurisdiction of the North Slope Borough, with the result that the borough's residents enjoyed a remarkable freedom from material want. Oil money brought houses, airports, hospitals, clinics, cops, bureaucracies, and schools on a scale unimaginable elsewhere in the bush.

It was certainly unimaginable in the Chukchi region,

where the only taxable property of any consequence was the Gray Wolf mine, and even that was minuscule compared to the golden goose at Prudhoe. Still, the Aurora Borough had been formed to take advantage of the opportunity to tax the Gray Wolf, and things were improving with the flow of jobs and revenue from the huge copper mine in the Brooks Range north of Chukchi. Now Chukchi and the other villages in the region were about to be absorbed into the borough. One day soon, the Chukchi police force would be dissolved, and Alan Long and the other city cops would find themselves employed by the borough's public safety department. Jim Silver had been tapped to organize the new agency as his last project before retirement.

Active paid the Filipino cabby, and they picked up their bags and walked into a lobby decorated with Eskimo masks made from dried caribou hide. Active recognized the masks as coming from Caribou Creek, an Eskimo village high in the Brooks Range, anomalously distant from salt water, seals, walrus, whales, and the other customary marine mainstays of Inupiat life. The village was known primarily for the caribou hunting in the nearby tundra valleys and high lakes of the Brooks Range. That, and caribou masks.

Active dropped his bags, checked his cell phone for service, found three bars, and dialed the Troopers in Chukchi. Evelyn O'Brien answered and put him through to Carnaby, who told him that Charlie Hughes, the District Attorney, had gotten an arrest warrant for Pingo Kivalina. They could fly him back to Chukchi, unless he managed to talk himself out of suspicion in the interview.

Two jailers showed them into an interview room like

every other one Active had ever seen: a table of blond wood, four chairs with shiny metal frames and black vinyl seats, one door, a trashcan, and a one-way mirror.

One of the jailers was a middle-aged Inupiat woman with a name tag identifying her as Mabel. The other was a younger white man named Ray, chubby and weak-chinned with a moustache that failed to lend authority or character to his round face.

Mabel told them to wait in the interrogation room while they fetched Pingo Kivalina, but Active asked to be put in the observation room to watch Pingo a few minutes before confronting him.

Mabel nodded, led them next door, and reminded them to keep the lights off. Then the two jailers left to get Kivalina.

Active and Long looked at each other in the dim light of the observation room.

Long grimaced. "This could be it, huh?"

"Could be," Active said, fighting down the urge to pace or drop to the floor for a few pushups.

Finally the jailers returned with an Inupiaq in short-sleeved orange jail coveralls. Mabel put him in a chair facing the one-way mirror, and the two cops finally got a look at Pingo Kivalina.

He had stringy black hair down to the middle of his back and an oval face with a long, heavy jaw under a wide mouth that appeared to grin reflexively when left to its own devices. His skin was black along the cheekbones, the mark of a hunter who had been repeatedly frostbitten while snowmachining in the cold. His left arm looked sunburned around the elbow, which glistened with some kind of ointment.

Kivalina surveyed the room after the jailers left, then got up and walked over to the trashcan and looked in. He came to the mirror, peered into it, and waved. Active couldn't tell if Kivalina was waving at himself or at the people he assumed were behind the mirror.

The jailers let themselves into the observation room.

"Think he's your guy?" asked the one named Ray.

Active shrugged and looked at Pingo Kivalina again, wondering why the face seemed vaguely familiar. Had he been in one of the pictures at Tom Gage's place?

"What do you think?" Active asked the jailers.

"There's no telling," Ray said. "He's totally gooned out as far as I can see. Keeps channeling his dead sister and telling her about this wolverine that's trying to kill him. My guess is, he'll confess to Nine-Eleven if you push him hard enough."

Active had watched Mabel as Ray spoke. She had a pleasant face, somewhat lean and angular; bright sharp eyes; and gray-streaked black hair worn in a braid at the back of her neck. Just now, she also wore the Eskimo mask.

"Thanks, Ray," Active said. "I guess we can take it from here."

Mabel headed for the door with Ray, but Active touched her arm.

"Maybe you could stay."

"Ah?"

"Do you speak Inupiaq?"

She lifted her eyebrows.

"How's Pingo's English?"

"You sure you don't need me?" Ray interrupted.

"No, I just think we may need a translator with Pingo."

Ray nodded with a relieved look and pushed out the door.

Mabel was smiling. "He always watch Howard Stern on cable this time of day," she said after the door had closed. "He like it when that Howard get those silly girls to take off their tops."

Active marveled for a moment at the New York shock jock's reach. But anywhere was everywhere these days, as long as there was electricity for a satellite dish.

"Will we need a translator with Pingo?"

Mabel turned and studied the man in the mirrored room. "I don't think so. His English is pretty good, all right."

"It feels strange to call you Mabel," Active said, "but I didn't get your last name before."

"It's Oktollik," she said. "Mrs. Mabel Oktollik."

"Oktollik? Isn't that a Cape Goodwin name?" Long asked. "Are you from there?"

"My husband's family was," she said. "But they move to Fairbanks when he's little boy, so I only been there a few times, when we visit his relatives."

Active nodded at the one-way mirror. "You ever know that guy when you were in Cape Goodwin?"

"Pingo? I think I must have seen him at the village, all right, but I don't remember if we ever talk or anything. I don't think so. Did he set that fire in Chukchi?"

"We don't know yet. You think he did?"

She glanced at Pingo, who was now slumped in his chair at the end of the table, arms crossed, chin on his chest. He looked to be asleep. "It's hard to tell what somebody can do," she said. "Somebody that's nice can do bad things, or someone bad can be nice sometimes."

"Is he crazy, like Ray says?"

"He sound crazy, all right, talking about that wolverine kill his sister and now it's after him. But at the same time, I dunno. Seem like he believe what he's saying, but crazy people are like that, ah?"

"That's right," Long said. "It's the difference between a crazy person and a liar. The crazy person believes it."

For a moment, Active thought Mabel was about to turn the Eskimo mask on Long, but she just lifted her eyebrows.

"A wolverine, huh?" Active asked.

"Ah-hah. *Qavvik*, he call it."

Active lifted his eyebrows. "And the sister? What's her name?"

"Budzie, I think. He's kind of hard to understand sometimes. He was pretty drunk when we got him, but he's sober now. Hung over too."

Active looked at Kivalina, then back at Mabel Oktollik. "Well, if his English is okay, you don't have to stay, unless you want to."

She shook her head. "No, I should get back to work. When you're done, call us to take you out." She pointed at a phone on a table by the door. Its one lighted button was the room's only illumination, other than what came through the mirror from the interrogation room. "Extension two-three-two."

"Thank you, Mrs. Oktollik. We will."

She left, and Active turned to Long. "Any thoughts?"

"Apparently he's not too crazy to remember his sister's name. Otherwise. . . ." Long threw up his hands.

Active peered through the glass. "I want to talk to him alone."

"What? I—"

"I need you to stay here and observe, watch his body language, listen for voice changes, that kind of thing, all right?"

Long gave a grudging nod, and Active walked into the interrogation room.

"Pingo Kivalina," he said as he closed the door. "I'm Trooper Nathan Active."

A shoulder twitched. Kivalina's eyes opened.

He blinked and peered about in evident confusion for a few seconds, then spotted Active by the door. His face went blank, and he screamed *"Arii!"* as he jumped up and knocked over the chair. Active braced himself, hoping that Long was on his way from the observation room to help.

But Kivalina didn't come at Active. He spun and slammed blindly into the mirror, leaving a smear of mucus and blood on the glass as he slid to the floor. The crotch of his coveralls darkened and the smell of warm urine filled the room. He twisted to look at Active and screamed again. *"Arii!* He come with you?"

The door opened, and Active sensed Long behind him.

"This is Officer Long," Active said. "Yes, he's with me."

"Hiya, Pingo," Long said. "How ya been?"

Kivalina stared over Active's shoulder at Long with no sign of recognition, then refocused on Active. "No, not him. That *qavvik*—he come with you?"

"There's no one else," Active said. "Just Officer Long."

"You never come with that *qavvik?*"

Apparently, Kivalina *was* crazy, perhaps crazy enough to have set the Rec Center fire. If he wanted to talk about a wolverine, perhaps that was the best way to get him going.

"What *qavvik?*" Active asked. "The one that killed your sister?"

Kivalina lifted his eyebrows.

"And now it's trying to kill you?"

Kivalina lifted his eyebrows again. "He try burn me up in that Rec Center."

"The wolverine set the Rec Center on fire?"

"Ah-hah."

"And that's how you burned your arm?"

Kivalina rubbed the red skin around his elbow. "Ah-hah."

"And that's how Tom Gage got burned?"

"Ah-hah, he got burned too, all right, except he never get out."

"And you were staying with him in Chukchi?"

Another eyebrow-raise.

"Some people are thinking maybe you're the *qavvik* that burned up the Rec Center and killed Tom Gage."

"Somebody say that?"

"What if they did?"

"They're lying. I never do it. I'm not no *qavvik*."

"The *qavvik*'s not around, so you don't have to be afraid. Now tell me about when the Rec Center burned and you got out."

Kivalina struggled shakily to his feet and leaned against the mirror, blood dripping from his nose. He glanced at his crotch. "Look like I piss myself. How that happened?"

"You don't remember?"

"Remember what?"

Active shook his head and looked at Long, who rolled his eyes. Active turned back to Kivalina. "You sit at the table there, and Officer Long will get you some dry clothes."

Active turned to Long, who raised his eyebrows and

slipped out the door. Active took a seat at the table. Kivalina righted his chair and seated himself across from Active, then jumped up as if it was no fun sitting in the sodden coveralls. He sat down again on the edge of the chair.

"Look," Active said. "We were talking about that fire in Chukchi."

"Ah-hah."

"You can have a lawyer here when we talk if you want."

"Yeah, they tell me that when I'm arrested, all right."

"Or you don't have to talk at all if you don't want to."

Pingo looked puzzled. "Why I don't want to?"

Active shook his head and plowed through the rest of the Miranda warning, one element at a time. When he was finished, he wasn't sure Kivalina had understood any of it, but it would have to do.

"All right." Active cleared his throat. "You said the *qavvik* burned the Rec Center?"

"I say that?"

Active lifted his eyebrows.

"Well, it's true. He try burn me up, all right."

"And who is this *qavvik*?"

"You know him already."

"I know him? How do you know that?"

Kivalina looked away.

"Can you tell me his name?"

Kivalina squinted in refusal. "I can't say it."

"Why not?"

"Too scare."

"Why would he want to burn the Rec Center?"

"He can do that if we try kill him, ah?"

"You and your sister tried to kill him? That's why he killed her and why he's trying to kill you?"

"My sister try kill him? She never tell me that."

Active frowned and rubbed his chin. Pingo Kivalina had the attention span of a flea. How to keep him on track? If there was a track.

"How you know my sister?" Kivalina asked. "I never remember you being around Budzie. You got the great weather in you?"

Active sighed and climbed on for the ride. "The great weather?"

"Budzie always say that what she's looking for, a man with the great weather inside him."

"What did she mean by that?"

"She have this song she always sing." Kivalina's face softened and looked suddenly feminine. When he sang, his voice was a woman's, and Active found the hair prickling on the back of his neck:

*The great sea
has sent me adrift,
it moves me
like a weed in the great river,
Earth and the great weather
move me,
have carried me away
and move my inward parts with joy.*

Kivalina was silent for a time, then was a man when he spoke again. "You move her inward parts with joy? That what she mean by a man with the great weather inside him. She always look for that man."

"I never knew your sister."

"Nobody really know her but me. We're twins, ah?"

Active lifted his eyebrows. "I heard that."

"But our *aaka* never know she got two of us in there. After Budzie come out, she think she's all done, then I pop out too. Like a pingo, what she always tell people. So everybody always call me Pingo." Kivalina smiled, and his face took on a distant look.

"Tell me more about your sister."

"Ah-hah," Kivalina said. "When we're little, we have our own language. Nobody else can't talk it, only us. You know what our *aaka* call it?"

Active shook his head.

"Twinupiaq, ah-hee-hee."

Kivalina paused, waiting for Active's response. Active smiled dutifully and, he hoped, encouragingly.

"You ever have a twin, Mr.—what your name again?"

"Active. Nathan Active."

"You ever have a twin, Mr. Nathan?"

Active was about to correct Kivalina, then decided against it. "No, I only have a half-brother."

"When we're little kids in Cape Goodwin, that's when we talk it, Twinupiaq."

Active nodded, trying to think of a way to snap Kivalina back to the present again. "Are you sure it was the *qavvik* that killed Budzie? I heard she died in a plane crash."

"Hah!" Kivalina snorted. "It was that *qavvik*, all right. She tell me."

"She told you? How could she do that if she was dead?"

"I hear Dad-Dad barking while I'm asleep, then I dream I'm awake and she's there and she say, 'We never *katak* in that plane.' Then I know that *qavvik* kill her, all right. That's why we go up there."

"Dad-Dad? Your father was bark—who's Dad-Dad?"

"That's our dog. Budzie's and mine. Dad-Dad is dead, too."

"Ah. So your sister came around with your dog?"

"Ah-hah, she come around while I'm dreaming, say, 'We never *katak* in that plane.' Then I know that *qavvik* kill her, all right. Her and Dad-Dad. That's why we go up there."

"You went up there?"

Kivalina lifted his eyebrows yes.

"You went up to where the *qavvik* killed her?"

Kivalina lifted his eyebrows again. "Ah-hah, that place they call Driftwood, where they never *katak* in that *qavvik's* plane."

Driftwood? It took Active a moment to remember. Driftwood was the oil-company airstrip Cowboy had identified as their best hope in the event of an engine failure in the Brooks Range. But why would Pingo Kivalina go where his sister had died? And how?

"You went to—" Active paused at the sound of the door opening behind him. Alan Long stepped in with a pair of the orange jail coveralls under his arm.

"Here ya go, Pingo." Long dropped the coveralls onto the table in front of Kivalina.

Kivalina put a hand on the jailwear and looked at the two officers. "I have to do it with you guys in here?"

"We'll give you some privacy." Active motioned for Long to follow him out of the room.

Through the mirror, they watched as Kivalina peeled off the coveralls with the stain at the crotch and tossed them into a corner. He looked down at his boxers, then stripped them off, exposing the scrawniest butt Active had ever seen.

"Look at that," Long said. "A real Eskimo, all right."

Active looked. "What?"

"He's got the blue spot. See, right there over his left cheek?"

Now Active saw it. A kidney-shaped patch the color of a faded ink stain in the small of Kivalina's back. "That makes him a real Eskimo?"

Long raised his eyebrows. "The doctors call 'em Mongolian spots. We call 'em Eskimo spots. I have one in the same place. Don't you?"

"Not there," Active said after a moment's reflection. "But I've got a blue birthmark under one arm. That count?"

Long raised his eyebrows again. "It does if it's blue, I think."

Kivalina had pulled on the fresh coveralls and was now attempting to sit back down at the table. But he overturned his chair and had to set it upright.

"What do you think?" Long asked. "Crazy?"

Active chewed his lip and studied their suspect, who had slid down in the chair and was leaning his head back, in apparent preparation for a nap. "Evidently."

"There's a lot of schizophrenia in Cape Goodwin," Long said. "You know, they say it's famous for—"

"Yeah, yeah, I know," Active said. "Everybody knows. And maybe they're right, at least in Pingo's case. He keeps talking about this *qavvik* who's to blame for everything. The *qavvik* killed his sister. The *qavvik* killed their dog. The *qavvik* set the Rec Center on fire. Pingo even tried to kill the *qavvik*, he says."

"You think the *qavvik* is Pingo's other self?"

Active shrugged. "It seems to fit. Pingo did get burned in the fire. Maybe that's how he tried to kill the *qavvik*."

Long shuddered as he looked at Kivalina through the mirror. "And got all of those other people instead."

Active was silent for a long time. "Maybe we can punch through it somehow, maybe talk to the *qavvik* himself."

"How?"

"Maybe Budzie's our lever."

"The sister?"

Active nodded. "She seems to have been a kind of mother figure to him. Every thread eventually leads back to her."

Long rubbed his chin and lifted his eyebrows. "You're right. But how do we use her? She died what, over a year ago?"

Kivalina was tapping his long, dirty fingernails on the tabletop and looking around the room. He seemed suddenly more alert, less hung over, the nap forgotten.

"You ever hear the exact name of the spot where she was killed?"

Long thought for a moment, then squinted the negative. "Doesn't seem like it, no."

"Pingo says it was at Driftwood."

"That old strip on the Utukok?"

"Uh-huh. Pingo says a wolverine killed his sister at Driftwood," Active said. "Not a crash, but a wolverine. And then he went up there. Pingo and somebody else."

"He say who the somebody else was?"

Active shook his head.

Long shrugged. "Driftwood, huh? Could be, I guess. Guys with airplanes go up there sometimes to hunt caribou. The

herds come through there on their way south in late
summer, early fall. But how would Budzie—"

"Tom Gage!"

"Sure," Long said. "He was a pilot and—"

"Shit, maybe he's the *qavvik* Pingo keeps raving about.
There's a crash, Budzie dies, Pingo blames Gage, and here
we are."

Long frowned. "But why would Pingo go up there
afterward?"

"Maybe he just had to see the spot," Active said. "Touch
it. Take a memento back. Maybe talk to her. She and the
dog apparently came to him in a dream and she told him
there was no crash. Maybe he wanted to camp out up
there, see if she'd put in a personal appearance."

They turned and studied Kivalina, who had risen and
was pacing the room.

"If you're Pingo Kivalina, it probably makes perfect sense
to barbecue eight or ten people alive to get the guy who
killed your twin sister," Active said. "And he was staying
with Gage—"

"He told you that?"

Active nodded. "So he could have taken a wire
twister."

"Sounds right," Long said. "But how do we get through
to him?"

They studied Kivalina some more. "Look," Active said at
last, "you go to North Slope Public Safety; talk to the
investigator on the crash; go through their files. We need
everything they have. Especially pictures. The more graphic
the better."

"And what are you going to do?"

Active chewed his lip again. He needed the details of

Budzie's crash before confronting Kivalina again, but it didn't seem like a good idea to leave him on his own for very long. He was still pacing and had begun shaking a finger in the air, as if lecturing an invisible audience. Was he rehearsing his story before trying it on Active? Or was he about to go over the cliff completely?

"I guess I should try to keep him talking," Active said. "Just get back as soon as you can."

Long nodded and started for the door of the observation room.

"Oh," Active said. "And take those, would you?" He pointed through the glass at the soiled coveralls piled in the corner of the interrogation room.

"Arii!" Long said. But he walked into the room with Active and left with the malodorous apparel.

Kivalina, who had halted the lecture when they came in, was now huddled in a corner, his eyes skittering around the room.

"Come back to the table," Active said. "Come on. No one will hurt you."

Kivalina walked over and perched on the edge of the chair opposite Active, coiled like a spring.

Active sighed inwardly and tried to think how to get him talking again. But not about the crash, not now. Now they needed a neutral subject.

CHAPTER THIRTEEN

"I HEARD THERE'S A lot of polar bears in Cape Goodwin," Active said finally.

"Ah-hah," Pingo said. "Used to."

"Used to? The bears don't come into the village now?"

"Not so much since that *nanuq* eat my cousin Ossie Barton few years ago."

"I heard that. He got it with a knife before it killed him?"

Kivalina raised his eyebrows. "He was a tough guy, that Ossie. After he's kill, we start hunting them more, all right, try keep them away from town. Village council even have a bounty from their bingo game and Rippies for a while. Then the government hear about it, make 'em stop."

"Mm-hmm. The white people Outside like polar bears."

Kivalina raised his eyebrows. "Me and Budzie never quit, though. We always like to be out on the ice hunting, even if there's no bounty."

"Your sister was a polar bear hunter?"

"I thought you never meet her. How you know she hunt *nanuqs*?"

Active, nonplused, tried to think of something to say. Evidently Kivalina's attention span was shrinking again. "Everybody talked about it," he answered finally.

"Ah-hah," Kivalina said. "She's pretty famous hunter, all right. Me and her and Dad-Dad and Susie, we always hunt them *nanuqs*."

"Dad-Dad and Susie?"

"You know about them already? They're good dogs, ah?"

"Susie was a dog too?"

"I thought you know about them."

"I might have heard about them." Active shifted in his chair. The demented conversation was clouding his mind. He felt like he needed a nap.

"Dad-Dad, she's the best dog in Cape Goodwin, all right. Big, strong, fast dog."

"Dad-Dad was a female?" Active felt like a recorder, playing back whatever Kivalina said.

"Ah-hah," Kivalina said with a lift of the eyebrows. "Budzie name her that because she's born right after our dad die. Budzie think maybe he'll come back in that pup little bit. That's why she name her Dad-Dad. You know what?"

"What?"

"When we're out on the ice, I never see that Dad-Dad asleep same time as Budzie. If Budzie's awake, then Dad-Dad might take a nap. But if Budzie go to sleep, somehow Dad-Dad will know and she'll wake up, keep watch." Kivalina sat up straight, widened his eyes, and stretched his neck, presumably to portray a dog on alert. "That Dad-Dad, she's Budzie's dog. Won't hardly have nothing to do with nobody else, not even me. But I got Susie, all right. You ever hunt *nanuq*, Mr. Nathan?"

Active shook his head in a largely futile attempt to clear it. "And Susie. Susie was a male?"

Kivalina recoiled with an indignant look. "Where you hear that? Susie was Dad-Dad's sister. She's not no male!"

"Right," Active said. "I must have gotten her mixed up with another dog."

"Ah-hah," Kivalina said. "Susie isn't no male, that's for sure."

"I'm sure she's not."

"You ever hunt *nanuq*, Mr. Nathan?"

"No, I don't think they have them around Chukchi."

"Not so much," Kivalina agreed. "All those white people you got in Chukchi scare 'em away, I guess. We used to get lot of them around Cape Goodwin till Ossie Barton get eat up, though. You heard about that?"

Active decided it would be pointless to remind Kivalina they had already discussed this. "Yes, I think I heard of that."

"That's when Budzie and me start hunting them a lot. You ever hunt them, Mr. Nathan?"

Active, sensing the conversation heading for an endless loop, just said, "Mmmm."

"It's pretty easy with dogs, all right, at least when there's not so many leads open and you can use a snowgo. Not so easy if there's leads. Then you gotta use your dog team and take an *umiaq* to get across them leads."

"Mmm," Active said again.

"But with snowgos it's easy. See, we just leave some old meats few miles out on the ice, maybe it's a seal we catch or some real old whale meats, too stinky to eat no more. Then in about a day or two, we go back out there on our snowgos to see if there's any bears. If *nanuq* is there, or if there's any tracks around, we chase 'im on the snowgos till he's kinda tire, can't run so fast any more. Then we stop, and them dogs jump off the snowgos and get the bear for us."

Active's skepticism overcame his resolve to let Kivalina ramble without interruption. "Two dogs could kill a polar bear? I never heard of that."

"Me neither," Kivalina said. "Why you ask about that?"

"Well, you said. . . ." Active sighed. "What did Dad-Dad and Susie do when you caught up with the bear?"

"Dad-Dad, she's the fast one. She can catch *nanuq* now he's tire. So she run up, bite him on the ass. *Nanuq*, he hate dogs and he's tire and now he's mad too, so he stop to fight them dogs. Dad-Dad and Susie, they just run all around him, barking like hell. One of them will run in and bite his ass while he's trying to get the other one. Pretty soon *nanuq* forget all about Budzie and me. So we just walk up and shoot him with our rifles."

It made a certain amount of sense, but this was Pingo Kivalina talking. Surely it couldn't be so simple to bring down the fearsome lord of the Arctic, the snake-necked emperor of the ice. "That's it?"

Kivalina raised his eyebrows. "Pretty easy, ah? We just take his fur and his gallbladder, leave the meats out there. Maybe when we come back tomorrow, another *nanuq* is already eating him, so we'll catch him too."

"You took the gallbladders?"

"Ah-hah, we get lots of money selling them bladders and the fur, all right. Budzie's our health aide in them days. She'll use the money to buy stuff for the clinic, or if somebody's real sick, maybe she'll get them or their family a ticket to the hospital at Chukchi or Anchorage. At first I never like to do it, but then Budzie say, 'Us Inupiaq always hunt that *nanuq* to live since early days ago. Now we just do same thing a different way when we use the money to buy medicine.'"

Kivalina looked sad and reflected for a long moment before speaking again. "She tell me them bears, they have their own village out on the ice where they go when they die. It's right by a big polynya with lots of seals and birds to eat, and they're real happy out there by theirself. A whole village with nothing in it but the ghosts of all them dead bears. You think that's true, Mr. Nathan?"

"I don't know. I haven't been out on the ice that much."

Kivalina flashed him a look of pity before continuing. "Well, we never find that village, but it's what Budzie say. Sometimes when I'm up on them cliffs by Cape Goodwin where we always get bird eggs, I look out to the northwest and I can see it, though."

"The village where these ghost bears live?"

"Ah-hah. And I can see Budzie and Dad-Dad out there with all them bears. Must be nice, that village on the ice, ah?" Kivalina looked at Active with an air of expectation, as though inviting him to explore this theory of the afterlife.

Active gave his eyebrows the slightest twitch, more acknowledgment than agreement, he hoped. "Your sister sounds like quite a woman."

The look of expectation vanished. "Too bad that *qavvik* kill her, ah?"

"You and Budzie sold the bladders to that Korean guy in Cape Goodwin?"

Kivalina looked away, as if the subject made him nervous. "Sometimes, I guess, till he go to prison. Now that *qavvik* kill him, too, ah?"

Active was tempted to name Tom Gage, in the hopes that Kivalina would explain Gage's motive for killing Jae

Hyo Lee at One-Way Lake. But he gave his head a mental shake.

Kivalina jerked his head up as the door behind Active slid open. "*Arii*, who's that?" Then he relaxed as Alan Long came into the room, steam wafting up from a styrofoam cup in his hand.

"Thought you might like something to drink, Pingo. Nathan and I need to go outside for a minute."

"Gotta piss, ah? Better not to wait so long like me, ah-hee-hee." Kivalina took the cup and downed a gulp of coffee.

Active stepped into the hall, eyebrows raised in inquiry. "Back so soon?"

Long clicked the door shut. "You better hear this for yourself."

He led Active into the observation room, where a short, fit-looking black man was watching Kivalina through the mirror. He wore a bristling salt-and-pepper moustache and a North Slope Borough Public Safety Department uniform.

Long made the introduction. "Sergeant Cave, Trooper Nathan Active."

Cave put out his hand. "Johnnell. Pleasure to meet you, Nathan. I hear you think your fire may be connected to our crash at Driftwood last year?"

"Killed a Cape Goodwin woman named Budzie Kivalina?"

Cave nodded. "Viola Louise Kivalina. Only fatality. Only injury, in fact."

"And the pilot was a guy named Tom Gage?"

Behind Cave, Long's face took on an expectant look.

Cave shook his head. "Duane Paniuk McAllister."

"Dood McAllister," Long said.

Active was speechless for a few moments. "Dood McAllister was flying the plane that killed Budzie Kivalina?"

Cave nodded again.

"I knew you'd want to hear it for yourself," Long said.

"So what—"

"We got a call from the Rescue Coordination Center in Anchorage a year ago August," Cave said. "The seventeenth, to be exact. The satellite had picked up an Emergency Locator Transmitter squawking somewhere between here and Chukchi. We launched our rescue helicopter and basically flew down the airway toward Chukchi with our radio tuned to the emergency frequency. About the time we started picking up the signal, Rescue Coordination radioed to say the satellite had pegged it as coming from the Driftwood strip."

"You went out on it personally?" Active asked.

"I like to see the country, and most ELTs are false alarms anyway. Some guy lands hard and it goes off, or he bangs it with a rifle butt while he's unloading the plane. Usually we have a chat, maybe wet a line for grayling or Arctic char from whatever creek or lake he's on, and then we're on our way. But this one wasn't a false alarm."

"So what happened?"

"We do a flyover, and there's this Cessna 185 in the Utukok River maybe a quarter mile downstream from the strip, basically crumpled up in a ball, just the tail sticking out of the water. And on the strip, there's this guy standing over a fire he's got going from those scrubby little willows that grow up there.

"The guy turns out to be McAllister. There's a hell of a wind ripping through the valley, and he's wet and shivering, so we give him some dry clothes, and he tells us the story. Basically, he and the Kivalina woman fly up in the 185 from his guiding camp on the Upper Katonak to knock down some caribou to feed these hunters he's got coming in a few days. But McAllister's wife starts—"

"They were married?" Active cut a glance at Long, who shrugged.

"That's what he called her," Cave said. "But her name was still Kivalina, so I don't know if they ever made it official. Maybe she was his common-law wife."

"And they were in a 185?"

"Yeah," Cave said. "Is that a problem?"

"McAllister's still flying one. How many did he have?"

Cave shrugged. "Beats me. But I think he said the one he rolled up at Driftwood was insured."

Active nodded. Cave went on.

"So all morning, the Kivalina woman is complaining of a bad stomach, and they land at Driftwood to make some tea, maybe catch some grayling out of the Utukok and spend the night. But the stomach keeps getting worse, and she wants him to take her back to Chukchi to see a doctor. By now, they've been there a couple hours, and it's really blowing. The way that strip lies, any wind coming down the valley rolls straight across it, and McAllister is a little antsy about trying a takeoff. But the Kivalina woman's stomach keeps getting worse, she's already thrown up everything she ate, and now she's into the dry heaves, so they climb into the 185 and crank up."

Cave tilted his hands to illustrate. "He lifts off with one wing low and lots of rudder to counteract the crosswind. They get a gust at the wrong moment, and, before he can compensate, the low wing catches some brush on the side of the runway and they're in the river, being rolled along by the current. He gets out of his harness, starts to yank her loose, then he's swept out of the plane and washes up several hundred yards downstream and on the opposite bank. By the time he finds a place to cross and gets back to the site, a couple of hours have passed and, anyway, the river's too fast and deep, not to mention too cold, to go out to the plane. So he blows the water out of his Bic lighter, starts a fire, and sits down to wait for somebody to come by."

"He was uninjured, you said."

Cave nodded. "We check him over. He's okay. But we don't know if the woman is still in the wreck, or washed downstream, or what. So we take off in the helo and search down river four or five miles—nothing. We end up having to come back to Barrow for some divers and equipment to get a cable on the 185 and haul it out. And when we do, she's in there, all right."

"You had her autopsied?"

Cave paused, a look of unease ghosting across his face. "Several broken bones, including a skull fracture that killed her."

"Any water—"

"No," Cave said sourly. "No water in the lungs—"

"But if she was underwater—"

"The pathologist said the head injury probably killed her instantly. She could have gotten it in the plane before they hit the river."

"And the stomachache? Any sign of—"

"Internal organs unremarkable," Cave said.

Active sighed. "So you—"

"Yeah, we called it an accident. The evidence didn't support any other conclusion."

"I suppose not."

This was the point where the conversation should have been over. Cave should have been offering his hand again, probably with a business card in it, and starting for the door, but he wasn't. And Alan Long's face had that expectant look again.

"And?" Active said.

Cave shot him a sour look. "And a couple weeks later, Pingo there"—Cave pointed through the glass at Kivalina—"comes into my office with a guy named Tom Gage. They've got this duffel bag. They pull out a dog's head, and they plunk it down on my desk."

"A dog's head."

Behind Cave, Alan Long lifted his eyebrows.

"With an eye shot out," Active said.

"Exactly," Cave said. "Officer Long tells me you've seen it too."

Active nodded.

"Anyway, they say it proves Dood McAllister killed Budzie Kivalina at Driftwood. They look like a couple of drunks that just staggered out of the Board of Trade bar in Nome, they smell like it, too, and I've got no idea what the fuck they're talking about." Cave paused, the look of unease touching his face again, but staying this time. "Then they dig into the duffel bag again—out comes a hunk of Visqueen for a tent, a couple sleeping bags, a camp stove, and some Mountain House freeze-dry."

Active sucked a breath through his teeth. "Camping gear?"

Cave nodded.

"You didn't find any camping gear in McAllister's plane?"

"McAllister said they didn't have much with 'em, and what they had must have washed out in the crash."

"But you didn't see any when you flew down the river searching for Budzie's body?"

Cave shook his head, looking testier than ever.

"And that didn't seem odd, for a bush pilot not to have—"

"We were looking for a woman, dead or alive, Trooper Active, not a bunch of damned Visqueen and sleeping bags. It was a fucking rescue mission. I mean, McAllister's got a hundred and eighty thousand dollars worth of Cessna folded up out there in the Utukok like origami, and he's about yea far from hypothermia himself." Cave held up a thumb and forefinger in a pinching motion to illustrate the dimensions of "yea."

Active nodded. "Sorry, I've, ah, we're—"

"Forget it," Cave said.

"So what did Pingo and Tom have to say?"

"Yeah," Cave said wearily. "Pingo and Tom, Jesus. I sit them down and get them some coffee and they tell me their story. Pingo, he's obviously crazy, as you know. And this Gage, he isn't much better by this point. It turns out he's been drunk pretty much continuously since the Kivalina woman died."

"What about the—how did they—"

Cave waved a hand. "Their story is, Gage comes to Chukchi, takes to the life, and starts going up to Cape Goodwin, where he and the Kivalina woman fall in love. But she's hooked up with McAllister, so she knows she's got to have it out with him. Gage offers to go with her, but

Budzie figures it would be safer to do it alone. So off they go to hunting camp, her and McAllister, and she's going to break it to him up there. He's always more relaxed out in the country, she says."

Active nodded.

"Next thing anybody knows, Budzie turns up dead in McAllister's plane at Driftwood. Gage hits the bottle, and Pingo is over on the Canadian border fighting wildfires with the Bureau of Land Management. You've heard of the Goodwin Hotshots?"

Active shook his head, hoping the detour would be short.

"It's this crack firefighting team they've got there. It's how the village guys make money in the summer, and Pingo's one of the Hotshots. Don't ask me how he got in, crazy as he is. Anyway, he comes home from firefighting, and Gage tells him his sister was killed in a plane crash up at Driftwood with Dood McAllister and that McAllister got out without a scratch. Then they both get drunk and pass out, and, while Pingo's unconscious, Budzie comes to him in a dream and says there wasn't any crash and he's gotta go find this dog of hers."

"Dad-Dad?"

"That's it," Cave said.

"Apparently that dog never left her side," Active said.

"I gather," Cave agreed. "Anyway, Pingo wakes up out of his dream, gets Gage on his feet, starts pouring coffee into him, and says they've got to go to Driftwood and find Dad-Dad, and off they go in Gage's Super Cub. Next thing you know, they're in my office."

Cave shook his head at the recollection. "God, you should have smelled them. And that damned dog's head."

"How did they find it?"

"They land at Driftwood, and Pingo starts to thinking he can smell Dad-Dad and he wanders off through the brush and, sure enough, he turns up the dog's carcass."

"The whole thing? Not just the head?"

Cave shook his head. "Dad-Dad was big, one of those Mackenzie River huskies, supposedly. Maybe a hundred and ten, a hundred and fifteen pounds, according to Pingo. Too big for the Super Cub with the two of them and a couple cans of avgas and their gear in it, anyway, so they cut off the head to bring in and show me how the eye was shot out."

"McAllister didn't mention the dog when you rescued him that day?"

Cave shook his head.

"And what about the camping gear? How'd they find that after you—"

Cave sighed. "I told you. We were looking for a plane-crash victim, not camping gear."

Active was silent, his eyebrows raised in the Western expression of inquiry.

"Instead of searching downstream, they go up, and they find the stuff stashed in the brush."

There was silence all around the room for a long time.

Finally, Cave sighed again. "So I ask Pingo and Tom, what do they think happened? How did the plane end up in the river and Budzie dead without McAllister getting himself killed too, or at least banged up? Gage laughs and says it would be easy if Budzie was already dead or unconscious. Just strap her into the passenger seat, crank up the engine, and set the throttle to a fast taxiing speed, then get out and grab the tail and steer the plane over the bank. It hits the water, the current takes it and rolls it up, and McAllister's home free. Then McAllister dunks himself in the river and waits to see if anybody hears the Emergency Locator Transmitter in the Cessna, probably figuring if nobody shows up he'll dig out the camping gear from where he hid it, douse it in the river for realism, then set up his Visqueen tent and hang tight till someone comes along."

"And what about the dog?" Active asked. "How—"

"Uh-huh," Cave said. "They figure McAllister is in the process of beating Budzie to death because she's dumping him for Tom Gage and Dad-Dad comes to her defense. So McAllister shoots Dad-Dad, but he only wings the dog, and it crawls off and dies out in the brush where Kivalina finds the carcass a couple weeks later."

Active looked through the glass at Pingo Kivalina, who had put his head down on his arms and was evidently asleep at the table. "Dood McAllister, huh?"

"You thinking he set your fire?"

"Pingo says somebody burned down the Rec Center to get him and Gage."

"Except Pingo got away," Cave said.

"Yep," Active said.

"Well, other than Pingo, what have you got that points to McAllister?"

Active felt depressed as he sketched the arson investigation for Cave.

"So the wire from the locker-room door is about the most concrete thing you've got?" Cave said after hearing him out. "And Pingo's roommate Tom Gage being a pilot and an aviation mechanic?"

Active nodded. "But McAllister's a pilot too, so maybe

he's got one of those safety-wire twisters, and maybe it'll match the marks on the wire. If we can find it."

Cave grimaced in sympathy. "But so far Pingo is all you've got that says it was McAllister?"

"He's too scared to name him. He just calls him the *qavvik.*"

Cave gave Active an odd look. "You don't know? That's what the people in Cape Goodwin call McAllister, according to Pingo and Tom. The wolverine. It fits too. You ever meet him?"

"He gave me a plane ride a few days ago," Active said.

"Plane ride, huh?" Cave stared at him, grinning a little. "And you didn't suspect a thing? Imagine that."

"We were just getting started," Active protested. "And we had no—Yeah, all right, point taken."

Cave nodded, as if accepting an apology, before continuing. "You notice how McAllister's always kind of grumbling to himself under his breath? That's supposedly—"

"Yeah, that's exactly what a wolverine does," said Alan Long from behind them. Active turned. He had forgotten Long was present.

"Always whining and snarling as it goes along the trail," Long said. "The old-timers think it's talking to the devil. Some of them think the *qavvik* is the devil."

"And he's got a hell of a temper," Cave added.

"McAllister?" Active said, thinking of the guide smashing the case of Solare on the tarmac at Chukchi.

"The *qavvik,*" Long said.

"Ah." Active turned back to Cave. "You talk to McAllister again?"

"Yeah," Cave said. "I paw through what Pingo and Tom have brought in, supposedly from Driftwood. Dog's head with its eye shot out, no collar, no tags. Bunch of camping gear with no I.D. on it. I get that sinking feeling, you know? It's a pretty big pile, but it doesn't add up to much."

Active nodded.

"But at the same time I got two guys sitting across the desk from me that obviously loved that woman to pieces, each in his own way, and they obviously believe every word of what they're telling me. One of 'em's a well-known wacko and the other one appears to be headed that way himself, he's so unhinged by her death. For a minute there, I almost envy them."

"Envy? Why?"

Cave shrugged. "Having something in their lives that gave them that kind of passion. That's rare, you know?"

Active looked away, uncomfortable.

"But maybe you got that in your life. I sure as hell don't, in Barrow."

"A seven-count," Active said.

"A what?"

"When she comes into a room of people who never saw her before, conversation stops. At first just close to her, then it spreads across the crowd. I finally started counting when it happens. One-one-thousand, two-one-thousand. . . . Usually I get to about seven-one-thousand before they start talking again." Active stopped, suddenly embarrassed. What had possessed him?

Long cleared his throat.

Cave cut his eyes back and forth between them, waiting for more. Finally he continued. "So I get Pingo and Tom to show us on the chart where McAllister's camp is on the Upper Katonak, and me and a couple of my guys pay him a visit in the helicopter. We go thumping in, set down on this little strip he's got on a gravel bar by his cabins, and he comes screaming up on a four-wheeler. He's pissed, says we're harassing him, we'll scare off the game, spook his clients, destroy his livelihood, there's no fucking way we're coming into camp. So I tell him we might have to fly around the area in the Bell and check for game violations the next couple days, and then he calms down a little bit and we have a talk there on the runway."

A defeated look came over Cave's face.

"No go, huh?"

"Nah, he denies the dog was ever with them, says they left it in camp the day of the crash and it disappeared a few days later when Budzie didn't come back."

"But what about the dog Pingo and Tom found at Driftwood?"

"McAllister said he had no idea whose it was, but it wasn't Dad-Dad. Maybe it got away from some of the floaters or hikers that get dropped off there, and then somebody else shot it later because they thought it was a wolf or it was scavenging food from their camp or something. Or maybe Pingo and Gage didn't even find it at Driftwood and they're trying to frame him."

"And the camping gear?"

"Same type of deal. Denied it was his. Either somebody else left it there or Pingo and Gage are lying." Cave shrugged. "About what I expected."

"What did McAllister say about Budzie leaving him?"

"Same type of deal again. Claimed she never mentioned it."

"So that was it? He walked?"

Cave shrugged again. "I worked the case for a while, then took it to the District Attorney. We checked for fingerprints on the camping gear, hired an expert to go over the wreckage of McAllister's 185, crawled through the autopsy results again . . . and there was just nothing to support what Kivalina and Gage were saying. We finally dropped it."

"You didn't even take it to a grand jury."

"Facts are facts. And we didn't have many."

"But what did you think?"

Cave's face took on a thoughtful look. "I ended up believing McAllister. His argument was, 'If I wanted to kill my wife, I wouldn't have to wreck a hundred and eighty thousand dollar airplane to do it. I could just push her off a cliff and say she fell, all right.'"

"I can see what you mean." Active paused, thinking back through the story. "And when was it you dropped the case?"

"I don't know, three, four months ago, maybe?"

"And you told Pingo and Tom?"

"You kidding? One or the other of them was on the phone to me every couple days about it. Tom . . . no, Pingo called the day after we made the decision and I told him then."

Active lined it up in his head. Cave and the Barrow DA had given up on the Budzie Kivalina case, and within a few weeks Tom Gage was visiting Jae Hyo Lee at the federal prison. A few weeks later, Jae was pike bait in One-Way Lake, and a couple of weeks after that, Tom Gage was dead in the Rec Center fire, with Pingo Kivalina a near miss.

He looked at Cave. "Either one of them mention a guy named Jac Hyo Lee? Korean, went to prison on a bear gallbladder case a couple years ago?"

Cave gave this some thought. "I don't think so. But I

believe I remember the case. A federal deal in Cape Goodwin, right?"

Active nodded.

"You think this Korean poacher's connected to all this too?" Cave gave his head a skeptical shake.

"We don't know. It's just that he fell off a cliff and wound up dead in a lake down on the Isignaq not long ago. And Tom Gage visited him in prison pretty soon after you guys dropped the Budzie Kivalina case. And Pingo and Budzie used to sell him gallbladders. And you said Dood McAllister mentioned the possibility of pushing somebody off a cliff."

Cave was silent for a time. "But why would Dood McAllister want to kill a Korean?" he asked finally.

Active shrugged, unable to think of an answer.

"Sometimes, if it looks like a coincidence, it is," Cave said.

He and Active studied Pingo, beneath whose chin a puddle of drool was forming on the tabletop.

"Oh, yeah," Active said. "So Alan told you we found what must be Dad-Dad's head in Tom Gage's freezer. They tell you what that was about?"

"Pingo wanted it back when we dropped the case," Cave said. "He was going to have it mounted."

"Guess I better wake him up," Active said.

CHAPTER FOURTEEN

ACTIVE SLAMMED THE DOOR loudly as he went in.

Kivalina's head jerked up and his eyes swept the room, making sure, no doubt, that Dood McAllister hadn't come in too.

Active pulled out his handkerchief and handed it to Kivalina, who stared at it with a puzzled expression. Active touched his chin to indicate where Kivalina's own chin glistened with drool. Kivalina felt the spot, wiped it, and pocketed the handkerchief.

And then Active remembered where he had seen the long, heavy-jawed face before and knew why Kivalina might think he would be accompanied by McAllister today. "You saw me come to Cape Goodwin in the *qavvik*'s plane that day, ah? You looked at me through the window."

Kivalina bared his teeth in a spasm of fear. "*Arii*, he's here now?"

"No, no." Active put a hand out, but Kivalina recoiled. "He's not here. He can't hurt you."

"He's tough, that *qavvik*. Kill Budzie, kill Jae Hyo Lee, burn up all those people in Chukchi." Kivalina shuddered. "I guess he'll kill me too, ah? That's why I go to Barrow after he come to Cape Goodwin with you."

Active shook his head. "You're safe here."

Kivalina looked at the mirror. "He's not in that other room watching me?"

Active shook his head again. "He's at his camp on the Upper Katonak."

Kivalina's face relaxed. "His camp, ah-hah. That's good. So you know about him, ah?"

Active raised his eyebrows yes. "Why did he kill Jae Hyo Lee? We know—"

"I tell her not to be with him. I tell her that *qavvik* is a man in rage, but that what she always like, a rough man. Budzie call it the great weather, that rage inside a rough man, say she want it inside herself. Some women are like that, ah, Mr. Nathan?"

Active resigned himself to another of Kivalina's detours. "So I've heard."

"Ah-hah, but this one, he's too rough, and he kill her at Driftwood, ah?"

"That's what we believe. Because she—"

"Because she find Tom Gage. He have that rage in him too, but it's different, like he wrap it around her, take her inside it, so she don't never have to be afraid of him. Ah?"

Active lifted his eyebrows again.

"Tom Gage, you know he pay Jae Hyo Lee to kill that *qavvik*, ah?"

Active stifled his surprise and merely said, "I forget how much."

"Ten thousand dollars, I think he say. Lotta money, all right. I guess he really love my sister, like me."

"That's why he visited Jae in prison? To hire him to kill Dood McAllister?"

Kivalina lifted his eyebrows. "But that Jae never want to do it till Tom tell him what I say."

"What you said?"

"Ah-hah, about that *qavvik* is the one get Jae arrested for gallbladders."

Active was silent for a moment. "McAllister told the *naluaqmiut* police about Jae buying gallbladders?"

"Ah-hah. For long time, that *qavvik* buy all our gallbladders in Cape Goodwin. Then when Jae start buying, nearly everybody is selling to him, even Budzie and me, because he pay more. That *qavvik* is real mad, tell us he'll take care of Jae. Then, next thing, Jae is arrested. After that, everybody is selling to *qavvik* again."

Active shook his head. "But what would McAllister do with the bladders? The Koreans control that whole market."

Kivalina frowned. "Not in Russia, all right."

"He sold the bladders to Russians? But how . . . where . . . did they—"

"All winter he'll keep them bladders in his freezer," Kivalina said. "Then in springtime, when the ice goes out and there's no more bears around, he'll take those bladders over to Russia in his Super Cub and sell 'em over there. His great-grandmother was one of them Anqallyt Eskimos from Russian side, and he still know some of them people, all right. He can even talk Anqallyt, little bit, from what I heard. And he got some kind of Russian papers he buy over there, a passport maybe."

The Russian coast lay a couple of hundred miles west of Chukchi, easily within Super Cub range. And it was true that people had trafficked back and forth across the Chukchi Sea until the Communists clamped down.

Supposedly, the traffic, even though still illegal, was coming back with the old Soviet Union gone and the new Russia not paying much attention to Siberia. And Active seemed to remember news stories about bear-poaching on the Russian side. Maybe what Kivalina said was true.

"One time he take Budzie with him," Kivalina continued. "She buy one of their reindeer hats while she's over there. Sure don't look like a normal hat, all right."

"But how did Jae Hyo Lee end up dead in One-Way Lake?"

"Tom Gage take him in there, all right. Fly over to Fairbanks in his Super Cub with some gear, meet Jae there after he get out of prison, fly him over to One-Way Lake to wait for *qavvik*, then kill him. But I guess—"

"Wait a minute. Why would Tom Gage think that McAllister would go to One-Way Lake? His camp is on the Upper Katonak, and that lake is way down on the Isignaq."

"Ah-hah," Kivalina said. "His main camp is on the Katonak, all right. But he have a spike camp there by One-Way Lake for sheep hunting back in them mountains along the Isignaq. Me and Budzie used to assistant-guide for him, and we been up in there a lot with him and his hunters. So I tell Tom, if Jae go up to One-Way Lake and hide out in them hills little bit before sheep season, *qavvik* will go in there pretty soon to set up his spike camp, and then Jae could shoot him."

Active studied Kivalina with new appreciation. "Sending Jae after the *qavvik* was your idea?"

"Not me." Kivalina squinted in negation. "I'm too much *kinnaq* for smart idea like that. Budzie tell me we should do it, all right."

"Another dream?"

Kivalina lifted his eyebrows. "I hear Dad-Dad barking, and there's my sister again. She say we could catch him at One-Way Lake if we're there right time. So we send Jae. But few days after Tom comes back from Fairbanks, me and him are waiting to hear if *qavvik* will turn up missing, then Tom will pick up Jae and take him back to Fairbanks, then Jae will go back to Anchorage and fly home like anybody, and no one will know he's been at One-Way Lake. But that *qavvik* show up at Tom's house in Chukchi. He's got Jae's wallet and Tom's ten thousand dollars he get off of Jae's body."

Kivalina's face stretched out in the terrified grin again. "He say he find it up at One-Way Lake, and he think we would want to have it, since Jae was working for us. So he give us the wallet, but he keep the money. Then he say, whatever happen to somebody working for us, it might happen to us too, and he leave. *Arii!* That's when we know he'll kill us like Budzie and Jae because we try to kill him."

"Why didn't you—"

"Dad-Dad and Budzie come back one more time. She say to put water in the gas of his airplane, then he'll crash and be dead like her and Dad-Dad. I tell her, no, I'm too scare; nothing can kill that *qavvik*. But she say I got the great weather in me; I should be in rage from what he did, so I put in the water, all right. But that *qavvik*, he land his plane even with the engine quit and never get hurt, just like I thought he would. *Arii*, he'll kill me even if there's cops around."

"We won't let him kill you. We'll arrest him."

"*Arii!* He'll be in jail with me?"

"No, you won't be in jail together."

Kivalina relaxed slightly, his face taking on a distant look. "My sister come here with Dad-Dad while I'm in jail here too. She tell me I should make that *qavvik* look like a clown, so people will think he's *kinnaq* like me."

"Like a clown?"

Kivalina lifted his eyebrows. "She say I should give him a red smile, all right."

"Like with lipstick?"

"Must be, ah?" Kivalina grinned. "He would sure look funny, ah?"

Active shook his head, trying to brush away the cobwebs of this latest detour. "Look, why didn't you talk to the police about this?"

As soon as the words were out of his mouth, Active realized the answer was obvious: Gage and Kivalina had tried with Cave and struck out. And Kivalina had seen Active arrive in the *qavvik's* Cessna. Why would they risk the police again? But Kivalina surprised him.

"We did, all right."

"What?"

"You know that Jim Silver, burn up in the fire?"

Active lifted his eyebrows. "Yes, I knew him."

"Pretty good guy for *naluaqmiu*, ah?"

Active lifted his eyebrows again.

"Somehow he find out about Tom went to see Jae in prison, and he come around asking us about it. At first, Tom won't tell him nothing. But when that water in the *qavvik's* gas never kill him, then we know he will get us if we don't get him some kind of way. That's when we decide to talk to Jim Silver, all right, see if we could get him to arrest the *qavvik* for killing Jae without getting arrest ourself. So Tom tells Jim maybe we could talk at the Rec Center at night, because we always go there to take shower or use the sauna."

"Why not at Tom's house? Or Jim's office?"

"We're afraid it might be too easy to arrest us if we're at his office. And Tom don't want him in the house because we still got Dad-Dad there in the freezer and Jae's wallet and we don't know if Jim will search the place."

"Jae's wallet is in Tom Gage's house?"

Kivalina squinted. "No, outside. Under that van by the house in a trash bag."

Active swore silently to himself. They had searched *in* Gage's storage van, but not *under* it. "So you met Chief Silver at the Rec Center?" It wasn't the first diplomatic conference held on neutral ground.

"Ah-hah. Jim and Tom are talking in the sauna, and I go out for a while to talk to that Cammie girl so they can be by theirself, but when I come back, that *qavvik* is going out the back door, and there's this board over the door to the locker room, and I can't go in. I try pull it off, and pretty soon I hear them guys screaming inside. Then the back door blows open, and fire comes in, and that's when I run. I can't help myself; I just run away, and I take that boat up to Cape Goodwin."

"Why didn't you—"

But Kivalina was lost in his terror of the *qavvik*.

"I think maybe I'll be all right if that *qavvik* don't know I got away, but then you come into the village with him, and I decide to run down to Anchorage and live on Four Street. Maybe he'll never find me there. But then I'm arrest trying to get ticket money to go to Anchorage."

Kivalina paused, and Active mentally picked his way

backward through the story. "But how would the *qavvik* even know you were in the Rec Center? Was he hanging around outside when you went in?"

"His house is right behind the Rec Center. He can see if somebody comes or goes from back side of town, like Tom and me, but we never thought about it that night we're seeing Jim Silver. That *qavvik*, he probably sneak in the Rec Center from the back, figure out how to put a board on the door, and start that fire, all right."

Active swore under his breath. McAllister had almost certainly been questioned when Dickie Nelson had canvassed the neighbors the day after the fire. Another if-only.

Active left the interrogation room and joined Cave and Long behind the one-way mirror.

"It's like McAllister never plans more than a step or two ahead," Active said. "He just acts and then cleans up afterward."

"And does a pretty good job of it," Long said.

"According to Pingo," Cave said.

"You still think McAllister wasn't involved?" Active asked.

Cave snorted. "I've been down the road with Pingo before. What he says makes sense as long as you don't think about it. Then it falls apart. So I don't know what to think, except for one thing."

"What's that?"

"Either way, you won't get McAllister. He may not be all that smart, but he's cunning. He's cornered, he thinks of something."

Active studied Kivalina, who was pacing the interrogation room again, and thought of how casually McAllister had pulled off ten homicides if Pingo was right. Budzie Kivalina, Jae Hyo Lee, and eight victims at the Rec Center. "Let's go get him," he said.

"McAllister?" Long said.

"You really believe that loon?" Cave asked.

Active nodded.

"Pick him up where?" Long said. "At his camp?"

Active nodded again. "If need be. If he's in Chukchi, Carnaby can have him brought in."

"But your only witness is a delusional half-wit who just confessed to cooking up two homicide attempts at the instigation of his dead sister," Cave said. He turned and looked at Kivalina through the mirror. "One of which was a murder for hire. Not to mention the fact that he admits to being in the Rec Center the night of the fire and then running up to Cape Goodwin in a stolen boat."

"Nobody's perfect," Active said. "You going to help or not?"

Cave stared at Kivalina and then at Active, who was drumming his fingers on the sill under the mirror. "Seriously. Other than the word of a nutcase, what have you got?"

Active ticked it off on his fingers: "A dog's head and a wallet back at Gage's place, plus the camping gear still in your evidence room, right?"

Cave shook his head thoughtfully. "Yeah, but your case against McAllister is like my Driftwood case. A lot of circumstantial evidence he can explain away, backed up by the sworn testimony of a *kinnaq*—is that what the Eskimos call him?"

Active waited, letting the silence build.

"I don't know," Cave said.

"Think long, think wrong, sergeant."

Cave drew in a ragged breath. "No, I'm out. I think your guy is sitting right in there." He pointed through the glass at Pingo Kivalina.

Active shrugged. "It's your call." He turned to Long. "Alan, let's get on the phone to Carnaby. We need an arrest warrant for McAllister and a search warrant for his home and his camp on the Katonak. And we'll need to get Dad-Dad's head and Jae Hyo Lee's wallet from Gage's place. That covers it, right? I'm not missing anything?" He stopped when he noticed the look on Long's face. "What?"

"I think Sergeant Cave may have a point," Long said. "There's more evidence against Pingo than Dood McAllister."

"Unless Carnaby finds the wire-twister at McAllister's place and—"

"Of course he's going to have a wire-twister," Long said, with unusual heat. "He needs it to work on his planes."

"—and it matches the wire from the locker-room door at the Rec Center." Active stared at Long. "Or the wallet has McAllister's fingerprints on it." Long lowered his eyes.

Active pulled out his cell phone, got Carnaby on the line, and briefed him on the interview with Pingo Kivalina and on what Johnnell Cave had told them about the Driftwood crash. Then Active asked the Trooper captain to get the necessary warrants from the Chukchi District Attorney.

"I don't see any problem with the search warrants," Carnaby said. "But I don't know about the other. You think we've got enough here to arrest McAllister?"

Active took him through the evidence again.

"Okay," Carnaby said. "I'll see what I can do. What's your next step up there?"

"If you guys don't find McAllister at home when you get there with the warrant tonight, we'll fly down to his camp on the Katonak and arrest him tomorrow."

"This guy Cave sending somebody along for backup?" Carnaby asked.

Active hesitated.

"Nathan?"

Active felt Long and Cave watching him.

"You there?" Carnaby said.

"Yeah, yeah, I'm here," Active said finally. "No, Cave doesn't plan to send anybody along."

"No?"

"He doesn't like McAllister for the Rec Center fire. He likes Pingo Kivalina."

Cave perked up at this, and watched intently as Active awaited Carnaby's response.

"Pingo, huh?" Carnaby said. Then he was silent for a time, presumably turning this over in his head. "Makes a certain amount of sense, doesn't it?"

"I think it depends on what you find at McAllister's place," Active said.

Cave shot him a told-you-so look.

Carnaby sighed. "All right, I'll see if anybody from the Trooper detachment in Barrow can go along. Your cell phone work up there?"

"I'm on it now," Active said.

"Yeah, I'll call you when we're done at McAllister's."

Active closed the phone and checked his watch. A little after six. He looked at Cave. "Jose's still open? And the Roscoe?"

Jose's Midnight Sun was a legend in the Arctic, a full-blown Tex-Mex restaurant on the tundra: two big dining rooms and a coffee shop, limitless quantities of refried beans and enchiladas suizas, all presided over by a septuagenarian blonde named Jean Hoyt who had come to the Arctic in the early days of oil exploration and somehow missed too many planes out.

The equally legendary Roscoe Arms, as Active knew from his previous visit to Barrow, was the only hotel in town cheap enough to be covered by the state per-diem allowance. It was a ramshackle assemblage of Atco construction trailers that afforded guests all the space and comfort of a jail cell, with bath and showers down the hall and signs everywhere warning against walking around town alone because of prowling polar bears.

"Absolutely," Cave said with a grin. "I'll drop you at Jose's, and you can grab a cab from there to the Roscoe."

Two and a half hours later, Active and Long were ensconced at the Roscoe, sharing an Atco to stretch their per-diem. Long snored on one bunk, while, on the other, an envious Active read a two-year-old *Time* magazine and waited for his stomach to forgive him for the plate of tortilla chips and steaming goop he had dumped into it at Jose's. He was on his way down the hall for the second time since check-in when his cell phone went off.

"That you?" Carnaby's voice said.

"Yep. How'd it go at McAllister's?"

"It didn't, as far as he was concerned. Nobody home, but he has a neighbor girl watching the house. She said he's at his camp on the Katonak."

"And otherwise?"

"So-so. We did find a safety-wire twister, which we're sending down to the crime lab tomorrow along with the dog's head and wallet we found at Gage's place."

"Not a bad evening's work, boss. So we'll fly down—"

"Yes, you can go down to his camp tomorrow, but all you

got is a search warrant, which I'm faxing to Cave's machine as we speak. The DA wouldn't go for an arrest warrant yet."

Active eased open the door to the rest room and stepped in. "Maybe we'll get lucky, and he'll do something a little off, and we can—"

"Nathan?"

"Yeah?"

"Think about what you're doing."

"What?"

"Any time you're with Cowboy, you push too hard if there's a crook involved. Remember when you jumped out of his Super Cub?"

"I didn't jump. I stepped. Cowboy was hovering in a high wind."

"Whatever you did, you ended up with a dislocated shoulder, so listen to what I'm saying: you two play to each other's pathology. And for backup, don't forget, all you got is Alan Long."

"None of the Barrow Troopers are available?"

Carnaby swore in disgust. "Apparently the detachment there is down three positions because nobody wants to work in Barrow, if you can imagine. And the other two are over in Prudhoe Bay wrapping up a drug bust. So you walk into McAllister's camp and politely show him the search warrant and politely search the place and get the hell out. Right?"

"And we'll arrest him if he gives us any trouble."

"Nathan!"

Active closed the cell phone and opened the door of the one stall that didn't have an Out of Order sign on it.

CHAPTER FIFTEEN

THEY GATHERED AT SIX the next morning in Cave's office at the North Slope Borough Department of Public Safety. The building perched above the tundra on the usual stilts and had a snow-blasted plywood exterior of faded blue, set off by fire-engine-red doors.

Cowboy Decker and Cave were there already when Active and Long showed up fresh from their night at the Roscoe. Cowboy wore an uneasy frown.

"Apparently you got yourself a situation here," Cave said with an air of malicious satisfaction as he passed around cups and poured coffee. He nodded toward Cowboy.

Active and Long looked at the pilot.

"McAllister may know we're coming," Cowboy said with a sheepish look.

"How could that be?" Active asked, feeling like he already knew the general outline of it.

"After we landed yesterday, I called Delilah to let her know we'd be bringing Pingo Kivalina back with us," Cowboy said. "Then, after you called and briefed me last night about the search warrant and all, I called her again to say we'd be coming back by way of McAllister's camp."

"And?"

Cowboy paused and sighed. "She told me McAllister

was there to pick up a client and get some gas when I called the first time, and he overheard her say Pingo's name. He asked her what the deal was after I hung up."

"And Delilah told him?"

"Well, you know how women are," Cowboy said. "Can't keep a secret."

"Women, huh? How about bush pilots?"

"It was a prisoner transport," Cowboy said in an offended tone. "I had to let the boss know. What was I supposed to do?"

"It's probably on Kay-Chuck by now," Long said.

Active shut his eyes for a moment, pinching the bridge of his nose. "Did McAllister say anything?"

"He told Delilah he heard Pingo was killed at the Rec Center."

"We never released anything about him being in the fire," Long said heatedly. "We never even heard of Pingo till we called the health aide in Cape Goodwin, and he was already here in Barrow by then."

"Exactly," Active said. "But if McAllister set the fire—"

"Then he would know Pingo was there that night," Long finished.

Active lifted his eyebrows, yes. "McAllister tell Delilah where he was going?" he asked Cowboy. "Carnaby told me just now he heard McAllister was up on the Katonak."

Cowboy nodded. "Loaded up the client and blasted off for his camp, according to Delilah."

"At night? Is that doable? It was nearly dark when we landed here."

"It's doable if you want to bad enough and you know the strip," Cowboy said with a shrug. "His 185's got landing lights, of course, and whoever he left in camp probably went down with a four-wheeler and parked at the end of the runway for reference when he buzzed the place."

"Well, I don't see that this changes anything," Active said after some thought. He swung his gaze around the room. "If he's figured out we're coming, it's all the more reason to get there before he runs."

"Your call," Cave said in a tone of malicious satisfaction. "He's got hunters in camp, maybe a cook, and an assistant guide. You could end up with a big fucking hostage crisis a million miles from nowhere."

Active chewed his lip and thought it over. "We can't just leave him out there, and if he's going to take hostages, he's already done it. I still say we've got no choice."

He turned to the pilot. "Cowboy, you been in there?"

Cowboy nodded. "I've hauled clients in and out for him a couple times." He walked to the map on Cave's wall and swept a hand over the fantastic corrugations of the Brooks Range, which ran like a dragon's back across the top of Alaska.

He stopped with an index finger on the point at the state's northern tip. "Here we are at Barrow, and south of us we got the Keating Mountains, with Driftwood along here, halfway between." He touched the spot, then swept his hand south. "Down here below the Keatings is the Katonak River valley, and south of that you cross the Laird Mountains into the Isignaq River valley, where Nathan found his dead Korean at One-Way Lake."

He looked up and everybody nodded again.

"All right," Cowboy said, moving his hand back up the map a little. "McAllister's camp is here, in these foothills north of the Katonak." He tapped the spot. "Kind of midway between the Driftwood strip and One-Way Lake."

Active stepped up and studied the map. Even though he had known all of this in a general way, the whole thing came into focus as Cowboy sketched it out visually.

"His camp's on what they call Lucky Creek," Cowboy continued. He still had his finger on the spot, but the scale was too small to show much detail. "It's in a big, broad valley that drains into the Katonak. Strip's about twelve hundred feet long, reindeer moss with chert gravel mixed in. About a hundred yards upstream from that, he's got the lodge, a couple cabins, a john, and a meat cache. It's in a fairly thick stand of willows along the creekbed."

"So how do you do it?" Cave looked skeptical as ever. "You go roaring in there and land on his runway, maybe he's waiting with a sheep rifle and a three-by-nine scope, and he picks you off as you come out of the aircraft. You can't risk a flyover, so you'll be going in blind."

Cowboy spoke up. "You know, he's got a radio there. We could call him when we get within range."

"What if the radio's off?" Cave said. "Or he tells you to go screw yourselves?"

Cowboy studied the map. "We might be able to make a flyover without getting shot. There's a little side canyon that opens on the creek just above his camp. We could circle around behind the ridge and drop down through the canyon, then blast out of it at full throttle and come screaming along the creek, right above the willows." Cowboy considered it for a moment, then nodded with a satisfied look. "He wouldn't even know we were in the neighborhood till we were overhead. Nobody can aim and shoot that fast unless they're up on the roof waiting for you."

Cave shook his head. "What if he is?"

"If we see somebody up there when we come out of the

canyon, I'll peel off and head across the valley, and Nathan will think of a new plan."

"Why not park down the creek and hike up?" Cave asked. "That's what our procedures call for in a case like this."

"When we can do a flyover?" Cowboy snorted. "You want us to hike through a couple miles of niggerheads?"

A shocked silence filled the room. Long cleared his throat and said, "Cowboy."

Cave threw up his hands and swiveled his chair to look out his office window. "Jesus," he said. "First I got all these village kids calling me taaqsipak, and now this half-assed captain of the clouds comes around talking about niggerheads."

Cowboy's jaw took on a stubborn set. "I didn't mean anything by it. That's just what they're called."

Active vaulted into the breach. "Not any more, Cowboy. Remember the fight over, um, that creek down by Fairbanks?"

The name of the stream in question had, in fact, been Niggerhead Creek, but Active wasn't about to repeat it in front of Johnnell Cave. The term referred to the infuriating hummocks of grass, interspersed with icy water, that made traversing the tundra a nightmare until winter froze the puddles and filled the hollows with snow.

"What creek?" Cowboy asked.

"Well, there was this creek that had that name on the aviation charts, and there was a big ruckus—"

"And then what did they name it?"

Active struggled to remember. The Anchorage Daily News had covered the controversy in some detail, but what was the creek's new name? "Actually, I think they just erased it," he said at last.

Cowboy looked incredulous. "They erased a creek?"

"The name, yeah."

"There's a creek on the map with no name?" Cowboy looked accusingly at Cave. "You happy now?"

"As a pig in shit," Cave said. "Don't I look happy?"

Active, now regretting his effort at pacification, tried to think how to get the conversation back on track. "I doubt we'll need to hike through anything, Cowboy. Let's do a flyover and see what we see."

Cowboy growled his assent with a gratified look. Cave shook his head and looked aggrieved but did offer them a ride to the airport.

"We taking Pingo?" Cowboy asked.

The others looked at him. "Why should we?" Active said.

"You might need him," Cowboy said in his bush-pilot growl.

"What for?" Active asked.

"He'll just be in the way if you get into it with McAllister," Cave said. "We can hold on to him for you."

"I dunno," Cowboy said. "Didn't I hear he used to assistant-guide for McAllister?"

Active nodded. "And?"

"Then he oughta know that country around McAllister's camp pretty good. Might come in handy if you end up having to track the guy."

"He's scared to death of McAllister," Active said. "He wet his pants yesterday because he thought I had brought McAllister to the jail with me."

Cowboy shrugged. "Still and all."

Active considered. However the thing with McAllister played out, it was a fact that Kivalina wouldn't stay in the Barrow jail long on the bootlegging charge. It would be

safer to stash him in the Chukchi jail than to trust the
North Slope Borough to hold him indefinitely in Barrow
on the Chukchi warrant, Johnnell Cave's offer notwith-
standing. The ancient tradition of the bureaucratic foul-up
was more deeply entrenched in the Alaskan bush than
any other place Active knew of.

"All right, let's take him," Active said.

Cave sighed, picked up his phone, and soon was
instructing the jailers to bring Kivalina to the airport.

"All right, yeah, we'll meet you there," he concluded.
He stood up, pulled on the parka that had been draped
over the back of his chair, and led them out to a Ford
Explorer.

Forty-five minutes later, Cowboy's Cessna lifted off into
the blue predawn haze, a few last stars still glinting
overhead. They speared through the clear morning air
toward the crests of the Brooks Range serrating the
southern horizon. The sun flared in the southeast, then
climbed into view, shooting long, deep shadows across the
tundra beneath them.

Cowboy clicked on the intercom in a spray of static.
"You know, there's one thing I feel bad about."

"Other than Delilah tipping off McAllister that we're
coming, you mean?"

The pilot grunted in acknowledgment. They were
climbing steadily to clear the peaks ahead. Cowboy
thumbed a little wheel mounted between the seats, and
the nose of the plane lifted slightly. "I knew about Dood's
crash at Driftwood. I just wish I would have told you."

Active looked at the pilot. Cowboy kept his eyes on the
horizon. "Me, too," Active said.

"You never asked."

Another if-only. Active sighed and turned his gaze to the terrain ahead. They were still over the Arctic coastal plain, with its stippling of pothole lakes and the weird permafrost pimples for which Pingo Kivalina was named. They looked like volcanoes just emerging from the earth, but they had hearts of ice, not fire.

"You know McAllister very well?" Active asked.

Cowboy was silent for a few moments before answering. "He's a hell of a pilot. He flew helicopters and Twin Otters for the Air Guard here before he went into guiding full-time. I always wondered how he let it get away from him like that at Driftwood."

"How about as a man?"

Again, Cowboy thought it over before speaking. "Lot of rage there. I never knew why."

Active glanced into the rear of the plane to make sure Kivalina wasn't plugged in to the intercom system. He was without a headset and peering out a side window, shackled to the seat, seemingly oblivious to what went on inside the Cessna.

Active turned to the pilot. "That's how Pingo described him. He called McAllister a man in rage."

"Fits."

"He says his sister liked that in a man," Active said. "She called it 'the great weather.' You understand that about women?"

"Not really," Cowboy said. "I've seen it, but I don't understand it. Maybe only a woman would."

"Or Pingo, maybe," Active said. "Even crazy and hung over, he figured out that Driftwood thing while Cave was getting nowhere. I'm starting to think quite a few of his brain cells still work."

Alan Long spoke up from the back seat. "Unless Cave was right. Maybe Pingo did burn down the Rec Center. He does admit being there at the time. And hiring Jae Hyo Lee to kill McAllister. And watering McAllister's gas."

"Nah," Active said. "I don't buy it. I can imagine Pingo burning McAllister's house down, but not the Rec Center. He wouldn't have had any reason to think McAllister was there. Plus, he wouldn't set the Rec Center on fire with all those other people in it."

"Yeah," Cowboy said. "Especially Tom Gage."

"Unless his sister told him to," Long said.

Active was silent for a time, chewing this point over. With Pingo, questions of good, evil, and motive were sideshows. All that mattered was the disordered world inside his head and the phantasm of Viola Kivalina who visited his sleep.

Finally, Active grunted. "In any case, we have to talk to McAllister. Cowboy, you think he could do all this?" He considered enumerating McAllister's presumptive body count, but couldn't bring himself to wade through it again.

"I don't know how anybody could," Cowboy said. "But somebody did. So, yeah, of the people I know, if somebody could, I guess it could be Dood."

In another hour, they began to see over the peaks of the Keating Mountains into the Katonak Valley. Cowboy bent over the chart on his knee, then hunched forward and peered past Active at the white folds off the right wing. "Driftwood's over that way," he said. "Thirty, thirty-five miles maybe."

They crossed the crest and Cowboy dropped the Cessna's nose slightly, angling right to follow the black braids of a river down a white-floored valley running southwest. He checked his chart again and pointed at a barren, snow-plastered crag looming above them as they followed the river downstream. "Mount Bastille," he said. "How do you reckon they came up with that?"

Active shrugged, and they continued along the river, the valley opening out as they passed the snowline and the country faded from white to brown. Cowboy rolled left to point the Cessna's nose at the tip of a long, rumpled ridge descending from the mountains like a crocodile's tail, then jabbed at the chart on his knee.

"Here's McAllister's camp on the near side of that ridge up ahead. We've gotta come around back of it, drop over the crest, and dive down through this canyon here." Cowboy's finger traced it out on the chart. "When we pop out, we'll be about a quarter-mile from the camp and doing around one-sixty, one-seventy, so we'll be overhead in about five seconds. That's how long we've got to look things over, maybe five seconds, because once we're past, we sure ain't coming back."

Active nodded. "Okay."

"We don't want to fly right over it," Cowboy continued, "because we won't be able to see anything directly under us. So I'll angle to the left a little bit, and the camp will be off our right wing when we go past. That way I can concentrate on not hitting a mountain while you look it over. Sound right?"

Active nodded again. "Sounds right."

Cowboy grinned. "Fun, huh?"

"Yeah," Active said after some thought. "It is, actually."

Cowboy worked his way toward the foot of the ridge behind McAllister's camp, staying low and using the terrain for cover. Finally he made a turn and started along the back side of the snow-draped ridge. In another seven minutes, Cowboy pointed the Cessna up a draw toward the crest. As they sailed over the top, Active caught a momentary glimpse of a little cluster of buildings three miles or so ahead on the valley floor. Then McAllister's camp vanished behind a rock wall as Cowboy dropped the Cessna into the canyon and began his downhill run.

Behind him, Pingo screamed "*Arii*! That's Qavvik's mountain! We can't go here." Active's seatback jerked. Pingo must have been kicking it. Active turned and lunged for Pingo's throat over the backrest. Pingo threw himself as far back as his restraints would allow and kicked Active's seat again.

"You gotta get him under control," Cowboy shouted over the intercom. "We're committed here."

Active was unbuckling himself when he saw Pingo jerk, then slump into his seat. "You're carrying a Taser, Alan?"

"Roger that," Long said. "Good thing, ah?"

Active settled back into his seat and returned his attention to their descent through the canyon. The needle on the airspeed indicator swept through one-fifty, one-sixty, one-seventy, and finally came to a quivering stop between one-eighty and one-eighty-five, the wind screaming through the wing struts as they plunged toward the valley floor.

The ridge to their left dropped away, and suddenly they were out of the canyon, G-forces jamming Active into his seat as Cowboy jerked the Cessna out of its dive and rocked into a hard left turn.

He leveled the wings just above the willows and they barreled down the little creek that trickled out of the canyon. Ahead on the right, McAllister's camp was a big two-story lodge and a cluster of smaller outbuildings. Active registered impressions more than information: nobody on top of the lodge or the other buildings; on the tundra in front of the lodge, a man pausing, knife in hand, over what might be the rib cage of a caribou, his face turning up, flashing white and surprised as they roared by; another man, in the act of opening the outhouse door, letting it swing shut as he looked up to watch them.

Then they were past the camp and roaring toward McAllister's landing strip on a patch of slightly elevated ground along the creek bank. A landing strip that was devoid of anything resembling an airplane.

Active felt the tension drain out of him as he nudged Cowboy and pointed at the strip. "I don't think he's here."

Cowboy eased the Cessna's nose up and made an arc to the right as they gained altitude. "Guess not," the pilot said, peering under the right wing at the empty strip. "But where the hell is he? Delilah said he headed up here last night. Maybe we oughta land and search around the camp."

"I saw a couple of guys in the yard as we went over," Active said. "How about we try the radio?"

Cowboy looked like he wanted to say "Duh!" but he just switched on his radios and tuned one to a new frequency. "McAllister's Camp, this is the Cessna that was just overhead, over."

A minute or two passed as Cowboy repeated the call once, then twice. Then the headset sprayed static, and a woman's voice said, "This is McAllister's. Who's that?"

"Probably his cook," Cowboy said over the intercom. He tapped the little boom microphone on Active's head set. "You want to talk to her?"

Active nodded and identified himself to the woman.

"We're attempting to contact Dood McAllister. Can you tell us his whereabouts?"

"What you want him for?"

"I'm sorry, that's confidential. Can you tell us his whereabouts?"

"He take off maybe couple hours ago, say he's going to pull out his spike camp over there at One-Way Lake."

Active gave the cook a roger and looked at Cowboy.

"You want to go in?" the pilot asked.

"We've got our search warrant," Long said from behind them.

After a moment's thought, Active shook his head, then realized nobody had seen him do it. "No, let's go after McAllister," he said over the intercom. "If he's running, this may be our last good shot at him."

"All right," Cowboy said. "But I gotta have a pit stop."

Ten minutes later, the Cessna was bounding to a halt on a rolling ridge a few miles from McAllister's camp. Cowboy and Active jumped down, stepped away from the plane, and relieved themselves on the tundra. Long hauled a still stunned-looking Pingo out and allowed him the same relief.

"Why would Dood go to One-Way Lake?" Cowboy asked after Pingo had been reattached to a rear seat—ankles, too, this time. "If he knows you guys have him figured out, why doesn't he just run for cover somewhere? Or go hire a lawyer?"

"Maybe there's evidence over there," Active said. "Maybe he took something off Jae Hyo Lee. Maybe he lied to the cook and he's not even there. All I know is, we have to stay on him."

"I don't know," Long said. "Go after him at One-Way

Lake without backup? Serving a search warrant on his camp would be one thing, but—"

"If he's running, I don't see where we have any choice."

"But he'll hear us coming and—" Long stopped as he caught the look on Active's face. "Yeah, yeah. Think long, think wrong."

Active gave a slight nod of approval, wondering about Long's reluctance to confront McAllister. He filed it away and turned to the pilot. "How far is it?"

Cowboy leaned into the Cessna and retrieved his chart. He spread it on the plane's tail, holding it down with a forearm so the wind wouldn't take it, and calipered the distance to One-Way Lake with a thumb and forefinger. He eyed the span for a moment. "Seventy miles, plus or minus. Half an hour, maybe."

"So what's your plan?" Long said in that same reluctant tone.

"Fly in there, look it over, figure something out," Active said.

"And if McAllister's waiting?"

"Figure something out. Okay, Alan?"

Long said nothing. Cowboy grunted and bent over the Cessna's tail again. Active and Long leaned in to follow his finger across the map.

"This one may be a little dodgier. If he's at One-Way, his Cessna's going to be parked on the ridge above the lake." Decker tapped the spot on the map. "Here. And there's no way to come at it without being seen ourselves."

Active studied the chart. One-Way Lake was in the foothills on the south side of the Laird Mountains above the valley of the Isignaq River. One of the canyons radiating from the mountains appeared to open onto the top of the cliff above the lake. He drew a forefinger along its route. "How about we come down through here and pop out over the ridge, like we did just now?"

Cowboy shook his head. "We got two strikes against us. Number one, McAllister's spike camp is probably right up that same canyon. That's why he uses that ridge to get to it. So we come down through there, he's gonna see us. And number two, you see what's moving in over there?"

Cowboy turned away from the map pointed at the Laird Mountains on the far side of the Katonak River. The peaks were topped with shreds of cloud and the dangling veils of gray that meant falling snow.

"In order to get over the Lairds and into that canyon above One-Way, we'd have to go right through that stuff. And even I don't fly around in the clouds if I know there's rocks in 'em."

Active studied the clouds, which appeared to be moving toward the Katonak a little as he watched. "So how do we get over there?"

"We might be able to sneak through Igichuk Pass to the Isignaq side, all right. But seriously, what do we do when we get to One-Way?"

"You got binoculars?"

Cowboy nodded.

"Let's stand off at a safe distance and glass the situation, then decide."

Cowboy nodded again. "About all we can do, I guess." He glanced at Active with the bush-pilot grin he got at moments like this. "Let's jet. We're burning daylight."

CHAPTER SIXTEEN

THEY CLIMBED INTO THE Cessna and cranked up. The engine still had some heat left, and Active opened his parka gratefully as warm air filled the cockpit. Cowboy taxied uphill a few yards, then locked the left wheel, goosed the throttle, and rotated the plane into takeoff position. Soon they were bounding along the whitish mat of reindeer moss and chert that covered the crest.

A gust caught them, and the plane soared off the ridge, the right wing lifting in a way that made Active think of McAllister's account of the crash that had killed Budzie Kivalina at Driftwood. Cowboy corrected the roll and climbed southward toward the Katonak River. The climb continued until the plane was level with the bottoms of the clouds draping the slopes of the Laird Mountains on the far side of the Katonak. Cowboy hunched forward to peer at the approaching peaks. Active had learned that this hunch was a bad sign in a bush pilot.

"Trouble?"

Cowboy gave one of his rumbling grunts and looked at the chart on his knee. "Fifty-fifty on Igichuk Pass," he said. "If it's closed, we gotta go way around like this to get over there." He traced a long arc on the map, running along the north slope of the Lairds to where the mountains sank into

the Katonak Flats less than fifty miles from Chukchi. From
the Flats, Cowboy's finger indicated, they would have to
double back and fly up the Isignaq along the south slope of
the Lairds to reach One-Way Lake. The pilot tapped one of
his gas gauges. "But if we have to do that, we'll have to run
in to Chukchi and refuel first."

"It's your call," Active said.

"Can't hurt to take a look." Cowboy continued his
scrutiny of the Lairds as they reached the Katonak,
followed it upstream to the mouth of the Igichuk River,
and headed into the mountains. Now they were skimming
the bellies of the clouds spreading north from the Lairds.
Snow streaked past the windows. Active peered ahead but
could not spot the pass, or guess the chances of it still
being open.

Active studied Cowboy, trying to decide how serious
the situation was. The pilot seemed to have relaxed a
little. He was farther back in his seat and even looking out
his side window at the valley below. He dipped a wing as
they passed a spot where a creek fed into the Igichuk near
a long, silky gravel bar. "There's a nice little hot spring
down there," he said. "Good place for a getaway with
someone sweet when the weather's nicer. I could drop you
guys in there."

"I'll keep it in mind," Active said.

They continued up the Igichuk until a hard left turn
around the end of a rocky granite ridge put them in a
mountain bowl of gray talus slopes whitening with snow.
Clouds capped the bowl like a lid on a pot.

Active looked for a way out and finally spotted a saddle
up ahead that looked as if it might lead through to the south
slopes of the range. It was at the same altitude as the

Cessna and pretty much socked in, so it was hard to see over. "That the pass?" He pointed.

Cowboy nodded.

"The clouds are right down on it. Maybe it's time for a one-eighty."

"Ah," Cowboy growled. "We came this far."

Cowboy rolled the plane into a turn and followed the curving wall of the bowl. Active wondered about this indirect approach for a moment, then realized they would have no escape route if they flew straight at the pass and found it closed. This way, if it was closed, they could complete the circle inside the bowl and backtrack down the Igichuk.

Active watched as the pass crawled closer on Cowboy's side of the plane. Through the mist and snow, he thought he glimpsed a rock-walled valley on the south side, with a thread of water in its center diving toward the Isignaq River far below. Cowboy yelled "Here we go!" over the intercom, and the world rotated ninety degrees as he snapped the plane into a punishing left turn. He leveled the wings just in time to skim across the saddle so low that Active thought for a moment he had decided to land and taxi to the far edge.

Then the terrain fell away, Cowboy dropped the nose, and they were under the clouds and in relatively clear air, hurrying down the rocky valley Active had glimpsed moments earlier. He let out a long breath and looked at the pilot, who was lounging back in his seat and scratching his nose with a thumbnail.

"Nice work," Active said.

"What was?" Cowboy asked, all nonchalance. Then the bush-pilot grin spread over his face, and he raised his eyebrows. He consulted the chart and peered down the valley ahead. "Another few minutes and we'll pop out of this canyon. One-Way Lake will be eight or nine miles off to our left. That ridge above the lake will be closest to us, so I'm gonna head straight for it while you glass it with these."

He reached into the pouch on the back of Active's seat and dug out a set of compact Nikon binoculars. Active took them, draped the strap around his neck, and adjusted the focus for his eyesight.

"You got a plan yet?" Cowboy asked.

"First let's see if he's there."

They continued down the canyon, jolted occasionally by turbulence, as the snow diminished almost to nothing. The wall to their left dropped away, and they could see in the distance what even Active's unpracticed eye recognized as the ridge above One-Way Lake.

Pingo shouted "*Arii!*" and there was a commotion from the back seat, followed by silence.

"I showed him the Taser," Long said over the intercom.

Active lifted the binoculars to his eyes and scanned the ridge ahead.

"Yeah?" Cowboy prodded.

"Nothing yet. Well, one speck that could be—hold on! Yes, it's definitely a 185."

"Anybody moving?"

Active was silent, the toy plane on the ridge growing in the binoculars as the Lienhofer Cessna ate away at the distance. "Nope," he said finally. "Nobody around it. I think I can see tiedown ropes under the wings."

Cowboy grunted. "Let me take a look." He put the glasses to his eyes for a moment and gave a chuckle of satisfaction. "He fucked up."

Active took the glasses back and studied the plane on the ridge. "How's that?"

"He parked it at the end of the strip."

"Eh?"

"If he would have parked in the middle, I wouldn't have had enough room to land. This way I can."

Active said nothing, still glassing McAllister's Cessna.

"Do you want to land?" Cowboy asked.

"Let's look it over first."

Cowboy banked the Cessna into a wide circle a couple of miles off One-Way Ridge, and Active scanned the make-do landing strip on the crest and the valley climbing into the mountains above. The snowline was a couple hundred feet higher than the ridge and the lake was still open, except for a crescent of ice under the bluff at the upper end.

"McAllister must be back in there at his spike camp, right?"

Cowboy nodded. "Seems like."

"And we can't flush him out from the air?"

Cowboy peered at the clouds shrouding the peaks above the ridge. "Negatory. It's socked in tight up there."

Active chewed the situation over in his mind.

"We could land on the ridge and wait him out," Cowboy said. "He's gotta come back to his plane eventually. And when he does, there'll be three of us to his one. Not counting Pingo."

"Maybe," Long said. "Unless he waits till dark and sneaks up and picks us off."

"No problem," Cowboy said. "We'll just leave at sunset and—shit, look at that!"

A red four-wheeler with a little trailer in tow was bouncing down from the mountains toward the Cessna parked on the ridge.

Cowboy was at the outside of his circle, the farthest point from the ridge. Active looked at the pilot, now hunched forward in the seat again. "Can you land and block him before he gets rolling?"

"I think," Cowboy said. He dropped a wing, and the Cessna wheeled to the right, heading for the lower end of the strip on the ridge.

Active swore under his breath as the seconds ticked past on the clock on the Cessna's instrument panel and the ridge loomed larger in the windshield.

Cowboy rolled into a tight left turn and snapped out on course for an uphill landing on the ridge, pointing straight at McAllister's plane squatting at the far end. By now, the four-wheeler was parked beside it, and there was no sign of the tie-down ropes Active had seen earlier. Nor was there any sign of McAllister. He must already be inside, Active was thinking when the propeller jerked, then spun into a blur. McAllister's plane began to roll, a plume of powdery new snow streaming off the ridge behind it.

The Lienhofer Cessna bounced onto the crest, once, twice, and then was down and rolling fast.

"Cowboy?" Active shouted as the planes closed in on each other.

"Hang on," the pilot said, his hands a blur at the controls. "I got it." The windshield filled with McAllister's plane, just lifting off. Cowboy swerved the Cessna left. The engine roared and, so fast that Active couldn't sort it out, McAllister's plane vanished, and they were headed straight for the tundra at the foot of One-Way Ridge. Then Active realized what had happened: Cowboy, rolling too slowly to take off, had plunged the Cessna off the side of the ridge and was now diving down the slope to get up to flying speed.

"Cowboy."

"No sweat," the pilot said, easing the Cessna out of its dive a few yards from the bottom.

"We should maybe be a little more conservative about some of these things in the future," Active said after a long silence.

"You bet." Cowboy bared his teeth in the bush-pilot grin. He pulled the Cessna's nose up and started a climbing turn back toward the ridge. "You see Dood anywhere?"

Three pairs of eyes scanned the horizon. There was no sign of a Cessna 185, other than the one they were in.

"Where'd he go?" Long said from the back seat.

"Let's just see." Something in Cowboy's tone said he already knew the answer. He pushed the throttle forward, and the Cessna roared over the ridge above the lake. "Whattaya think?"

Active didn't say anything. He just admired the view. A quarter-mile out in the lake, McAllister's plane was sunk up to its wings, with McAllister himself huddled on top, in the snow spitting down from the ragged gray overcast.

"I didn't figure he had enough room to get up flying speed before he hit the lake," Cowboy said. "That's why I went left."

Active regarded the pilot in silence. How could a man who consistently talked liked a fool—who had actually said "Let's jet" only a few minutes earlier—be such a genius in an airplane? An idiot one moment, the most competent member of the group the next.

Cowboy rolled the Cessna into a slow circle above the

lake. "I gotta give him credit, though. Most guys would end up on their backs if they had to ditch a 185, but Dood kept 'er upright."

"We better get down there before he swims ashore and takes off," Active said.

Cowboy snorted.

"I don't think so," Long said. "Most Eskimos can't swim, all right. They never learn. The water's too cold."

McAllister looked up at them as they passed over, then stepped down onto the engine cowling, grabbed a propeller blade sticking out of the water, and jumped off. His head went under, and for a moment only the hand grasping the propeller was visible.

Then he surfaced, hauled himself onto the nose, and made his way back to his place atop the wing.

"See?" Long said. "He can't touch bottom. He's stuck."

"How long will it float?" Active asked.

"Maybe long enough to ground out if he hadn't filled his tanks yet when we chased him off the ridge. Plus, he's got that cargo pod on the belly, so, if it was empty too. . . ." Cowboy pointed at the waves rolling down the lake. "And One-Way's pretty shallow at the lower end."

To Active's eye, it did appear the plane had already moved a few yards toward the outlet at One-Way Creek. "I think we better get down there."

Cowboy nodded, broke out of the circle, flew down the lake, made a tight turn to the right, and set them down on the ridge again.

"Alan, you stay here and watch Pingo," Active said as they bounced to a stop near McAllister's four-wheeler with its trailer-load of red jerry jugs. Cowboy jumped out and used McAllister's tie-downs to tether the Cessna against the wind rolling out of the hills.

"Stay here?" Long said. "You're going to take on McAllister by yourself?"

"I doubt he'll be in any shape to cause trouble." Active nodded toward the Cessna in the lake. McAllister was huddled on the wing-top, hugging his knees and betraying no inclination to test the water again.

"I could help," Cowboy growled. He rummaged in the duffel compartment at the back of the cabin and came up with a big revolver in a leather holster. "This is a .357 Magnum. It stopped a grizzly once, so it sure oughta stop Dood McAllister." He flipped out the cylinder and spun it to check the loads.

Active glanced at Long, then at the pilot. Who would he rather have at his back if McAllister turned out to have some fight left?

"Alan, keep Pingo handcuffed to the seat till we get McAllister in custody, then bring him down."

Long's face fell, but he climbed back into the plane.

"Let's go, Cowboy," Active said.

Decker had parked the Cessna at the upper end of the ridge, beside the cliff where Active had found Jae Hyo Lee's rifle stuck in the rocks five days earlier. The sides of the ridge here were nearly as steep as the cliff, so they hurried along the crest to the foot of the ridge, then made their way down the slope to One-Way Creek and forded the stream at a spot slightly shallower than their boots.

The Cessna was no longer moving, presumably grounded. The wing was just under water, and the only part showing above the surface was a propeller blade. McAllister was still on the wing, standing upright and slapping himself in an apparent effort to fight off the cold. Active and Decker raced to the nearest spot on the shore.

"What the hell you assholes doing?" McAllister yelled. "You wrecked my plane. You gotta rescue me now."

"*You* wrecked your plane. And you've got bigger problems than that," Active yelled back. "You're under arrest."

"What for? I didn't do anything."

"You killed Budzie Kivalina and Jae Hyo Lee and then eight more people when you set the Rec Center on fire. That's not wrong?"

McAllister didn't say anything.

"Take off your clothes and swim ashore," Active shouted.

"Fuck you, I can't swim," McAllister yelled back. "You gotta come get me."

Decker and Active looked at each other. "You got a raft in the plane?" Active asked.

Decker shook his head.

"I guess we wait him out," Active said. "Maybe he'll decide to swim for it after all."

But McAllister stayed on the wing. As the minutes dragged by and the wind continued to whip down the lake, he stopped slapping himself and dropped to a sitting position. Soon he was flat on his back in the water lapping over the wing. Had he passed out? Active wondered.

"We have to get him off of there. If he's not faking, he's going to die of hypothermia or wash off of that wing and drown." Active looked at Cowboy and pointed at his gun. "You can actually hit something with that thing?"

Cowboy lifted his eyebrows and drew the .357 from its holster.

"All right. I'm going to wade out there and drag him back. Don't shoot him if you can avoid it."

"What the hell does that mean?" Cowboy growled.

"Only shoot him if I tell you to or if he renders me unable to do so."

"Ah."

"You stand off to the right, and I'll come in from the left. That way you should be able to keep a clear line of fire."

"Got it." Cowboy waded into the lake until the water neared his boot-tops, raised the .357, and drew a practice bead on McAllister. Then he holstered the gun. "Maybe we should just let nature take its course."

"What?"

"We could leave him out there and say we couldn't get to him in time."

Active studied the inert figure on the wing, then turned to Cowboy. "Just let him die?"

Cowboy shrugged. "What about Jim Silver and those people at the Rec Center? Cammie Frankson and those other kids? He'll never get enough prison time to pay for that."

"That's not how we do it, Cowboy. Besides, what if it wasn't him? Alan and Sergeant Cave still think it was Pingo."

"You don't believe that."

"There's what I believe, and there's what I know. What I know is, that's not how we do it."

The pilot shook his head and stared into the water at his feet. But he drew the gun again. "Yeah, go ahead. I got you covered."

Active studied his route out to the plane. He would have to swim the last few yards, which meant it would be impossible to keep his Smith and Wesson dry. He kicked away the snow to make a clear spot on the moss by the lakeshore, then unbuckled his belt, wrapped it around the holster, and dropped the gun onto the moss. Then he realized he would have to take off far more than his gun belt. He probably wouldn't be able to swim at all once his Sorels filled up with water, besides which, he hadn't brought any other boots. Plus, his other clothes were still in the Cessna parked on the ridge at least fifteen minutes away, through the wind and snow.

"Christ," he said, and began stripping.

"You didn't tell me about this part," Cowboy said. "I never saw a naked Trooper before."

"You just keep your eyes on McAllister," Active said.

He studied the gear at his feet, grabbed his handcuffs, and clenched them between his teeth. Then he screamed as he imagined Pickett's Rebels must have screamed on the charge up Cemetery Ridge and plunged into the water. As it reached chest level, there was a moment of cold shock when he lost his breath and couldn't move and thought he wouldn't be able to finish. But the paralysis passed, and he could breathe and move again. He walked until his feet lost the lake bottom, and then he swam the last few yards, his skin burning with the cold, his breath coming in gasps, saliva spraying around the handcuffs. From the corner of his eye, he saw Cowboy off to his right, arm raised, the .357 trained on McAllister.

Active reached the plane and used the propeller blade to heave himself onto the cowling, feeling colder than ever now, the wind burning his bare, wet skin even more. McAllister was still motionless, his head near Active, his feet pointed at the wingtip. His hands, bobbing slightly in the water, were beside his thighs.

How to do this? Bending over to reach McAllister's wrists and snap the cuffs on would block Cowboy's shot at McAllister's upper body. There would only be his legs for a target. What if McAllister was faking? Could one of those hands conceal a weapon?

"McAllister," Active said, his teeth starting to chatter. "Raise your arms. I'm going to handcuff you. Dood!"

There was no response.

Active deliberated, shivering, then grabbed the hood of McAllister's anorak and yanked him off the wing. McAllister slid into the water and finally came to life a little, thrashing weakly and scrabbling at the wing. Active grabbed one upraised hand and cuffed it, then the other, and pulled up on the cuffs to keep McAllister's head above water.

"McAllister. Dood! Can you hear me?"

Recognition shone in McAllister's eyes for a moment, then flickered out.

Active dived over McAllister's lolling head and made for shore, towing the guide behind him like a log.

"Come on, Cowboy," he shouted when his feet hit bottom and he could raise his head clear of the water. "We have to get a fire going."

Active dragged McAllister onto the moss and dropped him. He felt himself shivering, but the wind didn't seem so cold now, which presumably meant his skin was going numb and he was approaching hypothermia himself. "See what you can do for him," he told Cowboy. "I've gotta get something on."

He dried himself as best he could on the outside of his anorak and, shuddering violently, began pulling on his clothes as Cowboy hurried into the brush nearby and returned with an armful of branches.

The pilot kicked the snow off a patch of moss, built a little teepee of branches, and pulled a Bic lighter and a wad of crumpled paper out of his parka pocket. Active saw a greasy napkin, a Snickers wrapper, and an envelope that appeared to have a shopping list on the back of it. Cowboy caught him watching and explained needlessly: "I always carry some fire-starter. Good habit to get into."

"Thanks," Active said. He was dressed now, but shuddering as much as before. He slapped his shoulders and jogged in place as Cowboy tucked the fire-starter under the branches and applied the Bic. A tiny flame began to eat at the base of the teepee, and a wisp of smoke curled up. Cowboy blew on it, added more twigs, then larger branches, and they watched the fire grow.

Active jogged into the trees and returned with a bundle of larger branches, including a couple of chunks that qualified as logs in the Arctic. He tossed them beside the fire, and they dragged McAllister closer to the blaze.

Cowboy shook his head. "He's gonna need dry clothes too. I've got some stuff in my emergency kit in the plane—another parka, some sleeping bags, probably a pair of snowpants. Maybe I better get on up there."

"Let me," Active said. "I need the exercise." He bent and went quickly through McAllister's clothing, turning up nothing more sinister than an Old Timer jackknife on his belt. He pulled a set of plastic FlexCuffs from his own pocket and fastened them around McAllister's ankles. Then he removed the metal cuffs from McAllister's hands and refastened them behind his back.

"Watch him," he told Cowboy. "Not that he's in any condition to do much, but—"

"Yeah, you never know with a guy like this," the pilot said.

Active turned and looked down the shore toward One-Way Creek. He was still cold, still shuddering as hard as ever. How long had he been in the water? Ten minutes, fifteen at most. That should be survivable. Once cooled past a certain point, he knew, the body couldn't re-warm itself. External heat was required. But he thought he recalled reading that you hadn't reached that point if you were still conscious and shivering.

He set off at the best sprint he could muster, feeling out of it at first, a little uncertain about where to put his left foot down, a little slow remembering how to lift his right foot and bring it around past the left, almost drunk. But it seemed to get easier as he went, and the shuddering seemed to be letting up.

By the time he crossed One-Way Creek and started up the ridge toward Cowboy's Cessna, he figured his body temperature was approaching normal. By the time he reached the plane, he'd probably be sweating.

Halfway along the crest, Active found himself jogging through fog and realized the descending clouds had now covered the upper end of the ridge. He peered ahead but Cowboy's Cessna was invisible, swallowed up in the mist.

"Alan," he called. "Alan!"

No answer, but it probably wouldn't matter. The crest was narrow enough that he surely couldn't miss the plane, even in the fog.

But he did, realizing his error only when he stumbled into a rock outcropping. There was nothing like that around McAllister's tiedown, though he remembered seeing rocks farther up the hill. He stopped and opened his parka, happy to find himself actually hot. He let his breathing calm for a moment, then called Long again, again without result. The fog must be muffling his voice, he decided. But how to find the plane in the murk?

He turned and pointed himself directly down the ridge, as best he could judge, then set off. He tripped twice as he peered into the void trying to spot the plane. After that, he kept his eyes on the reindeer moss and gravel at his feet, trusting gravity and his sense of direction to lead him down the crest of the ridge rather than over the side.

The next minute, he stumbled into the tail fin of Cowboy's Cessna. "Alan," he said, rubbing the bruise on his forehead.

There was no answer, no movement inside the plane. He circled the tail and opened a rear door. The plane was empty.

He stepped back and called Long again, then Pingo.

Silence, except for the faint sigh of wind sweeping down the ridge. Where—but wait, hadn't he told Long to bring Pingo down to the lake once McAllister was secure? That was it. They must have missed each other in the fog.

He dug through the storage area behind the seats and found Cowboy's survival gear: two pairs of snowshoes, a nylon backpacker tent, the clothes and sleeping bag the pilot had mentioned, a tiny gas lantern, an equally tiny single-burner camp stove with fuel and cooking utensils, the inevitable roll of Visqueen plastic sheeting, a hank of nylon camp cord, a folding saw, and a canvas bag with a seemingly random assortment of Mountain House freeze-dry and military-surplus MREs. He thought it would be too much to carry in one load, until he found a pack frame at the bottom of it all. He lashed everything but the snowshoes onto the frame, closed up the Cessna, and started downhill.

He was nearly to the foot of the ridge when he came out of the fog. He turned and studied the shoreline near McAllister's grounded Cessna. McAllister was still stretched out by the fire, now covered with what appeared to be Cowboy's parka. The little blaze had become a bonfire, and Cowboy was hunched over it with only a wool shirt and a down vest covering his upper body. But that was it. No sign of Alan Long or Pingo Kivalina.

Active swiveled and surveyed the tundra on the other side of the ridge. The snow was heavier now, and there appeared to be some fog in the air, even here below the clouds. No sign of human presence was detectable in the limited range of his vision.

He swore and jogged the rest of the way down the ridge, the pack frame flopping against his back and throwing him off balance. He was out of breath by the time he crossed One-Way Creek and sweating when he reached the fire. He dropped the pack frame, and Cowboy knelt and went to work on the lacings.

"You seen any sign of Alan or Pingo?" Active asked.

Cowboy looked up in surprise. "What?" he said, peering down the shoreline. "I thought they'd be with you."

"Jesus," Active said. "The plane was empty when I got there. Absolutely no sign of them, no response when I called, nothing."

The pilot looked up at the gray wool draping the ridge across the lake. "Where the hell could they be?"

Active shook his head. "God knows. That Alan. . . ."

"Maybe Cave was right about Pingo," Cowboy said, shrugging on a parka from the load Active had brought down the hill. "Maybe he really did set our fire in Chukchi, and now he's. . . ."

"Yeah, he got the drop on Alan somehow and took off?"

"Uh-huh, and, ah, Alan is, ah, lying out there somewhere. . . ."

"Yeah." Active looked around at the weather closing in on them. "And right now there's no way to search for them."

"Huh-uh. Not in this."

Active chewed the inside of his cheek for a moment, then nodded at McAllister, motionless beside the fire. "How's he doing?"

Cowboy grimaced. "No change. I gave him my coat, but he's not any warmer that I can tell. He's still breathing, at least."

"Well, let's get him into dry clothes and a sleeping bag and see if we can get him warmed up."

Cowboy kicked at the edge of the fire. "I found some rocks and put them in there to heat up. We could stick them in the sleeping bag with him."

Active nodded, impressed again by Cowboy's competence within his own universe.

They undressed McAllister, got the dry clothes on him, worked a sleeping bag around him, and slid in the rocks from Cowboy's fire. Active watched as snow dusted the sleeping bag and McAllister's nose and mouth, the only part of him they had left exposed. "We probably ought to get him into the tent."

"Nah," Cowboy said. "I'll build him a Visqueen lean-to. We can put the open side toward the fire and he'll get more heat that way."

"I'm thinking I'll go back up to the plane and get your Emergency Locator Translator."

Cowboy raised his eyebrows. "Yeah, I guess we could use some help finding Alan and Pingo."

"And you probably ought to keep the .357 handy. In case Pingo is our guy."

"Jesus." Cowboy looked into the trees around their campsite. "I hadn't thought about that. There's no telling what he's liable to do."

"Yep." Active checked the Smith and Wesson on his hip and set off for another trip up the ridge.

CHAPTER SEVENTEEN

HE WAS FORDING ONE-WAY Creek when the voice came from the trees.

"Hi, Nathan."

Active froze and peered into the cottonwoods. "Alan? Are you all right?"

"Not really."

"What? Are you hurt?" Active looked Long over as he approached. There was no sign of blood, or of an arm held stiffly, or of a limp.

Or of anyone else.

"Pingo. Where's Pingo? He got away, is that it?"

Long averted his gaze and raised his eyebrows. "I was watching you take off your clothes and bring Dood in from the plane, and when I looked around, he was gone."

"Gone? But he was shackled to the seat. Did he rip it loose somehow?"

"Not exactly, no."

Active closed his eyes and waited for the urge to throttle Alan Long to subside. "What the hell happened, then?"

"He had to take a leak. When I put him back in the plane, I guess I forgot about shackling him to the seat again."

"You *forgot?*"

Long lifted his eyebrows, his chipmunk cheeks drooping in dismay. "I tried to follow him, but it's too foggy up there. I couldn't see anything."

"So he's gone."

Long raised his eyebrows again. "But he is handcuffed, at least."

"Well, he can't travel very fast," Active said. "Not on foot, and with his hands shackled. Soon as this weather lifts, we can go up in Cowboy's—" He noticed the look on Long's face. "Pingo is still shackled, right?"

"Pretty much."

"Pretty much?"

"His hands are cuffed, but I don't think they're shackled to his waist any more."

"You don't think. You forgot that too?"

Long nodded his head with a miserable expression.

"Gee, Alan, a guy in handcuffs can move about as well as anybody else and do pretty much whatever he needs to, can't he? That's just. . . ." Active stopped as the thought entered his head that maybe Long's letting Kivalina get away was no accident.

"At least he can't move very fast on foot," he said, studying Long's face. "Plus it'll be dark before too long, so he probably won't get far tonight. If we can get in the air at first light, we should—"

Long had raised his head and was looking intently up the ridge, into the fog, toward where Cowboy's Cessna was parked.

"What?" Active said. Then he heard it himself. *Br-r-r-r-p. Br-r-r-r-p. Br-r-r-r-p.* Like someone pulling the starter cord on a snowmachine. Or a—

"I bet he's taking Dood's four-wheeler," Long said.

"Come on," Active shouted, and sprinted up the slope. But, even over the sound of his own feet scuffing over the tundra, he could hear the four-wheeler catch and settle down to a steady r-r-p, r-r-p, r-r-p, then rev up and gradually fade into the distance.

He stopped in the fog. Long bumped into him from behind.

"Damned fine job, Alan," Active said, unable to check himself now. "Pingo could be a hundred miles away by the time this stuff clears."

"I don't know if a four-wheeler can hold that much gas."

"You happen to notice what was in that trailer McAllister was towing?"

"I can't remember. Oh, yeah, a bunch of gas jugs, right?"

"Uh-huh."

"*Arii.*"

"Uh-huh."

Active debated whether to continue on to Cowboy's Cessna or get back to the fire and see to the perhaps-dying, perhaps-reviving, McAllister. Long was safe and Pingo apparently bent on clearing out of the country, so the situation probably no longer qualified as an emergency. Unless—

"Come on. We gotta get up there."

Long looked into the fog shrouding the ridge. "What for? Pingo's gone, like you said."

"In case he did something to the plane. I'm not sure anybody knows we're here. If we can't fly out, it may be a while before anybody figures it out." Active set off up the slope at a fast trot, leaving Long to follow. Or not.

"YOU SURE my plane's okay?" Cowboy asked a half-hour later. "Maybe I oughta go have a look myself."

"If you like," Active said. "But I think Pingo just snuck up, started McAllister's four-wheeler, and took off. There's no sign the plane was touched. In fact, the keys were still in the ignition. I locked up and brought them back with me."

He pulled the keys from his pocket and dropped them into Cowboy's hand with a mildly accusing look.

"I always leave 'em in the switch," Cowboy said, sounding defensive. "You take 'em with you and they fall out of your pocket on the tundra, then where are you?"

"Good point," Active said. "Except this time."

Cowboy grunted and swung his gaze to Alan Long. "And how exactly did Pingo get loose, Alan?"

Long hedged and stumbled his way through the story.

When it was over, Cowboy shook his head. "I never knew anything like that to happen with Chief Silver."

Long said nothing. He turned and walked to the lakeshore.

Active studied McAllister's figure in the Visqueen lean-to. The sides and rear were closed off, so the only opening was the front. It faced the fire, which Cowboy had extended with more fuel from the nearby spruces until it paralleled the makeshift shelter for most of its length. It looked to be about as warm an arrangement as could be devised with the resources at hand.

McAllister was still covered except for the nose and

mouth poking out of Cowboy's sleeping bag. The bag was vibrating visibly.

"McAllister's shivering now?" Active said. "That's good, right?"

"I think so," Cowboy said. "Assuming we want to keep him alive."

"Yes, Cowboy. We do."

The pilot turned and pointed at a coffeepot nestled in the coals at one end of the fire. "Got some hot water here. Ready for an MRE?" He turned and looked toward the lake. "Alan? Want some chow?"

Cowboy dumped several of the brown pouches into the coffeepot and poked at them with a spruce branch to make sure they were immersed. "Couple minutes," he said. He handed out what passed for treats in MRE-land, and Active munched on something called Fortified Snack Bread as the entrees heated.

"What ab-bout me-he-hee?" McAllister said from under the lean-to, his teeth chattering.

Active checked the impulse to jump in surprise. "You're hungry? We've got—"

"I'm cuh-hold. I need something huh-hot."

Cowboy pawed through the food bag and came up with envelopes of powdered hot chocolate and clam chowder. "These'll be the fastest," he said, eyeing Active.

Active nodded.

Cowboy emptied the envelopes into cups, added water, and stirred the chocolate. He glanced at McAllister. "Who's going to do this?"

"I could," Long said from behind them. Neither had noticed him come up from the lake.

"Take off your gun first," Active said.

Long unbuckled his gunbelt and dropped it into the tent Cowboy had set up. Active unsnapped the flap of his holster and held the Smith and Wesson at his side.

Long crossed to the lean-to and slipped the sleeping bag off McAllister's head, then got an arm under his shoulders, and raised the hot chocolate to his lips.

"I could d-do i-hit myse-helf," McAllister grumbled, trying to shrug the sleeping bag off his shoulders. "Unloose my ha-ands."

"Your hands stay where they are!" Active stepped forward a couple of paces and showed McAllister the gun, though he didn't raise it.

McAllister relaxed, and Long fed him the hot chocolate. Then Cowboy fixed the clam chowder and Long fed that to McAllister too.

"Thanks," he said. It sounded as if his teeth had stopped chattering. He glanced around the camp. "Did you say that *kinnaq* is here? I thought he burned up in that fire back in Chukchi."

"He got out," Active said, watching as McAllister digested the news.

"Where is he now?"

Cowboy cleared his throat.

"He got away," Long said. "He took off on your four-wheeler."

"Wonder where he went," McAllister said with what sounded like a snicker.

"Don't worry about it," Active said.

Cowboy pulled the MREs out of the coffeepot and passed them around, with plastic spoons. They ripped open the pouches and dug in. Active found himself with one labeled Cajun Rice/Beef Sausage and another that identified itself as Western Beans. They tasted about the same—pretty much like he imagined boiled sawdust would taste. How did the military fight wars on the stuff?

Cowboy collected the empty pouches and dropped them into the fire. Then he passed out official MRE napkins. "Just wipe off your spoons and put 'em in your pocket for later."

He looked across the lake at the falling snow and into the fog covering the ridge where his 185 was tied down. "I gotta go have a look," he said. "You never know."

"You never do." Active shrugged. "I doubt Pingo's anywhere within ten miles by now, but—"

"Yeah, yeah, I've got the .357." Cowboy grabbed one of the MRE snacks from the food bag—some sort of chocolate bar—and, munching, headed down the shore to the crossing of One-Way Creek.

"I guess I could wash these," Long said. He picked up the cups he had used to feed McAllister and walked to the lakeshore. Active heard him splashing water and was glad he had suppressed the impulse to say "Think you can handle it?"

McAllister shifted in the sleeping bag, trying to find a comfortable position for his legs. It was evidently difficult with his ankles tethered by the FlexCuffs and his hands shackled at his back. Eventually, he rolled onto his side, drew his knees up nearly to his chin, and studied Active. "You could take these things off my hands. They're cutting off my blood."

"They're supposed to be tight. Just keep them under the bag. Alan can check them when he's done with the dishes."

McAllister only grunted, his leathery face masklike, the dark eyes warier than ever.

AFTER LONG returned from the lakeshore and stowed the two cups with Cowboy's gear by the fire, Active pulled him a few feet into the spruces. "I'm going to see what I can get out of McAllister," he said. "I need you there too, for a backup witness to anything he says."

"Can I ask questions?" Long said.

Active eyed him. "You think of something you want to ask, let me know and we'll step away and discuss it first, okay?"

Long looked unhappy but raised his eyebrows yes. They walked back into the firelight and Active prodded McAllister with the toe of a Sorel.

"You know why we're here," he said.

McAllister grunted.

Active recited the Miranda warning.

"Where am I going to get a lawyer?" McAllister said.

It wasn't actually a request, Active decided. "We know you killed Jae Hyo Lee up here."

"I don't know anything about that."

"Then how did he end up here in One-Way Lake with his neck broken?"

McAllister's shoulders jerked under the sleeping bag. "Maybe he fell in the lake while he was coming in to rob my camp."

"How would he know where it was?"

McAllister shrugged again. "Maybe the *kinnaq* told him."

"Why would he do that?"

McAllister shrugged again, but said nothing.

Active waited a while, but McAllister maintained his silence as the snowflakes fluttered down, leaving the taste of metal on Active's tongue when he breathed in. He wiped his eyebrows and saw that snow had collected on McAllister's eyebrows as well. Because he couldn't wipe, it was melting and trickling into his eyes.

"It would have been self-defense to kill him," Active said at length, watching for McAllister's reaction. "Tom Gage and Pingo sent up him here to kill you. They paid him ten thousand dollars."

The shadow of a grin flashed across McAllister's face. "Nobody could kill me out here."

"That's how you got Jae's wallet and the money you showed Tom and Pingo?"

"I don't know anything about that."

"Did you throw him off the cliff, like you told Sergeant Cave you could have done with Budzie if you wanted to?"

McAllister's shoulders twitched again.

"Was Budzie trying to kill you too?" Long said suddenly.

Active looked at Long, who flinched, presumably realizing he had violated protocol by asking the question without clearance. But Active decided it would have been his next question anyway.

"That was an accident," McAllister said. "I loved Viola."

"An accident?" Active said.

"That dog."

"Dog? What—"

"She told me about Tom Gage, and we got into it, and I hit her one, all right, but not that hard, not even with my fist, just the back of my hand. She didn't even fall down, just her lip was bleeding a little. But then Dad-Dad jumped me, and I shot it before I could think about it. She loved that goddam dog, and when I shot it and it ran off yelping, then Viola, she jumped me, screaming in my ear, and then when I shoved her off she went down and hit a rock. She couldn't wake up, so I put her in the plane to take her back to Chukchi, and then we went in the Utukok. It was an accident."

"If you're telling us the truth, then why was your emergency gear stashed on the creek bank?"

McAllister flexed his shoulders. "I heard they call you *naluaqmiiyaaq*. I guess you don't know anything."

Active heard splashing from the lower end of the lake and surmised Cowboy was crossing One-Way Creek on his return from the ridge. He looked down the lakeshore, saw nothing but snow and the ghostly silhouettes of trees, and turned back to McAllister.

"We know Pingo put water in your gas."

"Ah-hah. I knew it was him, that *kinnaq*."

"If he's such a *kinnaq*, how come a smart guy like you didn't find the water?" Long said. "Whenever Cowboy does his preflight, he drains some gas out of his tanks to check for water."

It was another protocol violation, but again the question made sense. Active waited for McAllister's answer.

McAllister looked disgusted. "Yeah, I always check, all right. But it takes a while for water to work its way through the system. I think it kind of mixes with the gas at first. So I guess it hadn't reached the drains yet when I was checking. I know that engine ran quite a while before it quit over the Flats."

"And that's why you burned up the Rec Center," Active said. "To get back at Pingo and Tom?"

"I don't know anything about that."

"Pingo saw you in there."

"That *kinnaq*? He doesn't know what he sees. From what I heard, he talks to Viola in his sleep."

"The Troopers are searching your place in Chukchi for your safety-wire twister. I think our lab will match it to the wire you used on the door to the men's locker room at the Rec Center."

McAllister's eyes got warier, and he was silent for a while. "You said I could have a lawyer, ah?"

"You can. But we'll still have the wire twister. And Jae's wallet that you left at Tom Gage's place."

"Is that what the *kinnaq* said? Too bad you don't have him, ah?"

"We'll find him."

"Maybe you think so."

"Think what?" Cowboy growled, emerging out of the mist like a ghost. He walked up to the fire and spread his hands over the flames. "Plane's fine. Maybe you think what?"

"That we'll find Pingo," Active said.

"I dunno. Guy like that, he's pretty good in the country." Cowboy stuck a cigarette between his teeth and lit it. "Plus, he's got the four-wheeler now."

"He doesn't have any gear," Active said. "What's he going to do?"

"Go steal some, probably. There's lots of camps down there along the Isignaq, and he's got McAllister's four-wheeler."

McAllister snickered. "Yeah, and he knows where my spike camp is back in them hills."

Active shook his head. "How much stuff is left up there?"

McAllister snickered again. "Anything he needs."

"Should we go up there?" Long said.

"How far is it?" Active asked.

"Few miles," McAllister said. "Too far for a *naluaqmiiyaaq*. You couldn't find it in this snow and fog, anyway."

"He's right," Cowboy said. "It's like swimming in soup up there, plus it's nearly dark now. If the weather clears tomorrow, we can find it from the air. Piece of cake."

"Ah, he's probably already been there and gone, all right," McAllister said. "You won't see the *kinnaq* again."

Active sighed. McAllister was right. There was no reason to think they'd find Pingo in the spike camp, though it would have to be searched eventually.

Active pulled Long into the spruces again. "Thoughts?"

"I guess I've come around," Long said. "Seems like it had to be McAllister, all right."

"We're going to have to guard McAllister," Active said. "Do I have to stay up all night and do it myself?"

"I can take a shift," Long said. "What happened with Pingo . . . well, it won't happen again."

Active nodded and they returned to the camp. Cowboy and Long crawled into the tent, while Active took the first watch at the fire.

"*Arii*," McAllister said. "I can't sleep on my hands like this. Put 'em in front."

Active stripped off his gun belt and left it on the far side of the fire, then walked over to the lean-to, unzipped the sleeping bag, and checked McAllister's wrists. There was no damage that he could see. "You'll just have to gut it out. If you're good, we'll put them in front while you're eating breakfast tomorrow."

McAllister grunted and rolled onto his side, facing the fire. He drew up his knees, wriggled for a couple of moments, then settled down. The position might not be comfortable, but it didn't look agonizing either. Certainly nowhere near prisoner abuse.

Active buckled the gun belt back on and dropped onto a boulder near the fire. The wind was still building out on the lake, but the camp was relatively sheltered. It was comfortable, but not enough so to put him to sleep, he judged. He settled in to ride out the hours until it was time to wake Alan Long for a turn.

But should he let Long take a watch? Was there any way even Long could screw up guarding a prisoner who was bound hand and foot? As Active knew from having tried it in training, the best pace a man could make with his feet shackled was a maddeningly slow, noisy, exhausting shuffle. A few inches per step; that was it. Hopping was faster, but, as he had also discovered, you couldn't hop and maintain your balance with your wrists cuffed behind your back.

A gymnast or a contortionist, maybe, could work his hands past his feet or over his head and so get them around in front to make slightly better time. But McAllister was built more like a scaled-down linebacker, and he was wearing a parka and snowpants inside the sleeping bag. No, there was no way McAllister could escape. The big risk would be if he talked Long into unshackling him to answer nature's call. Well, Active would give emphatic directions to be awakened immediately if McAllister asked for anything whatsoever. For insurance, he would take Long's handcuff key into custody before leaving him in charge of McAllister.

"That Viola had a sweet mouth," McAllister said from the flickering shadows in the lean-to.

"What?"

"It was like kissing a Hershey bar, even if she just woke up."

CHAPTER EIGHTEEN

"NATHAN."

Active heard the voice in his sleep, but didn't wake. It came again.

"Nathan."

This time he drifted up into awareness. The tent was shaking. Somehow he knew this was from someone tugging on a guy rope. But what was he doing in a tent? Where was the tent? Who was snoring in the other bag?

Then he opened his eyes and was awake, mostly. That was Cowboy in the other sleeping bag. The tent was on One-Way Lake. They had chased Dood McAllister here and caught him. It was light now, a dim morning light, and misty blue inside the blue nylon tent. And that was Alan Long's voice saying "Nathan" again.

"Yeah." Active rubbed his eyes and sat up. "Yeah?"

"You better come out here."

Active pulled on his snow pants and Sorels, slung his gun belt over one shoulder from habit, and crawled out of the tent without his parka. The snow was still coming down and now lay perhaps three inches deep around the camp. Fog still blanketed the lake, and it wasn't possible to see to the outlet at One-Way Creek. Well, maybe it would lift as the day came on. That had been the forecast as of yesterday, according to Cowboy.

The fire was out, he saw as he rose to his feet, and the bottoms of Alan Long's Sorels and the knees of his snow pants were red. He puzzled over these things, trying to shift his mind out of low gear. "I need to piss. You let the fire go out?"

Long looked at him, wearing the same expression as when he had reported Pingo Kivalina's escape. He pointed at the lean-to. Active saw that McAllister was still asleep, his back to them, the sleeping bag pulled up over his head. Active was remembering his promise to let McAllister have breakfast with his hands in front when he noticed there was a great deal of red in the snow and gravel around McAllister's sleeping bag, the same red as on Alan Long's Sorels and snow pants.

Finally Active's mind kicked into Drive. He raced to the lean-to and knelt at McAllister's side, dimly aware of putting his knees in the depressions left by Alan Long's knees. He lifted the sleeping bag off McAllister far enough to see the slash across his throat and the dead pallor of his face. He felt for the left carotid, realized it was severed, and didn't bother reaching under McAllister's neck to look for the right.

He pulled the sleeping bag back up over McAllister's head and turned on Long.

Alan Long, who had let their only witness get away. Who had the blood of their suspect on his knees and boots. The alpha pup who had wanted Jim Silver's job. Active unholstered the Smith and Wesson.

"You did this."

Long shook his head, backing away, hands raised. "What? Me? Are you crazy, Nathan? I fell asleep. The fire went out, and I got cold and woke up, and he was like that. It has to be Pingo. He came back and killed McAllister while I was asleep."

"Bullshit! You and Pingo cooked this up together. He set the Rec Center fire for you so you could get Jim Silver's job, and you were supposed to kill Dood McAllister for him because of his sister, right? Except Pingo's lying out on the tundra somewhere, isn't he? Now he's dead, McAllister's dead, and there's no witnesses left. And you steered us toward Jae Hyo Lee because you knew he was already dead. Who killed him, you or Pingo?"

"No, listen—"

"Drop your gun. I'm going to give you your handcuff key back, you go over and get the handcuffs off McAllister, you throw me back the key, and you handcuff yourself to that spruce while I figure this out." He waved the gun at the biggest tree around the camp.

"But, Nathan—"

Active raised the Smith and Wesson.

Long's hands went to his belt and his own weapon—the Glock semi-automatic favored by Chukchi Public Safety— tumbled to the snow. Active tossed him the key. He walked over and knelt beside McAllister, unlocked the handcuffs and, in a few moments, had shackled himself to the tree.

Active pocketed the handcuff key Long had tossed back, then patted him down and recited the Miranda warning. "Care to take me through it, Alan?" he said.

"Listen to me. Think about it for a minute. If I would have known Jae Hyo Lee was up here dead, why would I have still tried to say he set the Rec Center fire after you and Grace found him in the lake? Of course I would have known he'd be identified. And why would Pingo set the Rec Center on fire and burn up Tom Gage? That was his best friend and his sister's boyfriend. And why would anybody in their right mind throw in with that *kinnaq* Pingo Kivalina anyway? Nathan?"

Active turned it over in his mind, feeling certitude leak away.

"Just look in the snow." Long pointed with his manacled hands at the end of the lean-to nearest McAllister's head.

Active walked over and saw the tracks. Someone had come around behind the lean-to and knelt at the end, presumably to cut McAllister's throat, then gone back the way he had come. The tracks were a couple of hours old at least, covered by an inch or two of snow. He compared them with Long's fresher tracks around the lean-to. The killer's were bigger.

He followed them from the back of the lean-to to the edge of the spruces and got a clearer look at the trail. The tracks crossed the little clearing to the lake and then headed down the shore toward One-Way Creek.

Cowboy emerged from the tent, tousle-haired and sleep-addled. "What the hell's going on out here?"

Active pointed at the lean-to. "Alan fell asleep. Pingo snuck into camp and killed McAllister."

"But why is Alan handcuffed to a tree?" Cowboy asked.

"A misunderstanding. And now Alan and I are going to go catch Pingo."

"What?" Long's eyes widened.

"Dammit, let's go." Active unshackled Long and raced to the tent, strapping the gun belt into place. He threw on his parka, then raced back to the boulder and sat down to lace his Sorels.

Long looked along the shore, into the gray wall. "But he's got a couple hours' start on us. And McAllister's four-wheeler."

"We'll see," Active said. "Let's go."

"Um, do I take my gun?"

Active nodded. "But you stay in front of me."

Long lifted his eyebrows, strapped on the Glock, and set off down the lakeshore at what struck Active as a pretty good clip for who a guy who didn't want to be going. Active sprinted after him, trying to ignore the protests from his bladder as his body revved up to full power, lungs burning, heart booming.

They lost Pingo's trail in One-Way Creek, picked it up on the other side, and followed it over the ridge to where a set of four-wheeler tracks took off across the tundra. Active pulled up beside Long, panting.

Long was stooped over, hands on his knees, gasping. "See?"

Active peered into the murk. "Yeah, he's gone."

Long was silent for a moment.

"Sorry," he said.

Active turned away, unzipped, and relieved himself onto the snow. "You learn to swim in the military?" he asked over his shoulder.

"Sure, but—"

"Somebody's got to dive on McAllister's plane and find out what's in there. And it's not going to be me this time."

"No way. I—"

"You let him get killed. You get to search his plane."

They climbed back over the ridge and started down the slope toward One-Way Creek, Long still protesting at the idea of jumping naked into the lake. He pointed at the steel-gray water, a few last flakes of snow still drifting down onto it, ice skimming the shoreline. "I'll get hypothermia."

"We'll put you in the lean-to. Just like McAllister."

After that, Long was quiet until they reached the spot on the shore nearest the grounded Cessna. There, he took one last look at Active, muttered "Arii," and began stripping.

"What's this?" Cowboy grinned. "Another naked cop? What's with you guys?"

Active jerked a thumb at McAllister's Cessna. "We have to get McAllister's stuff out of there and search it. This time, Alan gets to swim."

"Maybe we could go to Chukchi and get a raft or something and winch it out," Long said.

"By then the lake will be frozen and we won't be able to do anything till spring," Active said.

"What could happen to it, way up—" Long caught sight of Active's eyes and fell silent. Then his face took on a look of inspiration. "Maybe Cowboy's got a winch in his plane." He turned toward the pilot, who shook his head, seeming lost in thought.

Long sighed, slipped out of his snowpants, and was unsnapping the uniform pants underneath when Cowboy finally spoke.

"I don't have a winch, but we might be able to make a come-along if we've got enough rope," Cowboy said. "I saw a couple old guys from Ebrulik do it once to get a snowmachine that went through the ice on the Isignaq."

They turned in unison to look at the Cessna in the lake. It had stopped with the left wing pointed to shore.

"If we could get a rope around the tailwheel, we could

probably swing it around and drag it ashore," Cowboy said.

"I'd rather do that than have to swim around inside the cabin," Long said. "We got enough rope?"

"I think so," Cowboy said. "I've got my tiedown ropes in the plane, plus we've got the ones McAllister was using, plus we've got a couple more hanks of camp cord that should work if we double it up. That oughta be enough."

"I'll get the ropes from the plane," Long said. He took off down the shore, as if to get away before Active could veto Cowboy's idea.

"You really think this will work?" Active asked.

"Pretty sure," Cowboy said. "What we need is one standing tree for a fulcrum and a decent-size log for a lever." He walked to a spruce a few feet from the shore and kicked it. It was perhaps six inches in diameter, big by Arctic standards.

"This oughta do for the fulcrum," he said. "Why don't I look for a lever while you trim the branches off this one to about yea high?" The pilot karate-chopped a spot at about waist level on the spruce.

Active fetched the saw from camp and went to work.

Cowboy disappeared into the woods and returned dragging a log nearly as big as the fulcrum tree. He dropped it in the snow, sawed off the branches, then trotted up to camp and returned with the cord from McAllister's lean-to. In a moment, the big end of the lever log was lashed to the fulcrum tree, about three feet off the ground. Cowboy lifted the lever, swung it through a horizontal arc of about ninety degrees, and grunted in satisfaction. "That oughta work."

Active looked from Cowboy's come-along to the Cessna in the lake and began to think Cowboy might be right. If they could run a string of ropes from their lever to the tailwheel, the three of them might indeed be able to heave the Cessna toward shore a couple of feet at a time. It would take a while, but, from the look of the fog hovering just above water level, they couldn't hope to get Cowboy's Cessna off the ridge in the near future, anyway.

There was still no sign of Long with the ropes. Active wondered what was taking him so long. They returned to camp, where Cowboy rummaged in the food bag and came up with an MRE packet of peanut butter and crackers. He offered to share, but Active shook his head and walked into the spruces to forage for firewood, figuring they'd be there at least one more night.

When he dragged his load back into camp and dropped it on the pile by the fire, Long was just coming into view at the lake's outlet, his shoulders draped with tiedown ropes. Active and Decker walked down the shore and met him at the fulcrum tree. He dropped the ropes and studied Cowboy's come-along, then McAllister's Cessna. Finally, he lifted his eyebrows. "Yeah, I see what you're doing here."

They knotted the ropes together, and Long took one last look at Active, then shucked out of his clothes, exposing his Eskimo spot in the process.

"Tie it good," Cowboy said as Long waded out. "You don't want to have to go back and do it over."

Active watched as Long hit that spot where cold-water shock set in. He froze for several seconds, gasping, then started moving again.

Finding the tail was a little tricky, as it was fully submerged. Finally Long kicked over and disappeared, the rope in his hand. In less than a minute, he was back up, without the rope and looking a little confused. Active swore under his breath, figuring he was in for another swim, but then Long dove again. This time he was down longer and gave them a thumbs-up as he surfaced and began paddling for shore.

Cowboy took up the slack in the line and lashed it around their lever, a few feet out from the fulcrum tree. Long waded ashore, rubbed himself dry on the outside of his parka, as Active had done, then dressed and jogged in place.

"Come on," Cowboy said. "This'll warm you up."

They applied themselves to the lever and heaved. The plane didn't budge. "Tailwheel's probably buried in the mud," Cowboy said. He counted one-two-three, and they heaved again. This time they felt something give, and the lever swung through its arc.

"I think we got 'er," Cowboy said in a satisfied tone. He moved the lever back to its starting position, retied the rope, and they arranged themselves for another heave. "One, two, three," Cowboy chanted. "Go!"

Two hours later, the Cessna's tailwheel was on the bank, the main gear still resting on the lake bottom, the cabin floor at water level. Active decided it would do, and looked at Cowboy, who, as he always did until real winter set in, wore hip waders folded down at the knees.

The pilot nodded, pulled up the boots, and stepped into the water beside the Cessna. He unloaded the cabin, ferrying the contents to the bank an armload at a time, then pulled the keys from the ignition and opened the little cargo compartment behind the cabin. It was empty, as was the belly pod.

They spread the waterlogged haul on the bank beside the fire: a trash bag with some MREs, a couple of sleeping bags, a stove and some other camping gear, a dappled silver sealskin pouch with aviation charts inside, a .30–06 rifle and two boxes of ammunition, and a gray canvas knapsack that Cowboy had pulled from the front seat.

Active quickly went through the other things, then opened the knapsack and dumped out the water that had collected inside. With it came a Colt semi-automatic pistol in a clip-on holster, a sealskin wallet, a little red booklet, and a fat, heavy pouch covered in sealskin like McAllister's wallet and chart case. Active flipped open the booklet and realized it was a passport. McAllister's picture was there, surrounded by a foreign script.

"This has to be Russian, right?"

Long shrugged and Cowboy reached for the passport.

"Think so," Cowboy said. "I took a Russian photographer into the Gates of the Arctic park a couple years ago. His passport looked like this."

Active took it back and looked at the name fields beside McAllister's picture. Even in the foreign script—Cyrillic? was that what the Russians used?—it seemed reasonably clear that he hadn't been known as Dood McAllister on the far side of the Bering Strait.

The wallet contained a driver's license, McAllister's pilot's license and medical certificate, a Visa card, and a few bills Active didn't bother to count. He undid the drawstring of the sealskin pouch and shook the contents out onto the canvas of the knapsack.

Long whistled. Cowboy said, "That's something you don't see every day."

Active picked the stack up by its edges and flicked through a few of the bills. "Looks like about ten thousand, huh?"

Cowboy nodded. "If all of 'em are hundreds, yeah."

"We should count it," Long said.

Active considered, then shook his head. "The chances are infinitesimal, but there could be fingerprints on some of these, even wet. No touch." He slipped the bills back into the pouch.

"Ten thousand bucks," Cowboy said. "Just like Pingo said they paid Jae Hyo Lee to kill McAllister."

"Apparently," Active said.

"And a Russian passport," Long said. "I guess he was headed over there to stay with his relatives on the other side. Just like Pingo said."

"Lucky we ran him off the ridge," Cowboy said. "Otherwise, we never would have known for sure what this was about."

"Technically speaking, he never confessed," Active said. "Without that wire-twister, or some other direct evidence, I'm not sure we do know that McAllister started the Rec Center fire."

"Geez, even with all this?" Long said. "I thought you believed Pingo."

Active gazed silently at him.

Long wrinkled his nose in dismay. "*Arii*, you don't still think it was me, do you? Have we found one thing Pingo told us that didn't turn out to be true?"

"You mean like channeling Budzie in his dreams?"

Long's face fell. "But other than that?"

Cowboy scuffed a wader in the snow. "I believe him. Other than the stuff about Budzie giving him orders, I mean."

"We have to find two things," Active said. "Pingo and that wire-twister."

CHAPTER NINETEEN

THE SNOW STOPPED AT about two o'clock while they were eating lunch, but the clouds stayed low over the lake.

"Still no hope of getting off the ridge," Cowboy growled as he studied the rumpled gray belly of the overcast. "And we're way overdue on our flight plan. I oughta to get up there and see if I can catch Alaska Airlines or a military jet on the radio and let them know we're okay. Plus, we should see what we can do about clearing that runway."

Long groaned.

Active grimaced and tossed an MRE envelope on the fire. "And how do we do that? I didn't see any snow shovel in the plane."

"You found the snowshoes, right?"

Active nodded.

"That's our snow shovels," Cowboy said. "Or we can use them to pack it down if we have to."

Active started down the lake, but Cowboy spoke from behind him. "What about Dood?"

Active turned. Cowboy was pointing at McAllister's corpse, still encased in the blood-soaked sleeping bag under the lean-to. "We taking him back with us?"

"Yeah, I guess we are," Active said. "Any ideas?"

Ten minutes later, the sleeping bag containing Dood McAllister was lashed to his body with several turns of the camp cord, the Visqueen from the lean-to was wrapped around that and fastened in place with more camp cord, and Cowboy had rigged a harness from the tie-down ropes they had used to drag McAllister's Cessna ashore. The pilot lashed the tail of the harness to McAllister's ankles, grunted in satisfaction, and stood up, pulling on his gloves.

"There you go," he said. "He'll slide along in the snow so easy, we won't hardly know he's there. Till we hit the ridge, anyway."

Active slipped one of the loops in the harness over his shoulder and gave an experimental tug. Cowboy was right. Here on flat ground with several inches of new snow, McAllister's corpse offered practically no resistance. Lost again in silent admiration of the pilot's present-mindedness, Active hitched the other two loops over his shoulder as well, figuring there'd be no need for help from Long or Cowboy till they reached One-Way Creek.

At the crossing, Cowboy and Long each took a loop, and they dragged McAllister through the water and started up the ridge. Soon they were in the clouds, McAllister's corpse a hundred and eighty pounds or so of dead weight on the harness. Active calculated it was like dragging a sixty-pound pack uphill.

Finally they reached the crest and stopped, gasping, sweating, throwing off their parkas, bending over, hands on knees, too done-in even to curse.

Active's breathing finally slowed, and he peered along the crest of the snow-covered ridge. They were at the lower end. The Lienhofer Cessna was several hundred yards away and slightly uphill, invisible for the moment in the mist. "What about bringing the plane down here and picking him up?" he suggested.

Cowboy, still panting, lit a cigarette and squinted up the ridge. "I guess. Probably wouldn't hurt to taxi the runway after we get it ready, anyway. Just to be sure."

They left McAllister where they had dropped him and trudged through the fog to the plane. Cowboy lit a small catalytic heater and put it in the engine compartment, then draped an insulated cover over the nose. Active dug out the snowshoes and eyed the other two men.

Cowboy jerked a thumb at the plane, layered with the same four or five inches of snow as everything else around them. "I gotta get the wings and tail cleared off if we're gonna go anywhere. I'll do that while you fellas get to work on the runway."

Long groaned once again.

"Pilot's prerogative," Cowboy said. "Just strap on the snowshoes and sidestep down the hill. I only need about eight feet, just wide enough for the main gear. You come to any drifts or low spots, dig 'em out. Otherwise all you need to do is pack it down."

The gray around them was deepening toward black when they had finished the runway to Cowboy's satis-faction. He had even taken a turn on the snowshoes himself for the last pass, to be sure everything looked and felt right. Back at the top of the ridge, he pulled the nose cover off the Cessna, snuffed the catalytic, and stowed it all away.

They climbed in, and he hit the starter. The prop jerked and spun, the engine coughed, caught, and settled down to a steady rumble. Active was surprised how reassuring the sound was after a day and night in the cold with no machine noises to affirm their ability to keep nature at bay.

As the engine warmed up, Cowboy got on the radio and put out a call for "any traffic" in the vicinity of One-Way Lake. He tried four different frequencies before a lazy drawl came back from the sky. "Cessna Eight-Eight-Lima, this is Alaska One-Three-Five. That you, Cowboy?"

Cowboy looked at Active, raised his eyebrows, and spoke into the mike. "Affirmative, One-Three-Five. Who's this?"

There ensued a small-world, whatcha-been-up-to conversation, from which Active gathered that the copilot seat of the Alaska Airlines Boeing 737 now passing above the murk shrouding One-Way Lake was occupied by someone named Randy, who had done a year and a half in the Cessnas and Super Cubs at Lienhofer Aviation under the tutelage of Cowboy Decker.

"So the FAA in Chukchi asked us to keep an ear out for you on our way up to Barrow," Randy said finally. "What's the deal down there? They sounded kind of worried."

Cowboy explained their situation and asked Randy to advise the FAA they'd lift off for Chukchi as soon as the weather cooperated.

"Stand by," Randy said. "Let me see if I can get you a forecast."

A few seconds passed, then Randy was back. "You're looking good. That stuff down there is supposed to clear out tonight. Should be pussy weather by morning."

"Airline-pilot weather, you mean," Cowboy said. "Thanks for the help."

"Our pleasure," Randy said. "One-Three-Five, out."

"Eight-Eight-Lima, out." Cowboy looked at Active. "Good kid." The pilot paused for a moment. "But I wouldn't want his job."

Active stared at him. "You'd rather be stuck on this ridge figuring out how to put a dead guy in your plane?"

"Absolutely." Cowboy opened his side window and eased the Cessna down the crest, peering out at the trail packed by the snowshoes. When they reached McAllister's corpse, he pivoted the plane to point uphill, cut the engine, and grunted. "Not a bad runway, guys. I think we're good to go when the fog lifts."

They climbed out and horsed McAllister—who was not fully frozen and mercifully still free of rigor mortis—into the space behind the seats. Active and Long started back to camp as Cowboy restarted the Cessna for the gingerly crawl back up the ridge to the tiedowns.

ACTIVE AWOKE easily, warm in the sleeping bag, the pleasure intensified by how cold it was in the tent, the light seeming less blue and more yellow than the day before. Domestic sounds seeped in from outside: the fire crackling, a metallic scrape that sounded like somebody sliding the coffeepot off its rock in the fire pit. He closed his eyes. What if Grace was here? How warm her skin would be. Maybe she would use her magic hands again. He opened his eyes and, yes, the light was indeed more yellow than the previous day and, yes, it was cold as hell in the tent. Frost rimed the blue nylon overhead. Yellow light and cold weather? It could mean only one thing.

He unzipped the tent flap and stuck his head out and, sure enough, the day was breaking clear and cold, the dome overhead the same marine blue as year-old sea ice, sunlight starting to pour from the southeast into the bowl of One-Way Lake, the Cessna a toy on the ridge above, Cowboy at the fire filling his coffee cup, then scraping the pot again as he returned it to its rock. He spotted Active and raised his eyebrows. "'Bout time you got up. We're burning daylight."

"Looks like we've got plenty." Active pulled his head back inside the tent and zipped up the flap, then prodded Long awake and they dressed, shivering in the frost that showered down their necks when they bumped the tent.

By the time they emerged, Cowboy had a batch of MREs going on the camp stove. Active ended up with something that purported to be chicken tetrazzini. It tasted exceptionally good for an MRE, but perhaps that was only thanks to the thought that he wouldn't be eating any more MREs any time soon.

After breakfast, they burned the MRE wrappers, rolled up their sleeping bags, collapsed the tent, and started down the shore, Active hoping it would be his last visit to One-Way Lake for a while. True, they were leaving behind a half-submerged Cessna, but that was somebody else's problem. As he trudged along, he wondered: whose problem, exactly? McAllister's insurance company, he decided, though he supposed there was some doubt the salvage value would cover the cost of getting the plane out of the lake, back to civilization, and repaired. Maybe it would become another

Arctic legend as the years went by, with people passing over the lake and concocting myths about how it had gotten there.

The ridgetop runway, they were happy to see, was still clear from their efforts the previous afternoon, and soon they reached the plane. They tossed in the gear, then Active and Long untied the Cessna and threw the ropes inside while Cowboy took the heater out of the engine compartment, snuffed it, and did his preflight inspection.

Finally Cowboy gave the signal, and they piled in, Long crawling past McAllister's folded legs to take a seat in the back, Active sliding into the right front seat beside the pilot and slipping on the headset. "Any problem getting off here with this load?"

Cowboy shook his head and muttered, "Nah, not with this slope and the weather this cold." He tapped the outside air temperature gauge, which read twelve above. He hit the starter, and the engine settled into its reassuring rumble. Cowboy let it warm up for a few minutes, ran it through a final check, and then they roared down the ridge and lifted off, One-Way Lake dropping away to their left, the snow-covered tundra rolling off to the right, and the Isignaq River coming into view dead ahead as they gained altitude. The Isignaq was still blue and flowing, with just a little pan ice running in the middle.

Cowboy wheeled the Cessna right, paralleling the river and heading for Chukchi, out of sight a hundred or so miles to the west.

"Man," Cowboy said over the intercom, "I don't know if I want a steak first or a bath."

They were approaching the first of the numerous ridges, white with new snow, that crossed their course. Active let his eyes drift along it, following the crest back into the peaks where all the ridges originated, thinking that what he wanted first was to kiss Grace Palmer's neck and breathe in her lavender scent. But he said, "A bath for me, I think."

"How about you, Alan?" Cowboy was saying when Active realized that the little splash of color that had barely registered in his consciousness couldn't possibly be natural. By then they were past the ridge and it was out of sight, whatever it was.

"Cowboy," he said. "Come around. There's something up on that ridge we just crossed."

Cowboy craned his neck and tried to see it out the rear window on Active's side. "What? Where?"

"The back side, up near the head. Something red."

"Shit," Cowboy said. "Red? You mean like a four-wheeler?"

Long perked up from the back seat. "A four-wheeler?"

Cowboy rolled the Cessna into a hard left turn and started back for the ridge. As soon as they re-crossed it, they could all see the spot of red a few hundred yards away. Cowboy circled and passed over it a hundred feet above the snow and rock.

Now it was easy to see what it was: a red four-wheeler drifted over with snow, just the handlebars and the teardrop gas tank visible in the clear morning light.

"Can we get down there?" Active asked.

"No way," Cowboy said. "There's no telling how deep the snow is on that ridge, or what's under it. We'll have to come back with skis on."

They were crossing the ridge again, Cowboy starting a turn to bring them around for another pass, when Long shouted from behind them. "Hey, it's Pingo."

Active swiveled in his seat and peered back under the wing, where Long was pointing, and caught just a glimpse of the figure in the rocks above the four-wheeler before it slid out of sight behind the plane. "Is he naked? Did I see that right?"

"I think so," Long said.

"Naked?" Cowboy said. "What's he doing naked?"

"Was he moving?" Active asked.

"I don't think so," Long said.

Active had Long pass him the binoculars from the seat back, and he put them to his eyes as they approached Pingo's perch again. He had chosen a spot relatively free of snow, probably because it was sheltered from the wind, and he was seated on a pile of what appeared to be clothing. He was looking northwest, more or less toward Cape Goodwin and its polynya and the vast sweep of ice beyond, all out of sight over the folds of the Brooks Range.

"Any sign of life?" Cowboy asked.

"Nope," Active said. "He's all white. Frozen solid, I'd say. Probably been there since right after he settled things with Dood McAllister. Come around again, and I'll get some pictures."

Cowboy circled while Long dug the Nikon out of Active's bag and passed it forward. Active flipped out the bottom of the window on his side and shot unimpeded by Plexiglas as they approached Pingo's lookout point.

"Fucking loon," Cowboy said. "What the hell was he thinking?"

"I think he went to be with his sister," Active said.

CHAPTER TWENTY

"WHAT A STORY," GRACE said as Active finished his recap at the kitchen table in the Palmer house a day later.

The previous afternoon, Cowboy had had the Lienhofer mechanic install two big fiberglass skis on the Cessna. That morning, Cowboy and Active had flown back up the Isignaq and retrieved Pingo's remains, discovering in the process how difficult it could be to get a naked, frozen corpse through an airplane door. Now Cowboy was on his way to the upper Katonak to retrieve the cook and clients at McAllister's camp.

"So you're sure it was Pingo who cut Dood's throat at One-Way Lake," Grace said. "Not Alan?"

"Has to be. It just doesn't fit together otherwise."

She tilted her head, foxlike eyes intent. "But wasn't Pingo scared to death of McAllister? How would he get up the nerve to sneak into camp and do what he did?"

"He wasn't too scared to put water in Dood's gas," Active said. "And he—" Active slapped himself lightly on the forehead. "Duh. Budzie told him to do it, of course."

"What? How?"

"Pingo dreamed about her all the time. When I was questioning him in Barrow, he said she came to him in his cell and told him to give Dood a red smile. He thought maybe she wanted him to paint lipstick on Dood so he'd look *kinnaq* too. Pingo must have decided she meant something else." Active drew a thumb across his throat in the curve of a smile.

Grace shuddered. "Maybe he had one last dream out on the tundra that night and she finally explained it to him."

"That would fit."

"So he came back and finished the job."

Active raised his eyebrows yes.

"And then he killed himself on that ridge. But why? He sounds too crazy to have a guilty conscience."

"You ever hear that legend about the village of the ghost bears?"

Grace thought it over for a few seconds. "Yes, I think so—the one about where all the polar bears go when they die?"

Active raised his eyebrows again. "That's where Pingo thought Budzie went after Dood killed her at Driftwood. Their dog Dad-Dad too."

"Pingo said that?"

"Yeah. While I was interviewing him in Barrow."

"So he decided to kill Dood McAllister and join his sister and that dog of theirs in the village of dead bears?"

"To Pingo, it must have made perfect sense."

"I suppose it would." She shook her head and blinked, then frowned. "But if Dood was trying to run, why would he go back to One-Way Lake?"

"Seems pretty clear he planned to fly over and hide out with his relatives on the Russian side. He must have had something essential—the cash maybe—stashed at his spike camp so that woman he had cooking at his main camp wouldn't find it while he was out with his hunters."

"Ah," Grace said. "A woman would certainly do that. And the ten thousand ties him to Jae Hyo Lee's killing, right?"

"Right."

She was silent for a few seconds. "But are you sure Alan wasn't in on it somehow? You think he really let Pingo slip away, then fell asleep and let him sneak back in and kill McAllister? Sheer incompetence is the explanation for everything at One-Way Lake?"

"Apparently."

"And Alan had nothing to do with the fire?"

"There was a couple minutes up there when I was convinced it was him," Active admitted. "But there's just no way to make it all fit with Alan as the doer. Plus, the lab in Anchorage confirmed that the safety-wire twister Carnaby found at McAllister's place matched the tool marks on that wire Ronnie Barnes found on the locker-room door at the Rec Center."

Grace nodded again.

"Plus Carnaby found Jae Hyo Lee's wallet under the van, right where Pingo said it was. And it had Dood McAllister's fingerprints on it."

"So it was all Dood?"

Active nodded.

"Except," Grace said.

"Except?"

"Except, if Dood was going to run, why wouldn't he just do it right after the fire? Why hang around till you got on his trail?"

"There's no way to know for sure," Active said. "But he

probably figured the best way not to get caught was to lie low and act normal. He had hunters in camp and more coming in. He couldn't have bailed out and stranded them without stirring up so much trouble we would have gotten interested. And, remember, as far as he knew, Pingo had burned up with Tom Gage and there was nobody still alive that knew the story. Dood thought the slate was wiped clean and we'd never connect him to any of it."

"And he was almost right," Grace said after a moment.

Active raised his eyebrows.

"So nobody was after Jim Silver at all?"

"Apparently not. He was just in the wrong place at the wrong time."

"And none of it had anything to do with gallbladder poaching."

"Nope, not directly."

Grace nodded, and they were silent for a few moments, marveling.

"These people," Grace said. "They were living in the same space at the same time as the rest of us, but they were in a different reality, fighting their own private war all around us, and we never knew. And now they're all dead."

"Along with a bunch of innocent bystanders at the Rec Center."

Grace sighed, looking lost in thought. "This Budzie Kivalina," she said at length. "I wish I could have known her. She must have been something."

"She was like kissing a Hershey bar."

"Mmm?"

"That was the last thing I heard Dood McAllister say."

"A Hershey bar."

"Uh-huh."

"So that was the last thing he said in his life."

"Most likely." Active pushed his chair back from the table and stood. "I guess I've got some paperwork to take care of."

"Lots of it, I should think."

Active hesitated, fidgeting.

"What?"

"Are you really going to burn down this house?"

She shrugged. "I talked to the fire chief while you were gone."

"My God. What did he say?"

"I'd describe him as a worried man. He asked me if I was crazy."

"And what did you say?"

"I smiled nicely and explained it all to him in a calm voice, and pretty soon he was saying he could probably work something out. It might be good practice for the firefighters, he said."

"Seriously? He's going to let you do it?"

"Apparently."

Active was silent, astonished anew at the effortless persuasion Grace Palmer seemed able to work on any adult male with a normal testosterone level. He was about to head out when the doorbell rang.

He looked at Grace, eyebrows raised in question. She looked puzzled and went to answer it.

"It's the mayor," she said as she returned. "I forgot to tell you, he's been trying to find you."

Everett Williams, looking as hybrid as ever with his dark skin, curly hair, and Mongol features, followed her into the kitchen. They shook hands, Grace waved him into a chair, and Active sat down again.

After the good-to-see-yous, there was that awkward silence that means the person with something to say doesn't know how to start. Grace excused herself to make tea. Finally Williams cleared his throat.

"I talked to that Cowboy Decker last night. He's a good guy, ah?"

Active lifted his eyebrows. What could be said about Cowboy Decker?

Williams nodded in satisfaction. "After that I talked to Captain Carnaby. And just now I talked to Alan Long." Williams stopped and shook his head. "Sometimes it's pretty hard to talk to that fella, all right. I heard they call him alpha pup sometimes. What is that?"

Active masked a smile. "A little dog that wants to be the big dog."

There was another silence. The mayor seemed to be pondering something. Then, "He really let that *kinnaq* Pingo Kivalina get away, then come back and kill Dood McAllister?"

Active lifted his eyebrows. "Apparently so."

"And it was Dood that set our Rec Center on fire, kill all of those people?"

"That's right," Active said. "One of his airplane tools was used to wire the locker-room door shut. It can't have been anybody else."

"Then maybe it's good he's dead, but now we won't ever have a trial, ah?"

Active shook his head.

"Lotta people won't ever believe he did it if there's no

trial. Some of them still think it was the Koreans. Or maybe that *kinnaq* Pingo."

"I'll be going on Kay-Chuck tomorrow to talk about it," Active said.

"That might help, all right," Williams said as Grace brought the tea and joined them at the table. "You heard we're having a new public safety department in our Aurora Borough?"

Active nodded.

"Chief Silver was going to run it, but now he's dead. That Alan Long, he want the job, but—" Williams rolled his eyes and let it hang in the air.

Active looked at Grace, eyes narrowed. Grace looked into her tea.

"Well, our council had a meeting about what to do little bit ago, just before I came over here. And we voted to offer you the job of setting up our public safety department and then running it for us."

Active swung his eyes from Grace to Williams, his throat suddenly dry. "Me? But I'm transferring to Anchorage."

"We need an Inupiaq to run our department, all right, if it can't be Chief Silver," Williams said. "But we need somebody good, so we sure don't want that Alan Long, even if he's Inupiaq. That Alan, what he's good at is drinking coffee and riding around in Chief Silver's Bronco with that gun on his belt. That's what I think."

Grace snickered behind her teacup, and Active coughed, delicately covering his mouth with his hand.

"And that headset he wear all the time," Williams continued. "Blueshoe, what they call it?"

Active nodded, suppressing another smile.

"What is that, anyway?"

"Something for his cell phone, I think," Active said.

"And I bet the city's paying for it too." Williams shook his head. "Anyway, everybody tell me how hard you hunted that Dood McAllister. Alan, even Cowboy Decker maybe, they're a little bit scared of you, I think. That's good if you're going to be the top guy, ah?"

"Me be Alan Long's boss?" Active raised his hands. "Sorry, I'm going back to Anchorage. We are." He tilted his head at Grace.

The other two just stared at him.

"We'll see," Grace said.

"Ah-hah," the mayor said.

ACTIVE WAS still in a fog as he left the house and unlocked the Suburban. There was too much too think about, so he resolved to think about none of it till he was knocking on Nelda Qivits's door. The paperwork could wait.

He started the engine and was slipping the transmission into reverse when a four-wheeler pulling a little trailer puttered to a stop behind him. He put the Suburban back in park and stepped out to ask the driver to unblock him, but the driver spoke first, extending his hand.

"You're Trooper Active, ah?"

Active shook the hand and studied the man, a young Inupiaq with a vaguely familiar face wearing Sorels, a fur hat with the flaps folded up, and Carhartt overalls crusted with what looked like camp dirt and animal blood. He smelled like camp too, that combination of wood smoke and sweat.

"I'm Buck Eastlake," the driver said. "My sister said you came by to tell me about Rachel. I wanted to thank you for that."

Active nodded, embarrassed to have his lie turned around like this. "It's okay. Part of the job."

Eastlake went to the trailer and removed the bungee cords holding a blue tarp in place over the load. "I brought you some meat." He peeled back the tarp to expose two fresh caribou hindquarters, the gray-brown fur still attached. "We just brought it down from my uncle's camp up on the Katonak."

"I don't know if I can take it," Active said. "I—"

"Don't worry. It's from a female. They don't taste rutty like them bulls this time of year."

"That's not it. It's just that we're not supposed to—"

"You could." Eastlake said. He made eye contact and held it, unusual for someone from Chukchi.

Active shrugged and raised his eyebrows in assent. He could take one in to Grace and the other to Nelda. He leaned into the Suburban and pressed the button to unlock the tailgate.

Buck tossed in one of the hindquarters, and Active hoisted the other onto the tailgate. The boy rolled up the blue tarp and bungeed it into place, then mounted the four-wheeler. "It's good you caught Dood McAllister for burning up Augie and Rachel and them other people. She was a good person, even if some people around here didn't know it. She just wanted to be with the top guy, that's all." Eastlake was silent for a moment. "Lotta women are like that, ah?"

Active lifted his eyebrows.

The boy pulled the starter cord, and the four-wheeler sputtered to life. He made a wide semicircle and headed back the way he had come, the loadless trailer bouncing along behind.